Awakening passion ...

With a deep moan that vibrated from the depths of her being, she clasped her arms joyously around him and yielded, letting him lead her now into that glorious new world of love and passion that she had never dreamed existed.

Slowly he increased his rhythm. He knew he had finally brought her safely over that tumultuous sea of doubt and fear that had separated them. And the bridge had been love — a love that could no longer be denied. Unhindered at last, he plunged on to fulfillment, sweeping her along with him on the crest of their newly found joy in each other.

She met each thrust with increasing ardor, unable to restrain the tide of her own unleashed passion as her need for release became as urgent as his. She was now as eager as he to reach that final explosion, that moment when flesh and spirit are fused at last.

BELOVED OUTCAST

BELOVED OUTCAST

LORENA DUREAU

PaperJacks LTD.

TORONTO   NEW YORK

This book is affectionately dedicated to all my students who have taught me so much over the years, and especially to those who have given me their love and friendship: Louis and Bea Krieger, Linda Louise Coate, Michele Van Pelt, Vivian "Stef" Jackson, Sherry Harrison, Margaret Mehrtens, and Belinda Hutchinson.

And a very special dedication to my "bonus" families: Maud (G'ma N) Newsham and her clan, and Mary Distefano and Anna Pecoraro and her family.

AN ORIGINAL

PaperJacks

BELOVED OUTCAST

PaperJacks LTD.

330 STEELCASE RD. E., MARKHAM, ONT. L3R 2M1
210 FIFTH AVE., NEW YORK, N.Y. 10010

PaperJacks edition published April 1987

ISBN 0-7701-0508-4

ACKNOWLEDGMENTS

The author gives special thanks to the following people and organizations for their invaluable assistance: Miss Florence Jumonville, Head Librarian, The Historic New Orleans Collection; Mr. Russell Ruíz, Barn Manager, City Park Stables (New Orleans, La.); Mr. Norman Simons, Curator, Pensacola Historical Society; Miss Sheilah Bowman, Manager: Tourism Development, Pensacola Area Chamber of Commerce; Ms. Jean Getchell, Archives Chairman, Historic Mobile Preservation Society; Dauphin Island Tourist Association; Mobile Chamber of Commerce; Commander George V. Dureau, Sr., United States Power Squadron; TMT Shipping & Chartering of Louisiana; Louisiana Department of Wildlife and Fisheries; Louisiana Tourist Development Commission, New Orleans & Baton Rouge Offices; and Linda Louise Coate, my Girl Friday.

PROLOGUE

Louisiana Colony — 1719

The stranger strode boldly into the dimly lit bedchamber. Already he was unbuckling his sword and removing his frock coat. He obviously meant to take her quickly and get back to more urgent business in the parlor.

Nicole lay breathless behind the mosquito netting, desperately trying to shield her nakedness with her hands, yet all the while watching with fascination as the tall, broad-shouldered silhouette moved closer.

Though the intruder's face was hidden in the shadow cast by the solitary candelabrum, Nicole could feel his eyes penetrate the thin curtain that hung between them as he flung his coat and weapon on the back of the chair and sat down to pull off his boots.

A hot wave of rage and shame swept over her. If only she could run away. It didn't matter where, as long as it was far from this veiled bed in the heart of the swamplands and this giant of a man who was about to lie down with her!

He was rising now to take off the rest of his clothing. Even in the semidarkness, she sensed the vitality emanating from him. His presence dominated the room.

Instinctively she closed her eyes. She had never seen a man naked before. But when she opened her eyes all she could really distinguish was the frosting of candlelight playing around his tall, muscular frame and turning the gold of his hair into a shimmering halo.

So this swaggering buccaneer was going to be her first man. He was going to stretch out beside her now and make love to her. But no, there would be no love between them. He was simply going to take her, nothing more, and she would have to lie there and let him do as he willed. For she was a whore now, as the fleur-de-lis branded into her shoulder proclaimed.

The bed curtains parted and the shadowy form was suddenly a startling reality.

"Faith, lass, but you're a pleasant surprise!" came the appreciative murmur of a deep-timbred voice. "I'd have offered my services to the French long ago had I known you'd be here waiting for me like this!"

The mattress sank beneath his weight as he straddled her, and she bit her lip to keep from crying out. His powerful frame began to press demandingly against her, the gold-tipped hairs on his chest grazing her breasts, until the vigorous warmth of his flesh merged with the coolness of her own. The hardness of his body rippled firm and smooth against the bareness of her skin. It was a disquieting sensation, flesh brushing against flesh. His hands ran possessively over her body with a light, expert touch, and his tongue began to push boldly against her tightly closed lips until he worked them apart and the taste of wine and tobacco invaded her mouth.

Suddenly the taut cords of his muscles flexed, and his arms and thighs closed around her and held her fast. She gasped, startled to find she was no longer able to move or even utter a sound. The masculine scent of him, spiced with sandalwood, hung heavy in the air, overwhelming her. A flood of new sensations engulfed her, pulling her inexorably into a whirlpool of churning emotions. Rage vied with panic, curiosity with confusion. Her body no longer seemed a part of her.

So it was happening. She had resisted to the end, fighting desperately against the fate that had brought her to this moment. Yet she had always known it would come. Ever since that horrible morning in Paris when they had branded her an *incorrigible* and carted her off to the waiting ship, she had been destined to lie in the arms of this stranger.

PART ONE

Paris — November 1718

Chapter 1

Nicole swayed to the rhythm of the chains rattling against the railing of the open cart. She tried desperately to keep her balance as the tumbrel bumped over the narrow cobblestone streets, throwing her and her companions against each other on their journey through the jeering crowds.

Though many of the insults hurled at her and the rest of the prisoners were lost in the din, the shower of rocks and dung could not be so easily ignored.

Instinctively she lifted a shackled hand to ward off a piece of melon rind. It grazed her shoulder and slid down her dark woolen cloak to the hem of her tattered gown, adding another stain to the already foul garment. How could this be happening? What was she doing in the midst of this bedlam? She still couldn't believe it was real, that it wasn't just a bad dream. But then, nothing had seemed real since that horrible day when she had unwittingly killed the gendarme. From that moment on, she had found herself trapped in a pit where only shame and death awaited her. For she was a convicted murderess now, condemned to the labyrinths of the damned.

Well, at least it would soon be over. This time next week she would be hanging from a gibbet. She shivered and drew her ragged cloak tighter. How would it feel, she wondered, when the rope tightened around her neck? Would she suffer long? One of the women prisoners had assured her that by the time the murdered gendarme's regiment had finished taking turns flogging her, which the judge had decreed was to be part of her sentence, the hanging itself would be a blessed relief.

Nicole crossed herself. *Mon Dieu!* Was she really going to die so soon? If this was a nightmare, why didn't it end? Why couldn't she wake up?

Suddenly it occurred to her that perhaps she was on her way to the scaffold now. Her execution had been posted for next Saturday, but it could have been moved up. The guards had given no explanation when they rudely awakened her and the other women and herded them into the waiting carts. Now they were turning into the street that led to the Place d'Armes. She was sure she'd heard the roll of drums amid the shouts and laughter. Of course! The people were being called to the square to witness some spectacle — and she and her companions were going to be it!

Panic seized her. The dreaded moment had come even sooner than she had expected. She dug her nails into the wooden railing, trying to cling to this last vestige of reality. Everything in her screamed in protest. Oh, how she wanted to live! She was only eighteen. But if it had to be, then at least let it be over quickly!

One of the guards marching beside the tumbrel grinned maliciously at her as he warded off the curious townsfolk with his musket. She had seen that look before; it had been in the eyes of the gendarme when he and his companion had tried to rape her. Now that she was a condemned convict, all men looked at her that way.

She was glad her poor father would never know, would never see all the hopes he'd had for her end like this!

He'd watched over her so carefully all those years, given her the best of tutors and hired the most trustworthy chaperons.... If the sudden loss of his fortune had not killed Clement D'Arcenaux, certainly the sight of his only child being driven through the streets of Paris in chains would have done so!

At her trial she had tried to speak out in her own defence, telling how she had simply tried to defend herself. But it had been her word against the other gendarme's, and the latter had insisted that she had killed his companion while resisting arrest. After all, how could he, a sworn representative of the law, admit that he and a fellow officer had abused their authority, that on seeing a wench so young and unattended, they had decided to have a little sport with her before taking her off to debtors' prison? Of course, the judge had chosen to believe the "official version" instead of the one told by a penniless girl with no family or husband to back her up. The fact that she was being arrested for debts at the time of the crime had only made the case against her worse.

The one person who might have helped her was Marcel, and she had expected him at least to try. But he had done nothing. Even now, the heartbreak of that betrayal weighed more heavily on her than the chains binding her wrists and ankles. Was it possible Marcel had believed her capable of committing such a crime, or was it simply that he had not wanted to become involved? His family had pressured him, of that she had no doubt. After all, her fiancé had not even offered to help her pay off any of the debts she had found herself saddled with after her father had died, so why should she have expected him to come forward when she was being tried and condemned for murder? So much for the love of a man who had sworn his undying devotion one day and abandoned her the next!

The Place d'Armes lay directly ahead, and the impatient mob was gathering there to receive the prisoners. Nicole anxiously scanned the large clearing. But no, there was no scaffold in sight. Only a pair of burly, barrel-chested men, naked to the waist, stood waiting in the center of the square, flaming braziers on either side of them.

"Oh, my God!" wailed a bushy-haired girl next to Nicole. "Those brands they're heating up must be for us!"

Another woman near them snorted angrily. "You can lay odds on it, dearie. Them damn bastards mean to burn the fleur-de-lis on our hides!"

The wagonload of prisoners groaned and cursed. Several women made the sign of the cross, but Nicole just clung to the railing. Wouldn't the flogging and hanging be enough to satisfy even the most exacting defenders of the law? Did they have to subject her to this final humiliation as well? Only the most dissolute of whores and felons — the so-called *incorrigibles* — were so branded. Must they rob her of every last shred of dignity even as they wrested her life from her?

The tumbrel had stopped now, and the guard hurriedly lowered the gate. The women awkwardly scrambled to the ground, stumbling over their leg irons in their haste to obey the impatient guards.

The jailer with the nasty grin reached up eagerly to where Nicole stood and pulled her down beside him, his hands fumbling roughly under her cape.

"You little redheaded bitch," he sneered, his breath sour with ale, "I've got you in my sights. Before they put a noose around that pretty neck of yours, I aim to ram you good!"

He held her tightly against the hard bulge that attested to his ability to carry out his declaration, and bent his grizzled face close to hers, laughing evilly at her futile attempts to break away from him. "By the time we finish giving you your farewell party Friday night, you won't give a damn what happens to you on Saturday morning!"

He was groping his way into her bodice when another guard approached and tapped a coiled whip impatiently against his boot. "Hurry these strumpets along," he growled. "There's no time tor dallying. See those others over there? They're descending on us like the plague! Damn it! Must be over a hundred of these sluts! How the hell are we supposed to have them all branded and back in their carts by noon?"

"Why the rush?" Nicole's guard asked crossly. "The orders we got just said to bring every ablebodied wench between eighteen and thirty-five here to be branded. Why can't we give them a little extra attention on the side while we're at it?"

"Bah! You can forget about that. As soon as the smiths are through with their chores, these bitches will be off to the colonies. A boat's waiting for them now in Le Havre."

Nicole's jailer tightened his grip on her, like an animal unwilling to give up its prey just when it was about to devour it. "You mean we're not going to take these wenches back to the prison after we finish here?" he exclaimed angrily. "What the hell are they going to do with all these *chats* in Louisiana?"

"The same thing they do with whores anywhere, I guess," the second guard retorted with a shrug of his shoulders. "They say the men in Louisiana are so desperate for females that they'll snatch up — maybe even marry — the first ones they can get their hands on. That's why the Regent's given the order for us to empty the prisons, scrape the gutters, and strip the gallows of every pair of available buttocks in Paris."

Nicole stopped struggling. Was it possible she wasn't going to be hanged after all? But the wave of relief had barely swept over her when a sobering thought replaced it. Her life may have been spared, but she was far from safe. Even as the guards continued talking, a chill crept over her. What strange new destiny had been set in motion for her? As a branded outcast at the mercy of ruffians starved for women in an untamed wilderness, would she really be any better off?

Chapter 2

"Marry? You say the Regent thinks some fool might want to marry one of these sluts?" Nicole's jailer guffawed. "Our Duc d'Orléans must be daft if he thinks any man in his right mind would tie himself to gallows bait like these! Just because a wench is good for mounting doesn't mean she's good for marrying! Besides, why should he send harlots all the way to Louisiana for the colonists to roll? If the Regent wants to hand out whores to deserving subjects, he can start right here with me! I already have mine picked out. See this little redhead? I got special plans for her."

He gave her breast an appreciative poke. "Look at the *mamelles* on her! I'm not about to let this one get past me without getting a few good rides off her, even if I have to push her behind some bushes on the road to Le Havre."

The other guard lifted Nicole's cape with his whip and swept an appraising glance over her. His dark eyes flickered, but then he withdrew the whip and let the cloak fall around her again. "Maybe if we make good time getting them to the ship, the higher-ups will let us have a few minutes alone with them before they're loaded on the boat," he mused, "but I know we won't be able to do any dallying along the way. As it is, we're going to have to keep these sluts moving night and day if we're to get them to Le Havre in time for the sailing."

The guard who held Nicole continued to fondle her under the cloak, despite her efforts to push him away with her manacled hands. "I sure hope there won't be any *religieuses* going along with us," he snorted.

Now it was his companion's turn to laugh sarcastically. "Nuns? With these? You must be joking!"

"Well, I heard tell how some of those Sisters of Charity will be taking a batch of whores from Salpêtrière to the colonies come January," he said, "although chaperoning a bunch of trollops makes no sense to me. Talk about closing the barn door after the horse is gone!"

"Oh, they might accompany the wenches who come from their correction houses" — the other guard shrugged — "but these here are nothing but convicts — branded *incorrigibles* at that, the lowest breed there is. Who cares what happens to them? I doubt more than half will make it to the colonies alive anyway. Ever see how they pack them in those pest ships? But you'd better stop pawing this one and keep the lines moving or you'll have the lieutenant coming over to see what's holding things up. This crowd's already got him in a bad humor, and he'd just as soon take it out on us."

Nicole's guard grunted a response, then reluctantly dragged her to the ever-lengthening queue of prisoners who had been unloaded from the carts. She barely heard the obscenities he whispered in her ear as he promised to return for her later; her mind was elsewhere, desperately trying to grasp the significance of what she had heard.

She still found it difficult to believe she was not going to be hanged. Dare she allow herself to hope? Perhaps the Regent's decree was not as merciful as it seemed. After all, shipping her off to some primitive land to fill the "needs" of a band of disgruntled settlers might prove a more cruel punishment. The guards said the Regent had spared her life only to make a whore of her! She swayed at the thought of lust-crazed men clutching at her the way that guard had, of ruffians violating the most intimate parts of her. Would it be better, she wondered, to face execution than to live in such degradation?

But a part of her was already clinging to life. At eighteen it was difficult to give up that last ember of hope. At least she would live now, and perhaps she'd find *some* way to escape in the New World. That hope had to be kept alive.

As the sun climbed, the women prisoners stirred restlessly. By now they had picked up enough information to speculate that they were about to be branded and deported to the Louisiana Colony. For some it came as a blessing, but there were many who lamented that it was no real reprieve.

Only one girl was enthusiastic. "Why all the wailing and complaining?" she asked in surprise. "I saw a leaflet that said Louisiana was a paradise. It said the mines there are so rich with gold and silver that the streets are paved with them."

A tall, buxom blonde laughed mirthlessly. "What dungeon have you been locked up in these past few months, *chérie*? Surely you know by now that it's all so much poppycock? They'd say anything to fleece the investors and trick people into going there. I used to work the docks before they caught up with me, and I tumbled with a lot of mariners who told me that most of the colony is nothing but a pesthole. If that's where we're being shipped, we'll be in a living hell, trapped in a disease-ridden jungle with rogues as wild as the animals that infest it!"

Nicole listened, more bewildered than ever. The longer

she spent with these new companions of hers, the more she realized how ignorant she had been of the world around her.

There was a nervous giggle behind her. "Well, I'll take my chances with a pack of lusty men any day over one hangman! Besides, I've never met a bastard I couldn't handle."

"*Bien*, any man who wants me to unload him will have to pay for the service," sniffed a pretty young brunette. "I'm not giving out free tumbles, Regent or no Regent!"

The plump blonde laughed again. "Who knows, the Duke of Orleans may have done us a favor. If they're really so desperate for a good roll, we might be able to make ourselves a fortune there."

"Don't count on it," snorted the bushy-haired girl. "From what I hear, most of the colonists are poor as church mice. Many of them are convicts, no better off than we are, so they'll be expecting a lot of free rides, you can count on it! No, *mes amies*, business will be bad there."

"I — I heard one of the guards say some might want to marry us," Nicole ventured timidly, more in an attempt to console them than because she believed it herself. She remembered only too well how her guard had reacted to the idea.

Her companions greeted her words with a burst of shrill laughter.

"Now that's a nice thought!" exclaimed the blonde. "And who'd want to marry the likes of us, pray tell?"

"For that matter, why should we want to marry the likes of them?" quipped a coarse-featured woman.

"Well, I say to hell with them all!" snarled a voice farther up the line, but a nearby guard shook his whip threateningly and the women fell silent again.

The menacing gesture suddenly reminded Nicole of the more immediate perils to be faced before the day was over. The ones awaiting her in some distant land were insignificant against the reality of the half-naked giants who signalled that the brands were hot enough to begin. They were glowing white-hot now, and Nicole shivered even as the hot noonday sun beat down on her.

Chapter 3

The crowd pressed in on the women like a pack of hungry wolves. The mood of the townspeople had been festive earlier, but as soon as word got out that the prisoners were going to be transported to the colonies instead of receiving their prescribed sentences, roars of protest shook the square. The people had come to see a good spectacle and demanded satisfaction. Was there no justice in France these days? they cried. Why should whores and criminals get off? What punishment was there in a harlot's being sent to the New World so she could continue plying her trade?

Several indignant matrons burst through the gendarmes ringing the plaza's center and hurled whatever foul matter they could find at the prisoners. The street urchins followed, flinging obscenities with their pebbles.

The big blonde shook her fist and rattled her chains at the crowd, returning profanity for profanity. Another cursed and spat at an old hag who was taunting her. Something grazed Nicole's forehead, but she just stood there, stunned and disbelieving.

The hatred was palpable. There was not a single word or gesture of compassion from the enraged populace or the callous guards hurrying her to the waiting brandsmen.

Suddenly she saw it all with a clarity that had eluded her until now. She was an outcast.

The smiths worked rapidly, methodically, taking the women in pairs.

The guard in charge, irritated by the disgruntled mob's constant heckling, paced back and forth between the lines of women, brandishing his whip whenever they hung back.

"Push those capes aside, ladies, and loosen your lacings!" he snapped. "Bare those shoulders well so the smiths can do their work, or I'll make you strip to your waists and be done with it!"

Nicole's fingers were cold and stiff as she pulled her cloak open and worked at the narrow black ribbon running from her neckline to the waist of her faded blue silk gown. Flushed with indignation and shame, she eased the dress off her shoulder. What a cruel joke fate was playing on her! Here she was about to be marked with the stigma of the most dissolute of women, and she was still a virgin! But in their eyes she was a condemned murderess, the lowest of harlots.

True to his promise, the guard who had first lifted her out of the cart returned, eager to be the one to escort her to the brandsman. He greeted her cheerfully even as he caught her roughly and pulled her out of the line.

"Come, my pet, your turn now," he grinned wickedly. "Walk in front of me ... that's it ... and let the people see how pretty you are." He pulled her cloak behind her so that the high, full cone of her partially bared breast could be better appreciated.

For the first time since the branding began, a hush fell over the crowd. They gaped as the guard prodded Nicole. Then an excited murmur began to gather momentum. Here was no ordinary strumpet! Even in her soiled garments, her bedraggled skirts shorn of panniers and starched petticoats, Nicole D'Arcenaux stood out from the others, the proverbial pearl amid swine, a slender lily thrust up through the muck toward the open sky. She stood defiantly, her proud head with its delicately chiseled features and bold emerald eyes held high beneath her glorious mane of red-gold hair now blazing wild and free in the strong light. The mob stared as the tall, willowy figure moved toward the center of the square with surprising grace despite the leg irons. They exclaimed over the flawless perfection of the smooth white shoulder and half-bared breast, over the sweeping curve of the hips that undulated so tantalizingly beneath the tattered folds of her drab skirts.

As they pressed closer, men called out coarse compliments, proclaiming in no uncertain terms what they would like to do to so delectable a whore and urging the guard to pull her bodice down the rest of the way.

The women screamed insults more vehemently than ever, as though resenting the fact that one who had fallen so low could still be so beautiful — beautiful enough to arouse desire in their men and envy in themselves.

The shouting and heckling grew until it was a veritable symphony of lust and hate. Nicole shuddered before the brutal force of it. The mob was like a great animal, crouched and ready to pounce, its unsheathed claws reaching out to tear her to pieces, its foul breath fanning her cheek. She tried to steel herself. Somehow she must not give these vultures the satisfaction of seeing how afraid she was, but her heart was pounding so wildly she knew they must sense her fear. Her breath was coming in short, rapid spurts now, searing her parched throat with every gasp.

"Don't fret, my sweet," the guard snickered in her ear. "I'm right behind you."

A wave of intense heat engulfed her as she neared the brandsman waiting beside the brazier. She was suddenly aware of the smith's naked chest before her, and she stared mindlessly at the rivulets of sweat coursing through the wiry black hairs on the glistening bronze torso. The roll of the drums and the cries of the feverish crowd were muffled now by the roaring in her own ears. Even the shrill screams of another girl being branded a few feet away seemed distant.

The brandsman stoked the coals, and little tongues of flame leaped from the fiery depths of the brazier. He chose a fresh iron and slowly drew it forth.

She fixed her eyes on the iron shimmering in the smith's hairy hand. It was her only reality now. The snap and crackle of the brand's white-hot tip sounded louder than all the noise around or within her. She swayed, nearly losing her balance, as she fought to keep the gray mists swirling before her eyes from closing in.

The guard's grip tightened. "Don't be afraid, *mon petit chat*," he whispered with mock tenderness. "I'll hold you up by your teats!" He cupped the fullness of her breast roughly with one hand while he buried the other deep in her long hair and forced her head back until her exposed shoulder was lifted high to receive the brand.

"If you want to wiggle, go right ahead," he hissed. "I've got another hot poker for you right here!" He pressed himself against her buttocks, and a wave of nausea swept over her as she felt the hard bulge of his bloated shaft.

"Hold the bitch still!" the smith ordered crossly. Before Nicole could brace herself, he brought the iron down on her shoulder.

The fire pierced her flesh, then tore through her being, searing everything in its path. The sea of jeering faces dissolved into the cloud of gray that was slowly swallowing her. She would have crumpled to the ground, but still the guard held her.

A sickening odor jolted her back — her own flesh burning! She no longer heard what the crowd was saying to her, and she didn't care. Only the guard's whispered obscenities penetrated her agony as he continued to rub himself against her buttocks with increasing fervor and clutched her tighter in a paroxysm of delight.

Nicole knew the horror of that moment would solder her rage to her pain and indelibly record on her flesh this final descent to a place where human dignity no longer existed. For as the brand had burned into her shoulder, it ignited a bitter hatred in her. How she despised them all — the shouting, merciless mob that had come to gloat and make of her suffering a diversion, the callous judge who had turned a deaf ear to her pleas for justice and condemned her to this inferno, the licentious Regent who had ordered that she be branded and cast into the wilderness to live her life as a whore, the faithless suitor who had vowed his undying love, yet abandoned her utterly, and all those leering, sadistic men who lusted after her now, eager to take advantage of her helplessness. In the infinity of that moment she cursed each and every one of them.

Nicole looked at the three-petaled fleur-de-lis emblazoned raw and red against the whiteness of her skin. She was a branded felon now. Till the day she died this stigma would be with her. It would never allow her to forget what she had become.

Once again the guard was urging her along, his lewd soliloquy as unending as the taunts of the crowd. He led her to a cart loaded with women. With a parting tweak to the smarting breast he had clutched so tenaciously, he relinquished her to another guard who was busily checking off the names on his list.

Nicole was vaguely aware of sweaty hands rudely tugging at her. Something hard and cold encircled her waist and snapped shut with frightening finality. There was the harsh sound of metal grating against metal, and to her dismay she realized that still another shackle had been added to her body. A master chain attached to a band around her waist joined her to the others, as her destiny henceforth would be bound to theirs.

Someone impatiently shoved her into the tumbrel and slammed the gate into place. "Done!" a gruff voice called out. "Take them away!"

The boards beneath Nicole's feet rumbled and shook as the wooden wheels clattered over the rough cobblestones once more, and she groped for the railing to steady herself. But the cart was so full she could hardly find a place. Someone brushed against her burned shoulder, but though she winced from the unexpected pain, she did not cry. She had no tears left.

Securing a place at the railing, Nicole leaned wearily against it and crossed herself. The road would be long and arduous, and she knew that many who set out upon it that day — perhaps even herself — would not see its end. But then, this was really just one more lap on a journey that had begun months ago — a journey that was carrying her ever deeper into the depths of hell.

PART TWO

**Louisiana Swamplands
April 1719**

Chapter 4

Despite the warmth of the early spring afternoon, Nicole shivered. The strange new world was strange indeed. As far as she could see, there was nothing but wilderness. She and her five companions had been traveling in a crowded dugout for almost a week now, crossing rush-filled lakes and bayous surrounded by forests flooded with the swollen river's backwash. Always there was that same feeling of vastness and isolation, of unknown perils lurking around each bend and in the depths of each thicket.

Even now that they had reached the mighty Mississippi, the swamp was everywhere, flanking the irregular banks and spilling over into the river itself. At night when they stopped to make camp, the impenetrable wall of trees and tangled vines and the inescapable muck and shifting sands were there to lay claim to the travelers. Even the sturdy, weather-beaten cypresses that marked the edge of the ragged shoreline had to fight to hold their own against the treacherous currents that constantly besieged them.

Nicole had seen a few huts and several large frame houses boldly perched atop cypress posts. Yet how futile were these attempts of man to take root in this maze of marshlands! The invincible wilderness seemed to be biding its time until it could swallow it all.

Nicole shuddered. There would be no hope for escape here. She simply had been exiled to another kind of prison.

Her chains clanked as she shifted the folded strips of cloth under the iron bands on her wrists. All her petticoats and finally her cloak had been sacrificed to these makeshift cushions, but now the strips were fast becoming ragged and worn. What would she do when they no longer served? Only her bodice and skirt were left, and they were so tattered that they, too, would soon be in shreds.

At least it was warm here in the colony. She wished she could adjust the cloths around her ankles, but she dared not bend forward. The new jailer, Monsieur Legarde, had warned them to sit still else they might capsize the boat. And if the long snake whips that he and his huge black slave carried tucked in their wide leather belts were not enough to impress them, the roar of the river and dragonlike creatures sunning themselves along its banks were an even greater incentive to obey.

Limited movement was a way of life for Nicole and her companions. They had worn chains for so many months that the weight of them had become an integral part of the women.

Certainly they were all better off than they'd been on the cargo ship. After the inhuman conditions of the four-month crossing, with well over a hundred women crowded and shackled together in the dark, foul-smelling hold, Nicole had to admit that her present discomfort gave little cause for complaint. At least here she could fill her lungs with clean air and see the blue sky above her.

Nicole looked down at her shoulder. Every time she thought of the stigma barely hidden beneath her torn sleeve, the spot — though only a scar now — would begin to throb and the nauseating odor of her burning flesh would fill her nostrils. Paris might be far away, but that awful moment in the public square still haunted her.

Many of her companions had died along the way. Between Paris and Le Havre over a dozen unmarked graves were dug in the ditches along the roadside.

Villagers and farmers had stared in awe, then made the sign of the cross and turned away as the sorry caravan laboriously made its way past them.

When the carts had broken down, the women had walked the rest of the way, stumbling in their leg irons as the snap of the ever-present whips set the pace, regardless of the stinging wind and rain.

But the hated chains, especially the one around her waist that shackled her to the others, had proven a blessing as well as a curse; though they made escape impossible, they prevented lecherous guards from stealing off with any prisoner to some secluded spot.

But even after the horrendous death march, there had been that hellish voyage. The women had huddled half starved in their own filth, prey to disease and vermin.

It was all a blur to her now, a kaleidoscopic nightmare. In the festering hold, where days and nights melted into an endless twilight amid the weeping and curses of the sick and dying around her, Nicole had fought to stay alive week after week, month after month, losing all sense of time, of identity, and intent only on self-preservation.

Once a day, when the pitiful rations of watery gruel and stale, weevil-infested bread were lowered into the hold, the captain or one of his officers called roll to see how many were still alive. The only time the ship's doctor ever descended into that pit of misery and death was to see whether someone who didn't respond to her name had died.

When the weather was nice enough, the captain would order the prisoners topside for an hour; when there were storms, even the grating was covered over, and the stifling darkness closed in on them with the terrifying finality of a tomb being sealed. Nicole didn't know which she hated more — being buried alive in that foul hole while a storm raged, or enduring the insulting scrutiny of the crew when they threw buckets of water on the women, more to see what their wet garments would reveal than to keep them clean.

Not that some of her companions didn't flirt or make coarse jokes of their own, lifting their skirts high or tugging at their bodices to show their breasts in hopes of getting extra rations or special privileges. At such times Nicole tried to stay out of sight, but finally one of the officers spotted her and pointed her out to his comrades. After that, she was always on the list of women that the captain ordered be brought to his cabin to entertain him and his lieutenants once a week. It was only by pretending to be too sick to answer the summons that she had been able to ward them off. As luck would have it, by the time they began to suspect she might by lying and sent the doctor to examine her, she really had taken ill.

There had been moments when she had been certain she would be one of the corpses heaved overboard. And she probably would have been, if not for Murielle. Dear good-hearted Murielle! She had scrambled into the heap of desperate women time and again to get enough food and water to keep both of them alive! Without Murielle's years of "training" in the back streets of Paris, neither of them would have survived.

Nicole cast an apprehensive glance at the tall, angular man in front of her. Monsieur Legarde, with his elegant frock coat and breeches of mulberry silk, the richness of the color highlighted by frothy lace ruffles, seemed ridiculously out of place in the wilderness. But the enterprising representative of the newly formed Company of the Indies had boldly gone to meet the *Dolphin* before it had reached the main island at the entrance of Mobile

Bay. With an eye to making profit, he had offered the captain so much per head for the "choice ones" among that ship's human cargo.

There had been no lust in Legarde's eyes as he had picked his way among the women, a perfumed kerchief pressed to his nose, and quickly selected the ones he wanted. There had only been greed in the cold, calculating way he had studied her before he had ordered his slave to unchain her. He had, he confided to the captain, a group of "discerning clients" who would be willing to pay handsomely for the privilege of having first choice from among these "latest Paris imports."

Nicole wondered whether it augured good or ill for her to have been Legarde's first selection. She wondered, too, what the crafty Company official would say if he learned just how inexperienced one of the "whores" in his boat really was! But then, it might only make him raise his asking price for her. Murielle had advised her to keep her virginity a secret. Wise in the ways of the world, the one-time prostitute, who had fallen into thieving as her beauty began to fade, had warned her that some men were sadists where first-timers were concerned, a maidenhead causing many rakes to lust all the more after a wench.

At least Legarde had been feeding them well these past few weeks. Although he continued to keep them in chains and treated them scornfully, he made no attempt to molest any of them. They were his "investments," so he urged them to rest and eat all they wanted. He readily admitted that he hoped to "fatten them up a little more in the right places" before his clients got a look at them. Regardless of their jailer's motives, Nicole found it a welcome change to be able to lie down at night on a pallet of moss or to be out in the sunlight with a full stomach.

She hoped Murielle and the others had fared well. She wondered if they had been distributed to the men waiting on the docks or if any had found husbands. Would she ever see any of them again? Six months from now, how many of them would even be alive?

She suspected that officially she was dead now anyway. She had seen the captain strike her name and those of the five others off his list as he turned their documents over to Legarde. The records would probably show they had died at sea. It certainly would not occur to anyone to ask questions. Human refuse was cheap. There would probably be more fuss made over a missing keg of rum from the cargo than the loss of a few more harlots.

So Nicole D'Arcenaux had become a nameless object — merchandise to be sold to some stranger for his pleasure. But whoever bought her would get no pleasure from her, she vowed.

Legarde's voice jolted her back to reality; he was ordering the black to pull in at the next landing. That nagging fear of the unknown crawled into the pit of her stomach and stayed. They were about to meet the first "client"; for one of the women in the boat, the journey had ended.

Legarde was the first to jump ashore. He glanced disdainfully at the women sitting dejectedly in the dugout. Annoyance frosted his finely chiseled countenance. How was he going to get good money for jades like these? But then, any man who would pay even a sou for a wench was a fool. Give him a smooth-cheeked lad any day!

He strode rapidly and purposefully up the path that led through the trees to the raised house at the end. "Wait here," he called over his shoulder to his black overseer.

But as he spoke, a short, stocky man in nankeen frock coat and breeches walked out onto the gallery of the house and, on seeing them, hurried down the staircase. The large silver buttons on his coat glinted in the bright afternoon sunlight as he neared them, impatiently trying to straighten an outdated wig of shoulder-length black curls that did nothing to improve his sallow, heavy-jowled face.

The roots of Nicole's hair tingled uncomfortably, and a wave of repugnance swept over her. God in heaven! No wonder their jailer had been treating her and her companions like lambs being fattened for slaughter! To be owned by such a man would be the same as death!

Chapter 5

"No time to fool with wenches right now!" snapped Jean Renaud as he mopped the beads of sweat off his face with a crumpled lace-edged handkerchief. "You've caught me with a house full of guests — important guests on important business."

The two men shook hands and sought the shade of a huge oak while the black man remained in the boat.

"Oh, come now, Jean, I've traveled a long way to accommodate you," Legarde scolded with a wave of his lace-cuffed hand. "Besides, I've never seen you so busy that you couldn't find time to sample a few wenches. Wait till you see what I've skimmed off the top of the *Dolphin*'s cargo."

"I already got myself a good *chat*," grumbled Renaud. "What I need are some husky blacks to work my fields. When are you going to start bringing them in?"

"The first shipment should be coming in any day now," Legarde replied, nonchalantly brushing aside the topic, eager to get down to business as soon as possible. "Don't worry, I'll see to it that you get the pick of the lot. They'll come high, though. You know how hard it is to get a good African in the colonies. But meantime, don't pass up the prize merchandise I've brought you today. Wenches like the ones I've got now for you aren't easy to find either."

"Don't tempt me," spat the planter, although he couldn't resist craning his neck to look at the women in the boat. "There's just too much at stake to let myself be distracted. You'll never believe who my guest of honor is." He dropped his voice. "None other than Paul Dawson—you know, the notorious buccaneer captain himself!"

He dabbed nervously at his forehead, as though the mere thought of it was too much for him.

"Dawson?" Legarde's usual composure was momentarily ruffled. "You mean the one the Spaniards call *El Diablo Dorado*?"

Renaud shook his head so energetically that his jowls and curls bounced in unison. "That's right, the Golden Devil himself! He's up there in my parlor with two of his officers, sipping my best port and discussing possible strategies against the Spanish with some of the colony's best military men."

Legarde shot him a quizzical look. "Since when are you trafficking with pirates?"

The planter smiled smugly. "Ah, but this one is here at the governor's invitation, mind you." He lowered his voice even more and drew Legarde deeper into the shade of the oak. "I guess you heard about our being at war with Spain?"

"Yes, Governor Bienville's brother Sérigny landed in Mobile with the news the day before I set out on this journey. But what's Dawson's interest in our quarrel? He's British, not French."

"Ah, but war makes strange bedfellows, *mon ami*," smiled the planter. "France and England are fighting on the same side this time, and you know Dawson's fetish for Spanish ships. He seems hell-bent on sinking every damn galleon in the Caribbean. As far as the Spaniards are concerned, he's the devil incarnate."

"But what's he doing here? Where's his ship?"

"Anchored somewhere near the mouth of the river, I suppose. He hasn't said exactly, and I doubt he will. But you can be sure, if he's taken the trouble to come here to meet a couple of Bienville's top brass, there must be something big going on. From what I can tell, he's offering to help us, now that we've declared war against his sworn enemy."

"I guess he'll expect a handsome fee for his services," said Legarde, "but once he learns how impoverished this damn colony is, I doubt he'll be willing to make any pacts with Bienville."

"Who knows?" The planter shook his head. "I really don't think money's the only object with a rogue like Dawson. He's probably got so much booty stashed away that he could buy the whole Louisiana Colony, lock, stock and barrel. No, if he's offering to pitch in with us, it's more likely because he's got it in for the dons, that's all. Of course, the governor feels it might be to our advantage to have someone like Dawson on our side. After all, he knows the coastline from the British colonies to New Spain like the palm of his hand."

Legarde glanced uneasily from his boatload of contraband "merchandise" to the house. "Don't tell me the governor's here?" he said nervously.

Renaud laughed. "Don't worry, *mon ami*, Bienville's too busy meeting with his brothers in Mobile to prepare for the defense of the colony. He thinks the Spanish are sure to attack us, what with their fort at Pensacola being so near, and those at Havana and Veracruz not that far away, either. That's why he's sent two of his best men to meet with Dawson. If they think he can be trusted and has something worthwhile to offer, Bienville or one of his brothers will probably formalize a liaison with him."

Legarde was visibly relieved. "Well, it's just that I prefer not to attract any undue attention to our little, ah, business arrangement. I came here from Mobile my usual way, through Lake Pontchartrain and then Bayou St. John. The portage is flooded now. Looks like it's going to be bad again this year. At least we were able to use the dugout the whole way, but I was careful to enter the river to the south side of that one-hut settlement Bienville started last year, *Nouvelle Orléans*. Not that I think the governor would raise too big a fuss over a few whores, but he might feel obliged to do so for appearance's sake if he found himself in a situation where he couldn't look the other way."

"Oh, Bienville has no love for these sluts," scoffed the planter. "He's always complaining about the trash the Regent's dumping on us, but until he can get something better, what can he or any of us do? He has to keep his men content so they'll stay here. As long as wenches like these can do that without stirring up too much mischief, I don't think he cares what happens to them. He's not much of a ladies' man himself, you know. He seems able to take them or leave them."

"*Voilà!* So there you have it!" nodded Legarde. "After all, these strumpets have been transported here to 'comfort' you settlers, *non*? And as an official of said *Compagnie*, it's one of my duties to see that they're distributed to those who will appreciate them the most. So, shall we get down to business? I promise I won't keep you."

The planter looked about nervously. He was glad the house was set back far enough from the river to screen Legarde's clandestine visit from his guests. Nevertheless, he was anxious to get back to them. It was important that they speak well of his hospitality when they met with the governor. Perhaps then Bienville would grant him those extra *arpents* of land he wanted for that crop of indigo next year.

"I — I really shouldn't...." he muttered, although he

couldn't resist casting another glance at the women in the boat. "The governor asked me to be sure to make the buccaneers welcome and keep them in a receptive mood. Dawson's known to drive a hard bargain, even when he makes the first move. He's no cat's-paw, I can tell you that!"

But now that Legarde had been reassured that the governor was nowhere around, he had but one thought in mind.

"From what you've told me, Jean, I'd say I've arrived just in time," he said, smiling condescendingly. "I know how famous you are in these parts for your hospitality, so I'm sure that you plan to serve your guests a lavish meal. Why not offer them one or two of these wenches for dessert? Surely this would satiate their more sensual appetites as well."

"Oh, I've thought of that. I plan to let Mignon attend them," the planter replied. "Now there's a whore who knows all the tricks. She'll keep them happy."

Legarde's smile broadened. "Aha! You've said it yourself, *mon ami*. I didn't steer you wrong where she was concerned, did I? Then-trust me when I tell you I've brought you an even more succulent tidbit this time."

He caught Renaud by the arm and pointed toward the boatload of women. "See that pretty wench over there — the one sitting near the prow? That's the one I have in mind for you."

He called to his overseer, "Virgo, stand that redhead up so Monsieur Renaud can get a better look at her."

The boat rocked precariously as the black picked his way to Nicole and pulled her to her feet.

The planter stared at her, his mouth agape, his wig slightly askew.

"There, my friend," said Legarde triumphantly. "You see, there's no need to lose time. You can tell at a glance she's the best of the lot. I wager just the sight of her makes the sap rise in you, *n'est-ce pas*?"

Although Nicole couldn't hear everything the men were saying, she could feel Renaud's eyes appraising her from head to foot.

"She's pretty enough," the planter conceded, "but a little scrawny. In fact, they're all rather scrawny. I like a *chat* with something I can grab when I'm riding her. That must have been a sorry cargo if these are the best!"

But Legarde waved aside his client's complaints. He had dealt with the planter before and knew the man's tactics only too well. From the way Renaud was running the tip of his tongue over his lower lip, it was evident that the guests in the parlor — even the governor himself — had already been forgotten.

"Now, now, Jean, don't play difficult," Legarde chided with a knowing smile. "The girls may be a little peaked from their voyage, but they're already beginning to fill out again. I've brought you choice merchandise and you know it. I went out to meet the *Dolphin* personally and hand-picked these wenches before anyone else could get at them. That shapely little filly has a lot of meat on her where it counts. Why not see for yourself?"

Before the planter could find his voice, Legarde motioned to the overseer to bring Nicole ashore.

Chapter 6

The Negro deftly lifted Nicole from the boat and waded through the shallow water, then carried her up the muddy bank to where the two men waited under the oak. Knowing what was expected of him, he set her down in front of Renaud and held her there, pinning her arms to her sides so the planter could examine her.

Renaud leaned forward, his eyes bulging until they seemed ready to pop out of his head. The damp, mud-spattered gown clung more closely than ever to the girl's softly rounded form, her undergarments having been discarded. Nicole stood angry and defiant despite the weight of her chains.

"Look at the fine buttocks on her," Legarde urged his client in a low voice. "And those *mamelles*! She's not wearing stays to prop them up, either. Feel for yourself. Nice, no?"

Renaud's stubby fingers eagerly sought one of her breasts. Nicole closed her eyes, trying desperately to blot out the paw probing her flesh. Would the day ever come when she would grow accustomed to such degradations — when she would no longer cringe at the touch of a lustful hand?

"She does have a fine pair . . . bigger than I expected," Renaud mumbled under his breath. "But she seems a bit squeamish. For a harlot, she sure has an air about her!"

"Oh, she'll come around," Legarde quickly assured him. "It's just that she's better quality than most of the jades they've been sending us. Her papers said she came from a good family. She can read and write, too. That ought to be worth a few *louis* more."

Renaud growled impatiently. "I don't give a damn about all that! When I climb in bed with a *chat*, I'm not interested in her reciting the alphabet for me! All I want is a good tumble. What this slut needs is a lesson in how to be sociable with a man!"

He was fondling her breast now, and Nicole reeled. Rage welled up within her and overpowered her caution. She began to struggle against the black's implacable hold, but he only tightened his grip. Frustrated, she tried to kick the planter away from her, but the leg irons interfered.

"You disgusting animal!" she hissed. "Try to climb in bed with me and I'll scratch those horrid eyes of yours right out of your head!"

Renaud jumped back as if she had struck him. "*Sacre bleu!* What an ill-tempered strumpet!" he exclaimed. Then he turned to Legarde, his tone accusing. "So you're trying to pass off a bad one on me, eh?" He reached over to Nicole again and yanked the tattered sleeve from her shoulder. "Aha! As I thought — the fleur-de-lis! She's an *incorrigible*. I might have known a wench as pretty as this was too good to be true!"

Legarde shifted uneasily. "I wouldn't try to deceive you, Jean," he said defensively. "You know I got these sluts from that batch of convicts they shipped here last month. Of course she's branded. They're criminals and whores, not convent girls. Why lie about it? This one's a condemned murderess, plucked from the gallows in the eleventh hour. She killed a gendarme while resisting arrest for debts. But what difference does that make? For what you want of her, she doesn't need impeccable character references."

"But a felon? I — I thought she might be like Mignon — one of those correction girls from Salpêtrière. God knows they're bad enough!"

For a moment Nicole glimpsed a faint ray of hope. Never in her wildest imagination would she have thought the day would come when she would be glad to have that brand on her shoulder! Perhaps he wouldn't want her after all.

"Ah, my friend, where's your sporting blood?" chided Legarde. "If the wench still has some spirit left in her, so much the better, *non*? Surely a beauty like this is well worth taking the trouble to tame!"

"Granted, she's a looker, but . . ." The planter's naturally suspicious nature was at war with his lust. "Damn it all, man, I'd have to think twice before sleeping next to a shrew like this. No tumble is worth getting killed for!"

He looked longingly at the swell of her breast, now partially bared. Already he was lamenting the fact that he might not have the pleasure of tasting it.

"Oh, you're man enough to handle her," Legarde cajoled.

"I suppose so," grumbled Renaud, "but look at the sullen bitch! I dare say she'd murder us here and now if she could! Why, your black has all he can do to hold her down, chains and all! She's a bad one, all right. They don't decorate them with the fleur-de-lis for trifles."

Legarde could see his profits slipping through his fingers. In desperation he decided to change his approach. He had dealt with this client enough to know that all he had to do was fan the fires this girl had started in his loins and the fool would end up taking her, no matter what she was.

"Come, *mon ami*, all this little filly needs is a few hours of rough riding. She might buck a little in the beginning, but a man of your experience knows what she needs to calm her down, *n'est-ce pas?*"

Legarde watched a sinister grin steal over the planter's coarse features and knew he had him. "Why don't you let those rascals you're entertaining break her in for you," he went on quickly. "Run her through the gauntlet with them a few times and I assure you she'll be docile enough when they're through with her. It'll be good sport for your guests on their final night here and will leave you with a *chat* purring at your every command by dawn."

"Perhaps you're right," Renaud sighed. "Giving them a wench as pretty as this ought to impress them with my hospitality."

"And certainly help keep them in an amiable mood for their negotiations," Legarde pressed. "Why, you might say they'll be bedfellows in more ways than one by the time the night is over!" He winked slyly and Renaud guffawed in agreement.

Nicole was stunned by the turn their conversation had taken. *Sainte Vierge!* This horrible monster was going to buy her after all.

She looked around quickly for some means of escape, but even if the black weren't holding her, what could she do? Who could she turn to for help? Her companions were as defenseless as she was.

The men were still haggling. "Of course, I wouldn't want to risk her kicking up a fuss and causing trouble with my guests," Renaud whined. "It might be simpler just to let Mignon attend them...."

"No, no," Legarde argued quickly. "Why, you can't even compare the two! Take my word on it; if you want to show your guests that you're a man of exquisite taste, offer them this one. You'll be the envy of every man in the colony when they see her. Why, this is a whore fit for a king's bed!"

"You know damn well I'd never buy a wench without seeing all of her, and I have no time to..."

"I can assure you there's not a blemish on her — perfection itself."

"The hell with your assurances! With sluts like these, you never know what mementos they might have brought from the brothels of Paris. I'd have to see her stripped so I can look over every damn inch of her."

"Of course, of course. I only mean if you're in a hurry ... but you're welcome to examine her as much as you want, even sample her if you wish." Legarde's voice was velvety now.

His harsh command electrified Nicole. It was really happening after all — he was ordering her to disrobe in full view of everyone at the landing!

"Come on, be quick ... we don't have all day! Show this gentleman how well made you are."

The black had eased his grip on her so she could unlace her gown, but she stood there too stunned to obey.

"Get on with it," Legarde prodded her angrily, "or I'll rip those rags off you myself!"

The planter's eyes were bulging, his face an unattractive dark crimson. "I hope your man doesn't lay his whip too hard on these wenches," he fretted. "Not that they don't deserve it, but they usually have blemishes enough on their hides without adding whip scars to them as well!"

"Virgo is an expert," drawled Legarde with a wave of his slender hand, as though the mere discussion of such things offended his delicate sensitivities. "Rest assured, you won't find signs of his lash on my wenches."

Anxious to complete the sale and move on to his next client before nightfall, Legarde reached out to hurry Nicole along with her lacings, but she instinctively covered herself.

"Look at the bitch rear up like a wild filly!" exclaimed Renaud. "*Mon Dieu!* How I wish I had time to mount her right now! I'd break her fast enough!"

Legarde smiled and, with a mock bow, stepped aside,

motioning to the planter to do the honors. "Go ahead, Jean, strip the wench yourself. My black will hold her still for you."

"You'll be wasting your money," Nicole suddenly cried out through scalding tears of humiliation and rage. "All you'll ever get from me will be contempt."

Legarde stepped up to her, whip in hand, anxious to silence her before she ruined the sale beyond any chance of repair. "Hush, or I'll lay my lash on you until you remember who you are!"

Nicole's pulse pounded wildly. Had she survived the insults and abuse of all these past months only to end up the chattel of a man like this? Far better they had hanged her in the very beginning and been done with it!

Now Renaud plunged his hand roughly into the torn neckline of her gown, impatient to clutch the breast that had so fascinated him during the bartering. She let out a cry of protest, but he held on to her greedily while he fumbled at the lacings of her skirt with the other hand.

"Let me see your shanks, wench. If they're half as good as these *mamelles*, I'll take you and be done with it."

The feel of his hard stubby fingers digging into her bare flesh sent a fresh surge of blood through her veins. Something deep within her had snapped. Even the fear of the whips no longer deterred her. Let them beat her to a pulp. Perhaps then the planter wouldn't want her ... perhaps no man would want her, and they would leave her in peace at last!

With a shot of renewed energy, Nicole broke free of the black man and struck at the planter with her shackled hands. Caught off guard, Renaud released her and stepped back, momentarily blinded as his wig slipped over one eye.

Quickly Legarde tried to intervene, but Nicole lashed out at his long arrogant face. For her he was the embodiment of every jailer who had ever tormented and abused her. Shouting to his overseer to come to his aid, Legarde threw up his hands to ward her off, but it was too late. Her ragged nails had already slashed their course down his smoothly shaven cheek.

He let out a shriek, and the ugly red gash was even more vivid as his face paled.

"Bitch! You've scarred me for life!" he wailed as he pressed his handkerchief to his wounded cheek and looked at the drops of blood staining the delicate linen and lace. He turned to his overseer in fury. "You black bastard! Why didn't you keep a better hold on her?"

The Negro put a quick end to Nicole's violent but brief bid for freedom. She winced with pain as he forced her arms back until the chain dangling between her wrists spanned the flat of her belly so tightly that she could feel its metal links bite into her flesh through the thin silk of her gown. But she kept her head high, all the while knowing that Legarde's uplifted whip was sure to fall. Far better the sting of a lash to the vile caresses of a lout like Jean Renaud!

"One moment, *mon ami*, don't let a fit of temper rob you of your wits. You have just convinced me that there are better ways to tame a wench. Now that I've made up my mind to take her, I don't want her scarred."

Legarde was torn between rage and greed. A purse of gold would be his if he could forgo the pleasure of avenging himself.

He lowered the whip slowly, but his face remained hard. "It'd almost be worth losing the sale, just for the joy of leaving some scars of my own on this damn bitch's hide! After what she's done to my face . . ." he choked.

Renaud smiled. "Don't forget, *mon ami*, you were the one who put the idea in my head. Console yourself with the thought that she'll have little fight left after we've finished with her tonight."

Legarde reluctantly tucked the whip into his belt.

"*Bien*, we'll close the deal then," he acquiesced, dabbing

his cheek and looking at his spotted handkerchief again in dismay. "I'll take my usual fee, though frankly, she's worth a lot more."

Legarde turned to where Nicole stood against the dark form of the overseer.

"I leave you in Monsieur Renaud's capable hands, madame," he sneered. "I hope those buccaneers split you in two with their mastheads!"

"You can count on that, my friend," Renaud assured Legarde as he set his cumbersome wig straight again. "I'll see to it that they take the wind out of her sails. Come dawn, she'll be flying at half-mast!"

Chapter 7

Nicole felt light, almost giddy. After having worn the shackles for so many months, it seemed strange not to feel their weight bearing down on her anymore, not to hear their incessant rattle.

Most of all, there was the joy of feeling well fed and clean again — really clean, at last scrubbed free of the grime and lice. When Legarde had first taken the women off the ship, he had had his overseer throw several buckets of water on them, clothes and all, but it had not been the same as getting out of their filthy gowns and soaking in a steaming tub of perfumed water.

With the help of Renaud's concubine, Mignon, and a sullen Indian woman called Baba, Nicole had scrubbed herself until her skin shone radiant and smooth in the late afternoon light filtering through the gauze that covered the window. Mignon, who seemed friendly and eager to chat, explained that there were few luxuries in the colony, though Renaud had more things than most of the settlers there. Even glass for windowpanes could not be gotten at any price, she said.

At first the young brunette, who was about the same age as Nicole but not quite as tall or well proportioned, had brought only a bowl of water and a vial of perfume for her new companion's "ablutions." When Nicole had insisted that nothing less than a tub of hot water and a bar of soap would do, however, Mignon had been horrified.

"But so much bathing will be the death of you!" she exclaimed. "Of course, you should get out of that horrid old rag you're wearing, but then, if you just sponge off a little and anoint yourself with this perfume, that should be enough. It's a very fine oil. Renaud had Legarde get it for him in Paris. You know the doctors say too much bathing can weaken you, and ... and soaking like you want to do might even make you come down with something!"

Nevertheless, Nicole won out, and after a bowl of spicy stewed chicken, which she ate while the water was being heated, she submerged herself gratefully in the tub.

Now, with her hair combed and cascading in a perfumed mist around her shoulders, she readily accepted the woman's suggestion that she lie back on the bed and rest awhile. Her aching body welcomed the soft moss-filled mattress and the feel of the fine linen sheet beneath her bare skin, even though she knew this rare moment of respite would not last long.

As dusk fell, the Indian woman lit a two-stemmed candelabrum on the bureau in a far corner of the chamber and proceeded to burn a handful of dried herbs in a small clay dish, mumbling that it would "help ward off the evil spirits of the swamps." Mignon, however, only laughed and observed philosophically that the real evil of the swamps was not any spirit but *los maringouins* — the mosquitoes which besieged them every summer and probably would be returning any day now.

"Then you'll know you're really in hell!" she exclaimed with an emphatic shake of her dark curls.

Mignon's words suddenly reminded Nicole why she was receiving all this special attention, and a chill crept over her. This smoky room with its flickering light and encroaching shadows was her new prison!

Though this particular evening seemed pleasant enough, with a touch of summer warmth already in the air, she wished she had a gown or something to cover herself with as she lay there. But when she asked if they could find something for her to wear, or at least another sheet, Renaud's concubine chuckled. "Of course you're chilled," she called over her shoulder as she paused in the midst of gathering up the discarded chains and clothing. "I warned you about bathing so much." Then she grew more serious and cast a sympathetic glance at Nicole. "I'm sorry, *chérie*, but Jean ordered us not to give you any clothes or bed covers until tomorrow morning, and we dare not disobey him. But don't worry," she added, resuming a lighter tone, "you'll be well covered before the night's over. Won't she, Baba?"

The squaw's ruddy face remained expressionless as she shrugged her shoulders and continued to tidy up the room.

Mignon laughed. "As you can see, Baba lives up to her name, Babbling Brook. That's what the Indians called her when Jean bought her from them to use as his concubine until that fop Legarde brought me to him last year. Jean says that if Baba is a babbling brook, then I ought to be called Still Waters!" She giggled and moved closer to the bed to get a better look at the girl who was to share the chores with her in the future. There was no resentment in her manner, only surprise. She couldn't understand Nicole's being forlorn.

"What's the matter?" she asked, her quick brown eyes scrutinizing the gracefully curved figure stretched out on the bed. When she noted how Nicole made an effort to cross her arms to shield her nakedness, she smiled, then added, "There's no need to hide yourself. God knows you're pretty enough! I wish I had that tiny waist and breasts as firm as yours. Mine are as big, but they're like overmilked udders now. That's what a year with Jean can do!" She sighed and then, taking advantage of Nicole's continued silence, blithely went on as though delighted to have someone with a common bond to talk to. "I guess you're a little nervous, this being your first night here and having to attend Jean's guests right off, but you needn't be. With that body of yours, you'll have them eating out of your hand. Some of them are not really that bad, you know. They're not all monstrosities like him." She put a dimpled hand to her lips as she shot a quick glance toward the door. "He'd beat me if he heard me say that, but it's the truth. Take that Captain Dawson, for example. I wager the Spaniards aren't the only ones who call him a devil! *Quel homme!* I caught sight of him when he arrived yesterday. He must be almost two meters tall — big and golden all over — with an air about him that makes you tingle just to look at him! Imagine having a man like him breach you! That's something to tell your grandchildren about — how the famous *Diablo Dorado* made love to you! Maybe Jean will let me take a turn with the guests, too, and I'll have a chance to be with Dawson. As it is, you'll have your hands full. If this soiree ends like the ones Jean usually has, you'll have them coming at you fore and aft before the evening's over!"

Mignon chattered merrily on while Nicole stared at her, trying with difficulty to follow what she was saying.

"I — I'm afraid I won't know what to do," she confessed at last, making an effort to speak over the knot lodged in her throat.

"Don't be frightened," the girl said easily, not realizing the extent of her new companion's ignorance in such matters. "They're not any different here than they are back home in France. A man's got the same equipment the world over. Actually, most of the bastards here in the colony are so starved for a good roll, they'll just go at you quick and leave off the frills. Of course, later on, as the wine goes to their heads, they might start piling up on you and getting a little rough, but the best advice I can give you is to let them do what they want and just keep on smiling. Remember, no matter what happens, just laugh and act like you're having a good time. Jean isn't going to let anyone do any real damage. After all, he paid Legarde a goodly sum of money for us."

Nicole sank deeper into the moss mattress, wondering how she would ever live through the night.

"The one you have to watch is Jean himself," continued the talkative girl, lowering her voice a little, her brown eyes darting cautiously again toward the door. "He's a mean one when he gets his dander up, so you'd better keep him happy. This plantation's his private little kingdom, and his word is law. He especially enjoys throwing these little parties and showing off all he has because hardly anyone else around here has anything of value, much less a woman to share his bed. Frankly, I'm glad you're here now. It's a relief to have someone to ease the burden of keeping him and his cronies contented."

Mignon finally noticed Nicole's silence and misread it. "But look at me, trying to tell a fish how to swim!" she laughed. "After all, you must know a few tricks yourself or you wouldn't have that decoration on your shoulder."

Nicole's eyes were huge green orbs in her pale face as she lay trembling in the bed, wishing she could be anywhere else in the world except there — even hanging from a gibbet in France or buried somewhere at the bottom of the ocean.

"Hasn't it ever occurred to you or any of the other women to go to the authorities and register a complaint?" she asked, her voice quavering.

Mignon threw back her head and laughed harshly. "Complain? About what? If I wasn't here, I'd be in prison or locked up in Salpêtrière with those dreary nuns, wouldn't I? And you would probably be crow's meat by now. The way I see it, we've been dumped in this pesthole to serve our time, and compared to what those sentences were supposed to have been, we probably got off easy. Male convicts fare a lot worse than we do, you know. If you were a man, you'd have been condemned to a life of hard labor in the colonies, and at this very moment would very likely be out there working in chains alongside those salt smugglers Bienville's using to clear off the swamps upriver in New Orleans. On the other hand, all we have to do is lie back and let some man roll us every now and then, so all considered, we're not that badly off."

Mignon's words left Nicole more indignant than ever. Everyone kept telling her she should be *grateful* for this new life. Why, then, did she feel so abused and degraded?

"But Legarde sold us as though we were slaves —" she protested.

"Oh, he'd never admit to that, and it would be hard to prove," Mignon reminded her. "He calls his 'sales' part the 'distribution of merchandise' and refers to his profits as 'reimbursement of expenses' for 'services rendered' to those planters who can't go to Mobile in person when the ships arrive. Rest assured, he's clever and careful."

"Is everyone here corrupt?" Nicole asked in dismay.

"There's corruption all over these days, *chérie*. And the damn system — or rather, the lack of it — leaves so many possibilities for mishaps or even outright knavery. In France they're snatching people off the streets and even kidnapping them at so much per head just to fill quotas for the colonies. It's all a business, with some making the profits and others, like us, providing the means."

"But I thought the Regent wanted the men to marry the women he was sending here."

"Of course, that's what he and the *Compagnie* would like," Mignon said ruefully. "And it would be ideal if it were that way, with everyone paired off and living happily ever after. But the reality is quite different. Many do marry, of course, especially the correction girls from Salpêtrière. That's what I was, you know. We came here in chains like you, but a couple of nuns escorted us, and we were distributed to men who agreed to marry us. They gave me to a clod of a farmer, and a priest said a few words over us on the docks in a mass ceremony with about ten other couples. Then the *religieuses* sailed back to France, probably feeling they had earned their crowns in heaven for having risked the voyage to deposit us here in hell! The son of a bitch they married me to started beating on me every time he was in his cups, so I decided to run off and be on my own like I'd been in Paris. That was when that weasel Legarde caught me and sold me to Jean. And, like I told you, Legarde's one of the officials in charge here, so you can see how things are!"

Nicole's head was spinning. "But Legarde isn't the only official in the colony. Surely there must be someone we could complain to . . . someone who'd listen to us. . . ."

"How naive you are!" exclaimed Mignon. "Don't you realize that, even if you could find some official to complain to, he'd probably just laugh and then take a little 'comfort' out of you for himself? Face it, *chérie*, that's what we were sent here for. In the eyes of the law we're only whores and criminals serving out our terms in what amounts to one big penal colony. Remember, we're outcasts. If we fall into the cracks, no one gives a damn. The authorities really don't want us here any more than they wanted us back home."

"But surely you can't be very contented belonging to an animal like Renaud. Isn't he just as bad or worse than your husband was?"

Mignon shrugged her slim shoulders. "I've decided I might as well make the best of it here for the time being. A woman alone can't survive in this wilderness, and most men are going to mistreat whores like us anywhere we go. At least with Jean I have a good roof over my head, all the food and drink I want, servants to do the menial work, and even a few luxuries. Believe me, *chérie*, we could be a lot worse off."

"Is there no place else to go, then?" Nicole asked incredulously.

"Not that I know of," came the other girl's quick reply. "There isn't even a church or a convent in this part of the colony. It's so remote here that there's seldom a traveling priest or official around to even demand an accounting from anyone who might try to abuse us."

"But there's a governor . . . a militia . . ."

Mignon snorted. "Now that's a laugh! It's mostly because of the soldiers that the Regent is shipping women to Louisiana in the first place! You see, Bienville has been sending so many complaints back to France about the way his men are running through the woods after the Indian girls that the Duc d'Orléans, whoremonger that he is, simply decided to send over a few boatloads of harlots to placate him. But they say Bienville is still complaining. He wants no part of us here. He thinks we're troublemakers, so I dare say he often looks the other way where we're concerned."

"But if he were confronted with the facts," Nicole insisted. "If he really knew . . ."

"Don't expect any miracles," Mignon interrupted with a cynical smile. "The most the governor would probably do — *if* you could track him down — would be to order that those interested in getting a wife draw lots to decide who'd get you."

"*Mon Dieu!* Is he the same as all the others, then?" moaned Nicole.

"I wouldn't say that," Mignon replied with a shrug. "He doesn't seem to be as corrupt as most of the officials, and he's certainly no rake. Actually, where women are concerned, he has a reputation of being a rather cold fish, though he's no fop like our friend Legarde. Or rather, if he is, he's very discreet about it. But I heard the two men he sent here to meet with Dawson talking outside my door today, and they said they thought the governor was biding his time until he could go to France and convince some highborn lady to marry him and return to the colonies with him. Meanwhile I'm sure he'd rather abstain than consort with any of us."

"But he should at least . . . as governor . . ." Nicole spluttered.

"That's just the point," continued Mignon. "As governor, Bienville has more pressing problems than a bunch of castoffs he doesn't want here in the first place. We'll be lucky if he can just keep this damn colony from sinking back down into the swamps again. No, *chérie*, you can forget about him or anyone else around here worrying about us."

Nicole lay silent and felt cold again, despite the evening's pleasant warmth. So she would have to face her destiny at last. No matter how she resisted, it seemed she was doomed. There had been many moments in the past year when she could have lost her life, yet here she was — very much alive but destined to drink to the bitter dregs the cup fate had poured for her.

And it was still difficult for her to believe that this was the way all the dreams she had once had for the future were going to end. How many times had she wondered, while little tremors of excitement ran deliciously up and down her spine, about the way it would be on her wedding night . . . the way it would feel for a man to make love to her. She hadn't been certain of all the details, of exactly how it would be, for although her father had been good to her, there had been things she had dared not ask him or her prudish old governess. Nevertheless, she had always wanted to believe that the act of love would be pleasant between two people who really cared for each other.

From early adolescence she had been aware that she attracted men. She'd had more than her share of admirers at social functions, but the young men had never dared to offend her or take liberties, probably because she had always been well chaperoned. Her father's zeal where she was concerned had been well-known. So she had grown to womanhood unmolested, a carefree girl — a bit overly romantic and naive perhaps, but secure and full of hope for the future.

How happy she had been this time last year! Of course, her dream lover had worn the features of chestnut-haired Marcel. But what a rude awakening she'd had when he abandoned her.

She wondered if he ever thought of her now. But what did it matter? He was gone from her life, like everything else she had treasured. She no longer dreamed of him or any man. Most certainly she didn't dream about love.

The time had come. Her destiny had finally caught up with her. The most intimate part of her was to be brutally invaded by some nameless ruffian. An orgy with a bevy of drunken strangers was to replace the wedding night that would never be. But then, how foolish those childish fantasies of hers had been! There was no such thing as love. There was only lust.

Chapter 8

Long after Mignon and the Indian woman had gone and the key had turned in the lock, Nicole lay motionless in the semidarkness. Citronella spiced the air now, and the loud hum of crickets outside the window mingled with the sounds of laughter and voices.

The warm bath, along with the herb tea Baba had pressed on her, had left her drowsy, so Mignon had drawn the thin white mosquito netting that hung from the bed's canopy and suggested that she try to get some sleep, since it was almost certain she would have no opportunity later on.

She was exhausted but she was still too tense to let go and doze off. The pounding of her heart almost drowned out the ominous rumble of masculine voices echoing down the gallery from the main rooms. Try as she did to blot out those heralds of impending doom, she found herself listening intently, straining toward every sound, wondering at what moment that flimsy veil that shielded her from the world would suddenly be pushed aside.

She found herself thinking how each one of those gruff voices belonged to someone who would soon be lying there beside her — some man who would be using her any way he pleased. For to him she would be nothing more than soft flesh to clutch and bite, a warm sheath to give pleasure and release.

She wondered how they would look as their strange faces bent close to hers. What would they say? Would they expect her to talk? And how would they go about it? Would they line up there in the room and take turns falling on top of her, or would they steal in one by one? Mignon had spoken as though she might be expected to handle more than one at a time. *Sainte Vierge!*

Thoughts of escape flooded her mind again, yet she knew there was a guard outside her door, and beyond that the wilderness rife with deadly inhabitants. Renaud was correct when he said she might as well attend his guests without chains since there was no place for her to go.

If only she could look on her lot with the same philosophy as her friends Murielle and Mignon! They seemed able to take it all in their stride. Perhaps the day would come when she would accept it, too. But for the moment the thought of living that way was more than she could bear.

Yet something deep within her refused to give up completely. She had come this far and managed to survive. No matter what the future held, a part of her clung to life. She knew she had to go on and face whatever lay in store for her.

The night air that caused the netting to flutter gently was cool on her bare skin, yet the wild beating of her heart set her blood racing.

More and more boisterous laughter and an occasional oath punctuated the medley of male voices and clattering tableware. How long had she been lying there? Surely it was after midnight by now.

And then two voices emerged from the others and came closer until she suspected they were right outside her door. It was Renaud, and he was talking to someone about her. A second voice, equally deep yet more modulated, was muttering something in reply, but she couldn't catch the words.

She wanted to run, to hide, to cry out — anything but lie there in her fragile prison of mosquito netting. But at that moment the key turned in the lock and the door swung open. A slight breeze invaded the dimly lit chamber and set the candle to fluttering wildly.

Renaud's short, stocky figure was obliterated by the powerful frame of the second man, who filled the doorway completely. Nicole froze, then tried to peer through the white mist of the *baire* — the only wall that stood between her and the tall stranger who had just stepped into the chamber. She kept her eyes fixed on him and tried to rise to shield her nakedness, but her limbs were paralyzed. Oh, God, was this giant of a man going to be the first?

"No, no, *mon capitaine*." She heard Renaud's voice coming from behind the stranger. "I insist you take your turn with her. The others can draw cards to see how they'll follow."

"But if she just arrived this afternoon and you haven't even had time yet to be with her yourself —" the other was objecting politely. "After all, if she's to be your concubine —"

Nicole heard Renaud snort disdainfully. "Bah! Exactly! If the wench is mine, I can have her anytime I want to, so I can afford to be generous, *non*? What's a whore between friends? And we *are* friends after tonight, *n'est-ce pas, capitaine*?" Renaud's voice was oily and condescending now.

"So it would seem," came the courteous but less effusive reply.

"Then please, I insist you go ahead and enjoy her to your heart's content. She's here to please you, *mon ami.*

Use her as you wish. My overseer will be right outside the door, so if there is anything you want . . . ." A nervous note crept into Renaud's voice. "If the strumpet displeases you in any way, don't hesitate to let me know. She's a beauty, all right, and without a blemish on her. You won't need to use any of your English redingotes to ride *this* filly, though I warn you she'll probably need some coaxing. Remember, she's a convict, so don't expect much sweetness and grace from her. But then I'm sure there isn't a wench you can't handle once you've mounted her, *n'est-ce pas?*"

Renaud's voice was oily again, but the captain paid little heed to it or to the crudeness of his parting jest as the door closed behind him. His eyes were beginning to grow accustomed to the dim light, and what he saw behind the misty curtain had captured his immediate attention. Faith! Here was a wench he wouldn't mind coaxing one bit!

Chapter 9

The softly curved figure lying nude shone palely from
the dimness of the shadowy chamber. Her face may have
been a white blur in the frame of her abundant auburn
hair, but Paul Dawson knew she had to be pretty. How
could it have been otherwise when everything about her
was perfection itself?

In bold appraisal he followed the path of the capricious
candlelight as it illuminated the twin peaks of her rose-
tipped breasts and flickered along the sweeping curves
of the sensuous hips and thighs. In the pale golden glow,
the satiny smoothness of her skin reminded him of carved
ivory . . . ivory glimpsed through a delicate veil of moonlit
lace.

Renaud had told his guests that they were in for a
pleasant surprise, and Dawson had to admit his host hadn't
exaggerated. The wench must not have been whoring for
long. What a delightful sheen her skin had, and how high
and firm her breasts were! The sight of her sent a rush
of desire coursing through his veins.

He moved closer to the bed, unbuckling his sword belt and working at the various lacings of his clothing as he went, all the while keeping his eyes fastened on the girl who waited for him.

He had intended to remove only his frock coat and breeches, but now that he had seen how exquisite she was, he decided to disrobe and enjoy her to the fullest. How he'd like to linger awhile and delight in the perfection of her, exploring every nook and crevice of that sensuous body. But there were five others waiting in the parlor, so she would probably not be in the mood to dally too long with any one of them.

Nicole dared not breathe. Even as she wanted to disappear, however, her eyes strained against the dimness to see this man who would be her first.

She could tell he was not wearing a peruke. It was his own generous blond hair caught at the nape of his neck. Yes, he matched the description Mignon had given her of that pirate *El Diablo Dorado*. This had to be him — the Golden Devil himself!

Suddenly the bed curtains parted and for a long moment he stood there, his gaze frankly appraising.

"Faith, lass! But you're a pleasant surprise! I'd have offered my services to the French long ago had I known you'd be here waiting for me!"

She wanted to cover herself, then lash out and fight him, but she knew that to resist him was to tempt fate.

So she lay there, willing her body to be still, reminding herself that he was one of many. Refuse him, and there would simply be another to take his place . . . . then another . . . and another. And if she dared scream, it would only bring everyone else, and they would probably end up having one of those horrible orgies that both Renaud and Mignon had mentioned.

The buccaneer had pushed aside the net curtains and was bending toward her now. His scent was on her — strong, masculine, and not unpleasant.

She bit her lip to keep from crying out as he threw

himself on top of her. Now his skin was on hers, his body rippling firm and smooth against the bareness of her skin. It was a sensation unlike any she'd ever known — his flesh against hers, fire and ice. His touch was sure and deft, and his hands moved over her and owned her. His tongue sought her lips, forcing them apart eagerly.

He had her now, and his powerful body was a vise to her helpless one. He tensed, flexed, and she gasped. Holy Mother of God! It was happening. This brazen pirate was really going to take her! His hand closed over the fullness of her breast and fondled it in a way that stripped her of rage, of panic. Strange, unexpected sensations tugged at her loins. Instinctively she tried to strike out at him, no longer caring whether she brought down the wrath of Renaud and all his guests upon her. But it was too late. The blond demon had locked her in his powerful embrace and his tongue had claimed her mouth as his deft hands had taken over her body.

A burning hardness was pushing now against the apex of her tightly closed legs, and the buccaneer's caresses grew more passionate, more demanding. The hot, pulsating tip of his manhood seared her thighs. She tensed, knowing the inevitable moment was upon her.

Dawson was surprised to discover how tense the girl was. He had expected her lips to part, her arms to encircle him, and her legs to receive him. Instead, she was so rigid, so uncooperative! Despite the soft warmth of her body, she was unyielding. Perhaps it was because he was the first this evening. After all, even a whore needed some warming up. He had wanted her from the moment he had seen her, and he was eager to take her then and there. But how much more pleasant it would be for them both if she responded!

He ran his hands through the sweet-scented abundance of her hair, watching as the red-gold of it glinted in the candlelight. By Jupiter! He had forgotten there were women like this!

Suddenly his gaze was caught by the fleur-de-lis on

her shoulder, and that unexpected reminder of the girl's unsavory past momentarily disconcerted him. It seemed incongruous. Renaud had said she was a condemned murderess. How could a woman as soft and lovely as this ever have killed anyone? Besides, what did it matter whether she was a condemned felon or not? He wanted her so much now that he wouldn't care if she were Medusa herself!

Deliberately holding back his urgency to take her, he murmured and lowered his mouth to the nipple of the breast he had been caressing and began to tickle it gently with his tongue, then faster as his hunger grew. He moved to the other breast, his own breath coming fast, and it was then that he felt her begin to tremble beneath him.

A low moan escaped Nicole's lips. She could feel her body reacting as though it were no longer a part of her, responding in spite of herself. How was it possible for her to feel such things with a stranger whose face she had not even seen? How could her breasts swell and her nipples stiffen to his touch and her flesh tingle to the demands of his body pressing against hers? He seemed to be draining all the strength from her, drawing the very essence out of her.

She resented this assault upon her senses as much or more than the assault upon her body. She wanted control over this, the part of her she'd thought no man could touch, but this renegade who was so boldly trying to possess her definitely held the upper hand.

Dawson reached down again to see whether the girl was ready to receive him. Her thighs were quivering wildly against his, so he moved his knee between them and eased them apart, impatient to go on. His hand tightened on the swell of her breast, and his mouth found her ear in time to whisper, "Now," as he thrust at last.

Nicole cried out involuntarily as she felt him plunge into her, his lance tearing through her as it pushed unhesitatingly forward. She cried out again, but there was no stopping its impetus now. A strange mixture of pain and pleasure racked her from head to foot, even as Dawson, too, momentarily shuddered from the unexpected impact.

"My God!" he groaned, his voice husky and breathless in her ear, but he could no longer stem the tide. The force of his passion engulfed them both, sweeping them along in its all-consuming urgency. She was filled to bursting now with the throbbing hardness of him as he thrust again and again, ever deeper, gaining in momentum as he went, blazing a trail into the very core of her being. Instinctively she clung to him.

He grasped her buttocks, urging her to follow his rhythm. She was sobbing in short spurts as her own breathing quickened and the flood of strange, uncontrollable sensations finally overpowered her. Beyond reasoning, she lay there blindly obeying him, letting him do as he willed with her. It was happening and there was nothing she could do. He had unleashed his passion and was sweeping her along to fulfillment.

Suddenly a throaty moan shuddered from him as he gave a final feverish thrust and exploded deep within her, leaving her vibrating at the impact of his passion. He fell against her, spent from the overwhelming force of the long-awaited release, his face buried in her hair, his hand still on her breast.

In a frenzy of emotion — caught between panic and ecstasy — Nicole lay in his arms weeping softly. Their bare flesh moist from the emotions that had racked them both, they clung to each other, fused together. The experience they had shared enveloped them. The very room was charged with it.

Chapter 10

For a few moments only the sound of his labored breathing and her faint sobs disturbed the silence of the dimly lit chamber. When at last he pulled reluctantly away from her, he was aware for the first time how the girl was trembling. Curious, he lifted himself to his elbow and peered down at her, trying to see her face in the semidarkness.

"What a bloody fool I am! Did I hurt you, lass?" he asked incredulously.

In truth, he was sorry if he had been rough with her. That's what came, he supposed, of having been at sea too long. The girl seemed more refined, more sensitive than most prostitutes he had known. Actually, he would like to go on to a second time with her. He felt he could spend the whole night making love to her and still want more. Already he was swelling with renewed desire. Never had he enjoyed a woman so much!

He sensed, however, that something was amiss. For though he had enjoyed the brief but passionate encounter immensely, something bothered him about it. If he hadn't known better, he would have sworn he had just taken a virgin! Of course, he knew harlots had their tricks to please a man — special douches, skillful muscular contractions — but the girl's reactions puzzled him. Renaud had led him to expect an ill-tempered vixen, but instead the woman he held in his arms seemed surprisingly vulnerable, more like a frightened, confused young girl than a hardened whore.

He rose and brought the candle over to the bed. For a moment he stood there delighting in the closer look at the lovely, sensuous body he had just possessed. Her breasts were still taut and quivering, their rosy tips ripe and swollen from his kisses.

Suddenly he saw the red stains on the sheet. Swearing, he lifted the candle to the girl's face and stared in amazement. The largest, most luminous green eyes he had ever seen glared at him.

"Blast it all, girl! Haven't you ever lain with a man before?" he exclaimed in disbelief, still unable to accept what the evidence suggested.

She seemed unable to reply. Not knowing whether she had understood him or not, he repeated his question in French. All she could do, however, was shake her head and look at him accusingly, though her terror and confusion were palpable. And she still tried to shield her nakedness from the scrutiny of those disturbing blue eyes. Now that he was no longer faceless, she felt more ashamed than ever. In that fleeting moment, as their eyes met, the memory of how he had just possessed her so completely sent her blood rushing through her veins, and a hot flush colored her neck.

"I don't understand," he went on, using French now in order to be certain she knew exactly what he was saying. "Renaud led us to believe — Didn't you come over with that last boatload of convicts? That is a fleur-de-lis on your shoulder, isn't it? God as my witness, I'd never have taken you like that had I known ... I thought you were a ... were accustomed to ... My God!"

The circle of light bathed his ruggedly handsome features and caught gold lights amid the tangle of hairs on the broad expanse of his chest.

"Just because I've been branded a felon doesn't necessarily make me a whore!" she replied bitterly, finding her voice at last, though she hardly recognized its thin, quavering tone as her own.

"The truth is you don't look like either one," he admitted. "Why, you're scarcely more than a child ... a frightened one at that!"

"I'm far from being a child," she retorted. "I'm a woman who knows when she's just been raped!"

"Raped?" His jaw dropped. "Damn it all, wench! If you didn't want a man to breach you, what the blazes were you doing here like ... like this?"

"I — I'm not here of my own volition, I assure you."

"You mean this was ... you really were a virgin?"

"I *was* until ... until you forced yourself on me!"

"Forced? Now hold on there, lass. You were lying here ready to receive me. I've never had to force myself on any woman. Why in the devil didn't you tell me?"

"What difference would it have made?"

"It could have made some. For one thing, if I had known this was going to be your first time, I'd have been a little more gentle with you. As it was, I thought ... How the hell was I supposed to know?"

Nicole sat up, crouching in the middle of the bed, her legs drawn close to her body, still trying to cover herself with trembling hands.

Suddenly Dawson remembered Renaud and the others waiting in the parlor. He knew only too well what lay ahead for the girl as the night wore on and the wine continued to flow. She might be a condemned murderess and a branded outcast, but as he stood there looking down into that bewildered beautiful face, a wave of compassion swept over him.

The memory of his possession of her came back to him, and it warmed his loins just to think of how it had been. Somehow he couldn't bear the thought of those others mauling her, of rough, insensitive hands abusing that exquisite body. Perhaps he was feeling a little guilty, but now that he knew she wasn't a whore, it would be hard for him to sit by and watch the others merrily breach her. The poor wench ... she seemed so alone, so defenseless!

He rose and began dressing.

"Where are your clothes?" he asked as he relaced the points of his breeches.

"I have none," she replied sullenly. "They burned the ones I came here with and refused to give me anything to wear until morning."

He pulled on his boots and went to the door, opening it to say a few words to the guards. Then he returned to the bed and tossed her his red silk frock coat. "Put this on," he said in the manner of one accustomed to giving orders. He buckled on his sword once more. "I've sent for Renaud."

Chapter 11

Renaud came quickly, obviously worried that his new concubine had somehow offended his guest of honor.

He cast an uneasy glance at Nicole, but the buccaneer's tall frame blocked the doorway and prevented a closer view.

Except for his coat and jabot, the captain was fully dressed. A gold-embroidered vest of royal-blue silk finished off his white full-sleeved shirt, which was open at the throat.

"Something is amiss, *mon capitaine*?" the planter asked, anxiously mopping his brow with one of his finest lace-trimmed kerchiefs. "If this baggage has —"

"No, no, nothing like that," Dawson assured him as he passed a hand quickly over the golden tumult of his hair to smooth it back into place, "but I did call you to talk about her." His French was so perfect it was hard to believe he was British.

"Ah, then you liked the wench?" The apprehension on Renaud's face dissolved into a smile of relief. "Perhaps you'd like a little more time with her but are concerned over those who are waiting —"

"Forgive me if I interrupt you," Dawson said, holding up a hand, "but I prefer to come straight to the point."

"Ah, yes, I could see that from the way you handled yourself with the governor's men earlier this evening. I admire a man of your caliber, *mon ami.*"

"Several times you have been kind enough to speak of friendship between us ..."

Renaud's bulldog countenance lit up. *"Oui, oui, mon capitaine,"* he replied eagerly. "I'd like nothing better than to have the honor of calling you a friend."

"Then, if I may, I'd like to presume on that friendship, though I assure you I wouldn't ask for a favor I couldn't repay doublefold."

The planter was beaming. "Whatever you wish, *mon ami.* If it's in my power, I'd consider it a privilege to gratify you in whatever way I can."

"In that case, it would gratify me immensely if you'd let me buy this wench from you."

"Let — let you buy her?" Renaud repeated, his eyes bulging.

"Precisely. Since you say you acquired her today — only a few hours ago — you can't have formed any real attachment for her yet, at least nothing, I'm sure, that a bag of gold can't compensate. That's why I make so bold as to ask you to let me have her."

Renaud's jaw hung lax. "But — but the wench isn't for sale, *capitaine.* Why, the very fact that I just got her is all the more reason — as I told you, I haven't even mounted her yet myself!"

"I'm not one to haggle," interrupted Dawson in a calm, deliberate voice, ignoring Renaud's startled objections. "I'll pay you well. She tells me you bought her from one of the Company officials who brought her to you this afternoon."

Renaud's eyes narrowed. "I — I didn't exactly *buy* the

wench," he corrected the buccaneer. "I simply paid the man for the trouble and expense he went to to fetch her for me since I couldn't go to Mobile myself for the distribution. And believe me, *mon ami*, that rascal charged me a fortune for his services, though he assured me she was the pick of the lot."

But Dawson dismissed his host's explanation with an indifferent shrug of his shoulders. "I'll not quibble over how you came by her," he said coolly. "Let's just say I'll reimburse you for whatever the girl cost you and add something for any inconvenience this whim of mine might cause you."

Renaud couldn't hide his amazement. "*Mon Dieu!* I knew the wench was special, but I never expected this! She's that good, eh?" He tried again to look beyond Dawson's frame to where Nicole was sitting on the bed.

Dawson shrugged again. "I wouldn't go so far as to say that. I've certainly known whores more skilled at their trade than this one. But since she's the only one available to me at this moment, she'll have to do."

Renaud, however, was running his hand over his double chin while a lecherous grin slowly spread over his florid countenance. "So she gave you a good ride. . . ."

Dawson's face showed nothing. He realized he must proceed cautiously and not say anything that might make the planter more interested in the girl than he already was.

"I assure you I've had better," the captain said indifferently. "It's just that I need a concubine and this wench happens to be the nearest at hand."

Renaud shifted his gaze again to Nicole. The glow in his eyes intensified as he caught sight of the slim legs dangling from the protective folds of the buccaneer's frock coat. He knew his desire for this damn bitch was clouding his better judgment, but he was determined to breach her. All evening he had been anticipating the moment when he and his guests had finished with her and she'd be lying weary and bruised at his feet, pleading for him to call a halt to the orgy. Then and only then would she be ready for her final lesson in submission at his hands. Once his guests were gone, he would spend the next few days training her — riding her with a crop if need be — until she'd learned how to please his every whim. Never again would she dare give him a look of disgust when he touched her.

"I — I have plans for this wench, *mon capitaine*," he said at last, his voice gravelly. "I'm sorry. Ask me anything else you wish, but I can't sell her." Anxious, however, to stay in the buccaneer's good graces, he quickly added, "Of course, if you'd like to mount her again, you're welcome to do so. She's here to please you. Roll her as many times as you wish. There's no need to buy her. I'll always share my concubine gladly with a friend."

"I appreciate your generosity, but I'm afraid it'll do me little good after I leave here tomorrow," sighed Dawson, momentarily feigning resignation. "But then, I suppose I've presumed too much on our friendship. After all, it's still too new to put it to such an exacting test."

Renaud shifted uneasily. He didn't want to displease the man Bienville had asked him to keep contented at any cost. But did this include so magnificent a concubine? No, there had to be some way to keep the buccaneer captain happy and not lose the wench!

"It's not the money," Renaud hastily assured his guest. "It's just that she would be hard to replace. Women are scarce in these parts."

"And they're even scarcer on the high seas!" Dawson retorted wryly. "That's why the only practical solution is to have a wench on hand for whenever I might feel the need of female company."

Renaud grinned knowingly. "I can sympathize with you on that score, my friend. Men of our strong temperaments have difficulty satisfying our appetites here in the New World, *n'est-ce pas*? But if all you want is a *chat* to share your berth, I'll be glad to put you in contact with the same man who got this one for me. He had others with him when he came by this afternoon, and I'm sure he's spending the night just a few miles from here. I could send a servant to fetch him for you. Rest assured, that knave would travel to hell and back to make a few extra *louis*."

"I'm afraid I haven't made myself clear," said Dawson, working hard at patience now. "Tomorrow morning my officers and I must leave at the crack of dawn. I have over a hundred men waiting for me to rejoin them. If I don't return by the time I've specified, they might think there's been foul play, and that could be disastrous for all concerned, especially the French colonies. So you see, I wouldn't want to jeopardize the good relations between your governor and myself simply because I dallied here shopping for a wench! No, my friend, I don't have time for such frivolities. That's why I said this one would have to do."

"It — it's not that I don't want to be a generous host, but —"

"And I will be generous in the price I pay you if you do this small favor for me. Shall we say half again what you paid for the wench? You could replace her at your leisure and have a goodly sum left over to compensate for any inconvenience this impromptu request might cause you. Of course, I intend to pay you in gold — Spanish gold, the purest there is, as you know."

The light in Renaud's eyes took on a new glow as lust warred with greed. Money, especially gold and silver, was scarce in the colonies. Settlers hoarded any foreign coins they could get their hands on. Nevertheless, he wasn't ready yet to relinquish the pleasure of bending his feisty new concubine to his will. The defiance blazing in those bold green eyes of hers seemed to be challenging him to tame her!

"I wouldn't want you to leave thinking I'm an ungracious host," he said slowly, never once taking his gaze from the wild-eyed girl sitting on the edge of the bed like a wounded lioness ready to spring at the slightest provocation. "If you are set on taking a wench with you in the morning, I'll let you have Mignon, the only other woman on the plantation except for an Indian squaw who's my housekeeper. And I can assure you that giving up Mignon will be a sacrifice. She's a whore who knows her trade and enjoys it. Believe me, you'll be coming out better with her. I'm sure I'll regret my decision before the week is out, but I have too great a yen for this wench here to give her up just yet."

The captain crossed the room, then turned again to Renaud, his face as impassive as before. "And this Mignon . . . what does she look like?" he asked.

"I'll send her to your chamber this moment so you can sample her," Renaud offered eagerly. "Believe me, the wench will please your every whim. And she's not a bad looker, either — long dark curls —"

But the buccaneer lifted a large suntanned hand to silence his host. "One moment, *mon ami*," he interrupted. "Don't bother calling her. I should have mentioned it sooner, but I'm partial to fair-haired wenches . . . especially redheads like this one. Oh, I might lie with a dark-haired woman now and then, but I wouldn't want to put out a goodly sum of money for one that isn't to my taste. After all, I'll be cooped up for months on end with her once we're at sea, and if she's not completely to my liking, I'll tire of her all the sooner."

Renaud was noticeably crestfallen. "Then I'm afraid I can't —"

"Look, my friend, suppose we end this bickering once and for all. I'll give you double what you paid for this wench in doubloons. She's not worth it, but I refuse to haggle over something as insignificant as a harlot."

Renaud blinked. "I — I paid eight hundred livres for her. I can show you the receipt I got for the merchandise, so you'll see I'm not lying. Surely you won't pay sixteen hundred for her?" he asked incredulously.

"I agree no whore is worth such a price," said Dawson, his face as fathomless as ever. "But I said I'd double whatever she cost you, and I never go back on my word. So let's not waste any more time on the matter. Certainly that should be more than enough to console you for the loss of any concubine, especially when you already have another one to comfort you."

Renaud licked his thick lips greedily. To double his money in one day was more than he could resist. The wench, it seemed, was worth more to him out of bed than in it! The buccaneer must be mad to pay that much for a slut, much less a condemned convict like this one. Of course, women were scarce in these parts, especially pretty ones, so it was worth spending a little more to have the pick of what was available. But the equivalent of 1,600 livres in gold? A king's ransom! Only a pirate with the treasure chests of New Spain at his disposal could make such an offer just to gratify a whim.

"You drive a hard bargain, *mon capitaine*," the planter sighed. "But if buying this wench means so much to you, I have no choice but to acquiesce. After all, the governor asked me to be gracious to you. I'll have the wench sent to your room as soon as we've finished with her."

The captain's blue eyes hardened. "One moment, *monsieur*. No buttered buns for me! The wench is mine from this moment on or not at all," he said sharply. "I'm afraid I'm not as generous by nature as you are, my friend. As long as a woman belongs to me, no one else touches her. Call it vanity or caprice, but I think I'm paying a high enough price to be humored."

"But surely you can let us have just a little sip? It doesn't affect the taste of the wine to share it. After all, you'll still have the bottle in the morning."

"Aye, half empty or worse," growled Dawson, his patience wearing thin. "No, *monsieur*, I wouldn't want the wench after those ruffians have finished with her. Every man to his taste, of course, but personally I never touch a woman who's just lain with another man. Frankly, if you hadn't been so generous as to insist that I go first with this one, I wouldn't have accepted your kind invitation to lie with her at all."

"But the others are waiting. What shall I tell them? That I'm snatching the glass out of their hands just as they're about to drink?"

"You've just said you have another concubine and that she's even more skilled than this one. Let Mignon finish out the night with your guests. With the money I pay you for this one, you should be able to buy yourself a whole brothel. In my own case, however, I feel I can afford to be more generous with my gold than with my only concubine."

"*Bien*. As you say, every man to his taste. But at least let me have a tumble with the wench — just one ride, that's all I ask. I'd hate to give her up without having at least sampled her. Certainly you can understand that. I'll send for Mignon to attend the others, but I've had my sights on this *chat* since I first laid eyes on her. As one gentleman to another, you wouldn't deny me that one final pleasure, would you?"

He spoke with increasing speed as he saw the buccaneer's face darken. "Just give me a quarter of an hour with her — five minutes, if you wish. After that, I'll send her to your chamber. She'll be yours to do with as you please."

"Pardon me, my friend, but if your word is your bond, as I assure you mine is, the girl is mine now, and I definitely intend to do with her as I please," snapped the captain, his hand resting lightly on the hilt of his sword. I'm certain you are a man of honor, *monsieur*, and that you'll respect the terms of the sale we have just agreed upon. The wench is mine now, and anyone who touches her from this moment on must answer to me."

Renaud paled, his face more sallow than ever in contrast

to the harsh black curls of his shoulder-length wig. Dawson had a reputation for being deadly when crossed, and Renaud certainly had no desire to match steel with one of the most renowned buccaneers in the Caribbean. What's more, he wouldn't want to risk Bienville's displeasure by fighting over a harlot with a man whom the governor had asked him to win over to the French cause! Then there were those Spanish doubloons. . . .

The planter's barrel chest sagged in defeat. "Of course, *mon capitaine*, you're right," he purred. "I'll have the wench sent to your room immediately."

For the first time since the bartering had begun, Dawson walked over to the foot of the bed and looked down at Nicole.

She had caught enough of his conversation with Renaud to know that he had just bought her to fill his "needs," and she glared up at him with open hatred, but he seemed oblivious to it.

"One thing more," he said, directing himself to the planter, though he kept his eyes fixed on her. "The girl needs clothing. Perhaps something can be found for her in the other wench's wardrobe ... some kind of gown, shoes ... whatever is necessary."

"Of course, of course," agreed the Frenchman. "Don't concern yourself over it. She'll be ready for the voyage when she leaves with you in the morning."

Renaud went hurriedly to the door and gave a rapid order to the guard. Then he turned to the captain once more. "Will you be retiring now with the wench?" he asked with a sly grin. "I can understand how you might like to go on enjoying your new purchase, but permit me to remind you that the night is young, and I'd consider it an honor if you'd spend at least a few hours more with us in the parlor. You might even like to take a tumble or two with Mignon while you're at it. Who knows? Before the night is over, you might regret not having accepted her instead of this one!"

"I have no intention of being rude to you or your guests,"

replied the captain easily. "After all, my primary reason for being here is to meet with Governor Bienville's representatives, and there are still one or two matters I'd like to settle with them before leaving in the morning. But I would like to have this wench locked in my chamber for now and the key turned over to me."

"*Bien, bien*, it shall be as you wish," Renaud agreed, but as he turned away, he stroked his several chins. "I think it's my obligation to remind you, *capitaine*, that this wench can be dangerous." He went on more cautiously. "She may be a beauty, but she's a bad one. Remember, I told you about her being a murderess, and I'm sure you saw the brand on her shoulder. A slut like this is capable of anything — even murdering you in your sleep if you're not careful!"

The captain smiled. "Yet you bought her for yourself?"

"True, but with the intention of taming her as quickly as possible. The wench needs to be ridden hard. That's one of the reasons why I wanted her to attend all of you tonight. I'd hoped to keep her mounted and going at a fast gallop till dawn."

Dawson's smile turned slowly into a frown of annoyance. Everything the planter said convinced him that he had made the right decision in buying the girl.

"Frankly, I'm surprised the wench has had time to earn herself such a reputation since she's only been with you for a few hours."

"Ah, but you don't know this one, *capitaine*," the planter replied nervously. "She's an ill-tempered bitch, as brazen as they come. Believe me, she practically destroyed the official's face this afternoon when he tried to strip her for inspection. She took a few swipes at me, too. No, my friend, all I want to do is put you on alert. Don't be deceived by her pretty face. She's an *incorrigible*, deported here as an undesirable. A vixen like this belongs in chains. Never turn your back on her, and once you've finished using her, lock her up good. I wouldn't want to lose your goodwill because of something this slut might suddenly decide to do."

Dawson glanced at Nicole, who shot him a scorching look. A smile flitted across his suntanned face. "Thank you for your concern," he told his host politely. "I'll bear your warning in mind."

"*Bien*," the Frenchman sighed. "Just so you won't say I didn't warn you." He paused, then said, "You will remember to tell the governor what good friends we've become, *n'est-ce pas*?" His voice was velvety now.

"Of course, of course," replied Dawson hurriedly, weary of humoring his irritating host, who was obviously a twit as well as a schemer. "Now I'm sure you're anxious to return to your guests. I already feel guilty for having kept you from them so long."

Nicole had sat in stunned silence as she listened to the callous bartering between the two men. To be bought and sold twice in one day! And this new owner possessed her in every sense of the word — down to the very core of her being. The burning imprint of his hand lingered on her breasts ... her lips smarted where he had caught them between his own. She could still feel the overwhelming pressure of his powerful body bearing down on her, the pulsating hardness of his manhood as it penetrated her and set her throbbing to its demanding rhythm. How fragile her defenses had been when the moment of her final degradation had come! She cursed her womanly weakness that made her so vulnerable to brute strength. For once Renaud had been right. She did hate this British buccaneer enough to kill him. If she had really been the murderess everyone thought she was, she would have certainly run him through with his own sword in that instant when he had so brutally pierced her maidenhead!

Well, he may have bought her, but he would soon rue the day he had spent his ill-gotten gold on her! As far as she was concerned, this pirate was the sum of all the vile men who had lusted after her.

Chapter 12

Renaud's overseer took her immediately to the chamber assigned to the buccaneer captain and locked her in. Now she was alone again, waiting for her new owner to finish negotiating and partying with the other guests.

This bedroom was larger than the previous one, and there was at least a top sheet on the bed. Removing the frock coat, she wrapped herself tightly in the sheet and lay back wearily, hoping the captain would stay with the others long enough to give her the opportunity to sleep a few hours. Perhaps she then would be able to face him with renewed energy. *El Diablo Dorado* was in for a fight if he meant to take her again that night or any other night. He might have paid a fortune to get her, but he was going to have to pay dearly every time he tried to touch her. She didn't deceive herself; Dawson was a powerfully built man, well over six feet tall and hardened by the strenuous life at sea. He would undoubtedly overwhelm her in the end, but at least she could see to it that his pleasure cost him every step of the way.

Murielle had been right when she warned Nicole that some men took sadistic delight in breaking in a first-timer. As soon as Dawson discovered she was a virgin, he'd sent for Renaud and bartered with him for her. Given the price he'd paid, he'd surely want his money's worth from her!

The festivities in the front rooms had grown more bois-terous, and Nicole recognized Mignon's laughter rising above the wild chorus. She shuddered and crossed herself. But for a twist of fate, she would be the one out there!

Nicole wondered whether the captain was among the merrymakers. Was he making love to Mignon now per-haps? She stirred restlessly within the cocoon of bedding she had made for herself. It was difficult to picture him possessing Mignon the way he had just possessed her, but then, what did she really know about such things? Mignon probably responded in ways she couldn't even imagine. Perhaps Dawson would change his mind and ask Renaud to give him the other girl after all.

Fear trickled down her spine. What would she do if Dawson gave her back to Renaud? The planter left no doubt about what he intended to do if he ever got his hands on her again. She had to admit that almost anyone — even a pirate — would be better than a monster like Jean Renaud. Of course, the captain probably had some plans of his own for her or he wouldn't have been so set on buying her.

Suddenly the key turned in the lock and the door swung open. Nicole's heart sank; Dawson had come back sooner than she had expected, and she hadn't been able to sleep at all yet. At the sight of that familiar silhouette entering the candlelit room, her heart began to pound wildly. The size of him alone awed and terrified her. He was such a big man, broad-shouldered, hard, and lean, with the agility of a sleek, tawny-skinned lion. The Golden Devil — how well the Spaniards had named him!

Dawson's piercing blue eyes swiftly scanned the room,

taking in every detail with one glance — the frock coat hanging on the back of the chair, the silent figure lying in his bed.

He closed the door behind him and drew the bolt across it. A life of constant danger had taught him the value of caution. As his eyes began to accustom themselves to the dimness, he noted with an amused smile how the girl had pulled the sheet up to her chin so that all he could see of her was a splash of flaming hair on the pillow and those startling green eyes staring at him. He suspected she hadn't been given any clothing yet; on the contrary, she probably had been ordered to lie there and await his pleasure.

His first instinct was to climb into the bed beside her and make love to her all over again. The memory of her soft, warm body pressed close to his and those magnificent breasts swelling to his caresses as they betrayed the passionate nature beneath that icy exterior of hers stirred his desire.

She belonged to him now — and at what a price! He must have been daft to have paid that much for a wench, and a convict at that. But he had no regrets. He wanted her, and now she was his. He had every right to take her, and it was plain she expected him to do so. Then what was stopping him? Her eyes perhaps? Damn, but the girl seemed so terrified of him. She made him feel more like a villain than a savior! Didn't she realize he had rescued her from the slimy Renaud and his friends? Of course, she resented the way he had taken her maidenhead. But how in the devil was he supposed to have known? He had expected a whore and found instead a panic-stricken virgin. But whatever she was, he had her, and he wondered what he was going to do with her. A fighting ship was no place for a woman, despite what he'd told Renaud. There was a time and place for wenching; most certainly it wasn't on the high seas.

He ran a tight ship and demanded discipline of everyone,

including himself. What he ought to do was make love to her a few times and then send her on her way. Yet he knew he couldn't just leave her alone and helpless in the swamps. No, fool that he was, he had simply bought himself a problem. This ill-tempered wench, so obviously inexperienced in matters of love, and a deported murderess to boot, had suddenly invaded his world and he suspected he would never be the same again.

The girl's hostility was palpable, but he decided to ignore it. If only she would open her arms and smile at him the way Mignon had! Yet the thought of this one waiting for him in his bed had prompted him to leave the merrymaking and hurry to her.

He removed his sword belt and vest, and left them beside his frock coat on the large oak chair. Then he walked over to the four-poster and looked down at the girl.

"How nice of you to wait up for me!" he greeted her lightly, the hint of a smile playing about his mouth. He removed his jabot and loosened the lacings of his shirt and breeches.

But Nicole only stared back at him stonily, determined to hide from him how uneasy his penetrating blue eyes made her feel. Of course he knew she was naked under the sheet, and she suspected he was already thinking about stripping it from her, remembering how she had looked when he had made love to her. Something flickered in that level gaze of his and she knew he was toying with the idea of taking her again. She quickly drew the sheet closer to her chin and tried to look as belligerent as possible, hoping he'd be discouraged from coming too close.

Undaunted, however, Dawson sat down on the bed and proceeded to take off one of his boots. Nicole's face grew even paler in the candlelight.

Suddenly a roar of masculine voices echoed down the gallery, and Mignon's incessant laughter was shriller than ever.

Dawson let the boot fall to the floor and stifled a yawn. "That will be going on until dawn," he sighed, "but I prefer to call it a night. Love en masse has never held much appeal for me." He paused and looked at her over his shoulder before tackling the other boot. "You see, I knew you were here waiting for me," he added quietly, a playful smile tugging at the corners of his generous mouth, "so I just couldn't stay away any longer."

She continued to glare at him. When his boot dropped to the floor with a thud, he didn't turn to her but sat staring at the floor. He had to turn away from the hurt and anger he saw in that indignant little face peeping up at him. Obviously the girl was convinced he had raped her. Yet he felt he had made love to her — and longed to do so again. But this time he wanted to take her slowly, tenderly, enjoying every delightful second of her initiation into womanhood. He wanted to set that sensuous little body aglow with the passion he knew she was capable of feeling. Aye, for reasons he still couldn't fathom, he cared enough about this one to want her to care, too.

With a sigh he stretched out beside her, still clad in his breeches and open-necked shirt. Immediately he could feel her tense within her linen cocoon, so he fought the impulse to tear away the blasted sheet separating her from him and take her again. But the thought of her lying there naked beside him set his manhood to throbbing. He longed to plunge once more into the sweet depths of her, to linger in the intimate world of her loveliness. For that first taste he'd had of her had only made him hunger all the more.

He couldn't deny that it awakened special emotions in him whenever he remembered that this woman was his — really his — that she had known no man but him. The part of him that he had left deep in her drew him to her. But it was more than just a physical attraction. Something about this feisty little outcast fascinated him, made him want to hold on to her.

He had long since lost count of the women he had bedded. Why should he be so taken then with this one? Was it the desire pulsing in his loins that was robbing him of his wits? Why in the devil was he lying here wanting her, yet hesitating to take her?

But no, this wasn't the moment to try to make love to her again, and he knew it. She was still too afraid and too resentful of all the abuses she had so recently suffered. What's more, he didn't want to take her against a backdrop of Renaud's drunken guests diverting themselves with some boisterous whore. The girl was his now. He could wait ... wait until he could be truly alone with her. Perhaps tomorrow night, when they would camp under the stars along the banks of the river on the way back to his ship? In the privacy of his tent, with only the sounds of the marshlands around them, her mood might change. There they would be just a man and woman clinging to each other in the wilderness. She might turn to him then and let him make love to her the way he wanted to. He would teach her to respond to his every touch and match his passion with her own. Yes, this was a woman worth waiting for.

"Try to get some rest," he said gently. "We have a three-day journey ahead of us before we reach my ship."

He moved over onto his back and rested his head in the cradle of his arms, his clasped hands behind his neck. Within minutes his rhythmic breathing told her he had dozed off.

Only then did she venture to steal a glance in his direction. At least now she could look openly at this stranger beside her who had so suddenly taken over her existence.

How striking his profile was. The single candle backlighted the squared-off chin and strong Roman nose. His features were as generous as the rest of him. Nevertheless there was a muscular grace about him even in sleep, a suggestion of dormant power like that of a sleeping tiger, of sinewy strength that could easily spring into action.

His was a handsome face, rugged but not harsh. Most

of all, there was strength in it. Even in sleep, Paul Dawson did not strike her as a man to be taken lightly.

His soft doeskin breeches and cotton stockings clung snugly to his well-developed thighs and calves. She looked curiously at his large suntanned hands — hands that only a few hours before had run so possessively over her body and passionately cupped her breasts to his lips. How many other women, she wondered, had he caressed that way? And how many men had he killed with those same hands?

Now that his bold features were softened in sleep, however, she realized he was younger than she had thought. With his tousled mass of golden hair escaping from the ribbon that held it at the nape of his neck, he had an unexpectedly boyish air about him that made him, at least for a moment, seem more raffish than menacing. But then, the man was an enigma. He had just paid Renaud a fortune so he could have her for his concubine, yet now that he had her all to himself, he'd drifted off to sleep without even trying to touch her! What's more, despite Renaud's warnings about her being a convicted murderess, he hadn't tried to restrain her in any way, and he had even left his sword hanging on the back of the chair within easy reach.

For a fleeting moment she was tempted to try to make a break for freedom, but she realized, as he must have known she would, that she would be a fool to try it, what with all the men around and a guard standing watch on the gallery. And even if by some miracle she did manage to get off the premises, how could she find her way through the godforsaken swamps? No, this was not the right moment. She'd bide her time until a better opportunity presented itself.

It was at least another hour before she was finally able to go to sleep, and then it was from sheer exhaustion. Even so, she slept fitfully, always conscious of the lewd merrymaking in the parlor and, most of all, the strange man lying beside her who might awaken at any moment and demand satisfaction from her again.

Chapter 13

The revelry lasted until just before dawn, but Dawson was up at the first glimmer of pale light that sifted through the mesh covering the window. Nicole had momentarily awakened from her fitful dozing and watched him through half-closed lids as he put his boots back on and moved silently around the bedchamber, gathering his belongings. Then, without disturbing her, he slipped out to meet his men and prepare for the journey downriver.

Not long afterward, Baba roused her to announce that the captain wanted her ready to leave within half an hour.

The Indian woman had brought a steaming bowl of hominy with her, as well as one of Mignon's gowns — a simple one of periwinkle blue homespun with a starched white cap and fichu. But there was only a plain linen underskirt to go with it; the captain had said he could not permit too many petticoats within the limited confines of the rowboat.

A bleary-eyed Mignon, clutching a faded lavender silk dressing gown around her shoulders, came to wish her Godspeed.

An ugly bruise was beginning to darken on the swell of one of the darker girl's breasts. When she saw how Nicole stared at it, she shrugged her shoulders and smiled wanly. "You see, I have a couple of decorations of my own," she said. "At least mine will fade until the next time around!"

Her laugh was hard and brittle, but suddenly she broke off and reached for the bureau to steady herself.

"God! How I envy you — brand and all!" she exclaimed, putting a hand to her aching head. "And to think how I was trying to give you advice last night, when you obviously have quite a bag of tricks of your own. Imagine your snaring that magnificent captain! However did you manage to please him enough to make him want to take you along with him?"

Nicole shook her head. "I — I can't say I was trying to please him," she confessed.

"Well, I don't mind telling you *I* was trying!" Mignon hooted, "for all the good it did me! He was all business with Renaud and the governor's men, and though I did everything to get his attention, he didn't even seem to notice I was there! He just seemed anxious to finish whatever he was discussing and get back to you! *Mon Dieu, chérie!* What did you do to bewitch him so? I heard he paid Jean a king's ransom for you. Better give him his money's worth and try to hold on to him!"

Nicole had finished tying her fichu over the décolletage of her gown and was trying to see herself in the small streaked mirror on the bureau, which unfortunately did not match the quality of its ornate, gilded frame.

"How can you call a buccaneer a catch?" she asked as she set the cap on her head and let Mignon straighten it. "The man's an outlaw, a rogue ... "

Mignon looked at her in surprise. "And what does that matter?" she asked. "At least he's his own man — master of his own destiny. That's more than we can say for ourselves!"

Their conversation was rudely interrupted by Renaud's overseer, who declared he had come to put her chains on and take her to the boat landing where Dawson was waiting — a painful reminder that not even her body, much less her destiny, was her own anymore.

The once-familiar weight of her chains felt unbearably heavy that morning as the burly overseer hurried her down to the river through the mist-shrouded trees. Pale and sleepy-eyed, she stumbled along, cursing the fate that would not release her from its implacable grip.

The captain stood in his shirt-sleeves, bidding farewell to Renaud under the same giant oak tree where Legarde had sold her to the planter the afternoon before. *Sainte Vierge!* Had it only been yesterday? It seemed like a life-time ago! In less than twenty-four hours she had been bought and sold twice, lain naked with a man like a common whore, and now she was embarking on a journey as the concubine of a notorious pirate!

But as she came closer to where Dawson stood, he suddenly broke off his conversation and swept a disapproving look over her, his eyes flinty.

"What's this?" he demanded. "Why the devil has she been shackled? I gave no such order."

The overseer began to sputter, but Renaud quickly explained, "I'm afraid the fault is mine, *mon capitaine*," he said apologetically. "I thought you'd want to keep the wench in irons, at least while you're traveling. Remember what I told you; she's a tricky one."

"Well, you misjudged my intentions," Dawson said angrily. "She belongs to me now, so I should have been consulted." He turned abruptly to the overseer. "Get those damn chains off her as fast as you can and put her in the boat."

Once again the overseer shifted uneasily and looked at Renaud.

The planter was groping for words. "I — I'm sorry, *capitaine*, but it seems this oaf here has misplaced the key. Unfortunately, there's no way to get them off at the moment. But then, it's probably for the best, *non*? A shifty wench belongs in chains anyhow."

Dawson mumbled an oath under his breath and glowered at both Renaud and the overseer. The sky was a pale gray now, and he knew he was going to need every previous minute of daylight if they were to make the point in the river where he planned to camp that night.

"Damn! We can't lose any more time!" he exclaimed, exasperation edging his usually well-modulated voice. "Just put the girl in the boat and I'll file the blasted chains off her myself later."

The overseer roughly swept Nicole up in his arms and started to carry her down the bank while Dawson hurried off, shouting a last-minute order to his men, who were wading toward the boat, supporting a cask between them. No sooner had the buccaneer turned away, however, than Renaud came up quickly behind Nicole and the overseer.

"One moment," he said, detaining them at the water's edge. "Let me bid my former concubine a fond farewell."

The overseer paused obediently, holding Nicole suspended in his arms while the restless water licked at his ankles.

"No kiss for me, my pet?" the planter purred mockingly as he reached out to grab her by the chin, forcing her to look directly at him. When she saw the expression in his eyes, she knew at once that he had ordered his overseer to lose the key to her chains. She supposed it was his last petty effort to wreak vengeance on her for having rejected him.

"You planned this, didn't you?" she snarled, motioning to her fettered wrists and ankles.

The planter grinned triumphantly. "I think it's only fitting that you leave in the manner that most becomes you, my dear. Perhaps it will help remind you that a slut shouldn't give herself airs!"

"You really have no cause for complaint over me," she laughed harshly. "After all, you've made yourself a fine profit at my expense."

"That's true," he conceded, "but I wish I'd gotten a little pleasure out of you, too!"

He stepped nearer and boldly poked at her skirts with his stubby fingers. "I should have breached you here on the spot yesterday while I had the chance!" he growled. "I wish I'd rammed you good." He made a sign to the overseer to keep a good hold on her and, taking advantage of the fact that her legs were suspended in midair, he shoved a hand under her skirts and began to explore, ignoring her indignant protests.

"Still giving yourself those ladylike airs we were talking about?" He smiled evilly as she tried to push his hand away. "But you'll learn. My one consolation in losing you, my dear, is that Dawson will probably end up throwing you to his pack of sea wolves once he's tired of you. Then I wager you'll wish you'd been nicer to me."

He had worked his way up to her thighs when suddenly the captain was there, towering over them, his rugged face set like chiseled rock in the gray dawn and his cold, clear eyes contrasting sharply with the angry flush on his suntanned face. He had returned to discover the reason for the delay, and though Renaud had immediately stepped away from the overseer and Nicole, Dawson suspected that the planter was up to no good.

"We must get under way," he snapped. "Why isn't the girl in the boat yet?"

Renaud quickly resumed his fawning. "A thousand pardons, *capitaine*. I was only saying good-bye to the wench, wishing her Godspeed."

Dawson glanced at Nicole's flushed, angry face, but she simply drew her skirts around her with her shackled hands and said nothing. What good would it do? she thought bitterly. At most, this swaggering buccaneer would call Renaud to task for offending her and then turn around and do the same thing or worse himself before the day was over!

On receiving no complaint from Nicole, the buccaneer turned to his host, anxious to be away. It was all he could do to keep his annoyance with the planter in check.

"And I, too, must make my farewells," he said dryly. He didn't like the man, but the planter had tried to be a generous host, so a polite leave-taking was in order. "Let me thank you on behalf of my men and myself for your kind hospitality. Perhaps someday I can extend the same courtesy to you aboard my ship."

"I hope you'll tell that to the governor when you see him," Renaud was swift to interject. "I'd appreciate it if you'd speak well of me to him ... of how I even gave up my best concubine to accommodate you."

Dawson extended his hand to his host, hoping to keep the necessary pleasantries to a minimum. "I'll be only too happy to put in a word for you. I never forget a favor — not even when I've paid well for it."

By this time the overseer had turned Nicole over to Dawson's men. On seeing that everything was ready at last, the captain untied the mooring line and swung himself aboard. Positioning himself in the stern, he gave the order to shove off. A few pushes from Renaud's servants and the boat was soon in deeper water, pulling away rapidly.

Nicole settled back against a roll of canvas just as the sun began to tinge the early-morning sky with a rosy glow. She didn't know exactly where her new owner was taking her, but at least it was away from Jean Renaud. With a sigh of relief, she watched his chunky figure disappear from view and prayed that she was seeing him for the last time.

Chapter 14

Nicole watched the captain maneuver the boat with the tiller while his men rowed or poled their way down the river.

Just like this rocking boat of theirs, so perilously riding the unpredictable currents of the Mississippi, Nicole felt as though she, too, were being hurled headlong into the unknown future. For this Golden Devil with his tawny hair and suntanned skin was steering her destiny now. She wondered whether he would do it as deftly as he was guiding their bark among some barely submerged rocks.

It was difficult for her to understand what the buccaneers were saying; their English was spiced with a generous mixture of slang and nautical terms. Nevertheless, she could tell they were concerned about the rise in the river and the increasing threat of snags and cypress knees just below the surface.

She was surprised to note that one of the buccaneers was a Spaniard, and sometimes she heard the captain address the slender, dark-haired man in the latter's native tongue. Fernández, as she heard the captain call him, was probably a renegade or, like her, an outcast who had joined the freebooters for profit or simply a lack of any other place to go. Despite Dawson's reputation for despising anyone or anything Spanish, however, he was as amiable toward this officer as he was to the other one, a copper-haired, freckle-faced Englishman who was called Josh.

Dawson seemed able to slip with ease from English to French or Spanish. How was it possible that a sea-roving cutthroat could be so educated? But then, so many things about Dawson disconcerted her. The sight of him with a sword at his side, a musket slung over his shoulder, and a pistol and hunting knife tucked in his wide leather belt must surely strike fear in plenty of hearts, yet he wasn't dressed at all the way she had imagined a pirate would be. There was no earring, his face was freshly shaven, and his nankeen breeches were fashionably cut, accenting his well-shaped thighs without a sag or wrinkle.

Though his hair was ruffled by the wind and his boots mud spattered, he had started out the journey as neatly groomed as any stylish aristocrat off for an afternoon's boating party.

There in broad daylight, sitting tall and straight at the tiller, Paul Dawson reminded her more of one of his Norse ancestors than the shadowy phantom he had seemed in the dimly lit bedchamber the night before.

But whether bathed in sunlight or silhouetted by candlelight, a tremendous vitality radiated from him. It didn't surprise her that he could command obedience from a motley band of freebooters, most of whom probably had no morals or country to hold them in check; she was sure his presence could be as awesome to them as it was to her.

As the morning progressed, however, and she continued

to observe him with his men, she could see that a loose camaraderie appeared to bind them together, though she sensed there were certain limits which neither he nor they would cross. There was never any doubt as to who was in command.

Dawson's officers appeared to be as bewildered as she was by their captain's decision to take her with him. Every now and then they would steal curious glances in her direction.

The warm breeze gently fluttering the ruffled edge of her white lawn cap made Nicole very drowsy. The rocking of the boat was irresistible; no sooner did she close her eyes against the increasing glare off the water than she fell soundly asleep.

How long she slept that way she couldn't tell, but when she awakened with a start, she saw the captain's chiseled face inches from hers as he lightly touched her shoulder.

The buccaneers had made the boat fast to a large cypress rooted near the shore, and Fernández was already wading up the muddy bank, a pack on his back and another one in his arms.

"We're going to stop and refresh ourselves for a few minutes," Dawson told her. "Then we'll go on again until it's time to make camp for the night."

He helped her to her feet, but she swayed unsteadily.

"We're going to get these blasted chains off you as soon as we get ashore," he said, his voice sharp as he balanced her lightly against him and called out to Josh.

They quickly got her out of the boat without getting her wet, the captain standing in the shallow water that lapped his knee-high boots while his officer passed her to him.

Despite the added weight of her shackles, Dawson carried her ashore with an easy stride, but the feel of his arms holding her again made her uncomfortable. The familiar scent of him filled her nostrils as her cheek brushed against the soft lawn of his shirt, and the sight of that tangle of pale gold hairs at the open neck of his shirt brought back disturbing memories.

The open neck of his shirt also allowed her to glimpse a long scar that started below his shoulder and seemed to end in that same gold patch. It was just one more reminder that this man was a pirate — an infamous pirate who was said to show no quarter to those who crossed his path. No wonder even a villain like Renaud had feared displeasing him!

His voice interrupted her thoughts as he set her down on solid ground and released his hold.

"Now, lass, let's get at these shackles," he said, guiding her to higher ground and sitting her on a gnarled tree trunk.

While his men built a fire and hastily fried some fish they'd caught in the river, the captain pulled a file from one of the packs. Sitting down beside her, he took one of her wrists in his hand and went to work on the band that encircled it.

"Damn that Renaud!" he muttered, trying to keep from cutting her.

Such fragile little wrists to bear such a weight, he thought as the bands finally gave way and he forced them open enough to free her. Yet, delicate as those pretty little hands were, they had killed a man. He still found it hard to believe, but that's what Renaud's documents claimed. Of course, she was hardly more than a cub, but a frightened one, ready to show her claws if anyone came near her. He smiled to himself as he looked at her proud little figure sitting on the tree trunk, the red-gold of her hair tumbling rebelliously out of her frilly white cap and the huge green eyes anxiously watching his every move as he knelt and reached under her skirts in search of her ankles.

As soon as his hand came in contact with her foot, he could feel her pull back from him.

"Come, lass, I'm not going to hurt you," he reassured her, "but I can't file these leg irons off if you don't let me see what I'm doing."

She glared at him a moment longer, then finally eased her skirts up until the tips of the plain black slippers Mignon had given her were visible.

Dawson kept his face immobile, but his eyes twinkled. "Just a little more," he coaxed. "I have to see what I'm doing or I might hurt you."

She obeyed reluctantly. He knew it would be a mistake to remind her that he had already seen much more of those delightful limbs than what she was so unwilling to expose to him at that moment. No, this was definitely not the time to refer to anything that had happened between them the night before; yet for his part, he couldn't forget a single detail of it, nor did he want to.

The bands around her ankles were yielding now, and with a sigh of relief he removed them, glad to have the tedious job over at last.

"God! How I hate these damn things!" he muttered, more to himself than to her, as he picked up the shackles.

Suddenly he flung them away from him, hurling them with such force that they landed well out into the river. "There — and good riddance!" he growled with such intensity that Nicole stared at him.

Feeling the girl's eyes on him, however, Dawson quickly came back to himself. Smoothing his windblown hair once more and retying it at the nape of his neck with the black velvet hair ribbon, he turned back to her.

"There now, that's a lot better, isn't it?" he said as he helped her rise.

In an easy voice, as if he were pointing out the sights, he warned her against wandering away from the camp. She must watch out for snakes whenever the group came ashore and she must look before stepping or sitting anywhere. But Nicole only half heard him. She was too caught up in the exhilarating sensation of being free of her chains.

The shackles were gone at last, hurled to the bottom of the mighty Mississippi! She pulled herself up to her full height and threw back her white-capped head, filling her lungs with the clean sun-washed air of the wilderness stretching as far as the eye could see. At least she was one step closer to the freedom she longed for. Perhaps her new master would have thought twice about removing her chains had he realized he had only made her long for complete liberty all the more!

Chapter 15

Dawson was pleased with their progress. They had run with the current, so they had made good time and were able to stop with ample time to eat and set up camp before dark. According to the "marks" the captain had noted while traveling upriver, they were camping on the site he'd chosen earlier.

During the afternoon, Dawson had taken a long turn at the oars. Nicole marveled at how he could row hour after hour; his rhythm never faltered. His shirt did nothing to hide the steady rise and fall of his powerful shoulder blades as he bent over his oars.

The fresh air and hard labor of maneuvering the longboat had made them ravenous. As soon as they had made the boat fast, Fernández went hunting for their supper while the captain and Josh passed their machetes over the clearing and began to set up the tents.

Enjoying her new freedom of movement, and feeling just a little guilty over not doing anything while the others were working so hard, Nicole timidly began to help Fernández roast the rabbits he had caught and skinned. At first the Spaniard had cast a questioning glance at Dawson to be certain it would be all right to let her assist him, but the captain, pleased by her first gesture of cooperation, had readily nodded his approval.

Nicole's momentary surge of gratitude toward her new master for having removed her chains, however, was short-lived. As soon as the time came for them to retire and she realized she was to share his tent, her misgivings stirred anew, and they increased when she saw there was only room for one pallet.

Kneeling in the limited confines of the tent, she refused to lie down, even after the captain had lowered the flap and hung the lantern above them.

"But where else would you suggest you sleep?" he asked, stretching out on their pallet of moss and animal skins and pulling her down beside him with a playful tug. "We only brought along two tents — supposedly one for each man not on watch. Of course, if you'd prefer to snuggle up to one of my officers instead ..."

Nicole pushed him away angrily. "In other words, I'm to lie with you whether I want to or not!"

"I'm afraid that's how it is, lass," came his terse reply. "You see, I had no idea when I started out on this journey that we'd be returning with a fourth person, much less a female, so unfortunately we'll just have to make the best of these tight quarters until we get aboard my ship."

"Then you really intend to take me to sea with you?" An accusing tone had crept into her voice.

He heaved a deep sigh. "I don't like the idea any more than you do, I assure you, but there doesn't seem to be much else I can do for the moment. After all, I can hardly abandon you here in the middle of the swamps, and if I drop you off in Mobile when I go there to participate in military conferences with the French, you would be in danger of falling into the hands of someone like Renaud or that shady Company official again."

"So I'm to have the good fortune of enjoying your hospitality instead?"

He ignored the sarcastic tone of her voice. "You could do worse, you know."

"Then you admit you intend to keep me for yourself?"

"I'm afraid it's too late for me to do anything else. I hope I don't come to regret my impulse. The last thing I need right now is to get tangled up with a balky wench!"

He reached up and extinguished the lantern, leaving them in darkness except for the ruddy glow of the campfire on the canvas walls. The feel of her soft warmth lying there beside him fanned his desire for her all the more.

"I know we got off to a bad start last night," he murmured, his voice suddenly taking on a more intimate tone as he eased his arm across her shoulder and drew her closer to him. "But I promise it'll be different between us next time." He nuzzled the silken abundance of her hair and gently planted a kiss amid the tousled curls, hoping for some response, no matter how small.

Instead, she broke away from him and sat up. "You may as well not try to come near me," she declared. "You'll get no pleasure from me now or any other time!"

He chuckled good-naturedly and pulled her down next to him once more. "An idle threat, my sweet, since just the sight and feel of you already give me infinite pleasure!"

"Murielle warned me about lechers like you!" she suddenly exclaimed.

"And who the devil is Murielle?"

"She was one of the women chained to me during the voyage. She told me how there are men who lust after a wench even more once they know she's a first-timer."

Dawson smiled broadly. "And that's what you think I am, one of those — what did you call them — lechers?"

"Well, aren't you? As soon as you found out I was a virgin, you called in Renaud and started bargaining for me!"

"That's right. When I discovered the truth about you

I did call for him," the captain conceded. "Only, you have some of the details in reverse, my dear. Had I been one of those lechers, I'd certainly have not wanted to buy you after the fact. You're forgetting that when I bought you, you were no longer a virgin!"

Nicole had the feeling that those disturbing blue eyes of his were twinkling in the dark, laughing at her.

"Well, be that as it may," she said lamely, "you most certainly lusted after me!"

Dawson chuckled. "I suppose I have to plead guilty on that score. I wanted you from the moment I saw you, but that's putting it too simply. What I felt — and still feel — is a bit more complicated than that." He hesitated a moment and then went on. "What I marvel at is how in the blazes you managed to stay intact as long as you did. What about the guards while you were in prison? Talk about lechers. . . . Now *that's* a lecherous lot if there ever was one!"

"Oh, they tried often enough," she assured him. "They were even planning to give me a farewell party the night before I was to be executed, but then the unexpected change in orders came, and we were rushed to Le Havre."

"And what about on the boat over? I know those pest ships, damn their stinking hulls! But then, I suppose there were nuns accompanying you."

"No, no nuns. It seems that branded felons don't even merit the protection accorded the harlots of Salpêtrière!" she replied bitterly.

"Then how is it that the captain and his crew didn't take advantage of having a hold full of women supposedly of easy virtue who were at their disposal for months on end?"

"It was only thanks to Murielle that I evaded them."

"Ah, Murielle again?"

"Yes, she was a prostitute, but when I confided to her how inexperienced I was, she did all she could to protect me. Every time I was singled out to join the officers in their quarters, Murielle was quick to step in and lie or flirt or find some excuse to keep them from taking me. Then when I fell sick, she was the one who saved me again. . . ." Her voice faltered as the memories came rushing back. "If Murielle hadn't looked out for me the way she did, I know I'd have never survived. It was a living inferno." She shivered and buried her face in her hands.

Dawson tightened his arms around her, overwhelmed by a sudden desire to comfort her. "I'm sorry, lass, I didn't mean to stir up things better forgotten," he said gently. "But you're safe now. I won't let any harm come to you. You're not alone anymore," he told her quietly. "Let my love be your refuge."

He bent to kiss her, but she immediately stiffened and began to push at his chest.

"All right, all right, my little bobcat! Pull in your claws!" he admonished her as he caught the small fists pounding so futilely against the hard wall of his chest and held them fast. The poor wench! She was still so terrified. He had expected too much from her too soon. "There's no need to fight me," he told her with a patient smile, bending to brush his lips lightly against the cheek she had turned to him in an effort to move her head away. "I'm not going to force myself on you."

He lay back on the pallet, though he kept one arm around her. "In my profession I've learned it pays to bide my time when there's a worthwhile prize at stake."

"You'll never use me again!" she warned, struggling to work herself out of his disturbing embrace, but he didn't relax his hold. Instead he stroked her hair as though soothing a frightened child. After all, she was scarcely more than that, he reminded himself.

"Don't worry. I have no intention of doing anything against your will," he assured her. "We have a long day on the river tomorrow, and I still have to take the last watch tonight, so let's at least try to get some sleep, if nothing else."

He pillowed her head on his shoulder and fell silent, but she stirred restlessly, trying to work herself free of the confining circle of his arms.

For a few minutes he lay with his eyes closed, seeming to ignore her efforts, but suddenly the bands of his muscles tensed and she could feel them tighten around her.

"Be still, my sweet," he murmured drowsily. "If you don't stop squirming like that, you might start something you'll have to finish!"

She stopped, aware of how his manhood had sprung to life against her thigh. She lay there, tense and apprehensive, resenting the power this new master could exert over her. He was playing with her the way a cat enjoys toying with a mouse. He would take her whenever he was ready. Despite all his assurances to the contrary, she knew what his real intentions were. Hadn't she heard him tell Renaud how he wanted a woman to attend him whenever he felt the need of one?

His breathing was heavier, more rhythmic now, and though he still held her in his arms, his grip had relaxed. That hard length against her thigh, however, was still there, hot and pulsating as though it had a life of its own, obeying a primitive instinct that not even sleep could stifle. He wanted her, and when he awakened refreshed in the morning, he would surely want satisfaction.

She had to get away, escape while it was still possible. Once aboard Dawson's ship, she would be completely at his mercy, and there would be no place to run! If she was going to make a break for freedom, it had to be now.

An hour or two before they had stopped to make camp for the night, she had noted a small clearing with two or three thatched huts on the same side of the river. There had been two women, simply dressed, with babes in their arms, tending a crude outdoor oven. Perhaps she could make it back there and plead with them to take her in. They might have pity on her and let her stay, especially if she told them how she was fleeing from pirates who had been holding her prisoner. Of course, she would offer to earn her keep. No work would be too menial as long as she could be a free woman.

Dawson would probably be furious once he discovered his costly purchase had given him the slip. He might even go after her, and that single patch of humanity they had passed would certainly be one of the first places he'd look. But perhaps she could outwit him. If she hid in the swamps for a couple of days before she presented herself at the settlement, then the captain might not find her, even if he did go straight back to the settlement to look for her. One thing was fairly certain: Dawson would not have much time to waste scouring the swamplands for a stray wench while his ship and crew were waiting for him at the mouth of the river.

She tried again to disengage herself from the circle of his arm, but as soon as she moved, he tightened his grip and, murmuring something softly to her, buried his face deeper in her hair.

No, this was not the moment. The best time would be just before dawn when she could see her way; and best of all, the captain would be on watch.

So she lay there quietly, half dozing and half awake, waiting for what seemed an eternity, watching Fernández's elongated silhouette flickering against the tent wall like a demon dancing in the flames of hell — while she lay trapped in the arms of the devil himself!

Chapter 16

It was still dark when the captain rose to take his turn on guard. Nicole pretended to be asleep, but she could feel him linger a moment, and though she did not dare open her eyes, she suspected he was studying her intently.

All her instincts told her that he was trying to decide whether or not to take her, and she tensed in anticipation of his advances. But his touch never came. Before she realized it, he had lifted the flap of the tent and was gone.

For an hour or longer, she lay in the darkness waiting and listening to the sounds of the wilderness. The occasional cry of some distant animal on its nocturnal rounds sent tremors of fear down her spine, yet she reminded herself that it wasn't half as frightening as the powerful giant nearby. Besides, hadn't Dawson himself told her that most of the creatures in the woods were as afraid of her as she was of them?

"If you should ever find yourself face to face with one, stay perfectly still and don't startle him. Then he'll probably leave you alone," he had advised her earlier that evening as she sat eating with him and his men by the campfire. She'd been made uneasy when she had heard something moving about in the shadows.

When they had taken turns going behind a clump of tall ferns to attend to their personal necessities, he had cautioned her not to stray into the forest, but that warning had obviously been given because he hadn't wanted her to try and escape.

Now as she lay in the tent watching his tall silhouette smoking his pipe by the campfire, she trembled in spite of herself. How enraged he would be when he discovered she had run away from him after all!

She knew how alert he could be to any noise or movement around him, so she didn't dare try to sneak out the tent flap. Instead, she knelt and felt carefully along the lower edge of the rear wall of the tent, looking for a spot where she could loosen a tie from one of the stakes and crawl out. If only she had one of his knives to slash the back wall and just step through! But she was afraid he would miss it when he armed himself for the watch.

The grass was disagreeably wet, but at least the dampness made the earth soft enough for her to scoop some of it out from under the lower edge of the back wall. Lying flat on her stomach, she pulled herself to the other side. The tent shielded her escape into the woods. How easy it was!

It was still too dark for her to make much progress. The night air was cool and damp against her face, and the gray mist closed in upon her with frightening rapidity, almost immediately separating her from the camp. As she caught sight of the campfire flickering feebly through the veiled night, she suddenly realized the enormity of what she was about to do. But she knew if she hesitated she was lost.

Actually, she suspected that even if the visibility had

been better, it would have been difficult going. The terrain was simply treacherous, with obstacles every step of the way. After what must have been a half-hour of stumbling along the jagged shoreline, she had only been able to walk a short distance away from the camp, and already it was impossible to go any farther! The heavy curtain of fog suspended in the gray morning air was so thick she couldn't see more than a foot or two ahead of her. Though she knew it had to be near daybreak, she doubted even the sun would be able to find its way to that god-forsaken spot.

The branches of a bush hooked her skirt, and she slipped in the mud as she tugged impatiently to break away from its grip.

Never had she felt as alone as she did at that moment, with the broad expanse of the river on one side of her and the solid, closely knit rows of cypress on the other! Merciful God! She had expected some difficulty, but this was unbelievable! The unending fortress of trees extended right to the water's edge now.... No, it went beyond it . . . *into* the water, completely blocking the way! There was no longer room for her to walk!

But there was no turning back now. She had to continue in the direction of the settlement upriver. At this moment that little patch of huts was her only hope. Most certainly she could not return to the camp. The captain would be furious, and he wasn't the kind of man who would take desertion lightly. No, she had made her choice and would keep going. Even if she could not reach the settlement as soon as she had hoped, she would stay in the woods, eating berries and learning to hunt and fish, if need be.

She sensed more than saw something move among the cypress knees, and instinctively she retreated. As inexperienced as she was with this strange, hostile land, she immediately suspected it was an alligator.

Nicole looked about in dismay. If she kept retreating she'd soon be back at the campsite! But it wasn't possible for her to go forward. There was only one way left for her — the swamps.

Carefully she retraced her steps, searching for a chink in the wall of indomitable cypress. As the first rays of sun began to pick their way through the fog, she thought she could see a narrow space at last.

She approached the slender opening and peered through. God help her, this had to be the entrance to Hades! Row after row of trees like ghostly sentinels stretched as far as her eyes could see. It was a twilight world of gray mist and shadows that sunlight could not penetrate.

Well, she might not have to go too far into it — only far enough from the riverbank to be on dry land, safely hidden from anyone passing by. A flutter of startled herons greeted her as she entered the gloom of the forest, and for a moment she stood there as startled as the scattering birds. Gradually, however, her eyes began to grow accustomed to the dim light, and she could make out some sort of clearing ahead ringed by vine-covered trees and enormous ferns.

Relieved to find a hiding place at last, she made her way quickly toward the spot. At least she could wait here until Dawson and his men broke camp and left. Then she could return to the site where they had spent the night and stay there until she could find some means of getting upstream to the settlement.

She moved resolutely toward the clearing. Too late she realized that the ground was not as solid as she had thought; to her surprise, the earth began to move beneath her. . . .

She tried to step back onto more solid ground, but it was as though some giant hand had caught her by the feet and was determinedly pulling her down into the earth. Blessed Virgin!

She tried again to take a step, but she couldn't lift her foot. She only sank deeper, all the way up to her calves. Desperately she looked around her, but the tall trees and their branches were beyond her reach.

Chapter 17

She had no way of knowing how long her screams pierced the stillness of the swamplands before she thought she heard the familiar voice of the captain calling out to her. At first she told herself she was delirious. Even when she saw the tall, bright-haired figure coming toward her through the trees, she was certain she was hallucinating. But when the captain stepped out into the clearing, cutlass in one hand and pistol in the other, a cry of joy burst from her lips.

"Oh, thank God, it's you! Thank God!" she exclaimed, relief overwhelming all other emotions at that moment.

Dawson moved rapidly, apparently as relieved to have found her as she was to have been found. But he moved more carefully than she had.

"Stop thrashing around like that or you'll go down even faster!" he called to her sternly as he tucked his gun back in his belt and began looking for something to throw to her. Cutlass in hand, he began to slash away at a tangle of vines.

His men, who had been following him closely, emerged from the gloom, weapons drawn. Dawson shouted to them over his shoulder without missing a swing.

"She's over here, caught in a pit! Take care! No telling how deep it is. Let's get her out fast!"

The buccaneers reacted at once. "Black Jack's the best for that!" said Josh, skirting the treacherous clearing to where the captain was busy wielding his blade.

"Damn it! If only we'd brought a rope!" Dawson growled impatiently between breaths.

"Want me to fetch one?" asked Josh as his machete joined the rhythm of the captain's cutlass.

"No, we can't risk the delay." The captain's voice was controlled, but hard-edged.

"She's just a slip of a girl ... not much weight," the Spaniard muttered as he joined them. "She should stay up all right."

Dawson nodded. "That's the way I figure it, too, but you can never tell with quicksand. The danger isn't in going all the way under but in losing your balance and falling face down in it."

Josh grunted in response as he struggled to free the vine they wanted from a tangled mass of leaves and branches.

"We can double the vine so it'll be stronger and won't cut the lass too much," Fernández suggested. Then he turned and mumbled to Josh, "Jesus! The captain's really upset. This wench sure must be something special to him."

Nicole cried out that she had sunk another few inches. Her skirts were billowing around her in a puff of blue and white now, and her hair, free of the confines of her ruffled cap, spilled over her shoulders in a tumult of red-gold. Instinctively she extended her arms toward Dawson, but even as she did, she knew it was in vain. He was beyond her reach.

"Be still, lass. We'll have you out in a minute," he called back reassuringly, trying to keep his voice light, but he never stopped working for a moment.

He urged his men to go faster as they braided the vines into a long, thick rope and secured one end of it around the trunk of a large cypress.

Then Dawson walked to the edge of the clearing, holding the other end of the rope in his hand. "I'm going to throw this out to you," he called as he fashioned a loop. "As soon as you catch it, slip this around you, under your arms, then pull it tight. Do you understand?"

She nodded and lifted her arms to catch the vine as he sent it flexing through the air like a sinewy green snake.

But it barely grazed her fingertips and then fell out of reach. She leaned forward, but Dawson immediately shouted a warning. "No, no, don't lean over so far! My God! Whatever you do, don't risk falling face down! Just wait. I'll throw it to you again."

The unsuccessful attempt had cost her another couple of inches! The crushing pressure imprisoning her lower limbs was unbearable. Her breath was coming in short, terrified gasps now, and she began to sob in spite of herself.

"Don't give up, little bobcat. You'll get it next time." He talked to her calmly as he pulled the rope back in and prepared to throw it another time. "Watch now. Here it comes again!"

The vine sliced through the air and she stretched every fiber of her body to grab it. This time it landed in her outstretched hands.

"Now get it well under your arms and pull the knot tight! That's it, be sure it's tight enough."

Her fingers fumbled with the tough green rope that resisted her efforts to bend it, her panic mounting as she felt herself sinking ever deeper.

"That's it, my girl. Get it well under your arms. Now tighten the loop with all your strength. You don't want to slip out of it!"

Nicole was almost too paralyzed with fear to obey. The quicksand was up to her waist now, and her skirts were floating around her like the petals of a flower slowly opening.

"All right, hold on to the rope with both hands and don't let go," came the captain's command. He was determined to penetrate the gray haze of terror that he sensed was beginning to numb her. "Listen to what I'm saying!" he insisted. "No matter what, don't let go. If it cuts a little, let it. Hold on at all costs. Remember, you're safe as long as you hold on. Do you understand?"

She clutched the vine with trembling hands and held fast, praying that this last fragile link between her and life would not fail her. She could feel it tugging at her now as the men began to pull and the slack went out of it. All the while Dawson's familiar voice kept calling to her, reassuring her, urging her not to let go. But he sounded so far away, drowned out by the wild thunder of her own heart. At that moment all she knew was that she was caught in the middle of a tug-of-war between life and death.

"Keep your head up! Don't let your face get in the mud!" she heard Dawson yell.

In blind obedience to his persistent voice, she clung to the vine, fixing her eyes on his figure working at the edge of the pit, blotting everything from her mind except the sound of his voice guiding her back to life.

The buccaneers were pulling harder now, grunting and cursing. But the more they tugged, the greater the suction on the lower half of her body.

Time seemed to stand still. It could have been just seconds or an eternity, but slowly, painfully, she felt herself being lifted from the soggy grave.

Panic gripped her anew. The vine under her arms was easing upward, working its way over her extended upper arms. Oh, God! If she slipped out of the noose now, she was sure to land on her face! Then that overpowering weight of shifting mud and sand would close over her head and snuff out her life like a candle.

"Hold on to the rope! In God's name, don't let go, whatever you do!" The captain was shouting with an urgency she'd not noticed before.

She could see him reaching out to her, trying to grab her arms while his men continued to pull her closer to where he stood. Her arms and hands ached and stung from the chafing of the tough vines, but she held fast.

Vaguely she was aware of someone catching her by the wrists and dragging her roughly through those last few feet of quivering earth.

"You've got her now, Captain!"

"Don't stop pulling! Get her out!"

"The lass has guts, I'll give her that!"

Strong arms lifted her from where she lay gasping in the mud. "It's all right, you're safe now." Dawson's voice sounded close to her ear.

The light that managed to find its way through the overhanging branches struck her upturned face and closed eyelids, calling her back to consciousness, as the thin white lawn of a man's shirt, damp with sweat but still tinged with the faint scent of sandalwood, rose and fell in labored rhythm against her mud-stained cheek. She knew it was the captain who was carrying her.

So it had all been in vain. Her effort to escape had failed miserably, and she was still his prisoner. At least he hadn't left her to die in the quicksand. But then, why would he? He had paid a fortune for her. It was only natural that he would want to protect his investment. He obviously had no intention of losing such an expensive concubine.

Chapter 18

Now that she was back at the camp and safe in the tent, her narrow escape behind her, Nicole sat weary and dejected on the pallet. What a disaster her long-awaited escape had proven to be! She had been gone from the camp less than an hour and had spent half of that time retracing her steps. Then, when she thought she had found a place to hide, she had ruined everything by stepping into a pit of quicksand!

To make matters worse, Dawson was doubly angry with her now; not only had he caught her trying to run away from him, but the delay had cost him and his men precious time.

Everything at the campsite was loaded on the boat now and ready to go, except for that one tent. The captain, it seemed, had left it until last on purpose, thinking she was still sleeping and not wishing to disturb her any sooner than necessary. He hadn't discovered that she was missing until the last minute. He and his men had immediately set out to look for her. Thanks to the ruffle-edged cap she had lost along the way, they had at least had a clue as to which direction she had taken.

Although Dawson was visibly relieved to have her back, he was still annoyed about the incident. As soon as he had assured himself that she was uninjured and only needed to rest, he had ordered her to remove her mud-caked clothes so Josh could rinse them out for her in the river. Fernandez passed buckets of water under the flap of the tent so she could sponge off the worst of the grime.

The Spaniard must have felt sorry for her, because he warmed some leftover breakfast and passed it into the tent along with the bathwater, an attention which she greatly appreciated, since she was discovering how ravenous her brief misadventure had left her.

Since she had nothing to change into, and they couldn't sit around waiting for her clothes to dry, Dawson had once more extended her the temporary use of his frock coat. Nicole wrapped herself in it with mixed emotions, recognizing it as the one he had given her to cover her nakedness the first night.

At the sight of her sitting on the pallet enveloped once more in his garnet silk coat, her bare legs tucked under her, Dawson's eyes softened momentarily.

"Are you sure you're all right?" he asked, his concern winning out over his annoyance with her.

She nodded her damp curls like a weary child bracing herself for the scolding she knew was forthcoming.

He stooped to enter the tent and knelt on the pallet beside her, since his height did not permit him to stand in such confined quarters.

"Josh did the best he could with these under the circumstances," he said, handing her her still-wet gown and underclothes, "so I'm afraid they'll have to do until we get back to the ship. But you can use my frock coat as long as you wish. I have no need for it in the swamps."

The wet garments were still streaked with mud stains, but at least they were cleaner than they had been.

"They'll dry quickly enough in the sun," he assured her. Then, noticing how she tried to hide her bare legs, he added, "All I can offer you is a pair of my breeches. They will swallow you, of course, but you're welcome to them."

She colored, embarrassed that she should have such a problem and ashamed that the buccaneers should have even seen her petticoat and stays, much less handled them.

"Thank you," she replied coolly, "but I'll just put on my underskirt as it is and let it dry on me. In a few hours my dress and stays should be ready to use again and then you can have your coat back."

"As you wish." He was all business again. "If you're ready, I'd like to get under way without any further delay. We've already lost too much time, thanks to your antics."

"I'm sorry about the delay," she retorted icily, "but need I remind you that I never asked to be here with you in the first place."

How dare he be angry with her? Was this buccaneer so arrogant as to think she should be delighted to have been bought and dragged through the wilderness like this just so he could have her to attend him on land or sea whenever the fancy struck him?

Dawson frowned at her hostility.

"I suppose it would be too much to expect any thanks from you for having just saved your life," he said dryly. "But then you didn't show me any gratitude when I pulled you out of Renaud's lively little orgy the other night either, so why should I expect any thanks for having fished you out of quicksand! There's one thing, though, I would appreciate. Please tell me what the blazes you thought you were doing wandering around out there in the middle of the swamps!"

She looked at him contemptuously. "That should be obvious. I was trying to run away from you."

One eyebrow was lifted. "And why ever would you want to do that?"

She laughed harshly. "Are you so vain as to think I relish belonging to the likes of you?"

He colored, but his face remained expressionless.

"And what, may I ask, is your complaint? Have I mistreated you in any way?"

Now it was her turn to blush. "Can you really ask me that? You used me most vilely from the very first moment we met, and now here you are taking me God knows where so you can go on abusing me at your whim! Of course, I suppose I should be, as you say, grateful to be alive — though sometimes I wonder about that, too, since I'm well aware of the fact that you were simply protecting your investment. After all, I can understand how you'd hate to lose your property before you've gotten your money's worth out of it!"

She was seething with rage now — rage with herself for having failed to escape and rage with him for being so annoyed with her for having tried.

"I see where your trust is not easily given," he sighed at last. "But how in the devil did you expect to survive out here all by yourself? You were away from camp less than an hour and nearly got yourself killed. I shudder in my boots to think of all the things that could have happened to you if we hadn't found you!"

"I didn't intend to stay alone for long," she said defensively. "I—I was trying to get to that little group of huts we passed by yesterday afternoon. There were women and children there. They might have taken me in."

His jaw dropped in surprise. "You foolish child! You'd have never made it there by land! Why do you think people travel by boat around here? There aren't any roads. Even old Indian trails are flooded over during this season, and the way the river's rising, the very land we're standing on will probably be under water by tomorrow or the next day."

He saw the skepticism in her green eyes. She must be thinking that he was exaggerating just to frighten her. "Look, my innocent, many an experienced man has been swallowed up by these swamplands. What chance would a defenseless young girl like you have? Why, you wouldn't last twenty-four hours! If by some miracle you'd managed to escape drowning or being blown away in a hurricane, there would still be the wildcats and alligators and poisonous snakes, to mention a few of the creatures who inhabit these swamps. My God, lass, are you daft? Perhaps Renaud was right. You do belong in chains!"

She flushed angrily, resenting the sarcastic tone of voice he was using with her. "You yourself told me that most animals won't attack if you don't antagonize them," she reminded him indignantly, "and at night I could have always kept them at bay with a fire, even as you do yourself."

He chuckled, finding her naiveté amusing. "Ah, I see you learn quickly. But how, pray tell, did you plan to get that fire of yours going without a lantern or even flints to give you light? You have no idea how black it can be out here on a moonless night!"

He was laughing at her now, and she resented it. "I'm not entirely ignorant," she protested. "Even I know you can make a fire by rubbing two sticks together."

He ran his hand through his blond hair. "I see. And that pearl of wisdom makes you an expert woodsman, I suppose? And what if the sticks are wet? Did you think of that minor detail, my sweet?"

His eyes mocked her, and she looked away. "Frankly, I doubt I would have been on land for long. I'm sure someone would have come along the river sooner or later and been kind enough to take me to the settlement."

"Perhaps," he conceded, but his eyes were still making fun of her. "You might have been lucky enough to meet some well-meaning person — *if* you'd still been alive! Few people venture this far downriver unless they're expert navigators. Besides, what guarantee would you have had that whoever picked you up wouldn't have been as bad as Renaud or — heaven forbid! — as wicked as *I* am?"

"If you really have my welfare in mind, why didn't

you leave me off at that settlement yesterday?" she suddenly asked him, hoping to undermine some of that maddening self-assurance of his, but he didn't flinch.

"Because, as I see it, anyplace between here and Mobile would be too close to Renaud and that crafty official who sold you to him for you to really be out of their reach," came his quick reply. "What's more, as soon as one of those women spotted that brand on your shoulder, they probably would have driven you out of their settlement, even if they had similar decorations themselves. You're a very beautiful woman, my sweet. I mean no offense to you, but I don't think they would have trusted their menfolk around you, and I dare say they would have been right."

He leaned closer. "But do you really expect to find someone who would treat you better than I? If, as you say, I gave Renaud a fortune to get you, doesn't it stand to reason I'd be more inclined to care about what happens to you than someone who'd simply come upon you by chance in the wilderness? Am I really so terrible a protector that you'd flee to unknown dangers just to escape from me?"

His nearness, as always, disquieted her. She drew the coat closer around her.

"Almost any fate would be better than being a buccaneer's whore!" she flung back at him.

He colored as though she had struck him, and for a moment there was such a deafening silence she feared she had gone too far.

When at last he rose, the blue of his eyes glittered like cold steel.

"I don't have time to sit and argue with a silly wench all day," he said, his voice brittle and impersonal. "We're ready to shove off, so I'll send one of my men to attend you."

He turned and without another word threw the flap back and stalked out.

A few minutes later Josh came for her, and on orders from the captain carried her through the water to the boat while the Spaniard took the tent down and stored it on board with the other equipment.

Except for giving the necessary orders, the captain was stern and silent the rest of the day.

Chapter 19

That evening after they had made camp and eaten a tasty meal of roasted venison, Nicole retired alone to the captain's tent to change into her gown, which had dried during the long lap down the river. Although her dress was stained and wrinkled now and her fichu limp and not very white anymore, they were at least more comfortable and appropriate than the frock coat.

She had spent the day huddled against a roll of canvas in the stern, close to where the captain sat. Wrapped in the generous frock coat and wearing only her damp linen petticoat, which had soon dried in the brisk breeze, she had kept her eyes turned away from Dawson as much as possible. Nevertheless, she had felt him looking down at her every now and again, his gaze lingering whenever he thought she wasn't aware of him. Occasionally she blushed in spite of herself.

But when Dawson had carried her in and out of the boat during the rest of the day, he was noticeably reluctant to touch her more than necessary. He was terse and withdrawn, as though he had been making a deliberate effort not to react to her closeness.

Yet she knew he still wanted her. Perhaps he was so annoyed with her after this morning, however, that he preferred to avoid her for the present. On the other hand, there was also the possibility that he might go ahead and take her in anger, precisely to show her who was master.

She had just finished lacing the front of her bodice and tying the fichu in place when Dawson's voice sounded and the flap of the tent opened. A gust of wind momentarily set the lantern to flickering and stirred anew the citronella burning in the small copper brazier as his imposing frame filled the tent.

The large snakelike coil dangling from his hand sent an icy shiver coursing through her veins. By all the saints in heaven, was this pirate going to beat her into submission?

It wasn't until he flung himself down on the pallet beside her that she recognized it as a rope and not a whip.

For a moment Dawson studied her without a word, still undecided about his rebellious companion. He felt like a villain. How could he, of all people — a freebooter himself who took pride in his independence — not understand her burning desire to be free? But freedom was the one thing he could not give her at this moment.

He heaved a deep sigh and began in a conciliatory tone. "I'm sorry, my little bobcat, but since you seem so hell-bent on running away from me, I'm going to have to restrain you in some way while we're on land."

She drew back suspiciously. "What do you mean?"

"I hate to do it, lass, but I'm going to have to tie you up. It seems the only way to insure that we all get a good night's sleep."

"I might have expected as much!" she exclaimed. "All that show of throwing away my chains! Now you reveal your true colors at last!"

For a brief moment his eyes clouded, but the set of his mouth remained firm.

"I truly don't want to do this, lass, but you leave me no choice. This is only to protect you from your own folly."

"And it'll protect you from my scratching your eyes out while you're violating me again!" she added sarcastically.

The pained expression on his face deepened. "Believe me, I wouldn't think of trying to make love to you while you're restrained in any way."

"*Bien*, if that's the case, then go ahead and tie me up!" she exclaimed, surrendering her outstretched hands to him with a cynical smile. "At least I'll have some consolation if my bonds will discourage you from touching me!"

With a frown, he looped the rope as gently as he could around her extended wrists and pulled it into a knot. Then wrapping the long end once around the slimness of her waist, he paused and looked questioningly at her, but when he saw the answer smoldering in her eyes, he took what was left of the cord and, after measuring out a play of some two feet in length between them, looped the rest of it around his own waist.

"Just in case . . ." he murmured as he finished the knot. "This way I'll know at once if you try to sneak off on me during the night."

Nicole wilted noticeably. Dawson tested the rope again to be sure it wasn't cutting her, feeling more guilty than ever. But she simply sat there staring at him with such hatred shimmering in the green pools of her eyes that he had to look away. How lovely she was! She was made to be loved, not abused like this. If only he could find some way to penetrate that wall of hatred and mistrust she had built around herself. If only she would let him love and take care of her the way he wanted to! He turned the palms of her hands upward and noticed how chafed they were from the vine.

"My poor little bobcat, how hard you fight against your destiny!" he murmured, suddenly lifting her hands to his lips and planting a kiss on each palm.

"Here, I have something that might help you," he said. He reached for his pack. "It's a pomade," he continued, fishing out a small tin box and gently patting a cooling cream on her palms. "It may not be perfumed, but it's very soothing and should help you heal faster."

She didn't resist. Her hands were limp in his.

"What about under your arms?" he asked. "Would you like me to put some there, too?"

He felt her tense. "No, no ... that won't be necessary," she quickly assured him.

"As you wish," he smiled, "but I'll leave the pomade out so you can use it yourself in the morning."

She didn't reply.

"This is just for one night," he reminded her gently, "and you see, I'm tied, too," he added with a half-hearted chuckle as he touched the rope around his own waist. "Josh and Fernández are going to split my watch between them so I won't have to leave you tonight. They think we had a lover's quarrel last night and that's why you tried to run away this morning. It's best they go on believing that."

"What difference does it make what they think?" she shrugged.

"A great deal," he said quickly. "It's to your advantage if my men think you're my woman. They won't dare molest you."

He removed his weapons and was about to lie back when he saw how lost and bewildered she looked. If only he could find a way to protect her from herself without breaking that proud spirit he admired so much!

The light from the campfire filtered through the canvas and blended with the golden glow of the lamp, setting the bright mantle of her hair ablaze. Like a moth drawn to the flame, he leaned toward her and caught her hands in his, toying with the knot at her wrists.

"If — if you could give me your word ..." he said huskily. "If you'd just swear to me by your Virgin ..."

But she pulled her hands away from him. "Tied or shackled, I'll never stay with you willingly," she warned him in a voice that quivered with cold fury.

"As you wish," he sighed.

He loosened his clothing and extinguished the lamp. "I'm a very light sleeper," he told her as he lay back on the pallet, "so I advise you to close those big beautiful eyes of yours and go to sleep."

Because the rope that joined them limited their movements, he lay facing her and gently pulled her down beside him. She resisted at first, but he could see how weary she really was.

"Tuck in your claws and go to sleep, lass," he said softly. "I won't disturb you. You have my word on it."

The tension between them was as taut as the rope that bound them together. Too weary even to be afraid, Nicole tried to sleep, but the proximity of the buccaneer overwhelmed her. Every time she tried to move away from him, the rope would pull her back to his side. Though he had assured her he would do nothing to disturb her sleep, she could not relax. Just the fact that he was there — the mere essence of his masculinity — was enough to disquiet her. Well, he would not be able to go on dragging her around with him on a rope forever. There would be other days, and possibly better circumstances. Sooner or later she would find a way to escape.

Paul Dawson lay quietly beside the restless girl, but nothing inside of him was quiet. Each pull of the rope around his waist cut him to the quick. The obstinate little minx! Why did she force him to such measures? What a fool he had been to buy her from Renaud on impulse! If he had any sense at all, he would leave her at the first settlement he came across. She had made it plain that she wanted no part of him, that she preferred to fend for herself, and he certainly didn't want a woman he literally had to tie to him to make her stay by his side!

Usually he had to dodge the females — from barmaids to titled ladies — who pursued him whenever he dropped anchor. Why bother with one insignificant wench who was proving to be such a headache? His life was already complicated enough. There certainly was no room in it for a liaison with any woman, much less a troublesome one. Yet his heart went out to this incredibly beautiful girl. It was obvious she had been deeply hurt, and he admired that feisty spirit of hers which refused to compromise her inner dignity or bend in the face of adversity, no matter what the odds.

In the life he led he had encountered few women of true virtue. This wouldn't be the first time that a rogue found himself caught in the web of innocence. For though this wench was a convicted murderess, she most certainly wasn't the usual trollop that France was sending over to its colonies.

If only she would accept him. He longed to take her in his arms and comfort her, yet he knew she would neither accept nor believe him if he tried to tell her the feelings she had aroused in him from the first moment he had made love to her.

Well, she was his now, bought and paid for. He had even possessed that most intimate part of her where no other man had ever been. How could he just abandon her there in the swamps and sail away? What's more — why not admit it? — he *wanted* to keep her. He had never wanted any woman as much as he did this stubborn little *incorrigible*. He meant to save her in spite of herself — and if need be, perhaps even himself!

Chapter 20

Nicole slept fitfully, tormented by one nightmare after another. The tug of the rope brought back a flood of memories that penetrated her dreams. Even the darkness around her, illumined only by the fluttering campfire without and resounding with the wind's steady pounding, intruded upon her sleep, reminding her of other sounds and shadows she had known. . . .

In that phantom world the moaning and weeping of her companions came back to her. The symphony of creaking boards and clanking chains rang in her ears. The leering face of the gendarme she had killed was suddenly hovering above her once more, his laughter echoing down to her through the long tunnel of memory. But somehow, as dreams are apt to do, it began to blur and then double and redouble into a shouting, ruthlesss mob descending upon her with thousands of rapacious hands eager to strip and ravish her. She twisted and moaned, thrashing about, desperately trying to ward them off, but Legarde was suddenly there leading them in the attack, tearing off her garments while everyone watched and cheered him on.

Now he had placed her naked on a scaffold. With her arms tied high above her head, she hung suspended for everyone to see while Renaud, grinning broadly, was standing on the platform next to her, running his hands over her body and inviting the spectators to step up and join him in his inspection.

Immediately the guard who had held her that day in the public square came forward and, climbing up to the gallows, caught her roughly to him. She could feel his shaft, hard and brutal, penetrating her with one bold thrust, tearing her. . . . But no, it wasn't his shaft, it was a brand! He was branding her, burning the mark of the harlot deep inside of her! The crowd was cheering wildy and all her jailers were laughing heartily as they began to line up to take their turns branding her, too. Paul Dawson was even there, swaggering about among them and offering to buy their turns with her for himself.

The rope that held her dangling from the scaffold was burning her hands and wrists, and the chains around her ankles hindered her as she tried frantically to fight the rabble off. They reached up to pull her down from the scaffold into the mire — down into a bottomless pit of quicksand waiting to swallow her. The din was deafening — the boisterous laughter, the obscenities, the hissing whips, and above it all, her own desperate screams. . . .

Someone was shaking her by the shoulders. A familiar voice repeated her name.

"Nicole, lass. In God's name, wake up! You're dreaming. It's all right, it's all right!"

The lantern in the tent was lit once more, and Dawson bent over her anxiously. His two officers were shouting to him.

"Rest easy. All's well!" the captain shouted back. "The lass was just having a nightmare, that's all."

He turned back to Nicole, who was still gasping and

sobbing hysterically. "Please, lass, don't be afraid. It's all right," he told her again, trying to calm her.

But she stared at him with glazed eyes, not hearing anything he was saying. Still caught up in the middle of her nightmare, she continued to thrash about, crying out that there was a dead woman chained to her, that they were branding her....

Although she seemed to be babbling incoherently, Dawson couldn't help but suspect that his having bound her was what had set off her nightmare. Remorse overwhelmed him as he looked into her lovely face. Filled with self-loathing, he caught her wrists in his hands and tugged impatiently at the knot that held them lashed together. Then he drew her into his arms and continued to soothe her.

"There, lass, you're free," he reassured her, pulling the rest of the rope from around their waists and tossing it aside.

She had stopped screaming, but her breathing was still rapid and spasmodic.

"Don't be afraid," he said again as he gently folded her in his arms and continued to comfort her as though she were a frightened child. "You'll never be bound again, I promise you." A wave of tenderness swept over him as he felt her tremble. "My sweet little cub! How those bastards must have hurt you!" he exclaimed, stroking the burnished gold of her hair back from her pale tear-stained face. "And even I have unwittingly hurt you!" he added quietly. "But you're not alone and defenseless anymore. No one will ever harm you again."

"Don't be a hypocrite!" she suddenly flared back at him, trying to disengage herself from his embrace now that she had regained her composure. "You're as bad as the rest of them!"

He winced but dropped his arms from her so she would not feel he was forcing himself on her.

"I regret to say that in some ways I, too, have been

guilty of mistreating you," he admitted sadly, "but perhaps the day will come when you'll at least concede that most of my actions, bad as they might seem to you at this moment, have sprung from a desire to protect you."

She looked at him skeptically, but he went on. "I confess I let my temper cloud my judgment. After all, how can I blame you for wanting to be free? But you're not ready for that kind of freedom yet, my sweet. You need to learn so many things if you are to survive."

"Don't lie to me," she interrupted him. "You know very well you have no intentions of setting me free. You want to keep me bound to you."

He flushed under his tan. "Perhaps I do. I admit I'd like to bind you to me, but with chains of love, my sweet. No other way, I assure you."

"Yes, I suppose that's the way a man would prefer his concubine to be. . . ." she said bitterly.

"I said I wanted a concubine for Renaud's benefit," he corrected her. "It was the only way I could think of to get you out of there without creating an incident with the French, although I assure you I'd have drawn my sword if it had come to that, for I was determined to take you with me no matter what. God knows I paid a sizable amount to do it peaceably."

Nicole strained to see his face clearly in the lamplight. She found it hard to believe that a pirate could be so noble. "But no matter how good you might be to me," she said at last, her voice low and deliberate, "I still won't be free. No matter how exciting your caresses, I'll still feel used because I'll be the prisoner and you the jailer."

He stared a long time at her. "All right, lass, you win," he said suddenly.

"You mean you'll let me go?" she asked incredulously.

"No, I can't do that — for your sake as well as mine. I can't, in all conscience, just turn you loose in the middle of nowhere. After all, I do feel a certain responsibility for you, though you're right about one thing: I do want you to belong to me, but *only* if you want to. I promise I'll not take you against your will."

He stroked her shining hair, then extinguished the lantern and cradled her in his arms. "I'll give you time," he said softly, his voice husky with restrained desire. "Everyone and everything frightens you now, and justly so. But you must learn to trust again — to love and be loved. For that is your destiny, my little bobcat. So I won't force you. You have my word on it. But don't ask me to let you go. That I cannot do."

Chapter 21

The last day of their journey was overcast, with a cool, albeit humid, breeze ruffling the gray surface of the swollen river. Nicole was certain they would be drenched before they reached their destination, but the captain assured her that the storm was still too far out in the Gulf for them to feel anything more than its echo here in the delta.

Already he and his men had their hands full keeping themselves on a steady course against the increasing force of the current, as the boat bobbed like a cork on the heaving bosom of the river. Nicole was certain they would have long since capsized had the buccaneers been any less expert.

As it was, she clung tightly to the sides of the compartment where she huddled among the bundles and animal skins, growing damper by the minute and fearing they were all going to end up in the river before the journey was over.

But just when she thought things couldn't get much worse, the buccaneers surprised her by suddenly turning off the river and plunging into the swamplands.

Dawson smiled at her worried frown. "We're going to take a shortcut," he told her. "As you've probably surmised, there's a certain amount of danger involved in navigating the Mississippi from this point on, and it gets even worse the nearer we get to the mouth — or, should I say, mouths — of the river because of the crosscurrents that come together there. But fortunately we don't have to take such risks. My ship is anchored in a large bay southwest of here, so we can reach it by cutting across the swamplands and save a day or two while we're at it."

"But what of the dangers?" Nicole asked, remembering her own harrowing experience the day before.

"Don't worry, lass, I know this region like the palm of my hand," he reassured her with an indulgent smile. "Besides, I have too precious a cargo with me this trip to take any unnecessary chances."

He rummaged in his pack and took out a small jar.

"Put this on," he said, handing it to her. "It will help protect you from mosquitoes and such."

"What is it?" she asked, eyeing it with little enthusiasm.

"Bear grease. The Indians use it all the time. It helps, believe me, and it's not as bad as you might think."

She dipped a curious finger into the thick white oil, testing it hesitantly.

"Go ahead, lass," Dawson urged her. "It's fresh so there's practically no odor. We're all using it, and it'll only be for a little while. As soon as we get to the ship, you can wash it off."

While she reluctantly obeyed, the captain and his men took their oars out of their locks so they would be able to pole as well as paddle with them, and then began to cut a path with their machetes through the wall of tangled vegetation that blocked the narrow waterway they had just entered.

Nicole wondered how Dawson and his men could possibly know which route to take. Water was everywhere.

What had once been a forest floor was now a vast, silent sea reflecting in its stagnant mirror the multitude of towering trees rising out of its murky depths. But the captain assured her that the increased level of water could be to their advantage, since there would be less possibility of their boat running aground.

"And what happens if the water becomes too shallow for our boat to get through?" she asked.

The captain smiled. "We either find another way or get out and carry the boat until we reach deeper water again."

"*Mon Dieu!*" she gasped. The look of consternation on her face amused him.

"Don't worry, my sweet. There should be enough water at this time of year to get us through, but even if there isn't, we're close enough to our destination now that we could always leave some of our camping equipment behind. One thing is certain: I'll get you safely to my ship even if I have to carry you the rest of the way myself."

No sooner had they plunged into the swamplands than Nicole realized how little she had really seen of this mysterious world. It certainly had not prepared her for this part of the journey.

The twilight world extended as far as she could see. After the roar of the mighty river, a palpable silence descended upon them, disturbed only by an occasional bird call, the snap of a twig, or the gentle splash of their oars in the stagnant water. The swamp closed in on them, enveloping, almost suffocating them in its mossy arms.

Dawson's grin broadened as he watched her reactions. "Now you see this country as it really is, lass," he said, deftly pushing away some rotting debris with his oar. "There's a beauty about it, isn't there? But you must never forget that its embrace can be deadly."

The dampness had tightened the waves of his hair, and the wet tendrils fell rebelliously over his forehead, giving him a boyish look. He seemed in good spirits as he spoke to her of his ship waiting for him in the hidden cove — the ship which was obviously home to him.

Nicole had expected that at this time of the year the vegetation would be rampant, but she had not anticipated the endless network of narrow waterlanes and bayous. Sometimes their way was so completely blocked by over-hanging branches and tangled vines that she had to bend low in the boat while the men slashed through them before they could continue. The air was hot and sticky, and great beads of sweat coursed down the buccaneers' glistening faces as they wielded their blades. Nicole sat wet and miserable, dabbing at her own damp forehead, but not daring to wipe too hard for fear of removing too much of the oil that was protecting her from the swarms of insects that sailed out of the thickets when the buccaneers' machetes disturbed them.

The captain always seemed to know which way to turn, going forward with complete assurance — cautious, but never hesitant. He didn't seem to have as much interest in the tiller now as in controlling the boat with his oar.

Occasionally some timid fawn or small furry animal, startled by the intruders, would scurry quickly away, but the alligators were bolder. Like the lords of the swamplands that they were, the creatures would often swim right by them, and the buccaneers had all they could do to stay clear of the beasts. Nicole was certain they were doomed when one of the scaly monsters almost collided with the boat. They would have capsized had it not been for Dawson's skillful maneuvering.

But there were also pleasant interludes, when they traversed tranquil lakes and bayous, gliding over the sparkling, smooth-surfaced water with a steady, relaxed dip of their oars and making up for the time they had lost in the dense forests.

But just as Nicole began to breathe easily, relieved that the worst of the journey was over, they hit another difficult lap through a wooded area, and the captain had to exchange places with Fernández and go up front again with Josh to lend his strength to the task of hacking through the green wall blocking their progress.

"Damn it all, Captain, you'd never think we just cut all this down when we came through here less than a week ago!" grumbled the copper-haired buccaneer as he brushed away the sweat trickling down his freckled face.

"Aye, it's the season," Dawson agreed as he swung at the stubborn vines. "At least the mosquitoes aren't out en masse yet!"

But even as they spoke, Nicole spotted a long diamond-patterned snake slowly unwinding itself from one of the branches directly above the captain.

Instinctively she sprang to her feet with a cry, setting the boat to rocking precariously.

For a breathless moment the men grabbed their oars and worked feverishly to balance the teetering boat, while Dawson called out to her to sit down and be still.

She sank back sheepishly against the animal skins, as weak from fright as humiliation.

"For God's sake, lass, you nearly turned us over!" Dawson chided once the boat had been steadied.

"But the snake was right above you!" she protested lamely.

"Josh had already seen it and was about to kill it," he told her. "There was no need for alarm. Now in heaven's name, sit still and don't ever do that again!"

"*Mon Dieu!* Perhaps we'd have done better to have risked the mouth of the river!" she moaned.

Dawson gave a deep-throated laugh and his men echoed with more discreet chuckles. "But this is nothing, lass!" he assured her, his annoyance with her already beginning to dissolve. "It's all in a day's work! Today we fight the swamps. Tomorrow it'll be the Spaniards! It's six of one and half a dozen of the other!"

Then he added with a smile, "The truth is, that was the third snake that's been in the branches we cut down. You just didn't see the others."

"Don't worry, we're almost there now," Dawson called out to her as he rejoined Josh. Perhaps she wouldn't be so quick to try to run away from him again!

Besides, how could he be angry with her when she had reacted in part out of fear for his safety? Of course, he didn't deceive himself. It had only been an impulse — an instinctive reaction to what she believed was danger to all of them. But at least it was something. At this stage of their relationship, he was encouraged by even that small gesture.

They didn't stop at noon as they had done on the two previous days. Instead, they paused briefly to refresh themselves and then continued on their way. They were so near their destination now that the captain preferred not to delay their arrival any longer than he had to. Meanwhile they munched on fruit and chunks of jerked beef to keep them going.

When they finally came out of the swamp in the late afternoon, Nicole was surprised to see an imposing brigantine riding majestically at anchor in a large bay. There was much shouting and waving back and forth, but the closer she and her companions came to the brigantine, the more she could feel the curious stares of the men standing at the railing as they caught sight of her sitting next to the captain.

Suddenly a shadow fell over her, and she looked up to see the figure of a brightly painted angel with a flaming sword etched against the bright sunless sky. A chill swept over her as she read the name emblazoned in large gold letters — THE AVENGER.

Sneaking a wary glance at the captain, Nicole reminded herself that this new owner of hers — this golden-haired devil who called upon the angels to help him — was one of the most feared men in the Caribbean. He had promised not to harm her, had promised he would not force himself on her, yet he had never denied that sooner or later he meant to have her. Once aboard his ship, she would be more subject to his will than ever before. But there was no turning back. She had no place to go except to follow the course that this enigmatic buccaneer had set for her.

Chapter 22

While his men watched in open-mouthed amazement, the captain escorted Nicole to his quarters. No sooner had he safely deposited her there, however, than he excused himself, pausing only to give her a final warning that under no circumstances was she to leave the cabin without his permission.

Alone at last, she looked around the cabin. Its luxury took her by surprise. It was not at all the way she would have expected a pirate's lodgings to be. But then, Mignon had told her that Dawson was known to be fabulously rich. No wonder he had been able to offer Renaud a price for her that even the planter had not been able to resist!

Though not particularly large or ornate, the cabin was certainly ample enough for its owner's needs, and it was evident that he had decorated it to suit his taste and comfort. Everything suggested a paradoxical combination of abundance and restraint, a love of beauty tempered by an equal desire for practicality. But wherever she looked, there was a relaxed feeling of unpretentious wealth — from the highly polished silver and brass to the rich Oriental carpet extending from wall to wall, from the fine oak paneling to the scant but exquisite furnishings of well-waxed mahogany and rosewood. Of course, the mere presence of so many glass panes — twelve in each of the windows running along the back wall of the cabin — was in itself a sign of considerable means. They were closed at the moment, but the portholes on each side were open, admitting a pleasant breeze.

For a moment she stood admiring the sweeping panorama of the broad tree-lined bay, still finding it difficult to believe that just behind that ragged shoreline lay the wild world she had just traversed. But as she turned away from the window and caught sight of the simple yet comfortable-looking bunk on the far side of the room, she was suddenly reminded of the fact that this cabin was the captain's private domain.

Her uneasiness mounting, she paced the length of the room, wondering where she would be staying. Curiously, she tried the door to what seemed to be an adjoining room, thinking that Dawson would probably keep her nearby, but a peep inside revealed that it was a dining room. A long, polished mahogany table was surrounded by a dozen chairs, which she supposed must also serve the captain and his officers for meetings.

She turned back to Dawson's personal quarters and went over to a marble-topped night table, where there was a white porcelain bowl and pitcher with a shaving mug and razor beside it. She poured herself a little water and tried to rinse off some of the grease and grime from her face and hands.

No sooner had she finished her meager ablutions, however, when the captain returned, followed by a young boy carrying two buckets of steaming water. From a corner of the cabin Dawson rolled out a large metal tub elaborately enameled in white and gold and locked its wheels while the cabin boy emptied his buckets into it. Then he ordered the youngster to bring more water until the tub was full.

"I hope you like this scent," he said to her as he took a flask from the drawer of the marble-topped table.

A pleasant aroma filled the room, and she recognized it at once. It had lingered in his frock coat, in the lawn of his shirt, even on the gold-tipped hairs of his chest.

He could feel her eyes fixed suspiciously on his every movement. "If you prefer some particular scent, I'll try to get it for you the first opportunity that presents itself," he was saying as he let a few drops fall into the steaming water, "but meanwhile, I'm afraid this will have to do."

Nicole looked longingly at the tub of water, trying to ignore the inviting aroma of the sensuous perfume as it wafted across the cabin to where she stood. How she would love to remove her tattered gown and soak off the sticky bear grease and muck of the swamplands from her aching body! But she was afraid to accept. She didn't dare trust this buccaneer who had, on more than one occasion, admitted that he meant to find a way to take her again. How vulnerable she would be sitting there naked in the tub alone in his cabin! No, she had to be very cautious about such things if she hoped to keep him at bay.

"I — I have no desire to bathe just now," she faltered. He smiled slowly, a twinkle lighting his blue eyes. "If my presence disturbs your maidenly modesty, don't give it another thought," he said. "I have more important things to do than sit around ogling you like an adolescent school-boy while you take your bath."

"You don't have to leave on my account," she retorted. "I've already washed myself as much as I intend to do for the moment." She inclined her head toward the night table.

He looked skeptical. "Surely you can't be serious? Not after roaming the swamplands for three days!"

"It will have to do," she insisted. "I certainly don't want to risk catching my death of cold." She suddenly recalled Mignon's words and quickly decided to take refuge in them. "Surely you must know that most physicians advise against the practice of bathing all over. They say it weakens you."

Dawson frowned. "What the hell? Don't tell me you're one of those addleheaded wenches who believes in bathing only once a season?" he exclaimed. "I'd have never believed it of you! I see where your education is sadly lacking in more aspects than one!"

Nicole bit her lip. The tub seemed to be beckoning to her, and already she could imagine how delightful that warm scented water would feel lapping gently against her skin. But even if he left, he could always return at any moment. He was probably already planning to take her unawares ... though, of course, not until she was clean enough for his fastidious taste!

"I — I'm really too tired just now to do anything except rest," she persisted, but even as she spoke, her mind was racing on to meet the next dilemma. Where would he want her to sleep? The bunk seemed to dominate the cabin at that moment. The cabin boy had already prepared it for the coming night; its top covers were turned back to reveal clean linen sheets beneath, invitingly awaiting occupancy.

"You'd better take advantage of this opportunity to enjoy a good bath," he warned her. "Water consumption will be greatly curtailed once we're at sea, and you'll be limited to one bucketful at a time for personal ablutions."

He eyed her expectantly for a few seconds, but when he saw how immobile she remained, her chin resolutely set in her determination not to obey him, he suddenly scowled and strode over to her.

Before she realized what was happening, he swept her up into his arms and carried her over to the tub. By the time she knew what his intentions were, however, it was too late. The water rose all around her and splashed over the sides as he deposited her unceremoniously, kicking and protesting, into the tub.

"I'm sorry, my sweet. You leave me no alternative," he said. "It's bad enough you have the disposition of a bobcat, but I draw the line at your smelling like one!"

She sat there sputtering and glaring up at him with emerald fire in her eyes. Trying to grab hold of the sides of the tub, she fought against the weight of her soaked clothing and struggled to pull herself up.

He gave her a long, hard look. "I wouldn't do that." He paused. "Unless, of course, you'd prefer that I bathe you myself."

She stopped kicking and looked up at him. "You — you wouldn't dare!" she exclaimed.

He gave her a crooked grin. "Wouldn't I now?"

She shot him a venomous look. "Why, you probably would!"

"Well, I'm glad you believe me," he said tersely. "It'll save both of us a lot of time that way."

He sauntered over to a large chest beneath the wide window and threw back the lid, rummaging among its contents for a few moments. Finally he held up a silk dressing gown, its turquoise fabric shimmering in the late afternoon light slanting in through the myriad panes.

"When you've finished bathing, you can put this on," he said, tossing the garment across the bunk. "I have a lot of things to do topside before dark, so I'll be gone for awhile, but I'll try to send you something to eat in case you get hungry."

She shook her head. "Don't bother. I don't want anything," she mumbled crossly from the depths of the tub, hating to concede that she was so dependent upon him that even when and how she ate and bathed were subject to his command.

But he seemed oblivious to her mood. "Then go ahead and get some rest if you like," he urged her. "Actually,

I'd prefer that no one enter this cabin unless I can be here with you," he confessed, "so it would probably be better if you did wait to dine until I return. Once I've shed these garments and had my own bath, I'll be ready for a hearty meal, and I'm sure you will be, too."

He took up a tinderbox from among the logs and maps piled high on his massive desk and lit the gimballed lantern dangling from one of the overhead beams. Then he closed what portholes were open. "You see, I'm not entirely unmindful of your concern over catching cold while you're bathing." He smiled.

When he had finished, he bowed formally and, without another word, strolled casually out of the cabin, the twinkle in his eyes flashing as brightly as the anger in hers.

The turn of the key in the lock enraged her all the more. It simply confirmed what she had feared. She was a prisoner, at the mercy of this cynical pirate who probably wanted her to bathe and prepare herself to attend him on his return.

Chapter 23

Nicole had to admit, if only to herself, that she had never had such a delightful bath. Once she was alone and convinced that her jailer wouldn't be returning too quickly, she had shed her soggy, mud-stained clothing and lain back in the tub to enjoy the first moments of absolute privacy she had had in over a year.

As long as she could hear the sound of Dawson's voice far above her on the topdeck, she could relax and soak in the perfumed warmth of her bath. How wanton she felt as she sank down into the tub and let the water caress her all over — deliciously lapping against her bare skin and penetrating the roots of her hair as she tilted her head back and allowed her generous mane to cascade into the water.

By the time she had stepped out of the tub and slipped into the shimmering turquoise silk, she was wonderfully relaxed. The soft material felt pleasantly familiar to her body, bringing back bittersweet memories of days when her own wardrobe contained such luxuries.

Lethargy had suddenly overtaken her. How nice it would be to take advantage of this brief respite from the constant tension and steal an hour or so of sleep before Dawson returned.

She lay back on the bed and pulled the sheet over her, delighting in the soft, clean freshness of the linen after so many months of filthy pallets and bare ground. Once again there was the faint aroma of Dawson. In a few minutes she had drifted off into an exhausted sleep; she no longer had the strength to worry about what lay ahead.

She had no way of telling how long she had slept, but as she lay in the bunk drifting lazily between dreams and reality, she gradually became aware of the gentle rocking of the boat and the steady swing of the lantern above her.

The first thing she realized as she floated back to consciousness was that Dawson's familiar voice no longer came from the deck above her; it was much nearer — right there in the cabin, in fact!

Immediately she was wide awake. Her eyes adjusted to the dim light, and she could see Dawson's blond head and naked shoulders above the rim of the tub where he contentedly soaped himself and instructed Jeff, the cabin boy, how the evening meal was to be served.

How sound her sleep must have been for her not to have heard anything before this! Why, Dawson must have undressed and had that fresh tub poured for him while she had been sleeping in his bunk! He was speaking softly; under the circumstances, she thought it best to let him go on thinking she was asleep.

At last he rose from the tub, his smooth, sun-kissed skin gleaming in the light of the swaying lantern. The hard cords of his muscles rippled with his movements. She meant to close her eyes, but what looked like several scars on the broad expanse of his powerful back held her attention. He must have had his share of encounters and scarred a few men himself. How many men had he wounded and killed — and how many women had he raped?

He was drying himself briskly now with a huge linen towel, and the cabin boy held out a fresh pair of nankeen breeches to him.... She snapped her lids shut so tightly that her eyes watered in protest. *Sainte Vierge!* To peep on a naked man like that! Of course he had his back to her; all she had really seen were the scars on his back. But the thought that she had dared look even for a moment was shameful. Had the fact that she had been branded a harlot turned her into one? Was it possible she could find the anatomy of that swaggering buccaneer fascinating? Could it be perhaps because that same body had once been fused with hers? Even at that moment the memory of him as he had been on that night engulfed her in a flood of disquieting sensations.

She heard the cabin boy roll the tub out and the door close behind him. Though she kept her eyes shut, she knew Dawson was approaching the bunk. With pounding heart, she lay perfectly still, knowing his gaze was fixed on her. Finally she couldn't stand it.

Her eyes flew open, and she found herself staring into the penetrating blue of his gaze. For a fleeting moment his desire for her was plain — desire and something else she couldn't readily identify. But the instant he realized she was looking up at him, his expression changed.

He wore a clean, white open-necked shirt belted into his breeches and, instead of boots, cotton stockings and black shoes with gold buckles — the perfect picture of a young country squire, she thought. Perhaps in her honor, he had even combed his rebellious blond waves neatly back and tied them with a black satin ribbon into a short club. He seemed at ease now and pleased to find her lying in his bunk.

"Ah, so you were able to rest a little, I see." He greeted

her warmly, extending a hand toward her, but his eyes were guarded. "Come, little one, I've had a special supper prepared for us, one to make up for that long trek through the swamps. So get up, my sweet. You have all night for sleeping. You must eat now. The sea is no place for a finicky lass with airs. If you're to accompany me, you'll have to be strong and healthy."

Playfully he pulled her to her feet. She swayed unsteadily, slightly off balance from the ship's motion, still fighting her lingering drowsiness. He caught her to him and balanced her against his sturdy frame.

"You'll get accustomed to the rolling after a while," he assured her good-naturedly as he led her to the table that had been set in the middle of the cabin. He sat her down carefully and lit the candlelabrum, which brought into full relief the exquisite array of silver and crystal laid out against spotless damask.

The aromas escaping from the covers on the large bowl and platter suddenly reminded her of how hungry she really was.

"It's only turtle soup and roasted chicken with stewed rice," he said apologetically, "but our cook is quite good. I pay him an extra share of the profits just to keep him happy. After all, a man can't fight on an upset stomach!"

He opened a bottle of wine and filled their glasses. "I ordered this in honor of your first meal on board," he said, watching her closely to see her reactions. As he expected, the girl was obviously accustomed to such niceties, though she seemed surprised to find them here on his ship. Well, perhaps now she would realize he wasn't the barbarian she seemed to think he was.

The turtle soup was new to her, but she found its spicy taste pleasing. By the time she got to the chicken, she was thoroughly enjoying the first decent meal she had had since she had lost her way in France so long ago.

Dawson worked on a drumstick in silence, watching with undisguised pleasure the way his companion stripped a wishbone of its meat with relish. How lovely she looked with the blue-green of her dressing gown reflected in her eyes and the red-gold of her freshly washed hair cascading about her shoulders! She was meant to wear silks and satins; her beauty and bearing deserved no less.

Breaking the silence between them at last, he said, "Tomorrow, if I can find time, I'll take you to the poop deck so you can see the way the world looks from topside of a ship."

She grimaced. "I've only seen it from the bottom of one."

"I know, lass," he said gently, "but there will be no more black holes for you, on land or sea."

"Yes, I have to admit my new prison is more luxurious than any I've been in before," she conceded.

"Prison!" he exclaimed. "Is that the way you regard my quarters?"

"I heard you use the key," she said. "I know I'm locked in here."

"But that's for your protection," he protested. "You're a lone woman on a vessel with over a hundred men, many of them no better than brigands. I can't let you move around at will, not only for your own safety, but for the discipline of the ship."

She sighed. After all, she had expected as much. "But even if you must keep me under lock and key," she said, "why can't I at least have my own quarters?"

He rose slowly and walked toward the windows. Finally he turned and came to stand in front of her. "I can't begin to tell you how important it is that you appear to be my woman in every sense of the word," he said carefully. "Frankly, even if I had a cabin to spare — which I don't — I would insist on keeping you here. As long as it is evident to my men that you belong to me, that I care enough about you to keep you by my side, no man on board will dare touch you."

"You mean, as long as they think I'm your *concubine*?"

"When dealing with a man of Renaud's limited mentality, it's simpler to use such terms, but I hope you'll come to be something more than that to me," he hurriedly went on when he saw the look in her eyes. "My men are already curious about my relationship with you, so they'll be watching like a pack of gossips. That's why I don't think it would be wise even to have another bed set up in here for you. Such a move would only arouse speculation on their part.

"Not that I care what my men think about my personal life," he added hastily, "but things will be less complicated if they have no doubts about my interest in you. Once they are convinced that they'll have to get past me to reach you, they'll leave you alone. It's that simple, and I'm not looking for problems. A fighting ship is no place for a woman, and, believe me, if there were any other spot where I could safely leave you, I'd have never brought you on board. But since there isn't, we'll just have to make do with this arrangement as best we can."

Nicole recognized the futility of arguing with this man who obviously was accustomed to giving orders and being obeyed. After all, he was only confirming what she had known would happen once he had her on board his ship. Regardless of his glib tongue and high-sounding promises, she was still his prisoner and was going to have to share his bed whether it was a pallet in the swamplands or an elegant berth in his cabin.

"I'm sure we can work out some satisfactory sleeping arrangement," he said, well aware of her anger. "Once we set sail, I'll be too busy to spend much time here, so you'll have the cabin — and the bunk — all to yourself most of the time."

He poured himself another glass of wine and sat down, frustrated over his obvious failure to convince her of his sincerity.

"I can see those claws of yours getting set for another fight," he sighed. "You know, my little bobcat, the Spanish have an expression. "They'd call you *mal pensada* — always ready to believe the worst of everyone."

"What does it matter what I think?" she retorted. "You're the one who sets the rules."

"I'm afraid that here on board my word must be law," he agreed, "and frankly I'm not in the habit of explaining the whys and wherefores of my orders. If I'm taking the pains to do so now, it's only because I do care very much what you think."

He drained his glass and rose again. "Although I can't permit you as much freedom as you might wish, I'd still like to make you feel at home here. As far as it is within my power to oblige you, you'll want for nothing."

He walked over to the large oak chest and threw back the lid.

"Come, lass," he invited. "Feel free to choose anything you want from here. You'll never have to hide that beauty of yours again. You'll find some fine linens and laces in this chest, and here are bolts of silk and brocade, cloths of gold and silver. Perhaps you'd like to do some sewing? Of course, you can choose from these gowns, too. Unfortunately, the Spanish aristocracy can be very staid, so you might find some of these colors a bit somber, but I'm sure there are a few that will be suitable."

He saw her eyes widen, and encouraged by her reaction, lifted some of the gowns that she might see them better. He was truly boyish now as he showed off his treasures to her. "I've never shared any of these with a woman before," he admitted. "Usually when I have enough chests filled to the brim, I turn them over to my administrator in Virginia, who converts them into gold or property for me, but I'm glad I have something on hand at the moment to offer you. So choose what you will. I have jewels too. One day I'll let you see them and take your pick."

Nicole continued to stare into the chest, unable to believe her eyes. But when he handed her a gown of lavender silk, she drew back quickly.

"No, I — I can't ... I won't accept your bloodstained spoils!" she cried. "How many women have you killed and raped to come by these garments?"

He colored beneath his tan, as though she had struck him, and let the gown he had been holding drop into the chest.

"Watch your tongue, lass. You go too far," he warned her, his features hardening and a sharp edge she had never heard before creeping into his voice. "These things came from cargoes en route to or from New Spain — not off any women's backs! What kind of monster do you take me for?"

"Are you asking me to believe that you and your men have never captured women during your numerous exploits?"

"There have been occasions when we've encountered a few who were passengers, but as God is my witness, neither I nor my men have ever laid a hand on any of them. We don't wage war on women — not even Spanish women — and I'd certainly never allow a man who serves under me to rape any female, no matter who she is. It's in the articles they must sign when they enlist on my ship."

"Yet you raped me!" she flung back at him.

"Your case was quite different. I had no idea you weren't .. weren't who you seemed to be."

"A whore, you mean?"

"If you must put it that way, yes."

"And now ... now that you ... that I ..."

"Now that you're mine?"

She flushed hotly. "Now that you've violated me," she corrected him.

"I confess it's made me feel a certain responsibility for you. You certainly can't say I haven't tried to make it up to you. As soon as I realized your situation with Renaud, I got you out of there before you could be abused further."

Her laugh was brittle. "Saved from one rake to belong to another."

"You may not be aware of it, but there are degrees of raffishness."

"I don't think I'm going to find much difference between being Renaud's concubine or a pirate's!"

"A *privateer*," he corrected her with a scowl. "You'll please stop calling me a pirate. I'm a *privateer*."

"Pirate ... privateer ... what difference does it make?"

"I like to think there's a very big one," he retorted. "I may be an independent captain, but I'm in the employ of my government, with letters of marque giving me leave to attack Spanish ships and, when at war, any enemies of the British colonies. I don't consider myself an outlaw, and I'll thank you to remember the distinction."

He slammed the lid closed and turned on his heel. "I don't know about you, but I'm going to retire for the night," he said abruptly. He checked the oil in the lantern and then sat on the edge of the bed to remove his shoes. "I haven't had a moment's rest since last night, and there will be a lot to check on tomorrow before we sail, so I'll probably be up and gone from the cabin by dawn, if not before."

She continued to stand in the middle of the room, watching him warily as he stretched out on the bunk. "I usually sleep fully clothed when I'm on board ship. There's no time to get dressed when an enemy's sighted or some problem arises in the middle of the night."

"I — I'm not sleepy anymore," she protested. "I had a nice rest after my bath."

He gave her a knowing look but was too tired to try to convince her otherwise. "As you wish," he sighed, "but feel free to come lie down beside me. At least there's a lot more room here than we had on that pallet in the tent. It's certainly more comfortable."

When he saw she had no intention of joining him, he added drowsily, "There are some books on the shelves above the desk. You might find some of them dull reading, but there are several classics ... even a few in French...." His voice trailed off. "I wish you'd come lie here beside me," he murmured. "I miss your sweet warmth, lass."

Nicole sat quietly at the table, not moving until she heard his breathing slip into the slower rhythm of his slumber. Then she rose and went over to his desk.

A compass and several strange instruments lay on top of the logs and charts spread out over the surface. Off to one side stood a small rack with several pipes carved from different fine woods.

Carefully, so as not to disturb anything, she stood on tiptoe and reached over to one of the shelves lining the wall above the desk. The selection surprised her. She pulled down a volume of Molière's plays and settled back at the table.

The night was calm, the only sounds of life the occasional footsteps scurrying across the deck above her or the call of the watch. There was a faint creaking as the waves lapped gently against the hull, and gradually she began to feel her eyelids grow heavy.

When Dawson rose, he found her asleep, the book in her lap, her auburn head pillowed against her arm on the table. With a chuckle he lifted her gently and carried her to the bunk. She sighed contentedly as her head touched the pillow and he pulled the sheet over her carefully.

"My sweet, stubborn little bobcat," he murmured, his lips brushing her forehead lightly. Then he extinguished the lamp and quietly stole out of the cabin, locking the door behind him.

Chapter 24

Dawson kept the *Avenger* at anchor a few days longer. Now that he had agreed to join the French in their fight against their mutual enemy, the Spanish, he wanted to be certain his ship was in top shape.

One of the first things he did the next morning was order a curtain to be hung in his quarters so that he and Nicole could enjoy more privacy. Also, it would insure a more formal atmosphere on occasions when one of his officers had to consult with him there.

Nicole spent the following days looking out at the broad panorama of the bay, sprinkled with tiny islands and fringed with long, twisted fingers of wilderness desperately trying to cling to the shoreline despite the relentless assault of wind and waves. There were times when it all seemed unreal, as though she were dreaming and would awaken at any moment to find herself back in France, safe once more in her own bedchamber with her father asleep down the hall. Even the strange voices on the other side of the curtain, or those that drifted in from the neighboring officers' dining room, added to the feeling of vagueness.

Only the familiar voice of the captain was real, and often she found herself listening for him.

When she and Dawson were alone now, there seemed to be an uneasy truce between them. Out of necessity she soon had to avail herself of some of the garments in the chest, recognizing that she couldn't very well live on so limited a wardrobe as one mud-stained gown and a lovely but rather revealing dressing gown.

The captain had asked the cabin boy to find her some sewing things, and immediately she set about making herself a few much-needed undergarments and accessories such as caps and fichus from some lawn she found among the bolts of cloth in the chest. For her daily gown she decided to accept the lavender silk that Dawson had suggested, since it was the lightest one available; the weather was becoming increasingly warm with each passing day now that they were into May.

Dawson was more and more engrossed in preparations to join the French commanders in Mobile for a final military conference, and so was seldom able to linger very long with her. He had no set hours, but he did seem to make an effort to be with her for at least the evening meal and part of the night. Sometimes, if she was sleeping, he would draw the curtain and work at his desk well into the night.

At other times, however, he returned to the cabin, his face drawn and preoccupied and his body sore and in need of a few hours of rest. Then he simply flung himself on the bunk and went right to sleep. If by chance she was already asleep, he would simply climb in beside her as quietly as possible.

Nevertheless, there were a few awkward moments. Once on awakening to find the captain lying beside her, Nicole had just been about to slip out of the bunk, when suddenly he had thrown his arm across her and murmured her name. "Don't go, lass, stay with me," he whispered, his voice heavy with sleep.

For several minutes she had lain there, expecting him to swing on top of her. But as time passed and he didn't move again, she realized he was still asleep. Still, she lay motionless beside him, afraid to do anything that might remind him she was there.

When he finally did awaken, however, he rose hurriedly, rearranged his clothing, and dashed off to the upper deck, unaware of his actions the night before.

On the first night that the *Avenger* raised anchor and sailed out into the Gulf, however, it was she who disturbed his slumber. The more intense rocking of the boat must have crept into her dreams, for once more she found herself plunged back into the dark bowels of the *Dolphin*, crying out in vain to the Blessed Virgin to help her. When she awoke, she found herself in the captain's arms, instinctively clinging to him as she sought some measure of comfort in the solid reality of him. She was grateful when he did not try to press her further. Instead, he had just lain there, holding her in his arms until she fell asleep.

That following morning he took her to the topdeck for a few minutes while most of the crew was at mess. The vast emptiness of the Gulf awed her. As far as she could see, there was nothing but water and sky. How tiny their ship now seemed!

"It seems so lonely!" she exclaimed as she stood holding the railing tightly with one hand and her new white ruffle-edged cap with the other. The wind was strong against her face and whipped her skirts persistently, but Dawson kept a steadying hand on her arm. He seemed to be enjoying the view beside him more than the one around him.

"Aye, lass, it can be lonely sometimes," he agreed, "but it can be exhilarating, too. There's nothing like the freedom you feel out here. I've always wanted to share this world with someone like you, my sweet, who can appreciate as I do what freedom is...."

"And who won't be contented until she has it!" she retorted.

But he was in too good a mood to take offense. He simply smiled and tightened his grip on her. "Aye, that's my feisty little bobcat!" he teased. "Always ready to claw me at the drop of a hat!" His eyes swept possessively over her. "God, but you're beautiful!" he murmured in open admiration. "Do you realize you're the perfect embodiment of my world — a touch of the sea in your eyes and the rays of the sun caught in your hair? Take off your cap, lass, and let the wind caress you. This is your world now, too. You must learn to love it as I do."

She had to admit that there was something exhilarating about standing here in the open air with the warm wind kissing her cheeks and her hair streaming behind her. But there was still something frightening about it, too, even as there had been something awesome about the wilderness the first time she had found herself in the swamplands. For all its savage beauty and splendor, this fascinating new world still seemed strange and hostile to her. She feared it would never accept her.

Dawson stayed with her later for a meal of lamb stew and candied yams before rejoining his men. She nibbled at the peculiar orange potato the captain had put on her plate. He smiled at her reaction of pleasant surprise and urged her to take another one.

Dawson was becoming more accustomed to having her in his world, and he found himself looking forward to these brief interludes.

He loved his swift, sleek brigantine, but now it had a rival. For the first time he found himself resenting the time his duties as captain demanded of him — time he longed to be sharing with his fascinating little intruder.

There was so much, however, that he didn't yet know about her.

"I still find it hard to believe you could have ever killed anyone," he said suddenly. She stopped eating and looked across the table at him. He was sorry now that he had let his thoughts surface and destroy this rare moment between them.

"I mean ... is it true? Did you kill a gendarme?" he ventured cautiously.

She hung her head, the red-gold lights in her wind-tossed hair shimmering in the sunlight that poured in through the large portholes. "Yes, I killed him," she replied, her voice little more than a whisper. "I pushed him and he fell on his companion's sword. It was self-defense."

"What was the other man's sword doing unsheathed?" A deep crease had formed between his brows.

"He was threatening me with it," she replied.

"Were you resisting arrest, as your papers say?"

Her chin shot out defiantly. "I was resisting their attempts to rape me!"

The cord in Dawson's jaw was throbbing and the furrow between his brows deepened. "I'll have to teach you to defend yourself," he said in a tight voice.

She cast him a puzzled look, but said nothing.

"Were there no witnesses?" he asked.

"I was home alone the night they came to arrest me. Earlier that day I'd buried my father and dismissed the servants, for I had just discovered how destitute I was."

"But how could that have happened? Was your father such a blasted rotter, then?"

"Oh, no!" she quickly replied. "To the contrary, he was a God-fearing man and loved me dearly. If anything, he was too good! My father's only mistake was in trusting those around him. He was the victim of an unscrupulous administrator who had been cheating him for years. I'm sure that betrayal, together with the discovery that he had lost his fortune, was what brought on his heart attack. Most certainly it was *my* undoing. When the two gendarmes pounded on my door that evening, they had come to take me to debtors' prison, but as soon as they saw I was alone, they decided to have a little fun at my expense. I tried to fight them off, but one of them drew his sword and threatened me with it if I didn't submit to their demands. That was when it happened. In the struggle I pushed the one on top of me away and he fell back on the other man's weapon. But afterward the one with the sword said it was my fault that his companion had been killed, that no one would have been hurt if I'd just obeyed them. Of course, at the trial he insisted I had been resisting arrest and said nothing about the attempted rape, so it was his word against mine. Naturally, the judge chose to believe him. He wouldn't even listen to my plea of self-defense. The gendarme's testimony, plus the evidence that they were arresting me for debts, all went against me."

"The bloody bastards!" Dawson muttered between clenched teeth.

"Then you believe me?" she asked in surprise.

"Of course. Is there any reason why I shouldn't."

"No, but you're the first person who has."

"That's because you haven't been keeping very good company lately."

"But I could be lying. Most of the convicts I was with said they were innocent, too."

"And a few of them probably were," nodded Dawson. *Summum ius summa iniuria,*" he muttered in Latin, more to himself than to her. But Nicole caught what he said and her green eyes brightened.

"Yes, I know," she agreed. "*Extreme justice is extreme injustice.* Cicero said that."

It was Dawson's turn to be surprised. "You understand Latin?"

"I studied it ... along with other things. As I told you, my father was good to me. He gave me the best tutors he could find."

The captain wondered what other unexpected delights lay hidden beneath that lovely exterior. "I'm well aware of the type of justice being meted out in most of Europe these days," he said at last, "so I'm sure there are a lot of guiltless people walking around in chains. But in your case, my sweet, I haven't the slightest doubt of your innocence."

"And why not?"

"Because you're the most adorable little innocent I've ever had the good fortune to stumble across!"

Nicole looked at him in disbelief. How strange to hear a man speak that way to her after she had been branded a harlot before half of Paris and treated so miserably since then.

But this man was, in a manner of speaking, an outcast himself. Perhaps that was why he could sympathize with her. In the eyes of a buccaneer, she probably did seem an innocent.

"And how long have you been leading this kind of life?" she asked, her curiosity suddenly making her bold.

"For more years than I care to remember, lass." He looked out at the sea for a long moment. "My story is a long one, and every bit as ugly as yours." He rose and paced a few steps, noticeably uneasy that her attention was truly focused on him. "There's no time for it all now. Suffice it to say fate thrust me into this way of life, and now that I've grown accustomed to it and have made a fortune at it, I'd just as soon go on with it."

"I can't help wondering about your ship," she ventured. "Why do you call it the *Avenger*?"

His face hardened and the blue of his eyes darkened to sapphire as he poured himself another glass of wine and took a few sips before replying.

"I think the name says it quite plainly," he answered at last. "It means I've made a vow ... a vow that won't be fulfilled until I've found a certain man and killed him!"

For the first time Nicole realized that this buccaneer captain had a side to him she didn't know. She knew him to be a stern but flexible commander and a man bent on satisfying his desires, even though there had been moments lately, especially when he was alone with her, that she had seen a surprising gentleness and refinement. Now, however, she sensed she was glimpsing the Paul Dawson who had decided to turn to freebooting, the man who had earned the title of *El Diablo Dorado*.

PART THREE

Mobile Bay — Early May 1719

Chapter 25

Once they put down anchor at Dauphin Island, Nicole saw less than ever of the captain. When he wasn't in meetings with the French commanders, a group headed by Bienville's elder brother, Joseph Le Moyne, Sieur de Sérigny, Dawson was consulting with his own officers or was in the Mobile settlement tending to supplies and munitions.

Though Dawson seldom talked about himself or his affairs, Nicole gathered that plans were under way to attack Pensacola, the Spanish port closest to Louisiana. It was regarded as a constant threat to the French colony, especially now that war had been declared between France and Spain.

At that moment a fleet of four French ships lay at anchor in the shelter of Mobile Bay, waiting for Governor Bienville and his younger brother Châteaugué to finish amassing an army of settlers and Indians, which was to back up the naval attack with a simultaneous assault on the Pensacola fort by land.

Dawson was to continue acting as an independent captain, but was to complement the French operation in any way he could to help insure its success. In return he would not only have access to supplies and gunpowder for his own fight against the Spanish, but he would be guaranteed a friendly reception in French ports throughout that part of the Gulf of Mexico.

Dauphin, an elongated bar island some seventeen miles long, was the hub of the Louisiana colony. Extending its horny finger into the mouth of the bay, with a small wooden fort on the far eastern tip of the island, it guarded the busy little settlement of Mobile cradled behind it. Nicole found Dauphin Island especially fascinating, since this was the place she would have landed if Legarde hadn't taken her off of the *Dolphin*.

When they first dropped anchor, the thought did occur to her that she might be able to find someone there with whom she might register a complaint. After all, this was the most important port in the Louisiana Colony. It had all the rudiments of a civilized town — churches, forts, barracks. But she also remembered Mignon's comment that the best a branded convict could expect from the authorities would be a hastily arranged marriage with some stranger or forced labor on one of the plantations of the *concessionaires* in the interior. Dawson had warned her that there was always the danger of her falling back into the hands of Legarde or Renaud or someone equally as bad. Most certainly her own experience had taught her that those who were supposed to enforce the law were often the most corrupt.

She decided, therefore, to bide her time. As long as she stayed with Dawson, there was the possibility of landing in more advantageous ports.

Twenty years before, when the French had first landed on Dauphin, everyone had called it Massacre Island because of the mysterious pile of human bones found there. Even now she heard some of Dawson's officers refer to it by that name instead of the one honoring the late king's son, which Bienville had given it when he had founded a settlement there in 1702.

From what she could see of Dauphin through the portholes, the long, narrow island was far from being as gruesome a place as its former name might have suggested. Except for the military installations and the tiny, neatly laid-out settlement of some thirty dwellings, the island was covered with towering pine trees that seemed to span the distance between the snow-white sands and the blue skies — skies that were mirrored in the startlingly clear depths of the azure waters. The breeze wafting in from the island was pleasantly pine-scented — a welcome change from the salt and vinegar that clung to the ship from the frequent scrubbings Dawson insisted his crew give the brigantine to ward off mold and vermin. What a pity she had to be cooped up in the cabin! But she knew there was little hope of her venturing beyond its four walls.

Nicole had hoped to go ashore and make discreet inquiries about Murielle and some of her other companions, who had supposedly disembarked there. Dawson, however, absolutely refused to let her go, forbidding her even to set foot out of his cabin, much less the ship.

"Even if you gave me your word that you wouldn't be so foolish as to try to escape again — and I confess I'm not entirely sure whether I can trust you yet — there would still be the danger that you might end up in the hands of the authorities here, or worse yet, that scoundrel Legarde. Unfortunately, I don't have time to accompany you around Mobile, nor would I want to risk creating an incident with the French government over one of its women convicts, which I'd be forced to do if you were retaken. I'm afraid it's out of the question, lass."

"Am I always to be locked up in this cabin, then? Is this how I'm going to spend the rest of my life?" she shrieked, throwing her hands up in frustration. "Why, lately you haven't even let me go up on deck!"

"I'm sorry about that, too," he replied, "but I can't

permit you to go topside unless I'm with you. Unfortunately, I haven't had the time to attend you as much as I would have liked this past week."

He rose and began to pace — a sign which, experience had taught her, probably meant he had something unpleasant to say to her.

"My men are especially restless." He spoke slowly, as though weighing his words. "Not only are they feeling the usual tension that comes before any battle, but I haven't been able to give them shore leave, so they're hard to control right now." He paused a second and then plunged on. "Actually, I'm going to have to arrange for some women to come aboard to spend the night or at least a few hours with them so they'll be more content."

She could only stare at him. "You mean . . . ?" She groped for the appropriate words until he came to her rescue.

"Yes, I'm talking about prostitutes," he said uneasily. "They'll be well paid, of course. Contrary to what you might believe, I never allow rape on my ship, but I can't deny my men some female comfort. It's done all the time, and as captain, I occasionally have to choose the lesser of two evils to keep my ship running smoothly."

She drew her dressing gown closer around her. She had been sponging herself off in an effort to find some relief from the increasing heat when he had walked into the cabin.

"Under the circumstances, I can hardly refuse them their request," he went on, but she interrupted him.

"You mean, considering that you yourself already have your own whore on board, you can hardly justify not allowing your men the same privilege!"

His neck went dark red and the telltale muscle in his jaw began to twitch. "I was simply explaining that, since I can't let them go ashore to find their own diversion, the least I can do is bring it to them," he quickly corrected her. "But you, too, see the logic. Since you are on this ship ostensibly as *my* woman, I have even less of an excuse to refuse my men a few hours of female companionship. After all, they have no way of knowing how little companionship I really do get from you," he added, a touch of irony creeping into his voice. "But I have a reputation to uphold as a fair commander, and I'd lose the goodwill of my crew if they felt I was dealing unjustly with them."

Nicole smarted under the inevitable comparison between her and the women who were to be brought on board. "I suppose I should be grateful you're not asking me to attend them as well," she said caustically.

He turned livid. "By God, lass, if you're trying to test my patience, I'm warning you I'm damn close to my limits! You know bloody well I've been doing everything in my power to keep my men away from you. And stop calling yourself a blasted whore! From the first day I brought you on board, I told my men that you were here as my woman — not a casual buttock — and that any man who tried to take liberties with you would answer to my sword." He paced restlessly, running his hand repeatedly through his windblown hair. "My God! I shouldn't even be discussing the topic of my men and their — their carnal needs with you! Damn it!" He flung himself into one of the chairs.

The silence that hung between them fairly bristled. Nicole sat opposite him trying to regain her composure. She had seen that petulance was not the way to deal with a man like Paul Dawson.

"*Bien*, you have made your crew keep their distance," she conceded cautiously, "and I'm grateful to you for that. But I can't help resenting this arrangement between us."

"Is it really so distasteful to you?" He had composed himself once more, but his face was still flushed.

"You can't expect me to like being kept a prisoner, no matter how luxurious the cell!"

"And is that how you still think of yourself — a prisoner?"

"What else? I'm locked in here and forbidden to set foot out of the door without you."

"I thought we'd gone through all of that."

"Oh, don't be such a hypocrite! I'm being kept on this ship for one reason alone — because you want me here!"

"Of course, that goes without saying. If I didn't want you on my ship, you wouldn't be here."

"You know what I mean. You're keeping me here to use for your own gratification."

"And is that what I've been doing?"

"You've been playing your cat-and-mouse game with me, but I know your real intentions."

The ghost of a smile creased his handsome face for a split second. "My dear girl, I don't play games. If I really wanted to use you, as you so nicely put it, I'd have done so a dozen times by now. Do you honestly think those little claws of yours could stop me? Why, I could throw you down on that bunk and take you right now if I wanted to, instead of just sitting here and arguing with you about it!"

"I'm supposed to believe you really don't want me that way . . . for your pleasure, I mean?"

He smiled patiently. "I'm sorry, my dear, but I can't ease your mind on that score. Of course I want you. In fact, I want you constantly. I'm sitting here looking at you across from me, so lovely and desirable and only an arm's length away. But it goes deeper than that. I want more. There would be no pleasure for either of us in a one-sided affair. When the moment comes that we're together again, I hope the pleasure will be yours as well as mine."

"Don't flatter yourself! I'll never find pleasure in your or any man's lust!"

"How do you know?"

"I've already had more than my fill of men pawing and abusing me."

"Obviously you've never known a man who appreciated you."

"You're an expert, I suppose?"

"With the one exception being our, ah, unfortunate misunderstanding, I've never had any complaints."

She shifted uncomfortably in her chair and tried to pull the neckline of her gown higher, suddenly feeling the need to shield herself from the desire she saw in the depths of those clear, bold eyes.

"Would my making love to you again really be so repugnant?" he asked softly. "I confess I'd hoped that, in time, you might come to feel something for me."

"The only thing I feel is resentment," she retorted.

"There are many ways a man can make love to a woman," he said, his voice taking on a deeper, gentler tone. "Next time it will be very different between us, I promise you, my sweet. You'll never feel used again."

"Then you admit you're still determined to have me . . . to force me to accept you?"

"I admit I live for the day when I can be with you again, but I don't care for your choice of words. 'Force' is hardly the way I'd put it."

"Well, I don't know how else to say it, since I have no intention of giving myself to you or any man."

A crooked smile curved his generous lips. "We'll see."

Then he rose and leaned across the table, the nagging desire in his loins making him bolder. "You say you resent the thought of being mine," he said, the intensity of his gaze holding her fast. "But you don't seem to realize, my little Nicole, that I am yours, too. For what binds us together is stronger than any ropes or chains. That night in the swamps when I tied you to my waist . . . how furious you were with me! Yet remember the way it was? The cord that bound you to me bound me just as tightly to you!"

Chapter 26

His proximity unnerved her. After a moment of awkward silence, Nicole jumped to her feet and, in a whirl of blue-green skirts, took her turn at pacing the cabin floor.
floor.

"You speak very glibly," she said uneasily. "But if you mean to take me and you bought me for that purpose, perhaps it'd be better if you just stop tormenting me and go ahead and do it. You paid enough for the privilege!"

Annoyance crept over his features. "*Nicole!* How many times . . .? If I thought you were a harlot, I'd have breached you there in the swamps until I'd had my fill and then given you some money and left you off at that settlement you were so anxious to get to!"

Her expression didn't waver. "Considering what you paid for me, I doubt you'd have sent me away so quickly!"

"There are times, my dear Nicole, when I wonder if you resent me for having saved you."

"Are you claiming you did a noble deed?" She parried well, but he'd gotten to her; she wasn't so sure of herself now.

"I'm no saint, my dear," he replied, returning her sardonic smile with one of his own. "I admit the fact that you're so incredibly beautiful . . . that you had never belonged to any man but me . . . all of those things influenced me greatly. After the time I spent with you, I couldn't bear the thought of walking out and letting half a dozen ruffians go at you. Somehow I felt you belonged to me. I still do. I'm not talking about the fact that I paid money for you. I mean something deeper than that. I want you to be mine, but I'm not talking about ownership."

"What you're saying is you want my soul as well as my body," she said.

"Your heart, little one," he corrected her softly. "I think that's the word to use when speaking of love."

She stopped pacing and just looked at him. The word *love* sounded strange to her. After all that had happened, it seemed beyond the realm of possibility. Besides, was there really such a thing? She had encountered only lust. Yet here was the word *love* coming from this renegade captain!

She bent her head, grateful that the curtain of her hair hid her face from him. "Please . . . don't mock me," she begged, her voice barely audible.

Dawson looked at her in real surprise. How small and vulnerable she seemed without all that defiance.

"Mock you?" he echoed, quickly striding over to her. "I speak to you of love and that's all you can say?"

He reached through the veil of her hair and lifted her face to his. The anguish he saw there startled him. "What's wrong, lass? Do you doubt what I'm saying? Or is the thought of loving me beyond consideration? Believe me, I've known my share of women, but this is the first time I've spoken of love to anyone."

The emerald of her eyes glittered through her tears. "I don't believe there is such a thing," she murmured. She could not look at him.

"I told you you had a lot to learn, my sweet."

He cradled her chin in the palm of his hand and bent his head to meet her lips, all the while drawing her gently to him until he had molded her softness against the hard planes of his body.

Before she realized what was happening, the warm fullness of his mouth found hers and engulfed her with a passion she could no longer deny. His long, sensuous kiss rocked her very being. Boldly now he pressed her ever closer to him until she seemed to dissolve into the length of him.

"Believe me, little Nicole, love does exist," he whispered. "Can't you recognize what I feel for you?"

She wanted to stop him, to push him away, yet she couldn't. Whether it was from fear or from really wanting him, she could feel herself yielding.

Quickly he lifted her into his arms and carried her to the bunk and eased her down, never once taking his lips from hers. Now he had found his way into her bodice and was seeking out the taut fullness of her breasts, awakening first one and then the other. The sound of her heart pounding in her ears made her head spin and drowned out all reason. God forgive her! Could it be she really *wanted* this man? She could feel how her breasts were swelling and rising to meet his touch, their tips hardening at the thought of feeling his lips on them again!

His vibrant manhood quivered against her thigh, already throbbing with a rhythm she knew would soon be resounding deep within her. Something stronger than herself — even more powerful than his physical strength — seemed to hold her fast to him. She could no longer stem the tide that was flooding her senses. It was sweeping her on to its inevitable conclusion.

But suddenly that handsome face so close to hers began to blur. Now the twisted features of the guard who had held her at the moment the brand had seared her body leered above her. Her shoulder was on fire and the odor of burning flesh assaulted her nostrils. The word *whore* sounded and resounded in her ears. . . . Someone was fondling the nipples of her breasts and running his hands roughly over her body.

A wave of terror enveloped her and instinctively she began to strike Dawson. "No, no! Let me go! Leave me be!" She desperately tried to tear herself away from the arms that held her.

"But why, lass? I know you want me, too. I can feel it." The captain's voice was husky as he resisted her efforts to break away from him. "Why do you fight me so?"

"Love? You don't love me. You only want me, that's all!"

He laughingly dodged her tiny darting fists. "Of course I want you, you foolish darling. It's all part of loving you."

He bent to kiss her again, but her struggling increased. Catching her hands at last in his, he hovered over her for yet another moment, all his instincts urging him on to fulfillment. Her proximity day in and day out was driving him to distraction, and he knew the ache in his loins would never go away until he found sweet release within the depths of her. This maddening slip of a girl had completely taken him over.

He disengaged himself and rose slowly from the bunk. "I said I wouldn't force you and I won't," he acquiesced, though at that moment he regretted ever having made such a rash promise.

His clothes were disheveled and he made ineffective passes at the tangled mass of hair falling over his forehead. "God is my witness, how I wish I could erase that first time from your memory!" he groaned. "If you'd only let me make love to you . . . really love you the way I want to . . . it could be so different. . . ." His voice broke.

Nicole lay there looking up at him, trying to stop the whirlpool of emotions churning inside her. How could she make him understand what she felt when she couldn't understand it herself? Perhaps it was impossible for her to love anyone. . . .

A part of her had wanted him, still wanted him. She had been ready to abandon herself to the overwhelming passion that swept over her when he took her into his arms and kissed her. But all at once something had snapped inside her, and the demons from the past had appeared and crowded him out. They had reminded her of what she had become — of the reason why she had been bought and sold two times over, even of the way she had met this buccaneer who had already raped her once and was determined now to make her his willing concubine.

She looked at his tall, proud figure standing over her like some Viking god, and the wave of conflicting emotions surged anew. She had to admit that all those hours she had spent in this, his most intimate world, had not been without some effect on her. There were times when she *did* feel attracted to him, yet there were others when she continued to resent and mistrust him.

Perhaps she should forget about her feelings. This man wanted her. He had paid a fortune for her and had forced her to accompany him. But as he himself had said, she certainly could do worse. As an outcast she was destined to be used by someone, so why not by a man she at least found attractive? And she did find him attractive. He had asked her whether the thought of his making love to her was really so repugnant. If only he knew how just the sight of him sometimes affected her!

If she persisted in fighting him, he might withdraw his protection completely, perhaps even sell her to someone else. For her, that was unthinkable now. For she *did* want him, her whole being was clamoring for him to go on making love to her — and a part of her even yearned to love him back!

Her eyes were dark and luminous as fear warred once again with desire. "If you really want me, take me," she said softly. "You paid dearly for the right, and I certainly would prefer belonging to you. So do as you will. I won't fight you anymore."

But her words seemed to wound him. An oath escaped his lips and his face grew dark with rage. "Haven't you heard anything I've said? Do you think that's the way I want you. Is that all it would mean to you? A sacrifice? Just because I'm the lesser of two evils? Damn it all, madam, I wouldn't dream of defiling you with my lovemaking! As far as concubines go, I could send ashore for a whore right now and get a warmer response from her than you, so rest easy. I have no intentions of demanding any sacrifices from you!"

He snatched the lantern from his desk and strode toward the door. He had to get out of there, away from her maddening presence. Just the sight of her made the knot inside him tighten all the more. Hell and damnation! What did the wench think he was made of?

He paused at the threshold and looked back at her. "I'm taking the night watch," he said coldly, "so you needn't lose any sleep worrying over my trying to share the bunk with you."

The door slammed behind him, and she heard his footsteps hurry up the companionway. She had hoped to please him; instead, she had only made matters worse!

The cabin seemed unusually empty that night. It was strange to lie there in the dimly lit room and not hear his rhythmical breathing beside her or fall asleep knowing that he was on the other side of the curtain working at his desk. His absence weighed more heavily on her now than his presence had ever done. For the first time since she had met Paul Dawson, Nicole felt lonely.

Chapter 27

The *filles de joie* from the mainland paid the *Avenger* a visit the following afternoon, but though the sounds of the merrymaking echoed throughout the ship, Dawson made no reference to it when he stopped in the cabin for about an hour. Instead, he spent the time poring over his papers, and then left in a hurry, locking the door behind him as usual.

Nicole wondered whether he had joined his men but finally consoled herself with the thought that he probably would have been too discreet to have consorted openly with a whore while he supposedly had his own in his cabin.

Of course, he easily could have stopped off to see such a woman during any one of this many visits to the mainland, and it annoyed her to think he might have. The idea of his having touched another woman the way he had touched her made her uncomfortable, but now she was even more annoyed with herself than with him. If only she'd chosen her words wisely.

In the days that followed, he seemed to deliberately avoid her. Although the worst of her fears — that he might abandon her — did not come to pass, she was far from content.

At least he continued to keep her in his quarters and looked to all her needs. Actually, from all outward appearance the arrangement between them remained the same, except that she saw considerably less of him. He absented himself more than ever from his cabin, and when he was there, he went about his personal affairs, saying very little to her. Most of the time he seemed oblivious to her presence, as though he had decided to pretend she wasn't there. If she spoke to him, he would reply politely but briefly; for his part, he addressed her only when necessary. There was a cool formality about his manner that had not been there before. An invisible wall separated them now and, try as she would, she could not breach it.

He suddenly had a preference for the night watch and would return to the cabin in the morning when she was already up and about. Greeting her casually, he would go directly to his desk or throw himself wearily on the bunk and immediately fall asleep. Even so, she preferred the hours when he was there. It gave her a feeling of security to have him near her while she busied herself with mending or cleaning or browsing through his books.

She often watched him as he slept. Though she felt rather guilty for having violated the privacy of his sleep, she found herself beginning to know every feature of his face by heart. At such times the hard years at sea seemed to fall away from him as the stern lines around his generous mouth disappeared and the faint crinkle at the corners of his eyes softened.

Oddly enough, now that he seemed to be avoiding her, she felt more a prisoner than ever. She missed his company at the evening meal. Once when she asked him whether he had eaten or not, he had simply replied he had already dined with the French commanders. On one or two occasions she heard him eating with his officers in the dining room.

She missed the occasional walks she used to take with him on deck, but didn't dare approach him on the subject. There were times, however, when he would stand directly in front of her and, with the full impact of those brilliant blue eyes focused on her at last, ask whether she needed anything or had any preferences in the food being served her. But at such moments it was all she could do to muster one-word answers.

By the third day of strained relations between them, she decided in desperation to go up on deck and take at least a few minutes of fresh air. Though it was only the end of the first week in May, it had been unusually warm. The air hung heavy and still over the bay; even with all the portholes open, the cabin was stifling.

The captain was asleep, and she could tell by the fine lines around his eyes that he was especially tired, so it seemed like a good time to leave the cabin. After all, it was the hour she knew most of the crew was at mess, so with any luck she should have the poop deck to herself.

No sooner had she lifted the latch on the door and stepped into the companionway, however, than she nearly collided with one of the crewmen.

For a moment she hesitated, feeling foolish and out of place, but finally she decided to brazen it out and proceed to the topdeck.

With a polite smile, she gathered her skirts about her in order to get past him easily.

But there was even less space than she had anticipated, and the buccaneer held his ground instead of trying to step aside for her. It was impossible for her to get by without brushing against him.

The light contact ignited the seaman. His arm shot out and pinned her fast between him and the wall. Before she could cry out, he clamped his other hand over her mouth.

"Hello, now what have we here?" He grinned wickedly. "So the little bird has finally grown bored with her love nest! Or has the capt'n tired of you and set you adrift? I been noticin' how he's spendin' more of his nights on watch now than he did when he first brought you on board . . . probably had his fill of jockin' for a while, right? Or maybe a frisky little biter like you has him all wore out, eh?"

She pushed furiously against him, but he held her there, laughing at her futile efforts to break free. Although he was not a tall man, he was all brawn and hair. Even his hands were dark with hair. The odor of rum on his breath was strong, and the thought crossed her mind that he must have been coming from the storeroom, where he had probably been stealing a few nips from one of the kegs.

"Now don't go making any fuss till you hear what I got to say," he warned. "A pretty little filly like you must know how to give a man a damn good ride, since I ain't never seen the capt'n keep any buttock around him as long as he has you. But then, rumor has it round the mess table that he paid one hell of a price for you after he rolled you at some Frenchie's plantation on the Mississippi. I've always wanted to grind one of you fancy French whores. You're the best, they say. Bet a fancy tail like you can show even me a couple of new tricks!"

His hand groped clumsily for her breasts, unmindful of her struggling. "Now don't go playin' coy with me, ducky. Just as soon as I felt these diddeys of yours rubbing up agin' me, I knew I had to get my hands on them. And that's what you want, isn't it, you sly little doxy?"

Nicole fought against the hairy arms that had closed around her and were dragging her back along the companionway, past the closed door to the captain's quarters, and down toward the between-decks. The passage was too narrow for her to kick with any force, and the fullness of her skirts hindered her even more.

"The capt'n may be well hung, but I wager a cat like you needs to be wapped every hour on the hour to keep you purrin'. Come on to the storeroom where we can douse the glim and get our riggin' off. Then we can shag to our heart's content."

Her fists pounded against the hard mass of his chest, but her blows had about the same effect as raindrops splattering a rocky shore.

"Now, now, don't put on any of your uppity airs with me, you damn slut! A few nips of rum to put you in your altitudes and you'll spread your shanks quick enough for me!" His fingers probed her breast and finally closed over her nipple viciously. The pain stunned her, and her knees began to buckle, but he flattened her against the wall and smothered her moan of protest with his foul-smelling mouth.

His broken teeth tore into her lips as he pushed his tongue past them. She gagged.

Suddenly, acting on instinct, she caught the mariner's fleshy underlip and bit down with all her might.

Like the animal he was, he snarled in pain and slammed her against the wall, cuffing her with the back of his hand and showering her with curses. The shoulder of her dress gave way, and he clung to her breast. She finally screamed as she slid down the wall. The last thing she remembered was the door of the main cabin bursting open and the mariner's voice suddenly whining, "She rubbed her cat-heads agin' me, capt'n, and got my dirk to dancin'. All I was goin' to do was jock her a couple of times. I figgered you was tired of strappin' and about ready to scuttle her. . . ."

Dawson's figure filled the companionway. Trembling with rage, he loomed above them, sword in hand. Instinctively she reached a pleading hand up to him. Then she passed out.

Chapter 28

The first thing Nicole did was rinse the foul taste from her mouth. Now that the mariner had been taken off to the brig to await trial, she and Dawson were alone in the cabin, and he was pouring her a glass of brandy.

Looking at her forlorn figure, her torn dress, her disheveled hair, he couldn't make up his mind whether to give her a good tongue-lashing or just take her in his arms and console her.

"What the blazes am I going to do with you?" he said in exasperation as he sheathed his sword. "If you're so hell-bent on running away from me, perhaps I ought to go ahead and give you some money and let you leave!" His voice was tight and strained, and he poured another glass of brandy for himself. "A privateer ship is no place for a woman, especially one who is as stubborn and rebellious as you are, and I can't — I *won't* keep you in chains, so tell me where you want to go, and I'll give you whatever you need so you can go do whatever it is you're so hell-bent on doing!"

"I — I wasn't trying to escape," she told him tremulously while she sat sipping from her glass and trying to hold the torn piece of her dress over her breast. "All I wanted was a breath of fresh air."

So she wasn't trying to run away after all! His anger melted a little. He sighed and gazed into his glass.

"Well, perhaps someday you'll learn that when I give an order there's a good reason for it," he said finally, but most of the anger had left his voice. He didn't have the heart to scold her then. She looked so frightened.

"Come, lass, I know how shaken you must be," he said at last, setting his glass down on the table and taking her gently by the arm to help her rise. "You'd better lie down until supper so you can . . ."

But her stifled moan interrupted him.

"What's wrong? Are you hurt?" he asked anxiously. Quickly he drew up another chair and sat her down beside him. "Here, let me see."

He tried to take her hand away from where she held her dress over her breast, but she resisted.

"I can manage by myself," she insisted.

"I'm sorry, my dear, but I don't think you can. After all, this isn't the first time I've seen you without your bodice."

She blushed but let him ease the torn neckline of her gown farther down so he could examine her.

He swore when he saw the bruises already discoloring the smooth whiteness of her skin.

"Damn the bloody bastard! I'll drub the dog within an inch of his life for this!" he muttered.

Rising quickly, he went over to the nightstand and collected the porcelain pitcher and washbowl. Then he gathered together some towels and small vials and rejoined her.

"It's a pity I can't hire a servant girl for you — one who could wait on you and attend you in such things," he said apologetically, "but as you can see, one woman on board is already trouble enough!"

As he spoke, he poured some water into the bowl and mixed several drops from each vial into it. "I hope you'll bear with my clumsiness, but there isn't anyone else I'd trust to touch you," he said as he soaked one of the linen towels in the herb-scented water.

"Don't you have a physician on board?" she asked.

Dawson grunted. "Like most ship surgeons, he's a butcher. The truth is, I wouldn't even let young Jeff come near you. He may still be a young shaver, but the sea turns a lad to a man very quickly. That little rascal can get as fired up as any buck if you put him in the right situation."

He began with her back first, lightly pressing the wet cloth against her shoulder blade where the mariner had shoved her against the wall. It did help. Already she could feel the compress drawing some of the soreness out, and when he applied the pomade afterward, it was even more soothing.

The lightness of his touch surprised her. She marveled that such large powerful hands could still be so gentle. They had been very gentle when they caressed her breasts only a few nights ago. . . . How different his touch had been from the groping hands she had known! Why had she resisted him so?

The captain sensed her uneasiness. At the sight of the mark on her breast, the lines around his mouth deepened. "Flogging isn't enough for the dog! I should stretch his damn neck and be done with it!"

"You — you're going to hang him?" she asked in horror.

"That's what the bastard deserves," growled Dawson. "He's guilty on more than one count. Not only did he attack you, but he deserted his post, robbed the storeroom, and got drunk while on duty! Hanson's been a trouble-maker for quite a while, and the only reason I've tolerated him this long is because he's a good man in a fight — a bloody good gunner."

It was difficult for him to look at her breast and remain

unmoved. He started to apply the cloth, hesitated, and then suddenly handed it to her. "Here, put this over the bruise," he ordered, his face so colored now that she couldn't tell whether it was from anger or passion or embarrassment.

He turned away while she dabbed at the bruise and quickly drained his glass. "You must never leave the cabin again like that," he said stiffly, trying to assume a more formal attitude with her in an effort to relieve the tension of the moment.

"It had been so long since I'd been outside," she said as she sat holding the cloth to her bosom. "It's been stifling in here. Anyway, you have assured me on several occasions that I'm not a prisoner."

The telltale cord in his jaw twitched. "I realize I've neglected you of late, but you didn't seem to want my company."

"I didn't expect that animal to be slinking around in the passageway!"

"He shouldn't have been, and he's going to pay dearly for it. I don't tolerate such goings-on aboard my ship. Usually my men don't dare disobey me like that. Of course, he'd been drinking, which will only add to the charges against him, but it probably also explains his attacking you."

"He thought I was . . . just one of your — your doxies," she said bitterly.

He flushed even more beneath his tan. "That's no excuse," he said uncomfortably. "He knew better. No man who serves under me attacks a woman like that, no matter who she is, much less one under my protection."

"He probably thought you wouldn't mind," she said as she dipped the cloth in the bowl and reapplied it to her breast. "He said you seemed to be avoiding your quarters these days."

Dawson sat, his profile toward her. "I'm responsible in part for what happened," he admitted, finding it difficult to ignore the wave of guilt that had been nagging at him from the moment he had found her in the companionway. "I shouldn't have let my personal feelings interfere with my judgment. I might have known the men would begin to suspect how things were between us. Hell and damnation! They're worse than a pack of bloody fishwives!"

"He seemed to know about everything . . . even how you came by me." The long cascade of her auburn hair shielded her face as she bent her head and again put the cloth to her bruised breast.

"Damn his wagging tongue! I'll make him and anyone else who dares slander you pay dearly!"

"He may have put it crudely, but what he said was true," she reminded him. "You did buy Renaud's concubine for yourself — no more, no less."

"There's a lot more to it than that. You're not a whore, and I won't have anyone call you that — no one, not even you!"

"I may as well be, with this brand on my shoulder and documents that label me a condemned murderess."

"You're just an innocent chit who's been unjustly treated by everyone you've had the misfortune to encounter — everyone, even me!" At that moment his self-loathing overwhelmed him.

But her recent experience only served to bring home more forcibly than ever how the world regarded her and how helpless she was to escape it. Her future stretched out before her like a long, dismal corridor, an endless procession of episodes like the one she had just gone through. Wherever she went, it seemed, she was fair prey.

"I'm afraid I'm doomed to be passed from one man to another," she sighed as she began to apply the pomade to her breast.

The captain turned to face her, tenderness having replaced the anger in his eyes. "You're wrong, little one," he said softly. "If I have my way, you'll never know any other man but me."

"Oh, you'll tire of me sooner or later," she said sadly. "You'll end up sending me away, or perhaps someone will come along and offer you enough —"

But he smiled at her pessimism and pushed aside the pitcher and bowl. "My, but you're in a black mood!" he chided. "I think I prefer you as the rebellious little bobcat. Come, lie down and rest, and tonight we'll give you another treatment."

He helped her slip her arms out of the torn bodice and into her dressing gown. Then he gently drew her to her feet and, balancing her lightly against him, reached under the loose, flowing sacque and untied the lacings of her underskirt. She made no attempt to stop him. Somehow she sensed she could trust him — at least for the moment.

As soon as her petticoat fell to the floor, he lifted her into his arms and carried her to the bunk.

"I have to go topside now," he said as he placed her carefully between the sheets. "But don't be afraid. I'm going to lock the door so you'll be completely safe, and I'll be back to have supper with you later on."

A great tenderness swept over him as he stood looking down at her. His poor bruised and frightened little cub! "You're not alone, my dear," he mumbled lamely, longing to take her in his arms and console her, yet afraid to upset her. He fingered one of the red-gold curls that framed her lovely pale face. Aye, he was hopelessly snared! His whole being ached with the need to possess her . . . to make her really and finally his. But he knew too well that she would never forgive him if he betrayed her trust now.

"We'll be getting a fine breeze in the cabin by this time tomorrow night," he said suddenly, taking refuge in the mundane and at the same time hoping to cheer her up. "We'll be leaving Mobile Bay in the morning, my sweet. The waiting is over. If we have any luck and the Spanish don't give us too big a fight, we should be dropping anchor in Pensacola before the week is over."

Chapter 29

That night Dawson dined with her in the cabin, and for the first time since he had tried to make love to her again, things were relaxed between them.

After they had finished their meal and Jeff had cleaned off the table and left them fresh water on the nightstand, Dawson lit his pipe and sat awhile with her.

"This might be the last quiet meal we'll have until we've taken Pensacola," he said softly as he drew on his pipe. "I'm afraid I'm going to have to ask you to be patient and obey me to the letter from here on out, since there will probably be some fighting before it's all over."

Nicole felt a knot start in the pit of her stomach. "And what will your part be? Will you sail with the French ships as a part of their fleet?"

"No, I'm going on ahead. My job will be to keep any Spanish vessels headed for Pensacola out of those waters. The fewer enemy ships in the vicinity when the French attack, the better."

"But how will you be able to do that?"

"By either scaring them off their course or attacking them outright."

"But that will be dangerous for you, won't it?"

His hearty laugh rang out. "To a certain extent, yes," he admitted. "But don't worry, I know my business well. I'm accustomed to such risks. They go with the profession."

"If you've chosen the sea for your profession and are still so loyal to the British, I marvel at why you simply haven't joined their regular navy," she commented.

"I have my reasons," he assured her. "Not only is privateering more profitable, but I can keep my independence this way. Since I have some axes of my own to grind, I prefer to be able to come and go as I please."

"Ah, yes, I remember ... your vow," she said, drawing her turquoise silk sacque closer around her as she recalled the way he had looked the time she'd asked him about it.

"Do you feel better now?" he asked as he stretched his legs, which were splendid in his tan silk stockings and rust-colored breeches.

"Yes, a little," she said. "I'm still sore, but the nap I had this afternoon and the meal tonight seem to have done me some good."

"Then I have some news that should make you feel even better," he said. "I saw your friend Murielle while I was on the mainland the other day."

"Murielle?" Nicole's face lit up instantly. "Are you sure it was her?"

"Oh, yes ... a small, dark, shapely brunette with large black eyes?"

"Yes, yes, that's her. However did you find her? Is she all right?"

"Don't fret, my sweet," he smiled, pleased to see her more like her old self again. "She's well and speaks as fondly of you as you do of her."

"But how did you find her? Why haven't you mentioned it sooner?"

He puffed on his pipe. "Frankly, I haven't been quite

certain how to go about telling you, but since there's always been honesty between us, I think it's best I tell you exactly how it was. I came across her while I was in Mobile arranging for the women to attend to my crew."

Nicole paled. "*Mon Dieu!* Don't tell me she was one of those poor wretches...." She broke off. "Do you mean she was here — here on board with —? Oh, how could you?"

"No, no, lass," he answered quickly. "She was not one of them. But she was among the prostitutes living in a house near the barracks where some of the female convicts who haven't married yet are quartered."

Nicole moaned. "*Ma pauvre amie!*"

Dawson was silent for a moment and then went on carefully. "Well, be of good cheer, my sweet, for I don't think she's in her old profession any longer ... that is, I hope not. When I was satisfied as to who she was, I immediately assured her that you were alive and well and, in your name, made her a gift of enough money to help her set up some little business for herself or at least live on for a while until she can find a husband to her liking. So she shouldn't have to resort to whoring again if she doesn't want to."

Nicole stared at him in amazement. "You — you gave her as much money as that? But why? You say you didn't hire her, and you didn't even know her."

"But you did. That's why I gave it to her in your name. I hope what I did meets with your approval."

"But so generous a gift? Of course, it pleases me that it occurred to you to do such a thing, but what motivated you to give the poor girl so much?"

"She was good to you, wasn't she? Sometimes even at risk to her own well-being, she protected and helped you when you needed someone, so how can I not feel in her debt?"

This bold stranger had taken over her life completely, yet lately he seemed more of a stranger than ever before!

"What manner of man are you?" she blurted out, unable to keep her thoughts to herself any longer.

He gave her a lopsided smile. "I'm simply a man who loves you," he replied and calmly took another puff on his pipe. "Which reminds me of one other thing," he added as he rose and went to his desk.

He opened the top drawer and took out a small leather pouch. "I want you to have this," he said. "I'm not really worried about anything happening to me, but when there's fighting, there's always the possibility that something could go wrong, so I'd feel better if I knew you had this. It will be more than adequate to pay your passage to Norfolk in the Virginia Colony, which is where I handle all my business transactions. I've already dispatched a document to my administrator there, instructing him to see to it that you want for nothing, that ample funds be set aside for you from my estate in order to insure that you never find yourself in need again."

He held out the pouch, and as she lifted her hand to take it, he let a huge cabochon ruby fall into the palm of her hand.

"But I can't accept this!" she exclaimed, unable to tear her eyes from the magnificent stone.

"I don't know why not," he said. "I've wanted to give it to you since the day I brought you on board."

"But why would you want to give me such a priceless gem, when you haven't even made love to me since — since that night at Renaud's?"

"You're not a prostitute, my dear, and this isn't a payment. It's not contingent on whether you let me make love to you or not." He smiled. "Regardless of what you might or might not feel for me, I want you to have this, partly because of the responsibility I assumed for you when I forced you to share in my destiny."

"But I feel I've done nothing to deserve it!" she insisted.

"My dear, you'll probably never have need of it, except to adorn that pretty neck of yours. I intend to be around a long time to take care of you, but in the meantime, if you won't accept it for your sake, at least do so for mine. I want peace of mind where you're concerned."

"Well then, leave it there in your desk," she said reluctantly. "I know where it is now, and if an occasion should arise when I need it, I promise I'll use it. But not before."

He laughed. "It's yours, lass. Do with it as you please. You're welcome to keep it in my desk or anywhere else, but remember, it belongs to you now, not me."

That night, after he had helped her treat her bruises and stretched out next to her on the bunk, Nicole lay waiting, half expecting that he would try to make love to her again. It was hard to believe that he wouldn't try to press his advantage now that he had not only made her such an extraordinary gift, but won her gratitude as well with his unexpected generosity toward Murielle. But he simply brushed a kiss on her forehead and rolled over, his back to her.

As she lay there pondering the latest facets of Paul Dawson's character, she found herself once more trying to come to some conclusion about him.

But she was exhausted and dozed off in spite of herself. After the loneliness of those recent nights, she welcomed the familiar sound of his breathing. Nothing mattered now that she knew he was there beside her. Everything seemed right again in the little world that was fast becoming her own. Only the vague, gnawing fear that she might one day have to use the ruby he had given her because he would no longer be there kept her from sleeping as well as she might have.

PART FOUR

Pensacola — Mid-Day 1719

Chapter 30

The first day out on the Gulf was surprisingly uneventful. The only vessel they passed was one of the Company of the West's cargo ships, which looked suspiciously like one of the pest ships that had brought her and her companions to the New World.

Grateful for even the questionable safety of a buccaneer's ship, she stood by the wide window of the captain's cabin and watched the weather-beaten ship pass them, crossing herself as she said a fervent prayer for whatever doomed souls might be on board the other vessel.

Shortly after it had disappeared, Dawson stopped by the cabin. "Hanson was punished this morning," he told her as he gently patted ointment on her shoulder.

Her face clouded. "Don't tell me you hanged him?"

"He can consider himself lucky to have gotten off with Moses' law," he said roughly. On seeing her puzzled frown, he added, "That's forty stripes lacking one on the bare back. If I'd followed my own inclinations, however, I'd have had the bastard keelhauled or strung up from the nearest yardarm. Nevertheless, I had to take into account the fact that he wasn't the only one to blame for that deplorable incident."

Nicole drew herself up indignantly. "Meaning that I was, I suppose?" she said angrily, her cheeks coloring. "You believed him, then, when he accused me of deliberately flirting with him!"

"No, of course not. That isn't what I meant," he quickly assured her, "though you did disobey me when you left the cabin." But he didn't want to argue with her. She had suffered enough for her disobedience. "Frankly, I had myself in mind. I shouldn't have brought a woman on board in the first place, and to make matters worse, I let my emotions get in the way of my better judgment. Anyway, there were so many counts against him that I hardly had to say anything at his trial. He was unanimously found guilty by his own mates, and I think it was better that way, since I don't want the men resenting your presence on board. I did make it clear, however, that you're not my doxy but my woman, and as such, will remain here until I can make better arrangements for you. Meanwhile I warned them that anyone who offends you in any way must answer to me personally. Hanson knows damn well that he still has to give me an accounting for his attack on you as soon as he has recovered from his flogging, and I dare say he probably dreads that more than the punishment he got this morning!"

"I suppose I'm glad you didn't have him executed," she admitted. "Your gunner deserved to be punished, but the whip is cruel enough." She had seen the regulation ones used on male convicts — thick tar-coated thongs, up to nine at a time, designed to pull the skin off with each stroke. The memory of the many times she had been stung by the flick of the one-thong lash still haunted her, though at least those "kittens" or "colts," usually reserved for women and young boys, didn't break the skin or leave scars.

"No one hates flogging as much as I do," Dawson was saying, "but a weak leader is a bad leader. When you have a crew of well over a hundred ruffians on one ship, there would be mayhem without an iron hand. Rape is punishable by death on the *Avenger*, and if I hadn't come out and stopped that idiot in time, he'd be hanging now. I would have stretched him no matter who the woman was, but if it had been you, lass, I confess I'd have strung him up personally!"

The weather continued to be as warm as it had been in Mobile, but now that they were out on the open sea, the continuous breeze on the Gulf provided relief. At night, however, the captain insisted that the dark curtains be drawn over the windows and portholes so that no light could be seen by passing ships. The element of surprise means everything, Dawson told her, when stalking game or an enemy.

Their second day at sea started out as sunny and clear as the first. About mid-morning Dawson went below for a moment. He was in shirt-sleeves, booted, and heavily armed.

The curtains were open now and the bright sunlight streamed into the cabin as Nicole sat mending the torn bodice of her lavender gown.

How lovely she looked in the rose-print muslin she had made for herself, while the sun's rays ignited the red-gold braids coiled around her bowed head! How he had come to look forward to these stolen moments with her here. With each passing day he found it more and more difficult to think about the day when he might have to give her up. At times like this he was almost tempted to take her on any terms.

She looked up expectantly, and it pleased him to note that she no longer greeted him with a scowl.

"I thought I'd come down for a few minutes to freshen up and ... yes, I confess, to treat my eyes to the sight of you," he said as he quickly walked over to the decanter on the table and poured himself a small glass of red wine.

Only then did he notice that his garnet silk frock coat lay on the bunk instead of on the hook where he'd hung it. When she saw him looking she colored and quickly went back to her sewing.

"I took the liberty of reinforcing one of the buttons," she said lamely. "I hope you don't mind."

"Mind? Why, I'm flattered that you'd take the trouble!" He was trying to keep his delight in check.

"Well, you've lent it to me so often that I felt I might have been at fault." She blushed as though she had been caught with her hand in his pockets. "It would be a pity to lose a silver button."

"Whatever prompted you to do it, I thank you, lass," he said as he hung the coat in his clothespress, still making an effort not to let her see how moved he was by this rare gesture on her part. "The only person who's ever worried about my buttons is Jeff, and he's been rather negligent since I told him not to enter the cabin unless I'm here."

On seeing her embarrassment, he quickly changed the subject. "I know it must be boring for you to have to stay down here on such a lovely day, but we could be meeting Spanish ships at any time, so the men are at their battle stations round the clock now."

A knock on the door interrupted him, and the cabin boy entered with a large tray of cold roast beef and a loaf of corn bread.

"I thought it best you have something here to eat," he explained as he motioned to the boy to set the food on the table and leave. "If we encounter an enemy ship, there may not be time for anyone to bring you something, and since there's no telling how long the fighting might last, you could get very hungry."

Nicole was suddenly aware of the tight knot in her stomach. "I doubt I can eat anything," she protested as she watched him help himself to bread and meat. She marveled at how he could sit there eating so nonchalantly at a time like this, when she couldn't even swallow, much less digest her food.

"Come, lass. At least have a bite with me," he urged her, but she shook her head.

He sensed her unease and smiled sympathetically. "Then at least have a sip of wine," he offered, beckoning her to join him. "It'll help relax ..."

But at that moment there came a cry from aloft, and the whole ship began to tremble like a sleeping giant springing to life.

The captain gulped the last of his bread and beef as he pulled himself to his feet. His languor was gone now, his body alert.

There was a pounding on the door, and Fernández's voice rang out. "It's a galleon bearing down on starboard, sir!"

Dawson flung open the door. "Run out the guns," he told the Spaniard, "but don't strike our colors until I give the word. We'll put a shot across their bow at the same time as we present our calling card." He readjusted his sword in its sheath and checked the pistol and dagger tucked in his belt.

Fernández grinned his approval at the orders, and at a nod from the captain, was off again. Dawson turned toward the table but was surprised to find Nicole standing near him. Though she said nothing, the fear in her eyes was plain.

"Don't worry, my sweet, you won't be free of me so easily," he teased, pecking her cheek in an effort to ease her tension. On seeing that she didn't draw back, however, he caught her to him and kissed her boldly on the lips. The weapons in his belt pressed uncomfortably against her midriff, but at that moment it didn't seem to matter.

The feel of the firm sensuous mouth on hers left her reeling, yet before she could recover, he had dashed off up the companionway.

She ran to the door and looked anxiously after him. He paused at the end of the passage and looked back to where she stood in the doorway.

"Bolt the door, my sweet," he called as he paused in the open hatch. "Don't open to anybody except me or someone you can trust like Josh or Fernández."

When he saw how she still hesitated, a big smile creased his face. "Don't be afraid, lass. I wouldn't let anything happen to the two most important females in my life — you and my brigantine!"

She stood there a few seconds longer, but when she realized he wasn't going to leave the hatchway unless he were certain she was inside the cabin, she finally obeyed and closed the door behind her.

Dawson waited until he heard the scraping of the bolt falling into place. Savoring the taste of her that lingered on his lips, he turned his attention to the business at hand.

Chapter 31

Nicole paced back and forth, growing more anxious by the minute. She strained to single out the captain's voice from amid the scurrying feet and gruff shouts from the decks above and below her.

At first she stood glued to the portholes, watching with mounting apprehension as the Spanish ship slowly but steadily approached them, gliding across the sunlit water with its sails unfurled, the lion of Castile boldly emblazoned on its pendant. It certainly looked as if it intended to put up a fight.

The Spanish ship was larger than the *Avenger*, but she knew that too much bulk could often be a handicap. Of course, its cannon might be heavier, more powerful. . . . But how could she judge such things? All she knew was that the sight of the huge galleon bearing down on them scared her.

From the beginning, however, the *Avenger* played to the hilt its advantage of being the lighter and swifter ship, shifting its positions so rapidly that its enemy never had a dependable target and closing in to fire on the enemy's broadside, then quickly swinging out of range before the Spanish ship could return fire. After each volley, Dawson's men would cheer, but the captain and his officers would immediately shout out new commands, reminding the men of the urgency to come about before the Spaniards had time to recover. The *Avenger* creaked in protest at the demands its captain made, but it more than performed. Novice that Nicole was, even she could appreciate the skill and precision that was guiding the brigantine's every movement.

With each broadside, the ship groaned and vibrated beneath her feet, sending her clutching at the nearest piece of stationary furniture. She could see nothing now but the empty sea shimmering through the haze of smoke that filled the air.

If only she could hear the reassuring sound of Paul's voice again! The torment of waiting in the cabin, unable to see or hear what was really happening, made the anguish all the more unbearable. Was Paul all right? She hadn't heard him shouting out the usual orders after that last volley. Could he have been hit? Merciful heavens! He might be lying on the deck wounded at that very moment ... even dying!

Unable to bear the suspense any longer, she decided to go at least as far as the hatchway and see for herself. She doubted there would be any idle crewman lurking in the passageway to molest her this time. After all, she would only go as far as the ladder, take a quick peek, and come right back to the cabin, as Paul had told her to do. At times like this she wished she were a man. Then she could be up there by his side.

She made her way carefully to the door, holding on to anything that was nailed down to support herself against the lurching of the ship. Lifting the heavy bolt with some difficulty, she finally managed to step out into the dimly lit companionway and felt her way along the narrow passage. Her heart began to hammer as she neared the double doors of the hatch, which opened onto the quarterdeck. She lifted her skirts and caught hold of the railing so she could climb a few rungs up the ladder. Relieved to see that the hatch had not been fastened down, she timidly pushed one of the doors.

Afraid to open it more than a crack, she was nevertheless blinded by the bright light that hit her eyes, making it all the more difficult for her to discern anything through the wisps of gunsmoke that wafted over the deck.

Eagerly she tried to pierce the shimmering veil, searching for the familiar figure of the captain, but she hadn't expected the scene that met her eyes. The buccaneers were everywhere, working in clusters on the tiered decks, hanging boldly from the yardarms and rigging, and even straddling the bowsprit, balancing themselves precariously as they brandished their weapons at the Spanish ship. Many held knives in their teeth in order to leave their hands free to display their deadly assortment of cutlasses, grenades, axes, nets, and grappling hooks.

On a lower deck she saw the burly gunners frantically swabbing the still-smoking barrels of their huge black cannon and reloading them with fresh powder. Clad only in dirty cotton breeches, they darted about barefooted, their soot-covered faces streaked with rivulets of sweat despite the kerchiefs tied around their heads. Their glistening bronze torsos flexed to the rhythm of their frenzied movements as the master gunner urged them on with curses and threats one moment and praises the next.

And there high above it all, the banner of the *Avenger* fluttered in the breeze, an uplifted arm holding a flaming sword against a black background — the emblem of *El Diablo Dorado*!

With a cry of dismay, Nicole was about to turn and run back to the refuge of the cabin when suddenly she caught sight of the tall fair-haired figure she had been seeking. He stood directly ahead of her on the quarterdeck, looking surprisingly calm and controlled in spite of the seeming madness all around him. With a large megaphone in one hand and a spyglass in the other, he studied the enemy and called out orders alternately to his man at the helm and his master gunner on the deck below. The wind whipped his shirt, revealing the hard, robust frame beneath, and tugged persistently at his abundant mane until it tore free of its confining tie and rippled like ripening wheat in the sunlight.

The sight of him may have struck terror in the Spaniards, but it had a calming effect on her. Paul Dawson was indeed a center of gravity. Relief swept over her.

Suddenly feeling a little foolish and very much out of place, she knew she had better hurry back to the cabin before he spotted her. He would be furious if he knew she had ventured out like this!

But at that moment another broadside thundered from the galleon and roared across the water at the *Avenger*. The volley fell sort, but it caused the *Avenger* to pitch wildly, its hull quivering and its timbers groaning in protest.

Nicole clutched the railing and struggled to keep her footing. The hatch door banged shut in her face. Her feet tangled in her skirts as she tried to climb down the ladder, so she clung to the railing.

By the time the ship had stabilized itself she lay in a heap of muslin at the bottom of the ladder. But the instant she could disentangle herself and get to her feet, she grabbed the railing and began to climb up again. She couldn't return to the cabin without at least seeing what damage, if any, had been done. There was more shouting and heavier pounding on the deck than before. . . .

She lifted the hatch door cautiously.

The scene that met her was more confused than it had been the first time she had looked out on the quarterdeck. The smoke was thicker than ever, and she had to strain her eyes to make any sense out of what she saw. She stared anxiously at the spot where she had last seen Paul Dawson, but he was no longer standing by the rail. Quickly she raked the deck with her eyes, trying to pierce the veil of gunsmoke.

Two men had toppled from the bowsprit, and a few of their comrades were throwing them a rope. Here and there she could see mariners who had been wounded from a fall or some flying object that had come loose during the broadside. But nowhere could she see the unmistakable figure of her captain.

She recognized Fernández at the helm, struggling to hold the bark in position. But Paul — where was Paul?

She looked again toward the spot where she had seen him only a few moments before. Her eyes were growing more accustomed to the haze now. Suddenly she saw him! Her heart began to pound wildly. He lay on the deck near the railing, blood tricking down one side of his face! He was trying to raise himself on one elbow, but was obviously still dazed.

With a cry of dismay, Nicole pushed the hatch open all the way, and ran straight to where he lay. She stood swaying over him, too panic-stricken to realize what she had done. So engrossed was everyone in the urgency of the battle that her presence on the smoke-filled deck was hardly noticed.

Dawson, however, was already pulling himself up to a sitting position and was about to stand when he saw her. For a moment he sat there, more stunned by the sight of her than from the blow he had received.

"What the hell ...? How in blazes did you get here?" he shouted.

"You're wounded!" was all she could manage.

He reached up and pulled her down to the deck beside him. "You little fool! Do you want to be killed?" he scolded, almost crushing her beneath him in an effort to shield her.

"But you're hurt ... you're wounded!" she cried, reaching up to dab at the blood on his forehead with her handkerchief.

When he saw the terror in her face, the tears glistening

on her lashes, an incongruously boyish grin spread over his sooty, bloody face. "By all that's holy, I think the lass really cares after all!" he exclaimed. "But don't fret, my sweet, it's only a trifle," he went on to assure her. "You foolish, adorable child! To run out here like this!" He kissed her hungrily, and he felt a surge in his loins as he felt her respond to him.

It took all his willpower to break away from her. He signaled to Josh, who was anxiously observing them but was discreetly awaiting orders.

"Here, take her back to my cabin," Dawson said, rising and lifting Nicole to her feet along with him. He balanced her against him for a moment until his copper-haired lieutenant could come and take her from him, but his eyes swept the sunlit water to where the enemy ship lay half hidden behind the smoke of its last broadside. Quickly he put the speaker to his mouth and shouted orders.

"Come about ... stay to windward!" he called to Fernández at the helm, all the while brushing off Nicole's efforts to stem the blood on his forehead. He was relieved when Josh finally reached him and he could turn her over to him. "For God's sake, Josh, get her out of here!" he exclaimed, even as he shouted, "Mr. Simms, are you ready?"

"Aye, Capt'n, we'll have those sons of bitches floundering with the next blast!"

"Then aim for their mainmast. Bring down their spars and rigging!" Dawson shouted back. "Come on, lads, let's hit the bastards where it hurts this time!"

He turned again to Nicole, who still stood staring at him oblivious to Josh's nudging.

"What the devil?" he exlaimed. Then turning on Josh, he thundered, "Didn't I tell you to get her out of here?" But he murmured gently in her ear, "Don't worry, sweet, it's all right. All the demons in hell couldn't keep me from getting back to you tonight!"

He grabbed the bloodstained handkerchief she had been

trying to use on him out of her hand and wiped away the blood himself.

"Damn it, Josh, get her back to the cabin, even if you have to carry her there!" he said sternly. "And lock her in while you're at it!" He fished the key from his breeches and tossed it to his lieutenant. Then he turned to give the Spaniards his undivided attention. But a new vigor now surged within him. He felt like throwing back his head and shouting his joy until it filled the whole Caribbean! It was a glorious feeling! The lass really cared for him after all. He chuckled in spite of himself. He knew she was plucky, but to run out in the middle of everything like that — all because she thought he needed her! Well, he did need her. He ached to be with her. But first he had to get this damn galleon out of the way. Then he could go below to the even greater prize waiting for him!

Chapter 32

"Will you please stop fussing over me!" Paul Dawson protested, more amused than annoyed over the way Nicole ran to greet him, bandages in hand, the moment he returned to his quarters.

It was almost dusk now, and weary and begrimed, he instructed the men who accompanied him to place the large chest they were carrying next to the one already standing in the corner of the cabin.

The battle had ended shortly after Nicole had been ordered below. A few broadsides more, and the Spanish captain had run up the white flag, deciding it would be better to lose his cargo than his life.

"That's one of the advantages of having a bad reputation," Dawson observed with a knowing smile as he poured himself a glass of wine and proceeded to remove his weapons. "You see, my dear, one of the nice things about being notorious is that you usually have to fight less. Most people don't want to tangle with someone who is known to be deadly."

He tried to fend her off until he could retire behind

the curtain to refresh himself and change his battle-stained clothing, but now that he had emerged in a clean shirt and breeches, she would not be put off any longer. She insisted that he sit down and let her attend his wound once and for all; to humor her, he finally acquiesced.

"All right. Between you and that rogue who calls himself a ship's surgeon, I much prefer your gentle nursing." He sighed and drew a chair up to the center table, where she had a bowl of water and a pile of linen cloths already laid out for him. "Actually, it's only a scratch and I've already washed it off. That's all it needed."

The faint odor of gunsmoke had penetrated the cabin, though the cool breeze wafting through the open portholes was fast clearing the air. The sounds of the men celebrating their victory echoed and reechoed throughout the ship as everyone on board enjoyed the round of rum that the captain had ordered distributed before the evening watch, though he had made it clear he would not tolerate drunkenness.

Dawson sat back with his boots off and legs outstretched to enjoy Nicole's making such a fuss over him. When she began to press those attentions beyond what he considered necessary, however, he lifted a detaining hand.

"One moment, lass, you can stop now. You've done more than enough," he protested.

"But it should be bandaged!" she argued as he laughingly dodged her attempts to wrap a long strip of white linen around his head. "Look, my sweet, I've let you bathe and fuss over this blasted scratch as though my head had been torn open, but I'll be damned if I'll let you swath me in a turban like a bloody sheik! The piece of rope only grazed me!"

"Then at least let me put this compress on it for a few minutes," she insisted, bending forward again with a fresh poultice made from herbs that she had selected from the private cache she had seen him use for her.

"Now, that's something I won't object to." He smiled

appreciatively as he watched the mounds of her firm young breasts while she bent solicitously over him and held the cloth pressed to his forehead.

"Here, my dear, let me show you in what fine fettle I am," he teased, catching her playfully at the waist and pulling her down to his knee, smothering her startled cry with his eager lips.

"My sweet little Nicole," he murmured against the moist fullness of her mouth. "You have me half out of my mind! Just to get back to you as quickly as I could, I crippled a galleon, relieved it of its cargo, and divided the spoils with my men before suppertime! Now, instead of being up there celebrating, I'm here putting up with your over-zealous efforts to smother me in a bolt of linen!"

"And the Spaniards?" she asked, trying in vain to slip free of his hold. "Don't tell me you sank their ship and drowned them all?"

"Good Lord, no!" he laughed. "There you go — *mal pensada* again! Don't you know one of the first rules of privateering, my sweet, is not to sink the booty?"

"Then why didn't you keep the ship, too?" she asked. "Wasn't that part of the prize?"

"The point is well taken, which only proves what I sensed from the beginning — you're a bright lass." He smiled approvingly. "A ship is often a very nice prize in itself," he admitted, "but at the moment it's even more important that these Spaniards go forth and spread their sad tidings to their compatriots. Once it's known I'm operating off the coast of Florida, most prudent Spanish captains will avoid these waters for a while, all of which means there will be fewer enemy ships to oppose the French when they attack Pensacola."

"Then you simply set them free?" she asked incredulously.

"Aye, that I did, but they haven't gotten off as easily as you might think. Once we transferred the cargo from the *Santa Teresa* to our ship, we left the Spanish captain and his crew to the tender care of their galley slaves, many of whom were good English and Frenchmen who had been living out their miserable lives chained to an oar in the bowels of that stinking ship. There's nothing I enjoy more in my profession than liberating poor devils like them from the yoke of the Spanish dons. Actually, I've recruited some of my best men that way. I got three new ones today, in fact. But enough talk of war and strategy. I'm in no mood to discuss such things in these precious moments that I have with you, my sweet."

She squirmed to break free of him, though she kept the damp cloth pressed against his forehead.

He laughed and continued to balance her on his knee. "It seems to me I warned you before about wiggling," he teased as he grabbed the cloth out of her hand and flung it aside. "It's time you learned to purr as well as scratch, my little bobcat!"

He brushed his lips against the hollow of her neck and felt her pulse quicken as he planted a kiss in the sweet-scented shadow. Then he lifted his head to her lips and kissed her on the mouth, lingering there until her lips finally parted and her hands instinctively began to stroke his damp, windblown locks.

Encouraged by the passion he felt ripening within her, he increased the intensity of his kisses and let his hand drop gently to one of her breasts. For one fleeting moment she stiffened, as though trying to make one final effort to stem the tide that was engulfing her. But he sensed her resistance was directed more at herself than him. He knew she wanted him now, and her awakening desire was like a flame setting parched wood ablaze. He had waited so long — he would not be put off any longer. Yet he didn't want to do anything that might mar these first precious moments between them, moments that would remain etched in their memories forever.

Gently he cupped the fullness of her breast through the thin muslin of her gown, and as it began to swell against the tight confines of her bodice, he felt himself respond as never before.

"You do want me, don't you?" he asked softly, fondling the hardened tip of her breast.

She murmured against his lips, her hands still buried in the tousled mass of his hair. The green of her eyes was luminous now, glowing with a light that only love could give them.

"Then trust me, lass. I won't hurt you. I could never hurt you. Surely you know that by now?"

Slowly he bared the nipple he had been caressing and took it in his mouth. A quiver of delight shot through her, and trembling wildly, she pressed his golden head to the pillow of her breast.

"You must put aside the past and learn the joys of a woman who is loved and can love in return," he told her as he awakened her other nipple.

Pleasure rippled through her in ever-increasing waves, and she stirred, her body aflame with sensations that bewildered, even frightened her. She knew there would probably come a moment when there would be pain, as there had been the first time, but she wanted him so much now that she no longer cared. She would gladly endure any discomfort now, no matter how great, just to belong to him, just to know the wondrous miracle of his love.

"I'm going to make love to you," he was saying gently but firmly, "for I know now that you want me, too. There's nothing wrong with our loving each other, Nicole."

She sighed. At what moment had her hatred turned to love? How was it that the touch of his hand — the brush of his lips — could set her tingling with joyous anticipation, when all the others who had pawed her had only filled her with revulsion? His desire for her, hard and urgent against her thigh, filled her with an uncontrollable longing to receive him ... to be one with him at last. Her need had become as great as his. That thought shocked her, but it was undeniable. For something had ignited inside of her. All her yearning to love and be loved, all the stifled passion that had lain dormant within her was ablaze now, set off by the spark of love that this strange, enigmatic man had awakened in her. He was her whole world now.

Slowly he eased her off his knee and, putting an arm around her waist, led her the few steps to the bunk.

For a moment he stood there, pinning her to him, as he loosened the lacings of her bodice and skirts until they fell in a frothy heap of rosebuds and white muslin around her feet.

Sensing the emotions warring inside her, he knew how important it was for him to cross this last hurdle with her carefully.

But what a fool he had been! He should have realized that her resistance sprang from fear and not hatred. It had taken the events of that day to make him see how much she really cared for him. The poor lass was simply afraid to love, afraid of being hurt and betrayed. But she had to learn to trust him, to know that love and happiness could be hers if she would just accept them.

"I love you, my little bobcat," he murmured, his voice husky with desire. "I'll never let anyone hurt you ever again ... not even myself!"

He laid her against the pillows and brushed the fragrant abundance of her hair back from her lovely face, reassuring her as though she were a frightened child, yet never losing sight of the passionate woman he knew was longing to be set free.

He didn't disrobe but bent forward fully clothed and, lowering the flap of his breeches, gently slipped into her before she had time to react.

Immediately she tensed and her knuckles went white, but she clung to him, her desire struggling against the ever-present phantoms. He gritted his teeth against the urgency of his long deprivation, every fiber of his body aching to plunge on to fulfillment, but he paused and held her there, suspended on the firm rod of his manhood, reminding himself that he must temper his passion if he was to help her win this final battle with her past. His profession had taught him patience. How many times had he carefully steered his ship through a storm, sensitive to its every quiver, alert to its every reaction? Surely no vessel was as precious to him as this exquisite young woman.

"Open your eyes, lass, and look at me," he whispered, his breath coming in gasps now as he fought his own battle for self-control. "Keep your eyes on me." His voice was labored. "Forget everything but this moment. This is Paul ... Paul who adores you. Look at me and see the love in my eyes!"

She obeyed and looked up at him transfixed, unprotesting.

Slowly he eased deeper into her, continuing to kiss and stroke her hair. "Do you feel me now, my sweet? Between us, love and desire are one and the same. I'm giving you this most intimate part of me, even as you're surrendering your innermost self to me. You see, I'm not hurting you, am I?" His voice was ragged, but there was great tenderness in it, too.

Slowly he began to thrust, gently, sensuously, all the while caressing her breasts, his tongue languidly flicking her parted lips. "Do you feel how it is when there is love, my darling?" he murmured soothingly, afraid to leave her alone even for a moment with those phantoms that might still be lurking in the corners of her mind. "This is my manhood bursting with love for you. It belongs to you now," he reassured her. "I've never given it to any woman with love before. I'm yours, little Nicole, as you are mine!"

Now she had an overwhelming desire to follow his rhythm, to lose herself completely in this new world she was discovering in his arms. Instinctively she arched herself higher to draw him deeper into her, her panic and her inexperience dissolving in the heat of her passion. A flood of surprising sensations assaulted her senses, overwhelmed her. The gentleness of his touch seemed to blot out everything. His eyes bored into hers with unmistakable tenderness. The chains of the past were falling away, and she was emerging free — free to love and trust once more. She closed her eyes, and the ghosts were gone. Only Paul remained.

With a deep moan that vibrated from the depths of her being, she clasped her arms joyously around him and yielded, letting him lead her now into that glorious new world of love and passion that she had never dreamed existed.

Slowly he increased his rhythm. He knew he had finally brought her safely over that tumultuous sea of doubt and fear that had separated them. And the bridge had been love — a love that could no longer be denied. Unhindered at last, he plunged on to fulfillment, sweeping her along with him on the crest of their newly found joy in each other.

She met each thrust with increasing ardor, unable to restrain the tide of her own unleashed passion as her need for release became as urgent as his. She was now as eager as he to reach that final explosion, that moment when flesh and spirit are fused at last.

Chapter 33

Nicole lay breathless in Paul's arms, still trembling from the deluge of emotions that engulfed her. She could feel him deep within, he was part of her now. Even the weight of his body and the sound of his heavy breathing filled her with pleasure.

No matter what the future held, she was his now, bound to him with a passion that was stronger than any chains could ever be. The circle of his arms was her home.

And then the tears came. That hard lump which had been lodged in her throat for so long dissolved at last, and all the unshed tears rushed to the surface. And with them, the bitterness and hatred, the hurt and shame came pouring out of her as well.

Paul stirred. "Are you all right, Nicole?" he asked softly, gently withdrawing himself from her and kissing her forehead.

Nicole tried to reply, but she couldn't get past the torrent of tears.

He lifted himself to his elbow and peered down at her. He had felt how she had willingly responded to him every step of the way, and once that initial moment of tension had passed, had met his frenzied passion with a fierceness of her own, compensating for her lack of experience with a delightful abandon.

"It's nothing," she gasped.

"But why are you crying?" He bent nearer, but she sat up and covered her face with her hands. "What a silly goose I am! I can't seem to stop!" she exclaimed, marveling as much over her inability to check the flow of her tears as the fact that she was able to cry at all. "Please don't look at me!"

"Damn!" Paul growled. "If I've gone and hurt you in some way . . . I tried so hard not to. . . ."

"No, no," she assured him hastily, reaching out shyly to stroke his cheek. "I had no idea it could be like that," she whispered, her wet cheeks coloring at the boldness of her confession.

He gave her a pleased smile. "Nor I, my sweet, nor I." He gathered her into his arms once more. "You're probably just excited. You're a passionate woman, you know. I tried to go slowly but I'd waited so long —" He saw the puzzled expression on her face and broke off with a smile. "God as my witness, Nicole, you had me on the brink of madness. I've never wanted a woman so much in my life! I don't think I'll ever get my fill of you!"

She laughed in spite of her tears and gave him a playful slap. "You'd better not!" she warned him. "Remember what you said — you belong to me now, too."

"Aha! So you remember that?" he exclaimed. "My God! I see I'll have to watch everything I say around you from now on if you're going to hold me to every word!" he teased, dodging the indignant fists that flew at him.

But on seeing how the tears still glistened on her lashes, he sobered and cradled her in his arms. "But what's the matter, my sweet? Are you going to react this way every time I make love to you?"

"No, it's not that." She smiled through her tears. "It's just I hadn't cried in so long. I really thought I couldn't anymore!"

He tightened his arms around her. An overwhelming desire to shield her from the world swept over him. "Let it all out, my sweet."

Nicole lay her head against his damp shirt, secure in his nearness and drawing strength from the imposing breadth of his chest moving rhythmically against her cheek. The faint odor of gunpowder still clung to him, mingling with the familiar aroma of sandalwood and tobacco that she always associated with him.

Gradually she could feel herself relaxing, and soon she was dry-eyed and contented, a new feeling of well-being enveloping her. She no longer felt alone and frightened. The tears seemed to have washed her clean. Where there had been sorrow and pain, there was only love now. And love was Paul. She repeated his name softly, caressing it with her lips as she nestled closer to him.

He smiled at the sound and nuzzled her hair, savoring to the fullest these moments he had dreamed of sharing with her ever since that first night they had spent together.

"Don't get too comfortable, my sweet," he warned. "For the night has just begun and so have we."

She looked up. "You mean there's more?" she asked incredulously, her eyes glistening like huge emeralds as the prospect of his making love to her again immediately filled her with renewed desire.

"Much more, my sweet," he replied with an impish grin, and ran his hands possessively over the velvety smoothness of her skin, delighting in her sensitivity as he felt how she was already beginning to quiver at his touch. He lingered at her breasts and tweaked her nipples.

"Unless, of course, you have some objection?" he added playfully, then suddenly released her and rose from the bunk.

Her eyes widened and she sat bolt upright, clutching

the linen sheet to her still-tingling breasts. "Paul Dawson! Are you deliberately trying to torment me, just to see whether I'll beg you to make love to me or not?"

He laughed and came over to kiss her. "Don't fret, my sweet, for I'm afraid I couldn't pretend even for a moment that I don't want you. But I hope you won't mind if I remove my clothing this time. I feel like a blasted schoolboy making love to you through the flap of my breeches. I — we — will enjoy each other more if I'm free of them." He unlaced his shirt and lifted it over his head, exposing the broad, suntanned expanse of his chest as he tossed the garment to the floor.

He put his hand on his already loosened breeches, but paused. "Of course, if the sight of me disrobed really upsets you, I won't ..."

Nicole blushed and lowered her eyes, suddenly embarrassed. "I think you must be the most handsome man in the world," she said timidly. "I love the way your muscles flex and your body gleams all gold and bronze in the lamplight."

His delight at her words was obvious. "You saw so much that first night?" he marveled. "I hardly thought you'd noticed anything about me, much less something you liked!"

She was coloring more deeply by the minute, regretting her boldness. "There was one other time," she confessed, her voice barely audible.

His brows lifted. "When? I don't remember undressing in front of you except that one time...."

"That first evening you brought me on board, before you put up the curtain." Her voice was very low, and she was increasingly sorry she had ever brought the subject up.

A twinkle kindled his blue eyes. "You mean when I took my bath?" he asked incredulously. "But you were sleeping ... at least I thought you were...." Suddenly he threw back his head and laughed heartily. "Why, you little minx! You weren't ... were you?"

She covered her face with her hands. "I only saw you a fraction of a second," she assured him. "The light was very bad and ... and I was so ashamed ... I closed my eyes right away."

He sat on the bunk beside her and pulled her to him. "Why, you adorable child!" He tried to kiss her, but she continued to hide her blushing face from him. "I felt so guilty about peeping at you like that even for a moment. It was very wanton of me, I know."

He didn't have the heart to laugh at her anymore. "My sweet darling! If that is the worst sin you're guilty of, then you'll be the only one in Hades with a halo! I'm delighted you're such a passionate, sensual woman. I love your sensitivity ... the way you react to my every touch. God as my witness, I consider myself the most fortunate man in the world to have found such a treasure!"

He cupped her chin gently in his hand and, lifting her face to his, kissed her long and passionately, tracing the sensuous pout of her lips with his tongue until she slowly opened them. She found herself responding, her tongue darting past the even whiteness of his teeth into the warm recesses of his mouth, still sweet with the wine he had just drunk.

He swung himself over her and, lifting her breast to his eager lips, he drew first one and then the other into his mouth until she was moaning with delight and instinctively arching herself to receive him.

"My sweet, sweet little wildcat," he murmured as he eased his leg between hers and slipped again into the moist warmth of her.

This time she gave herself freely to him, with a passion she had not imagined possible. The feel of flesh against flesh set her pulse to pounding wildly, and she locked her arms tightly around his neck, drawing him ever deeper, her eager body learning quickly now, glowingly alive in places she had never suspected existed. Paul had been right. There was more — much more.

She lay back at last, as deliciously exhausted as he was, but reluctant to let him go. She enjoyed this intimate sensation of being one with him, of knowing that this golden giant who could set the Caribbean to quaking at just the mention of his name lay there trembling with passion in her arms. How boyish and vulnerable he seemed at that moment with his bright hair mussed and his sun-tanned face momentarily free from tension.

She unlocked her hands and ran her fingers over the smooth firmness of his powerful shoulders as he lay spent in her arms, lost in that dream world where he always seemed to withdraw in the first few minutes after he made love to her. How magnificent he was! The thought that she was the woman he had chosen to love filled her with pride. She remembered how he had looked standing on deck so tall and straight above all the others. Oh, God, protect him!

She ran her hands lovingly over the well-marked cords in his forearms and shoulders and kissed the half-hidden scar in the tangle of golden hairs on his chest. Gently she traced ridges here and there, and tears filled her eyes as she thought how she would kiss them one by one as he told her how he had come by them.

Paul stirred and sighed contentedly, instinctively tightening his arm around her. "Don't move yet, my sweet," he murmured drowsily as he shifted his weight so as not to bear down too heavily on her and dozed on for a few more moments.

But she couldn't sleep. Though delightfully relaxed, she didn't want to give up these precious moments just yet. She wanted to enjoy the vibrant feel of him, to revel in the strength of his masculinity, grateful that he was there alive and safe in her arms. Tomorrow would be another day, perhaps fraught with new dangers, but tonight, thank God, he was hers.

When he awakened several hours later and began to caress her with renewed desire, she responded with an almost desperate fervor, fired now not only by her ever-increasing passion, but also by the nagging fear that, though she had found love at last, it might be wrested from her at any moment.

Chapter 34

The next day they encountered another Spanish ship, but as soon as Dawson put a shot across its bow and ran up his flag, it turned and ran like a startled hind, the buccaneers close on its heels. But once Dawson was satisfied that the ship had changed its course and left the vicinity, he let it go. At that moment he was more interested in chasing away as many enemy vessels as possible than devoting all his time to fighting only one of them.

As long as the *Avenger* was at sea, however, he kept his men on as strict a training schedule as any ship-of-the-line in the British Navy. He insisted that his master gunner put the cannoneers through their paces until they could reload and run out their guns in no more than a minute's time. Extra lookouts were posted around the clock, and at night he continued to enforce the rule that all lights had to be kept hidden.

Though he often dined with his officers to maintain a good rapport, and he made personal inspections of every detail of his ship, he still managed to visit Nicole several times a day.

"I catch myself looking for the slightest pretext to come down here," he told her, "but then, it's so hard to tear myself away!"

In spite of the limited time he had to spare, however, he would pull her hungrily to him as she ran to greet him at the door, and soon they would be entwined in each other's arms, oblivious to the perilous world around them. He possessed her quickly and powerfully, and then reluctantly turned to his desk or went topside.

At night he would fall into an exhausted but contented sleep, cradling her in his arms, her head pillowed on his shoulder. But he would usually be gone before dawn, and when she awakened later, she would lie there in the bunk, still feeling his presence and tingling at the memory of his recent caresses.

Paul had agreed to rendezvous with the French commanders on the night of Saturday May 13 off the coast of Santa Rosa, a long, narrow island which, because of its strategic location as an integral part of the port of Pensacola, also had a small fort to supplement the larger one on the mainland.

Paul told Nicole, in answer to her anxious questions, that the French had chosen that particular spot to initiate their attack because it could not be seen from the mainland, and the element of surprise was one of the most important factors in their plans to take Pensacola.

Nicole had put out the lantern and opened the curtains so she could watch something of what was going on outside. From what she could see in the moonlight, she estimated the French had at least a dozen different kinds of ships. She recognized the three large ones as those she had seen in Mobile Bay. At the time Paul had commented on the fact that they were under the command of Bienville's older brother, Sérigny, and each one carried twenty pieces of cannon and 150 men. Then there were the four feluccas with a landing party that the governor himself had brought to the rendezvous, as well as a sloop and what looked like a transport boat, which probably held the food and supplies.

Meanwhile she knew that still another one of Bienville's brothers, Antoine Le Moyne de Châteaugué, was supposed to be on his way from Mobile, traveling overland with a force of some four hundred Indians and one hundred whites.

She smiled as she remembered how Paul talked about the governor's brothers. "As far as I know, there have been at least five of them, beginning with Iberville, who was one of the first Frenchmen to come down the Mississippi River from Canada and explore that region and who, incidentally, was clever enough to fool some of my compatriots into turning around and leaving all that territory to France. But then, the number of Le Moynes in Louisiana is not surprising," Paul had added, "when you consider that Jean-Baptiste, Sieur de Bienville, is number twelve of fourteen children!"

That night while the *Avenger* kept vigil, the French were to attack the smaller garrison on Santa Rosa. If all went well, they were to go on into the harbor and attack the main fort.

In their hurried offshore meeting, Sérigny agreed with the buccaneer captain that the French would send up a flare to signal that they were in trouble and needed him or to advise that it was all over. Either way, Dawson was to join them immediately.

When the night passed without gunfire or flare, Dawson confided to Nicole that he was puzzled. But after a long, quiet Sunday and a peaceful Monday, he was worried enough to send Fernández and another man in the longboat on a reconnaissance mission.

Their news was good: the attack on Santa Rosa had gone so well that not even a blow had been struck! After spiking the fort's cannon, the French had returned to their feluccas and joined the three larger ships, ready to enter the harbor and attack the large fort. But as luck would have it, the wind was so weak they had to postpone the second phase of their plan. They couldn't enter Pensacola Bay until Wednesday the seventeenth, but they still had the advantage of surprise, and it won the day for them. And thanks to Dawson's active campaign, there wasn't a single warship in the roadstead to defend the port.

The French ships lined up across the bay's entrance and the feluccas landed a hundred of their men with a warning that there were many more troops and Indians ready to attack the port by land as well. The Spanish commander surrendered immediately. With no ships to defend the harbor and the threat of a massive assault by land and sea, the Spaniard agreed to turn over the fort to the French after only one cannonade; by four o'clock in the afternoon it was all over.

Nicole was beside herself with joy. Ever since the expedition had begun, she had worried about the outcome, envisioning all kinds of terrible things happening to Paul, even to herself.

Paul had come to the cabin quickly to assure her that the victory was theirs and then had gone ashore with his two lieutenants to join the French commanders in a victory drink and to discuss the arrangements for the occupation of the port. He also wanted permission to talk to the Spanish prisoners in hopes they could give him news about a certain person. . . .

It was well after midnight when Paul returned to Nicole. While the sounds of rejoicing filled the night air, Paul and Nicole celebrated in their own way. Lying in each other's arms in the moonlit cabin, with the curtains drawn back to let the starlight spill into the room, they made love again and again, reveling in their own victory.

Chapter 35

Nicole's happiness knew no bounds. They had been at anchor for several days now, and at last she could have more time with Paul.

He took her up on deck often now and even let her stand at the helm for a while so she could see how alive the ship felt under her hands. He resumed his late evening meals with her, and he lingered a bit longer in the bunk with her in the mornings.

He gave his men turns at shore leave, but there was little to entertain them. Pensacola was a primitive outpost in the wilderness — a crude fort with hardly any town to complement it. There was no brothel, and the one or two camp followers who lived within the palisades preferred to stay with the Spanish prisoners; they wanted nothing to do with the victors.

The day after they anchored in the bay, Paul told her Hanson was missing. He had evidently preferred to jump ship rather than face the reckoning due him from the captain.

But Paul only shrugged his shoulders. "He's not worth hunting down. I'm better off without the coward. Besides, there's a good gunner among the three galley slaves who joined us last week from the *Santa Teresa.*"

Paul continued to meet with the French commanders. They had promised him a share of the food and supplies captured at Pensacola, but the Spaniards had not had as much on hand as the French anticipated, so Bienville could not spare anything yet. But he felt Paul had more than lived up to his part of the bargain, so he invited him to stay on at Pensacola until the supplies they were expecting from France arrived. Meanwhile the governor did give Paul a token amount to keep the buccaneers happy.

Paul's relations with the French were agreeable enough, but Nicole couldn't help noticing that something was bothering him. During the conference at Dauphin Island, it had been agreed that the prisoners taken at Pensacola would not be sent to Havana but to Europe, because the Spaniards were known to dishonor surrender agreements — a point which Paul had pressed at the meetings. Nevertheless, now that arrangements were being made for the transport of the prisoners, the two commanders and the Company director had decided to send the Spaniards to Havana after all.

"It's a mistake!" Paul exclaimed, pacing the cabin angrily. "Mark my words, they're going to regret this. France is going to have to take two of their large ships to transport the prisoners, no matter where they send them. If they go to Europe, at least they'll return. God knows what will happen to them if they sail into Havana!"

"Why can't they just keep the prisoners here in the fort until the war is over?" asked Nicole, finding war and politics too complicated.

Paul shook his head. "It's not that simple, my sweet. It costs money to keep prisoners. They need food and men to guard them. Actually, the lack of supplies is behind this new decision. Larcebault, the Company director here, insists that crossing the ocean on two ships with a total of some four hundred people would take more supplies than the French can afford, but I say the risk of sending them to Havana is one they can afford even less!"

"What should they do, then?"

"Scrape up what supplies they can, even if they only have enough to get them to Europe. As it is now, they plan to go on to France after they drop off the Spanish prisoners. Once they reach Europe, their Regent ought to be happy enough to give them provisions to return to the colonies. On the other hand, what good will their economical measures do if they never get out of Havana!"

"Don't you think the Spaniards in Havana might be grateful to the French for having taken the trouble to return the prisoners to their own people?"

Paul grunted. "If Rodrigo Escobar has anything to do with it — and after talking to some of the Spanish prisoners, I have good reason to believe he might be in Havana at this time — the French will be lucky to get out with their lives, much less their ships! As it is, the French are fools to risk losing two good vessels just to deliver prisoners. They'll need all the ships they can get if they want to hold on to Pensacola."

"It isn't over, then?"

Paul couldn't help smiling. "We only won a battle, my sweet — not the war. My guess is there's a lot more to come."

She paled. "Oh, no!" she exclaimed.

"I'm afraid so, my dear. From what I can see, the French position in Pensacola, and even in Mobile, is very precarious. They could lose the whole colony if they're not careful."

And you, my darling, could lose your life, she thought, but she knew if she voiced her fears, he would only laugh.

She looked up at him standing there so vibrant and strong, his golden head almost brushing the ceiling beams and the lamplight dancing in his blue eyes. What did she care about France, England, and Spain? Paul was all that mattered to her.

He noted her silence and read her expression accurately.

"Ah, my dear, forgive me. I've upset you with my talk of war. I didn't mean to worry you!" He lifted her and held her close. "Come, let's retire early tonight and forget everything except us. Our love is the only thing that anchors me in this sea of madness!"

As he began to pull at the ribbons of her lime silk peignoir, she threw herself against his chest and clung to him.

"Oh, Paul, please don't take so many risks. I don't want to lose you!" she begged. "I love you so! Hold me . . . love me!"

Her words ignited him. He tightened his arms around her and rained kisses down upon her lovely face. "God bless you, lass. You were well worth waiting for! You're the greatest treasure in my life!"

Their desire for each other was enormous, fueled in part by a desperate urgency to hold on to each other, to become an integral part of one another so that nothing could ever separate them — no matter what the future held.

Chapter 36

They lay deliciously entwined, their bodies still moist from the heat of their passion. She kissed the now familiar scar and fingered the ridges on the otherwise smooth expanse of his back. She knew every one by heart.

"My poor darling, I have to know," she ventured. "Are all these wounds from battles you've fought?"

"I'd hardly be much of a fighting man if I'd gotten so many wounds in just ten years, although my profession tends to scar body and soul."

"Ten years? I thought you said you'd been a privateer for only six years."

"Aha! So you remember that, too." He hugged her playfully. Just the feel of his bare flesh against hers sent a shiver of delight through her, and she snuggled closer to him.

"Please, I want to know," she begged. "I want to know everything about you."

"Everything?" he echoed, his smile broadening.

"Now stop teasing me!" she scolded, running her hands

deftly over his back and lifting her lips eagerly to meet his as she felt his arms tightening around her with renewed desire.

"All right, you little witch! You know I can't refuse you anything." He reluctantly disentangled himself from her and hoisted himself to a sitting position. "I'll tell you about these blasted scars, but you'd better stop running your hands up and down my back like that or I won't be able to keep my hands off you long enough to tell you anything!" He paused. "Yes, my sweet, you do have a right to know more about me, and I'm pleased I matter enough that you want to know."

Nicole lifted her peignoir from where it had been hurriedly discarded and wrapped it around herself. The lamp-lit cabin seemed unusually quiet. Only the gentle lapping of the water against the hull broke the silence at all.

"The scars on my back aren't from battle wounds. They're whip marks from the three years I spent chained to an oar in a Spanish galleon."

"God in heaven! No wonder you hate the Spaniards so!"

"If only that were all they did!" His voice was hard. "That was the least of it. They murdered my mother and father."

"*Mon pauvre amour!*" Nicole sat up straight and caught his hand in hers. "If it hurts you to speak of it . . . perhaps you'd better not go on. . . ."

"No, I've been wanting to tell you. You need to understand," he insisted. "The bastard who was responsible for the death of my parents violated every law of human decency observed by civilized countries. Even though it was in 1706, while England was at war over the succession with Spain and France, there were certain ethics then, as there are supposed to be now, concerning the treatment of prisoners of war.

"When the ship my parents and I were on was captured by the Spaniards, we had every reason to expect some semblance of decency from our captors. Instead, the Spanish captain seemed to be possessed with a savage ferocity toward anything British. He called himself Rodrigo Escobar y Villegas. I'll go to my grave with that name engraved in my memory." His voice cracked, but he went on. "The man behaved like the devil incarnate — more like a black-hearted pirate than a commander of a Christian ship. He ordered our vessel to be put to the torch, while many of its crew who were too wounded to leave it without help were still on board. Then he had the rest of the ablebodied prisoners chained to the oars of his galleon."

Paul wrapped the sheet around the lower half of his body and got out of bed and poured himself a drink from the decanter. "There were only two females among the passsengers of the captured boat — an awkward young girl of thirteen or fourteen, and my mother, who was still an exceptionally beautiful young woman. She was hardly more than a child when she married my father."

He took another sip, and Nicole sensed he must be coming to the part of the story he most dreaded. "The Spaniards were still celebrating their victory when Escobar, as drunk on rum as the lowest scoundrel in his crew, came out of his cabin. Unfortunately, the ship's priest had been killed during the battle, so there was no one to reproach them at that moment. When the crew began to call out to Escobar to let them have the women, he roared with laughter and promised they'd get their turns after he and his officers had finished with them."

Paul's voice was ragged now. "My father and I fought to save my mother, but the whole crew piled up on top of us. They killed my father and forced me to lie there on the deck with six men weighing me down while they dragged my mother kicking and screaming toward Escobar's quarters. But before they got her there, she broke loose, and in a frenzy of terror and grief — having just seen my father killed before her eyes and knowing she was about to be raped by over a hundred drunken ruffians

— she threw herself overboard." His voice had dropped to a hoarse whisper, and he sat down on the edge of the bed with the half-empty glass in his hand, unable to go on.

Nicole felt as though her heart were being torn from her breast to see how pain transformed his handsome face. Impulsively she took his hand in hers again, though she knew she was helpless to ease his anguish.

When he began to speak again, his voice was still strained. "Later, when the sounds of that poor young girl's screaming reached us down in the galley, I tried to console myself with the thought that my mother had at least been spared that ordeal. We never knew what happened to the poor lass, and we never heard her after that night. I doubt she survived till dawn. She was just a fragile little thing — a mere child!"

"Escobar is a monster!" Nicole exclaimed. "Is he the one you've been looking for all these years?"

"Aye, lass, and I'll find him, too. That much I know."

"So you were forced to serve on a galleon," she said at last. "It must have been horrible. And you were so young, too!"

"Yes, but I was a husky lad for my age — as strong as most full-grown men around me — and I had my hatred of Escobar to keep me going."

"And how long were you —?"

"Three years, though it seemed like an eternity," he replied bitterly. "Meanwhile Escobar, who was actually an adventure-loving son of a rich and powerful nobleman, returned to Spain to be rewarded for his gallant services by his grateful king and to inherit his father's lands and title. Another captain took his place, but I never forgot Rodrigo Escobar!"

"And how did you escape?"

"Pirates attacked our galleon and took it over. They killed the Spanish captain and his officers and then gave the crew and the galley slaves a choice of joining them or joining the others at the bottom of the ocean. Like everyone else, I accepted their offer and bided my time until I could better my situation. They were a ruthless, crafty lot, whose only law was the fist and the cutlass, but I learned two important lessons from them — how to stay alive and how to handle a ship.

"When their captain was killed, I fought for the leadership and won. Then the first thing I did was convince the men serving under me to turn to privateering instead of just roaming the sea as scavengers. Most of them, like Josh and Fernández, who had served on the galleon with me, accepted and signed the articles I drew up. Those who didn't want to stay under my terms were allowed to leave. I didn't want traitors or malcontents undermining my ship. For the past six years I've been operating under letters of marque in defense of the British colonies, but as a privateer I still have my freedom to come and go as I please and, of course, make a damn sight more profit than I could ever hope for in the regular navy."

A flush of pride brought back some of his usual sparkle, and in a surge of love, Nicole reached out and stroked his bright hair. "Oh, my dear, I'm so glad you told me. I understand so much now. When I think of all the terrible things I accused you of in the beginning. . . . You should have told me sooner!"

He smiled. "I tried to once or twice but, you may remember, you were hardly in the mood to listen to me. I doubt you would have believed me then anyway."

She hung her head. "I'd come to mistrust everyone," she admitted softly and fell silent while he drained his glass. Then she said, "You know, I was tempted once to jump overboard, too, on the voyage over. One girl actually did."

He caught her to him. "No, no, never think of such a thing!" he exclaimed. "Think of it, lass. What if you had jumped overboard! We'd never have met!"

"If anything ever happened to you, I don't think I'd

want to go on living," she said, clinging fast to him. "You are my life. Without you I'd have no reason to go on."

He smiled gently. "You're very young yet, my sweet. There will be many more reasons to live as time goes by, though I'm happy to know I'm one of them."

He kissed her soft cheek, but she remained thoughtful. "And in all these years, have you ever come across that scoundrel Escobar again?" she asked.

"Our paths have crossed several times. As the owner of some of New Spain's richest silver mines, Rodrigo Escobar is one of the most powerful grandees in Mexico and a favorite of the Spanish king. He travels to and from the court in Madrid and his villa about one hundred fifty miles inland from Veracruz, and during his voyages he often represents his king. Twice I nearly caught up with him. The closest I came was about two years ago. I had him in my spyglass — he was sailing home from Spain — but the wind suddenly changed and the vessel got away. The most I could do was fire on his ship. I learned afterward that he was wounded but had completely recovered. I'll get him one of these days. The latest news I have is that he's in Havana on king's business. You see, my sweet, I keep on Don Rodrigo's trail. I can tell you exactly where he's been almost every day of his life since that fateful day when our paths crossed."

Nicole stirred uneasily in his arms. "I don't like it when you talk this way," she said. "I can understand why you feel as you do, but it frightens me. I meant what I said. I'd be lost if anything happened to you."

"Don't worry, my sweet. You'll never want for anything. If something happens to me, you'll be a very rich widow."

Nicole shuddered. "Please, don't even talk about such things, much less joke about them!"

"I'm not joking," he protested. "Who else should inherit my fortune if not my wife? You mustn't forget what I've told you to do if . . ."

She shook her auburn head and tried to dismiss the

idea. "Yes, yes, I know. You've made me recite the name and address of your administrator in Virginia at least a dozen times. I know exactly what to do. But please, let's not talk about it anymore!"

He laughed. "Now that's a devil of a way to nip a man's proposal in the bud!" he scolded.

"Proposal?"

"Well, that's what I was leading up to, if you'd just let me finish! I know you'd prefer a more elaborate wedding than what we can have in this primitive port, but I think we should go ahead and do it now. I'd feel better if I knew you were my wife. Then you'd be completely under my protection while I'm alive, and my indisputable heir if something unfortunate should happen to me."

"You want to marry me?" she asked, dazed.

"Of course. Does that surprise you?" He kissed her parted lips roguishly. "Haven't you learned that when I say something I mean it? I told you from the very beginning that I hoped you'd become more to me than a — and you have. Much more. Surely you don't doubt my love?"

"No, not that. I don't think of you as a man who bothers much with formalities. I mean, you seem so —"

"You mean you didn't expect a black-hearted buccaneer like me to be the marrying kind. Well, I confess, my sweet, I'm not a churchgoing man. I've seen too much fanaticism — from the Papists to the Puritans — to embrace any one religion, but I do hold that we must all answer to some High Command for our actions." He was suddenly serious. "When it comes to a man and a woman, I think they should have their union blessed in some way — for the protection of the wife and children, if nothing else. In other words, my dear, I'm willing to put my head in the yoke to give you greater security and, I hope, to make you happy. For my part, I don't think it's a certificate that makes a marriage between two people. It's what's in their hearts, and my heart is already filled to overflowing with you, lass. It's as simple as that. So if you're willing to put up with an ill-tempered sea dog like me, I'll go ashore and make the arrangements tomorrow."

Chapter 37

The wedding was held on the poop deck of the *Avenger* and witnessed by the entire crew. The chaplain from one of the French ships performed the ceremony, and Paul's most trusted men, Josh and Fernández, were the official witnesses.

It was a typical June day on the Gulf — hot and sunny. A warm, steady breeze wafted across the deck and stirred the tall palms along the white sandy shore.

There was but one moment of sadness for Nicole — when she looked around at those assembled and realized there was no one there for *her*. But one look into Paul's eyes, and she no longer felt alone. He stood beside her, impressively attired in a silver-buttoned frock coat and breeches of royal-blue silk, set off by a gold-embroidered vest, a white starched jabot, and black polished boots. He had even donned his best tricorne hat for the occasion, but the moment he took it off, Nicole observed with a smile how the wind seemed to enjoy playing with the golden waves of his hair as much as she did.

Lost in his gaze, she rested her hand proudly on his arm and listened contentedly while the priest read from his worn leather Bible. Never had she been as happy as she was at this moment. In her other life, which seemed like a vague dream now, she had only been half alive, a child in love with love, more interested in planning her forthcoming wedding to Marcel than in Marcel himself.

Now she was gloriously alive, and all that mattered was this man she belonged to with her body and her mind.

Paul had done everything he possibly could to surround her with love and joy on her wedding day. He had Jeff gather wild flowers from the woods near the palisade, and had helped her pick her bridal gown and other accessories from the two chests in his cabin. The dress was of shimmering ivory satin, its overskirt caught up gracefully at the sides by huge clusters of silk tearoses, so that the panel of matching lace flounces on the underskirt could be shown off. Frothy cascades of lace adorned the cuffs of her elbow-length sleeves.

On her head she wore a long gold-spun mantilla draped over a tortoiseshell comb that she had perched atop the abundant coils of her red-gold hair.

It had been a long time since she had worn hoops, but the feel of her silk ruffled petticoats bobbing over them gave an added lift to her spirits. Once she had donned her clocked silk stockings and gold-embroidered satin slippers, she felt as though she were seventeen again, ready to preside over one of her father's elegant soirees.

Even Paul's friends seemed to make a special effort to keep her from feeling lonely on this most important day of her life. They complimented her gallantly and joked about which one of them she wanted for a bridesmaid. She felt they had accepted her now and not just out of loyalty to their captain.

Paul's final surprise was a priceless gold ring bearing

an impossibly large cluster of emeralds, which he insisted matched the color of her eyes.

After the ceremony, he ordered an extra ration of rum for the crew and invited his top officers to accompany him and his bride to his quarters for a celebratory drink. As they left the deck to go below, the crew gave a rousing cheer, and though she knew it was out of respect for their leader, it filled her with a warm glow to know that they could never again call her "the captain's whore."

There was considerable activity in the port throughout June and into July. Ships came and went. In early June a Company ship from Guinea landed there. It carried the first large shipment of Negroes for the colony — an arrival long awaited by the French, since nothing could be done without men to clear the wilderness, till the fields, build the homes and forts, and strengthen the riverbanks against flooding. There were simply too few colonists to handle the work, and in spite of the increasing number of convicts being brought over, the colonies were very short on laborers.

Paul told Nicole that there were close to five hundred blacks in the Louisiana Colony now, but though he understood the needs of the colonists, his own experience had instilled in him a loathing for slave labor of any kind — black or white. Nicole, who had also known her share of slavery, heartily agreed. She found herself thinking about Legarde again. He was probably busy making new profits in the distribution of these latest unfortunates.

On June 26 the two ships Bienville had been waiting for finally arrived in Pensacola with 350 soldiers and colonists, more convicts, and the long-awaited food and supplies.

True to his word, the governor gave Paul a portion of the provisions, but it was mid-July, after the ships that had brought the Negro slaves to Pensacola and Mobile had departed and the evacuation of Dauphin

Island had been completed, before Bienville and the Company representative could give their attention to the division of the supplies. The governor was especially anxious to distribute some of those precious new provisions not only to Pensacola, but to Mobile and his pet project near the mouth of the Mississippi River, *Nouvelle Orléans*.

Though Paul was annoyed over the unexpected delay in receiving the supplies, he and Nicole welcomed the extra time together. Their desire for each other still seemed insatiable, each coupling left them with greater hunger. Nicole had never dreamed she could love a man the way she loved Paul, that she could crave the feel of him until she ached. His caresses and exquisite sense of timing, his knowledge of every nuance and variation in rhythm made her shiver with delight. Yet there was a gentleness, too, almost a reverence in his touch that made her feel pure again. His love had washed away the violence and shame of her past.

The cabin she had once thought of as a prison had become her home. Even the vast expanse of sea and sky no longer seemed empty and lonely. For it was Paul's world, and where he was, she belonged.

But there were new fears. Every cry from aloft struck fear in her heart, for it might herald an enemy ship that could suddenly invade their lives and take Paul away from her. Before her father had died, it had never occurred to her that such basic things as freedom, happiness, security, even love could come abruptly to an end. Now she knew better. But at night as she lay contentedly in the circle of his arms, her whole body aglow, she would look out at the starlit skies and revel in the wonder of this new world she shared with the man who was her husband, her lover, her family, her everything.

"Aren't you asleep yet, sweet?" he asked drowsily as he gently fondled her breast.

"No," she sighed, "I'm just lying here thinking, that's all."

"Thinking of what?"

"How much I love you," she said simply, kissing his chest and snuggling up to him.

"Now *that* I like to hear," he said and was quiet again for a few moments. Then he broke the silence. "Do you ever think of going back to France?"

She looked up at him in surprise. "Sometimes, but I really have no one there to go back to. Why do you ask?"

"Because I'd hate to think you might be grieving for your homeland and wishing you could go back."

"I no longer have a country," she said. "The only place I want to be in the world is right here in your arms."

"I'm sorry I can't offer you much of a home yet," he said, "but I have a surprise for you, my sweet. I've had a little two-room cabin built for you on the mainland near the fort. It's very humble because there isn't any material available here at the moment except logs, but a little house will be better than living in this cramped cabin. Also, I've hired a middle-aged couple — they seem to be kind, decent folk — to stay with you. They came over on the *St. Louis* to settle in the French colonies, so you'll have your own people around you and won't be alone when I have to go back to sea."

Nicole gave a cry of protest. "But when you have to sail again I don't want to stay behind! I want to go with you!"

"Believe me, I'd like nothing better," he admitted, "but it's selfish of me to risk your safety. A fighting ship is no place for a woman."

"I've been with you all these months, haven't I? I promise I'll stay below and never complain again. Please take me with you, Paul!"

Paul smiled at her gently. "It seems to me I remember your complaining vehemently on more than one occasion about my keeping you cooped up in here all the time — 'like a prisoner' was the way you described it."

"*Mon Dieu!* You're not going to be cruel and punish me for having been such a silly *ra-ra* are you?"

He kissed her tenderly. "Believe me, my sweet, I wouldn't have the heart," he assured her, "but you know I've told you before that the only reason I've kept you in my cabin like this is because there was no other place I could leave you where you'd be safe and well cared for. But now that there is, it'd be foolish to risk that precious little neck of yours by dragging you around the Caribbean with me and exposing you to all the dangers of a privateer ship in the middle of a war."

"But what if the Spaniards should come back? You spoke as though you thought they might."

"Frankly, that is one of my worries about leaving you here," he admitted, "but it's the lesser of the two evils. No matter what we do, there will be some risk, but to take you with me where I *know* there will be fighting would be pure folly."

"Do you think the Spanish will return to Pensacola, then?"

"I'm afraid they will. But in my opinion they have even more reason to try to take Mobile, especially now that there's only a skeleton force left on Dauphin Island to protect the bay. I hope that Bienville and his brothers hurry and strengthen the forts here. I'm glad to see so much activity since the French have taken it over. The more ships sailing in and out of this port, the less inclined the Spanish might be to attempt to retake it."

"But why must you go now?"

"I've already been idle too long, my dear. Of course, officially I'm supposed to have been waiting for the supplies the French promised me, but I confess I've lingered longer than I should have because of you. Nevertheless, I do have an obligation to my men, as well as some unfinished business of my own, as you know. My country's at war with Spain now, so there's even more reason for me to go back to sea and track down Escobar and all the Spanish ships I can find. That's why I like the idea of your being here. You won't be so far away that I can't stop off and see you often. You'd like that, wouldn't you? I promise I won't be gone too long."

"Then you want to settle here? To make Pensacola our home?" she asked, but tears were welling in her eyes as she thought of leaving the *Avenger*. She had come to love this cabin where she and Paul had been so happy She had come to think of this as her home.

"Don't be so sad, my sweet," he comforted her as he wiped away her tears. "Pensacola will be our base for the time being. Our real home — yours and mine — will be in the English colonies, probably in Virginia."

She was too choked up with tears to argue.

"Please, my dear, don't make it more difficult than it already is. I hate the idea of being separated from you, you know. How I'm going to miss not seeing you when I come to my quarters! And my bunk will be intolerable when you're not here beside me. Everything in this cabin reminds me of you now — your sweet presence fills every nook and corner." His voice wavered and broke off.

"I'll be so alone without you!" she protested. "I have a horrible feeling I'll never see you again if you don't take me with you!"

He pulled her to him in a burst of passion. "My dear, sweet little Nicole! I assure you you're going to see a lot more of me. Now that I've found you, all the fires in hell couldn't make me give you up! You're my wife now. I'll always come back to you, no matter where you are! I love you, my sweet lass. Don't ever forget it!"

Chapter 38

Nicole tried to ignore the heat and concentrate on her sewing. The Baudiers had been so good to her that she wanted to help them in whatever way she could to get settled. Of course, Paul had paid them generously to attend her while he was at sea, and he had promised to give them this log cabin once she didn't need it anymore.

Her companions seemed to be a genuinely kind, hard-working couple, and she found Madame Baudier's motherly attitude toward her a new and pleasant experience. Her husband, however, was a quiet, reserved man, who seemed engrossed only in getting his vegetable patch going and making furniture for the house; all in all, it was nice to know there was a man around the place while Paul was gone.

She missed him so much. Today was only the fifth of August, which meant he hadn't even been gone two weeks yet, but it seemed like years to her. The nights were the worst. She had grown accustomed to his vibrant warmth lying there beside her. Now her bed seemed so empty — as empty as her days were without the prospect of seeing his tall figure saunter into the room at any moment.

While Monsieur Baudier was busy in the vegetable garden and his wife occupied with baking in the outdoor oven, Nicole decided she would try to finish making another pair of curtains for the room where the Baudiers slept. She had moved her chair closer to the window to take advantage of the bright light streaming in through the thin, transparent netting and, if possible, catch whatever breeze might be coming in from the bay. Now that it was midsummer, the temperature was warmer than ever. She paused a moment and removed her white lawn cap, brushing back the damp tendrils from her forehead. She let her sewing lie idle in her lap and looked longingly at the sunlit water beyond the glaring white sand. How she wished she could be with Paul on the *Avenger*! She wondered what he was doing at that very moment; in her mind's eye, she could see him standing on the quarterdeck with his shock of sun-bleached hair streaming in the wind and his azure eyes crinkling as he squinted at the endless horizon. She knew he had left her behind because he hadn't wanted to expose her to the dangers of his life at sea, but she would have preferred any peril to this anguish of being separated from him.

The fort stood baking in the midday sun. The tranquil bay was unusually calm for a Saturday afternoon, but there were only two large ships anchored there — the *Dauphine* and the *St. Louis*, which had brought the supplies and people, including the Baudiers, from France. Only a day or two before Paul had sailed, the *Philippe*, along with a transport boat, had been loaded with provisions and most of the newly arrived colonists, who were to be divided between Mobile and the new settlement on the Mississippi. A few, however, like the Baudiers, elected to stay in Pensacola, and from what Paul had told her right before he left, there were now about 250 French soldiers, 100 Company employees and some 60 Negro slaves in the port, not counting the crews on the ships and the few settlers who had remained there.

No one had bothered her and the Baudiers, probably out of fear of incurring the wrath of a man of Dawson's reputation. Also, she now had the cloak of respectability to discourage any unwanted advances; she was the wife of a valuable ally of the French colonies.

As soon as she finished the curtains, she planned to start making some things for Paul out of the bolts of linen and muslin he had let her take from his chests. Her gaze shifted again to the bay. For a moment she thought she saw sails in the distance, but the sun was so bright that it made the horizon shimmer. If only it were Paul coming back to her, but no, it couldn't be — it was too soon ... unless he had been wounded and had had to cut his roving short. Her heart began to pound. But what a fool she was! Paul was right. She was a *mal pensada*, always thinking the worst.

Madame Baudier came in just then, her round face flushed and beaded with perspiration from having hovered so long over the oven, but she wore a satisfied smile as she held out a tray of freshly baked buns in her plump, dimpled hands and urged her charge to help herself.

That delightful odor of freshly baked bread was too much to resist, so Nicole set her sewing aside and joined her housekeeper, welcoming the distraction.

The two women were still sitting and chatting over their cups of hot chocolate and buns when Albert Baudier walked in. From the expression on his face, Nicole immediately sensed that he was mopping his brow from more than the heat.

"God protect us!" he exclaimed anxiously. "I just got word that we should hold ourselves in readiness to take refuge in the fort. Those ships lining up at the entrance of the harbor are Spanish!"

Madame Baudier paled and made the sign of the cross,

but Nicole seized the spyglass from where it hung by a cord on the wall and ran back to the window. A whole fleet was descending upon them!

"They're Spanish all right!" she exclaimed. "But two of them look like our own vessels — the *Comte de Toulouse* and the *Maréchal de Villars*, the ones that were supposed to have taken the Spanish prisoners to Havana." Paul had taught her enough about identifying ships that she could recognize two of the vessels as ones she had seen anchored in the bay before. "The authorities in Havana must have done exactly what Paul predicted they would do. They've probably seized our ships!"

Baudier snorted. "Which only goes to show you what we can expect of them if we fall into their hands!"

Madame Baudier moaned and crossed herself again. "May the good Lord help us all! Let's gather our things and go to the fort at once!"

"For all the good that will do!" exclaimed her husband, displaying a show of emotion that was a rare departure from his usual undemonstrative self. "A pox on those damned Spaniards and on that motley band of thieves and salt smugglers that are supposed to help Châteaugué and his regulars defend us! They're little better than nothing!"

In spite of her own misgivings, Nicole tried to stay calm, though she feared that what Baudier had said was all too true. How often Paul had criticized France's policy of using men forced into service as punishment for real or imagined crimes, instead of encouraging them to give their allegiance freely.

"But we have ships anchored out there in the bay," she said. "Surely they will be able to offer us some defense."

"Ah, *ma petite*, what can two ships do against a fleet with hundreds, perhaps thousands of men?" The elderly man shook his gray head while his wife wrung her hands. "Our only hope now is that the governor gets word of our plight and sends us more ships and men immediately."

"If only Paul were here! He'd know what to do!"

Madame Baudier's white cap bobbed in agreement. "Would that he were!" she echoed. "But I'm afraid not even your husband could get us out of this dilemma! No, my dear, the Spaniards have come to take Pensacola back, and we're lost!"

Chapter 39

Although Nicole and the Baudiers took refuge in the fort with the few other settlers, they found no real security behind the palisades.

There had been no contest between the French and the returning enemy. Châteaugué was like a frustrated lion, chained and helpless before the superior numbers of the Spaniards and the treachery of his own men. The Spanish fleet had swung into sight of Pensacola that Saturday morning with three ships-of-the-line, nine brigantines, and landing forces of nearly two hundred men. They had had the audacity to include in their fleet the two ships that the French had sent to Havana, only now the captured vessels were manned by those same Spanish prisoners!

Almost immediately the pair of French ships anchored in the harbor were lost — the *St. Louis* was seized before it could even defend itself, and the *Dauphine* caught on fire.

To make matters worse, fifty of the convicts who had

been forced into service at the garrison had immediately deserted and gone over to the enemy, informing them that the rest of their companions were ready to deliver up the fort.

Elated, the Spaniards called upon Châteaugué to surrender, and the latter, having discovered that he no longer had any ships in the harbor and had lost a large segment of his troops, felt he had no other recourse but to do so. The French commander blamed his defeat more on the treachery of his soldiers than the greater numbers of the enemy, which he felt he could have overcome if he had had some good men to back him up. With tears of frustration in his eyes, Bienville's younger brother apologized to those men who had remained loyal and to the bewildered settlers and employees of the Company, who suddenly realized they were no longer under the protection of their countrymen but prisoners of the Spaniards! Châteaugué left the fort with his head held high, bitterly declaring that he felt so ashamed over having to surrender to the enemy that he doubted he would ever return to the colonies.

Nicole tried not to give in to despair. Instead, she clung to the hope that help was on the way, but in her heart she knew that even if it was, it would be too late. The day after the Spaniards sailed into Pensacola harbor, the French surrendered the port to them without a blow being struck.

It was evident that the Spaniards had more in mind than simply retaking Pensacola. As Paul had predicted, their true goal was the entire Louisiana colony. On Monday, even as they were loading the French prisoners on boats destined for Havana, Nicole saw three brigantines loaded with heavy forces departing for Dauphin Island.

She wondered where Paul was and what he would do once he heard what had happened. Would he be able to find her if she was transported with the prisoners to Havana or Europe? And even if he knew where she was, would he be able to rescue her? God in heaven! Was she never to know the joy of settling down in some place she could call home with the man she loved?

The prisoners had been waiting in line on the beach almost an hour for the longboats to take them to the brigantines to which they had been assigned, and the sun beating down on them was growing hotter by the minute. But now, just as she and the Baudiers were about to board, a mariner came up to her and called out to the officer in charge of the prisoners to pull her out and hold her under guard at the fort until the admiral called for her.

She was surprised that the order referred to her by name, but the mariner refused to give her any reason for separating her from the others. The Baudiers begged the officer in charge to let her accompany them, but he simply shrugged his shoulders and said the matter was out of his hands. He had to obey orders.

It was a tearful farewell; she embraced the Baudiers and told them not to worry, that she would soon be re-united with them. But even as she bade them good-bye, she knew it was doubtful she would ever see them again. Oh, Paul! Where was he? What could she do alone against a fleet of dour-faced Spaniards? And whatever could their commander want of her?

A horrible thought seized her. Was the lack of other young women in Pensacola the reason the Spanish leader had such an interest in her? Blessed Virgin watch over her! Would he order her to remain and attend him and his officials? After what Paul had told her about his mother and that poor girl, she could expect anything!

She walked beside the guard as he escorted her onto the Spanish flagship and then led her to the admiral's quarters. She half expected to find the Spanish command-er waiting for her alone in his dressing gown. But to her surprise, he was seated, bewigged and resplendent in his red-sashed uniform, behind an ornate mahogany desk with a pile of documents in front of him, while another important-looking official stood off to one side, looking out a porthole.

Though not quite as comfortable or tastefully furnished as Paul's, the cabin was nevertheless spacious and elegant. A large stained-glass window ran across its rear wall.

The guard led her to the desk and held her by the arm while the commander wrote, his quill scratching noisily in the silent cabin.

When he finally looked up at her, however, his face betrayed that he hadn't expected what he saw. "So this is the wench!" he exclaimed, his dark eyes springing to life as they swept over her. "Now I understand! She's enough to turn the head of any man!"

The tall official standing by the porthole turned slowly, his brilliant dark eyes narrowing in a more cautious appraisal as he followed the admiral's gaze.

"Aye, she's comely enough," he mumbled less effusively. "At least she's better than most of the trollops in these parts."

The commander cleared his throat and tried to regain his composure. "Of course, as a favorite of King Philip's, you've seen the best," he said quickly. "So perhaps she's not all that important to us after all, and we can put her to more, ah, practical use here among ourselves and perhaps later even with the garrison?"

The commander turned back to her. "Is it true you are Dawson's whore?" he asked.

Nicole stared at him in bewilderment, taken aback by the unexpected interrogation.

"*Andale, muchacha*, speak up!" he snapped. "And tell us the truth. We have ways of finding out anything we want to know."

"I'm Captain Dawson's *wife*!" she replied at last, drawing herself up indignantly.

The admiral snorted. "Ha! Listen to the airs this

strumpet gives herself! Perhaps what that scoundrel told us was so much bilge water, too!"

The king's representative continued to study her.

"Where's the ruffian who told you about her and Dawson?" he asked. "Send for him!"

"He's right outside," said the commander quickly. "I thought it best to have him on hand to identify her just in case she might try to deny it."

"Good, then call the wretch in and let's see what he has to say."

The admiral rang a small silver bell near his inkstand, and a mariner immediately appeared with a ready salute.

"*Está bien*. You can bring in that English brigand," he said tersely. Then he turned back to Nicole. "You, *señora*, are a French harlot, transported to Louisiana some eight or nine months ago as a condemned felon, *verdad?*"

But before she could reply, he went on, his tone accusing. "There's no need to deny it," he warned her. "All we have to do is pull your sleeve down, and I'm sure the brand will be there to confirm what I've said."

"Never mind about her," interrupted the other official impatiently. "I don't give a damn about the slut's past. Ask her about Dawson."

He strode over to the side of the desk and looked down at her with hard, penetrating eyes. "Is it true that be bought you from a French *concessionaire* on the Mississippi and kept you on board his ship for several months?"

A warning tremor rushed through Nicole as she looked into the tall Spaniard's cold eyes. So they were interested in her because of her connection with Paul. She had to be careful what she told them. Perhaps she had already said too much. She was glad she had had the foresight to remove her wedding ring and sew it in the hem of her petticoat along with the ruby. But how could they know so much about her?

The moment the door opened, however, and Paul's

ex-gunner, Hanson, strutted boldly into the cabin, she knew the answer.

He went directly over to where she stood in front of the admiral's desk and hiked his breeches up as he puffed out his chest and grinned a triumphant greeting.

"Aha, my little French biter! Bet you didn't expect to see me again, did you?" Then he turned to the two Spaniards. "That's her, your lordships. You see, I didn't steer you wrong. That's Dawson's rump, all right!"

The commander looked over at his distinguished colleague and smiled with satisfaction. "*Gracias a Dios!* It's true then. She's the one!"

But the king's representative slapped his sword impatiently. "Bah! So she's an exceptionally pretty whore that Dawson took a fancy to and breached a number of times. This rascal here is probably just exaggerating the facts to save his own neck and ingratiate himself with us. It doesn't mean Dawson gives a damn about what happens to her now that he's finished with her. He can find whores like her for a couple of centavos in any port."

"Beggin' your pardon, your lordship, you're wrong there," the buccaneer broke in quickly. "Dawson paid a hell of a lot more than centavos for this one! And he cares, all right. I have the scars on my back to prove it. You can count them — all thirty-nine of them! And all because this bitch here came on to me one day in the hatchway. She started pushing those blasted catheads of hers up ag'in me and gettin' me all hot and bothered, but when the capt'n came out his quarters and caught me feelin' her up a little, he got so mad he near ran me through on the spot. He's dotty over her, I tell you . . . wouldn't share her with none of us, not even his officers. He kept her locked up in his cabin, he did, like the most priceless swag he'd ever owned. He nearly hanged me, all because of this damn buttock here!"

The somber Spanish lord, however, was not so easily

convinced. "I can't see a man like Dawson behaving like that over any *ramera*, no matter how good a ride she might be!"

Hanson shrugged. "Oh, I'll give the devil his due. Dawson's usually got his noddle on straight, and as a capt'n is as pistol-proof as they come. He knows the sea and knows how to lead his men in a good fight, but this piece of baggage here has him dotty, I tell you. That's what a clever scut can do to a man — even a levelheaded one like Dawson. Once he got to cravin' her muff, he changed."

The admiral's face was creased in a frown. "You sound as though you admired your former captain well enough until he sentenced you to the cat for fraternizing with his whore."

Hanson flushed nervously. "Like I told you, your lordship, Dawson forced me into his service. I don't have nothin' ag'in you Spaniards. That's why I jumped ship first chance I got."

"*Como no!*" sneered the commander. "And you have your documents proving you were forced, of course?" It was obvious he didn't believe that part of the buccaneer's story in the least.

The ex-gunner shifted uneasily from one foot to the other. "I left the ship in such a hurry I couldn't take my papers with me. But surely I've proven my willingness to cooperate with you. Didn't I volunteer this information about Dawson and his doxy of my own free will?"

"Fortunate for you that you did," the commander said sourly. "That's the only thing that has kept us from hanging you. But I think you've exaggerated this wench's importance to Dawson just to save your own skin."

"But, your lordship —"

"Enough, rogue. Stash your lying tongue so we can see whether there's any truth at all in anything you've told us!" The commander turned impatiently to Nicole.

"And you, *muchacha*, what do you have to add to this man's story? Are you really Dawson's woman or just a *puta* he kept on his ship for a while and then sent away?"

Nicole seethed with rage, but her fear of hurting Paul in some way made her cautious. Obviously Hanson didn't know Paul had married her, so perhaps it would be better to swallow her pride and let it stay at that.

"He told me he thought of me as his wife, but then men say many things when in heat," she replied with a shrug of her shoulders, trying to assume a manner she thought Mignon or Murielle might have used under similar circumstances.

The admiral spread out his hands in exasperation. "*Vaya!* Now the *condenada muchacha* is changing her tune!" he exclaimed disgustedly.

But a sinister smile was slowly stealing over the other official's crafty face. "*Quién sabe?* This sudden desire of hers to lessen her importance to Dawson might be the best proof yet that there really is something more binding between them. I think she may have told us the truth the first time we asked her. Dawson just might have married her."

"So what do you want to do about her?" the admiral asked.

"The only thing we can do for the moment," replied the official. "Wait and see. If the wench means something more than a good roll to Dawson, he'll probably be back to get her. If not, it won't be the first time that devil has slipped through our fingers."

"You're wasting your time," Nicole said, feigning a nonchalance she was far from feeling. "He won't be back."

"*Vamos a ver*," smiled the official. "Time will tell." He turned to the admiral. "Meanwhile, we at least know that this wench belongs to Dawson, so I want her kept under lock and key."

"I'd rather hoped ..." The commander cleared his throat uneasily, not wanting to annoy a king's representative, yet unable to ignore the desire he felt spreading to his loins. "Perhaps she could be put to some practical use while we're waiting. My men and I certainly have need of the services of a good *puta*. There's not a female to be found in this *condenado* port, and nothing but wilderness between here and Mexico."

The official scowled. "As long as this woman is connected with that *pirata* Dawson, she's the king's business, and as such, my business, too. Once she's served her purpose, I'll decide what's to be done with her."

"Of course, the wench may be a prisoner-of-war," conceded the admiral, "but I'm sure we need not worry about any reclamations from the French where she's concerned." He leered at the official. "After all, she's just a prostitute — a convict they threw out of their own country, actually — so they certainly won't give a damn about what happens to her."

"But Dawson just might . . . ." muttered the official, stroking his strong chin as he fixed his dark eyes on Nicole. "If he wants her, he'll have to come get her from me and no one else."

"*Por supuesto*, it shall be as you say," nodded the commander. He turned and addressed the mariner who held Nicole. "Take her to the cabin next to Don Rodrigo's and stand guard there. She's to be confined until he orders otherwise."

The admiral watched Nicole's departing figure covetously, and hoped Dawson wouldn't return to claim her. If she proved to be just another insignificant harlot, perhaps Don Rodrigo would amuse himself a little with her and then pass her on down the line. That meant the admiral would be next. Of course, if she was really the wife or mistress of *El Diablo Dorado*, Don Rodrigo was sure to have plans of his own for her.

Chapter 40

Nicole spent that night and the following day locked in the cabin on the admiral's flagship, listening to the triumphant Spaniards celebrating their victory with French wine and brandy they had found among the supplies captured in the fort.

Every time she heard footsteps outside her door, she froze, expecting the commander to burst in.

From her porthole she had watched the other prisoners finally sail off. Eventually they would be released after some agreement was reached with the French for their freedom, but she had little hope for herself.

With a bitter smile she thought how right the admiral had been when he had said her government would have little interest in negotiating for her return. After all, who except perhaps the Baudiers would fret over a French whore that had been left behind in Pensacola?

Of course, she was certain that when Paul heard of her plight, he would come after her and demand an accounting of everyone who had had a part in holding her hostage. He would make them pay dearly.... But no, that was precisely what his enemies were hoping he would do! They wanted to use her as bait to lure him into a trap.

Don Rodrigo didn't come to see her until late the following evening, shortly after she had eaten the supper that had been handed to her by the guard posted at her door — a supper which, she suspected, had come from the captured French supplies.

The tall, dark Spaniard walked into the cabin without so much as a by-your-leave or an apology. For a moment he looked at her with open contempt.

"That buccaneer deserter said you bear the mark of the *incorrigible*," he said coldly, gesturing to her shoulder. "Let me see it."

Nicole just looked at him.

"If it were left to me," he continued, "women like you would be branded on the forehead or the cheek, where everyone could see at a glance what you are." He motioned again to her shoulder. "You heard me," he snapped. "Show me the brand or I'll look for myself!"

Her cheeks hot with rage, she uncovered the fleur-de-lis. Though she kept her eyes averted, she could feel his penetrating gaze boring into her flesh, his dark eyes, huge and heavy-lidded, seeming to echo the Moorish ancestry buried somewhere in his distant past.

After a long, taut silence, her skin began to crawl beneath the unrelenting stare. At last she could bear it no longer and lifted her head defiantly to meet his bold gaze. His eyes, however, were black, unfathomable pools.

"Perhaps Dawson will come back for you," he murmured, his voice strained now as his eyes lingered on the curve of her breast rising softly below the brand. "God knows, a good *puta* isn't easy to come by these days. That's probably why he ended up marrying you." He saw the sudden quiver of her breast as she caught her breath at his words. "Yes, I know you lied to my yesterday," he added in that same abrasive tone. "This morning while

I was checking over some papers the French left behind at the fort, I found a record of your marriage to Dawson. My revenge, it seems, is going to be all the sweeter...." His voice trailed off.

'Your revenge?"

"Surely, if you're Dawson's wife, he must have told you about me?"

Nicole felt the roots of her hair tingle.

"*Mon Dieu!* You're not...?"

"The same — Rodrigo Manuel Escobar y Villegas, *a sus pies, señora,*" he replied with a sarcastic smile and a mock bow. "I am none other than your notorious husband's fatal obsession and soon-to-be nemesis."

Nicole had all she could do to keep her wits about her.

"Then you must know that, whether you hold me prisoner or not, Dawson will hunt you down until he finds you!"

"That's exactly what I hope he tries to do," smiled Escobar, "but I'll be waiting for him on my own terms — and with his pretty little harlot bride as an extra weapon to use against him!"

"I doubt he'll come alone," Nicole replied, trying to keep her tone as steady and impersonal as his. "The fact that I'm the wife of a man who helped the French take Pensacola, and who will do so again if necessary, might be all the more reason for my countrymen to back him up if and when he decides to come after me. Perhaps you should reconsider your plans, for in your desire to bait Captain Dawson into returning here for me, you might very well lose this fort again in the process!"

"You have a ready wit, I see!" sneered Escobar. "But I, too, have considered that possibility. That's why I'm going to take you with me when I sail for Veracruz tomorrow."

Nicole tried to hide her dismay. "Veracruz? But that's in Mexico!"

"Precisely. It's a place where the French would never dare accompany him." The Spaniard's chest expanded with satisfaction as he went on, seeming to delight in her mounting despair. "Besides, the French are going to have their hands full taking care of their own problems. Even as we stand here talking, a fleet of our ships is launching a full-scale attack against the Louisiana Colonies. By now they should be off Dauphin Island, so even if your countrymen felt so inclined, I doubt they would be in any position to help a pirate ally track down his harlot wife! So you see, my little *francesita*, finding you among the prisoners here in Pensacola has been a godsend for us. In your own small way, you may very well serve to divide our enemies. By sending Dawson scurrying after you in the opposite direction from the already poorly defended French colonies, we will only insure a more rapid victory over Dauphin and Mobile, at the same time leaving Dawson to fight his battles alone in the best fortified port in New Spain!"

"That's ridiculous," Nicole retorted, though she was finding it more and more difficult to hide the effect his words were having on her. "My husband is no fool. He'd never attack Veracruz by himself — not even for me."

"Ha!" he retorted. "Even if he doesn't show up, I'll still have you. Either way, I'll have my vengeance — if not on him directly, then through you, his wife!"

"But why ... why in the name of God do you hate him so? Why do you feel such a need to avenge yourself against a man who has been vilely wronged by you?"

A growl rumbled in the Spaniard's throat. "That bastard has hurt me in ways that not even he can imagine!" He paused a moment to regain his composure. "He's hounded me for years now, ever since he took over that ship he rechristened the *Avenger* and began to roam the Caribbean announcing to the world that he was searching for me. Everyone knows of that damn vow of his by now, and every time he sinks a Spanish ship, I feel the weight of that scoundrel's curse like a lodestone around my neck!"

"You mean the weight of your own sins!" Nicole flung back at him contemptuously.

"Bah! So much ado over a queasy female and her foolhardy husband! If that Dawson woman had just let us have a few rounds with her without making such a fuss, nobody would've been the worse. But no. Instead, the idiot went and threw herself overboard. All she did was cost her husband his life and her son a sentence to the galleys. And the damn female wasn't even a virgin! But if I had known she'd spawned such a devil who was going to dog me for so many years afterward, I'd have thrown the bitch overboard myself!"

Nicole stared at the Spaniard in disbelief. "My God! That woman was his mother and the man you killed his father! What did you expect?"

"I certainly didn't expect a lifelong vendetta! I've raped dozens of women and killed double that amount of men and have never had anybody, not even their kin, react the way Dawson has!"

"Then you've known very few real men!" Nicole retorted, livid with rage. No wonder Paul hated him. The man was a reptile with no conscience or remorse.

Escobar threw her a cynical smile. "With what fervor you defend your pirate lover! I hope he cares as much for you."

Nicole remembered that momentary flash of lust she had seen in his eyes. "I care enough to do anything within my power to save him," she proclaimed, then faltered when she saw triumph leaping into his eyes.

"Ah! So you'd do anything to save him?" he echoed nastily.

Every pore of her body tightened, but she forced herself to go on. "If I had to ... if I could be certain no trap would be set for him ..."

Suddenly the Spaniard burst out laughing and caught her roughly by the wrist. "Oh, you would, would you?" he asked mockingly. "Are you, by any chance, offering yourself to me in return for your husband's safety?"

She couldn't reply. The words struck in her throat.

"So you think you can set the terms?" he scoffed. "*Por todos los santos!* What a brazen bitch you are! Why, if I wanted to breach you, I'd do so without as much as a by-your-leave, much less bargain with you!" He twisted her wrist until he brought her to her knees, tears of pain welling in her eyes. "But you can forgo your wiles with me," he went on. "I'm immune to them. I wouldn't soil my hands on a pirate's whore!" He threw her away from him, turned on his heel, and was gone, slamming the door behind him, his laughter echoing in the corridor.

She lay sobbing, the strength drained from her. At last, with great effort, she pulled herself to her feet and for a few moments stood swaying in the center of the cabin. Escobar's laughter still echoed in her ears, but she had meant what she said. She would do anything to save Paul — even die for him. But how does one reason with a man like Rodrigo Escobar, who obviously had no heart to move, or any sense of right or wrong to appeal to? Her wrist still smarted from where he had so ruthlessly twisted it, but the physical pain was nothing compared to the anguish that racked her being.

A part her of called out to Paul to come back for her, to save her from this evil man who had no regrets for any of the horrible things he had done. The other half of her prayed that Paul would stay away. No matter what happened to her, Paul must not risk returning to Pensacola, or worse yet, follow her to Veracruz.

How ironic it would be if the very love she and Paul had found in each other were the cause of their undoing.

PART FIVE

Mexico — August 1719

Chapter 41

Nicole crossed the Gulf to Veracruz in a little cabin next to Rodrigo Escobar's on one of the brigantines. Much to her surprise, no one, not even the grandee himself, disturbed her. Except for the guards who passed her meals to her and attended to the filling and emptying of the her water pitcher and night jar, she saw no one.

The week's confinement in such close quarters, alone with her thoughts and with nothing to distract her, made her fears and speculations all the more unbearable. Had her anxiety been only for herself, it would have been bad enough, but her worries over Paul were overwhelming. If the Spaniards caught him, it would mean certain death. Throughout the Spanish empire there was a price on the head of *El Diablo Dorado*.

La Villa Rica de la Veracruz — the Rich Town of the True Cross — was the oldest port in Mexico. It was there that Hernán Cortés had begun his conquest exactly two hundred years before. Built on a low beach of barren sand, it had been attacked and captured several times by pirates, been battered repeatedly by tropical storms, and even been abandoned for its unhealthy conditions, but it had tenaciously survived, mainly because it was the chief link between the Mexican colonies and Spain. Its two centuries of growth, however, seemed to have done little for it. Nicole found it a hot, dismal place. The heart of the town was the main plaza with the usual cathedral, *palacio*, and a few solid government buildings, but clustered along the muddy side streets were the fragile palmetto huts and one-room adobes of the poverty-stricken Indians and mestizos who eked out their livings on the docks, while beyond the town lay the thick tropical jungles where even the boldest of men hesitated to venture.

A grandee like Escobar, however, was invited to stay as a guest at the *palacio*, and he accepted, but only on the condition that he be allowed to keep his prisoner with him in an adjoining room under guard instead of turning her over to the port authorities to be imprisoned in the fort dungeons. This request, Nicole felt, was not made out of any consideration for her, but rather to insure that she would be accessible to no one except through him.

From her room she could sit by the window with a large palmetto fan and look out over the busy harbor. She had seen so many bays these past few months that they all looked alike to her now, but this one was by far the best fortified. No primitive wooden fort with a palisade around it, Fort San Juan de Ulua was a gloomy monster of brick and mortar crouching on a reef in front of the town, looking like a medieval castle with even a dungeon to complement it.

At the sight of that ominous fortress and the two galleons, the brigantine, and the three-masted square-rigged ship-of-the-line all riding anchor in the harbor, Nicole's heart sank. Paul would have no chance if he tried to sail into such an enemy's nest.

No, their only chance lay in her escaping and getting to him. Yet escape for her was all but out of the question.

Don Rodrigo stopped in once or twice the first day to have an Indian laborer put bars on her window, and the following afternoon he returned with the two bundles of clothing she had taken with her from Pensacola.

"I'm letting you keep your personal apparel," he told her acidly, "but the rolls of linen and muslin have been confiscated as property belonging to the Spanish government. Frankly, I expected to find at least one or two pieces of jewelry — a wedding ring perhaps. But then, why should Dawson waste anything of value on a *ramera*? As the Bible says, one shouldn't cast pearls before swine!"

Nicole gave him wry smile, determined not to let his barbs sting her. "Now I know what they mean when they say the devil quotes the scriptures," she retorted icily and turned away.

Rodrigo Escobar seemed to find pleasure in tormenting her. Sometimes she felt his hatred for her was a thing apart from his hatred for Paul — that he resented her for some other reason; not only because she loved his enemy, but because of her supposed past. Yet this man was a notorious rake. How was it possible that he could suddenly be so squeamish about a woman's reputation?

In some ways Escobar seemed to be a dark reflection of Paul Dawson. Though the Spaniard was some fifteen years his senior, he was nevertheless a formidable foe. Only a couple of inches shorter than Paul, he was still tall, well built, and quite distinguished looking. There was an agility in his movements, too, which, like Paul's, bore witness to years of living by the sword.

But there the resemblance ended. For the Spaniard's eyes were dark and hard, and his lips, though slashed boldly across his angular face, seemed to wear a perpetual sneer, as though he was scornful of the world around him. She wondered whether he was capable of love ... if there was anyone in his life who really mattered to him.

The third day she was in Veracruz, a *norte* hit the

port. Nicole listened uneasily to the wind howling and the shutters rattling, but the sturdy *palacio* weathered the storm as it probably had so many others.

Afterward, however, the town looked more woebegone than ever. Many of the huts had collapsed, and there was debris everywhere. At least the storm had cleared the air, and the temperature was a little cooler than it had been, but the gray skies and restless waves lapping at the fort continued to bear witness to the *norte* that had just passed through.

Don Rodrigo seemed to take the inclement weather in stride, arranging for another shipment of silver to be sent from his mines in Zacatecas to the port so it could be taken by galleon to his contacts in Spain.

Two days after the storm, another brigantine dropped anchor in the harbor. Later that same day, Escobar paid Nicole one of his unannounced visits. The heat was beginning to build again as the effects of the storm waned, so she sat by the barred window with her fan, trying to catch what breeze she could.

The look of elation on her captor's face unsettled her.

"I have news of your *pirata*!" he boasted as he approached her, waving a dispatch triumphantly. "Dawson was captured on the very same day we landed here! It seems he attacked one of the brigantines that was taking the French prisoners to Havana, thinking you were on it. They say that when he learned I had brought you with me to Veracruz, he was like a madman. He sent the liberated French settlers and employees home to Louisiana on the captured brigantine and immediately set out for Veracruz. Unfortunately for him, he ran into a bad storm in the Gulf — perhaps the one that finally worked its way down to us a few days ago — and crippled his ship. Meanwhile two of our vessels came upon him and after a brief fight were able to sink the *Avenger* and take him and most of his men prisoners. The larger ship went on with him and his crew to Havana, while the brigantine that dropped anchor in the bay this morning brought us the glad tidings. There's no more *Avenger* and no more *Diablo Dorado!*"

Nicole caught the back of the chair to steady herself. "That can't be true," she protested. "His capture has been rumored many times before, and it has always been just that — a rumor"

Escobar laughed, enjoying the anguished look on her pale face.

"Rest assured, *señora*, Dawson and his crew were taken in chains to Havana, where they were immediately tried and hanged for piracy. My only regret is that I wasn't there to have a hand in the execution. The sentence for piracy is hanging and beheading, so that impressive golden head of your lover's will be rotting on a pike over the palace gates for a long time to come — until it's only a sun-bleached skull hanging there to remind everyone of what happens to those who defy the might of Castile."

"I don't believe it," Nicole insisted. "Someone is lying. Perhaps it's you, just to torment me all the more."

"I doubted the news myself at first," the Spaniard admitted, "but they knew I would, so they sent me proof. You more than anyone should be able to verify the credibility of this dispatch for me. Was this cut from your husband's head or not?"

He held out his hand, palm up to her. Nicole stared in horror at the lock of familiar bright gold hair. A vision of Paul standing on the deck of his ship, his blond hair tousled in the wind, flashed across her mind as her knees buckled, causing her to clutch the chair.

"You know damn well if Dawson had been alive he'd have never let them cut this from his head, no?" She heard Escobar's gloating voice coming from a great distance.

"Guard! *Ven acá!* She's fainted."

Nicole could feel the cold tiles of the floor against her cheek. Escobar's gruff voice was in her ear. "Dawson was a fool," he muttered, "to have lost his life for a whore!"

Vaguely she heard him ordering the guard to pick her up and put her on the bed.

He was hovering over her now, loosening the lacings of her bodice and telling the guard to fetch someone to help attend her.

"So he was coming to get you," he murmured, more to himself than to her. "He was really going to try and rescue you!"

A woman's voice sounded in the doorway, and Escobar answered her, but at that moment the dark waves blotted out everything and she heard no more.

Chapter 42

Now that his archenemy had been apprehended and he
had finished arranging for his silver to be transported
to Spain, Don Rodrigo had no reason to remain in Veracruz. That very next morning, therefore, he decided to
hire a carriage to take him to his villa, where the climate
would be more agreeable and he could enjoy all the com-
forts of his luxurious home.

With his usual disregard for his prisoner's physical and
spiritual well-being, he ordered that she be carried to the
coach so they could proceed without further delay. When
his host suggested that the grieving widow might be too
ill to travel, Escobar had simply shrugged his shoulders
and replied that grief had never killed anyone.

The grandee was in high spirits — so much so that
he graciously invited a friend of his, also about to return
to his home in Puebla, to accompany him and Nicole
in their private carriage. Since Puebla was located halfway
up the same road that ran from Veracruz to Mexico City,
the route was fairly well traveled. It was dotted with villages and stagecoach stops, but there were also long

stretches of wilderness and, from what Nicole could gather, danger of brigands. Runaway slaves, hiding in the jungles of that region, were known to operate as guerilla bands who preyed on travelers, so the two Spaniards were heavily armed. As soon as dusk fell, they immediately sought the refuge of an inn.

Though Heriberto Moreno's rank was not as impressive as his friend's, he was a wealthy aristocrat, born in the mother country, which gave him superiority over those *criollos* of equal rank born in the colonies. Like Escobar, Moreno enjoyed the title of *grande* which, as the highest class of Spanish nobility, gave him vast influence and privileges, including the honor of being addressed as "my cousin" by the king, though he could not leave his head covered when his monarch spoke to him — an honor accorded only to a few lords like Rodrigo Escobar.

Of medium height, but appearing much shorter because of his corpulence, Don Heriberto was some seven or eight years younger than Escobar. As soon as he saw Nicole, he was completely taken with her, and much to her discomfort, kept stealing furtive glances at her. Even with her eyes closed, she could feel his dark gaze raking her from head to foot. He assumed, however, that she was his friend's mistress as well as his prisoner-of-war, and Escoabar did nothing to correct that impression. In fact, he seemed to encourage it.

Nicole sat beside Escobar in the coach with her head against the high back of the leather seat, deliberately keeping her eyes closed. Perhaps if she pretended to be asleep, Escobar would leave her in peace, and she could be alone with her sorrow. She didn't care where her jailer took her. Without Paul, nothing mattered. One place was as good as another. Escobar had said her grief would not kill her, but what did he know?

She wished Moreno would stop looking at her, though she wondered what he found so fascinating about her. Her face was unnaturally pale and drawn, and her eyes red and swollen from constant weeping. Her traveling dress of dove-gray silk did nothing to add color to her cheeks; she wore it because it reflected what she felt.

"The *muchacha* seems to be genuinely heartbroken," she heard Moreno comment to Escobar as their conversation swung around to her.

"She'll get over it," Don Rodrigo replied tersely. "The only feelings a whore has are in her vagina!"

They exchanged the latest news at court, the recent *novedades* of Puebla and Mexico City, and of course, Don Rodrigo's twin victories. He boasted of the recapture of Pensacola and especially about his personal triumph over his longtime enemy, the pirate Dawson.

Occasionally she could feel them glance in her direction, but she continued to keep her eyes shut, pretending to be asleep. From her knowledge of French and Latin, she had little difficulty in understanding what they said. And since they didn't realize how much she could understand, they spoke more freely in her presence than they might have done otherwise.

If only she *could* sleep, then perhaps she would be able to blot out Escobar and everything that had happened, perhaps she could dream and even seem to be with Paul again. The swaying of the carriage reminded her of the rocking of a ship ... of lying in Paul's bunk with his warm, hard body stretched out beside her.

Her dozing was cut short as she heard the men discussing her.

"And what do you plan to do with your *francesita* when you get to Puebla?" Moreno asked Escobar.

"Oh, I'll probably keep her with me for a while," Don Rodrigo replied easily. "The taste of revenge is too sweet for me not to savor it a little longer."

His friend snickered knowingly. "I can well imagine, especially when it comes in so lovely a package. But what about Doña Inés? How do you think she'll feel about your keeping a mistress under your roof when it's so close to your betrothal?"

There was a disdainful grunt. "We're not married yet,

and even then, I'm not going to let Inés or any woman dictate terms to me."

Don Heriberto chuckled. "Knowing you, I can believe that, but Doña Inés looks like she has the makings of a jealous wife."

"Bah! Our marriage will only be a political one."

"For you, perhaps, but I think your intended hopes it will be more than that. As a matter of fact, I wouldn't be surprised if she had something to do with the king's pressing you for the match in the first place."

"You think so?"

"*Vaya!* Don't you see how she looks at you? Maybe I'm wrong, but I have a feeling she's a fiery one under that frosty exterior of hers."

Escobar reacted as though the subject annoyed him. "Well, I'm sorry for her if she thinks she'll put a ring through my nose as well as on my finger! She should know me better than that!"

"*Tienes razón.* Surely she can't expect a man of your reputation with the ladies to be satisfied with just one woman. But she's a proud one. I'd at least be discreet."

"Oh, I intend to give her her place. I'll always give her the respect due her as my wife, of course, but my private life will be my own. She'll have to understand that."

"Has it occurred to you that you might pass the *francesita* on to some friend you could trust — like me, for example? In that way appearances could be served, yet you could continue to visit her on the sly as often as you wish. The wench looks like she has more than enough to serve both of us very well."

Escobar cleared his throat noisily. "We'll see. Actually, I've been toying with the idea of turning her over to the authorities when I've finished with her. After all, as Dawson's wife, she's an enemy of Spain — a prisoner-of-war."

"Give her to the Inquisition? *Qué barbaridad!* Surely you're joking? All that beauty destroyed on the rack? What a waste! Sell her to some bordello if you don't want to let her off too easy, but *en nombre de Dios, hombre*, not the Inquisition! A wench like this was meant to be stretched out on a man's bed, not the rack!"

"Yet it's what the harlot really deserves," Escobar scowled. "She might be pleasant enough to dally with for a while, but she should be punished for her complicity with Dawson. If it were left to me, I'd have hanged her right next to him."

"Come now, there aren't gibbets enough in the world to hang every whore a pirate's breached in his lifetime!"

"True, but this one was his wife, remember. And so close to him, it seems, that he was captured while trying to rescue her."

"Well, before you go surrendering her to the tender mercies of the Holy Office, at least let me have her for a few days. If it's punishment you want, two experienced rakes like us certainly ought to be able to think of some intriguing ways to make her repent her past sins. Believe me, she shouldn't be able to crawl out of bed once two *toros* like us finish giving her her daily comeuppance!"

Escobar's reply was a noncommittal grunt.

Moreno continued for a few minutes more, trying to rouse some enthusiasm from Escobar for the idea of sharing his captive mistress and describing in such vivid detail what he would like to do to her that she was afraid they would see her trembling and know she had been listening.

When no further response was forthcoming from Don Rodrigo, however, his friend finally fell silent, and soon the only sounds were the monotonous pounding of the horses' hooves and the steady creak of the coach.

Nicole's past was gone now, her present suspended in agony, and her future ominous. She didn't want to go on, but she had promised Paul that no matter what happened, she would continue her life. Even in this hostile country, she felt the cloak of his love around her. No matter where she was, he was there with her. Of course, she knew that the possibility of her getting away from her enemies was slim indeed, and the chances of her ever reaching the lawyer Paul had told her to seek out in Virginia were even more remote. The tiny linen pouch with the bright gold hair seemed to burn the spot where it lay hidden between her breasts. Whenever she felt unable to go on, she would touch it. It seemed to give her courage, to impart to her some of Paul's strength.

Chapter 43

Puebla might not have been the "City of the Angels" that its official title proclaimed it to be, but it certainly was a city of grandees. Its cool mountain climate was a welcome relief from the hot, humid lowlands and made it the choice spot for the cream of New Spain's aristocracy.

Nestled in the foothills of snowcapped volcanoes, it was the jewel of the Mexican colonies — home of the dons, those undisputed lords of the land. Already nearly two hundred years old, Puebla had an Old World atmosphere, and was reminiscent of Spain's fortress city of Toledo, with its massive palaces, arched doorways, huge stone churches aglitter with gold-leaf altars and bejeweled saints, and luxurious villas of gleaming tile and quiet patios adorned with verdant foliage and tinkling fountains. For Rodrigo Escobar and his countrymen, it was a world of ease and comfort, with legions of cowering brown-skinned servants to do their bidding.

The first thing Escobar did on arriving at his elegant villa near the entrance of the city was turn Nicole over to his elderly cousin, Señora Concepción Viuda de Guzman, who had been enjoying his hospitality ever since she had become a widow some nine years before. A huge raw-boned woman who always dressed in rustling black silk, Señora Guzmán hovered near her constantly and even slept in the same room with her. What's more, Don Rodrigo continued to post a guard outside her door.

Señora Guzmán made no secret of her repugnance at having to be the "chaperone of a whore," and she loudly protested to Don Rodrigo, with little regard as to whether Nicole heard her or not. Nevertheless, after all the years of protection and comfort that her cousin had extended her, she could hardly refuse his request. Besides, she adored her handsome *primo*, and though her piousness made her disapprove of his lifestyle, she had long since accepted his shortcomings with a tolerant shrug of her shoulders. She had conceded that a man of so virile a temperament naturally had his needs. Of course, he had explained to her that the wench was his prisoner, and intimated that he was holding on to her mostly for political reasons, but Concepción Guzman knew her relative well enough to suspect that his interest in so pretty a wench had to be more than just political. She consoled herself, however, with the thought that once he married Doña Inés, the *francesita* would have to leave the villa, so the arrangement couldn't last too long. Meanwhile she warned Nicole in no uncertain terms that, as long as she was in charge, she would not tolerate any trickery.

The day after Nicole arrived, Escobar ordered his cousin to see about obtaining an appropriate wardrobe for his prisoner so he could escort her around town "without being ashamed of being seen with her."

Dutifully the new *dama de compañía* went about her assignment, immediately bringing a dressmaker to Nicole to take the necessary measurements and discuss the designs. Escobar himself, however, chose the material from samples that the *modista* brought. He did so quickly and methodically, coldly appraising the bolts of satins and brocades opened out for his inspection. He fingered one or two, stared thoughtfully at Nicole, and then pointed hurriedly to a gold brocade and a dark olive satin.

"These will do," he said briskly. "I want one ready for Monday morning, the other by Thursday."

The dressmaker began to protest that it would be impossible to finish in so short a time, but he simply turned on his heel and was gone, leaving Señora Guzmán to placate the agitated *modista* with the promise of a special bonus if Don Rodrigo's deadlines were met.

Later the grandee returned. Immediately his cousin rose, intending to retire discreetly so he could be alone with his paramour, but he motioned to the woman to stay where she was. "I want the girl ready to go out with me to the *zarzuela* tonight," he said tersely. "See what you can do with what she has."

"By all the saints, Rodrigo! What's the hurry? How can I dress her decently on such short notice?"

"The wench isn't decent to begin with," he retorted curtly, "but she's pretty enough to get by in sackcloth if need be. I'll send you a necklace she can use. After all, everyone will know who she is and they'll make allowances."

Nicole knew her wishes didn't count in the least, yet she ventured to interrupt their discussion. "I don't care to go out all," she said, "but it you insist, I'd like to wear black."

Escobar glared at her, but shrugged his shoulders and acquiesced. "*Está bien*, be the mourning widow on your first night out. It'll only serve to remind everyone who you are and that your damned husband is dead now."

She winced and turned away to hide the tears that sprang to her eyes. The wound was still too fresh. Just the mention of Paul brought the dull ache back. The pain was always there.

Chapter 44

The light opera was only the first of a series of events in public places that Escobar forced her to attend with him. He paraded her around on his arm — a flamboyant badge of his manhood for all of Puebla to see and admire, while he gloated over his recent victories and presented her as his "prize-of-war." Yet when he was alone with her, he treated her contemptuously.

Everywhere he went with her, people stared — the women whispering behind their fans and the men raking her with covetous eyes. Yet when she saw how Don Rodrigo glowed with satisfaction as he strutted her before his peers, she understood at last why he had said that she would enable him to taste the sweetest fruits of his revenge. If Paul was watching them now, how he must be suffering to see her a captive in this hostile land and dependent upon the whim of his archenemy!

She thought of Paul by day and dreamed of him by night. Everything seemed to remind her of him — a head of yellow hair, a tall, broad-shouldered silhouette, a pair of striking blue eyes — and then suddenly she would realize it had only been her imagination. Then the wounds would open, and she would gently caress the golden lock of hair nestled close to her heart and no longer be able to focus her eyes for the tears that clouded them.

On Monday he insisted she don her new green satin gown and go to a fiesta with him at Don Heriberto's villa. It didn't take her long to realize that all the women present were either courtesans or concubines.

At least there was a little more propriety than she expected. Though the men drank freely and were less guarded with their language, there was no passing around of the women or orgies such as Renaud would have had. There were, however, many coarse insinuations and some crude advances made by the men on their respective partners, but the women coquettishly accepted such attentions and occasionally even stole away to the privacy of the patio or one of the other rooms.

Don Rodrigo sat with his arm around her most of the evening, joining in with a few gruff comments of his own. Though she couldn't understand many things they said, she suspected she was the butt of some of their jokes.

Once Escobar laughed and, with a comment that set his companions to guffawing, let his hand drop from her shoulder into her bodice, where he cupped one of her breasts. When everyone saw how startled and embarrassed she was, they laughed again, while Escobar continued to smile and tightened his grip on her breast as a warning to her that she had better not make a scene.

That had been the first time he had touched her since the first day in the cabin when he had made her bare her shoulder; as before, she felt the lust in his touch and saw the desire smoldering in his eyes.

When he took her by the arm to leave, she could feel his hand tremble and his breath quicken, yet as always, he sat apart from her in the carriage all the way back to his villa. On their arrival, he turned her over to Señora Guzmán and, muttering an oath, hurried off to his room.

Every morning he took her riding in his open carriage, but he would not let her cover her head with a hat or mantilla, since he wanted her flaming hair to be seen by everyone so there would be no doubt who she was — that redheaded *francesita*, Dawson's harlot widow, Don Rodrigo's captive mistress, and all the other even more insulting names she had heard people whisper when they pointed her out as she passed.

Strangely enough, Escobar had not tried to force himself on her yet. Somehow that fact did not make her feel any more secure. There was something about her situation with the Spanish grandee that made her uneasy — something that left her anxiously waiting for the ax to fall. His slurs about not wanting to soil his hands on her didn't match the expression in his eyes whenever he looked at her, nor did it ring true when she considered his notorious past.

It all seemed part of some cruel game. He obviously wanted to keep her on tenterhooks, awaiting the moment when he would finally give in to the desire she sensed increasing in him with each passing day. For though he might rudely shove her away with contemptuous sneers and accuse her of being too far beneath him even to touch, she knew he wanted her. Experience had taught her to recognize such things in a man. Rodrigo Escobar was no foppish courtier like Legarde. He was an animal who had raped many women over the years, and though he was in his midforties now, he was undeniably still in his prime. If he hadn't forced himself on her yet, it was probably because of his strange Spanish pride, which seemed to run the gamut from fastidious snobbery to outright brutality. There had been several times in the week since they had arrived in Puebla when she had felt him near the breaking point, but always he had thrust her away at the last moment.

Sometimes she was surprised at the self-control that this basically carnal man seemed capable of exerting when she knew only too well the degree to which he had so often indulged his sexual appetites. Of course, ten years could change a person. But in Escobar's case, she doubted it. She had encountered enough lust and brutality, and she knew they were seething beneath Don Rodrigo's seemingly indifferent exterior. He was a powder keg about to explode, and she dreaded the thought of what would happen when his true nature won out.

That following week he dragged her around on another whirl of social events, taking her to the theater again — this time to see a Cervantes play — and then to the bullfights, a concert, and several more *fiestas*. As an important nobleman, responsible to King Philip in the mother country, he enjoyed a prestigious position in New Spain. His actions were never questioned, and if he wished to flaunt his beautiful prize-of-war around Puebla, he was more envied than censured. Of course, some of the matrons might have cast disapproving eyes in Nicole's direction, trying to mask their jealousy of her bright young beauty with scorn while they watched the admiration kindling in their men's eyes. But then, the Spanish women of the ruling class seemed accustomed to hiding their true feelings behind an exterior of feminine submission to the unquestionable male dominance. For although they pretended not to be aware of it, they knew that virtually every man in the colony had a girl tucked away somewhere. But always it was the woman who was condemned in such liaisons, rarely the man.

Nicole found herself wondering about Escobar's fiancée, Doña Inés. If she was really as proud and taken with Escobar as Don Heriberto had said, she must be furious at being forced to sit on the sidelines and watch him squiring his mistress around town instead of her. If only that proud lady knew how little there really was between Don Rodrigo and his captive! For that matter, what would any of the people who were gossiping about her or envying Don Rodrigo say if they knew she shared her alcove with that black crow Señora Guzmán? And even Señora Guzmán would be amazed to learn that her cousin had never touched his prisoner all those times she had discreetly left them alone in the bedchamber!

Whenever Escobar made his crude jokes and rudely fondled her in front of the others, she sensed something in him that puzzled her, even frightened her. It was hard to believe that he could despise her so much that he would even deny himself his own gratification. What a strange, morose man this Rodrigo Escobar was! Trapped in his dark world of hatred and revenge, perhaps he was as much a prisoner as she was.

Chapter 45

At the start of her second week in Puebla, Nicole got her first glimpse of Doña Inés. Escobar had given her his permission to go to the *mercado* as long as she went well guarded, so for the first time since she had become a prisoner-of-war, she had finally been able to go somewhere without him. Of course, Señora Guzmán stayed close by her side while Escobar's henchman followed closely behind.

But Nicole knew that the moment to make a bid for freedom had not arrived, so she did nothing to make her jailers think that escape even crossed her mind. Let them think she had resigned herself to her situation; after all, she didn't want any more restrictions than there already were. If and when the right moment presented itself, she would have a better chance for success if no one expected her to make the attempt. Meanwhile, she listlessly went about the motions of living within the narrow confines of her captivity, caring little for the social whirl that Escobar imposed upon her to indulge his own warped sense of honor, and trying as best she could to ignore the contempt with which she was treated by everyone around her.

Yet despite her decision to pay as little attention as possible to things over which she had no control at that moment, she was not prepared for the hatred she felt directed at her when her path finally crossed with Escobar's *prometida*. The look in Doña Inés's dark almond-shaped eyes cut through the air between them like a sharp-edged sword as the black-haired, ivory-skinned beauty stared at her across the market stalls.

Nicole had sensed the Spanish woman was there before she had even turned around and seen her. She nudged Señora Guzmán discreetly. "Who is that woman over there who seems to be staring at us?" she asked in a low voice.

Her chaperone glanced in the direction that Nicole indicated, and her sallow complexion lost whatever color it had. With a quick flick of her fan, she turned aside and began fanning herself nervously, covering the lower half of her face as she replied, "You should ask! Now there's a *gran dama* — Inés María de los Angeles Ochoa Viuda de Alvarez!"

Nicole was duly impressed. She was beginning to get accustomed to the long, pompous names, but the length of this one with its strange-sounding assortment of names especially confused her. "Did you say *Viuda*?" she asked in surprise. "That's part of your name, too, isn't it? Is she a relation of yours?"

Señora Guzmán snorted. "Would that she were! What a *tonta* you are! Don't you know that *viuda* means 'widow'? I'm the 'widow of Guzmán' — Doña Inés is the widow of a man named Alvarez. The poor girl married young and she was left a widow with a year-old infant. But she'll have no trouble in finding another husband. If my cousin is foolish enough to let her slip through his fingers, there will be suitors galore to take his place. She's young, *bella*, and belongs to one of the oldest and richest families of New Spain."

"If she's so fortunate, why should she hate me so much — a poor widow held captive in a foreign land with no family, no money, not even a man to call my own. She does wrong to judge me so harshly. I know our countries are at war, but I'm not here of my own free will. Surely she must know that."

Señora Guzmán shot her an accusing look. "She knows a lot more about you than just your nationality, you little minx. Everyone in Puebla knows you were that pirate Dawson's woman and that now you're Don Rodrigo's whore. You've made yourself a powerful enemy in Doña Inés. For a saintly lady like her, your existence is an offense!"

Nicole flushed more from indignation than shame. "Doña Inés ... you ... of all the people here do me an injustice," she said, her voice quavering in spite of herself. "What do any of you really know about me to judge me as you do?" If that foolish, jealous woman only knew! If all of them only knew!

"For myself, I do what Don Rodrigo orders me to do." Señora Guzmán shrugged. "I try to keep my distaste for my task to myself, but Doña Inés is not one to stand idly by when she feels she's being slighted. Just wait and see. If she and my cousin contract nuptials, I'm sure one of her first conditions will be that he get rid of you."

Nicole shot her a cynical smile. "Believe me, I'd like nothing better. I do wish her luck!"

She cast another glance at the beautiful, elegant woman attired in black silk frosted with silver lace from the shoulder-length mantilla to the front panel dividing her panniers. The Spanish woman stood frozen beside one of her servants, a bolt of muslin in her hand. And she still glared.

Nicole tried to hide her burning cheeks behind her hand-painted fan as Señora Guzmán caught her by the arm and began to pull her down the aisle of vendors.

They were passing a display of religious items — votive

candles, small replicas of saints in brightly painted clay, and wooden carvings — when Nicole paused in front of a rosary of white-veined onyx with a silver cross hanging from its center, and fingered it admiringly.

"Do you think Don Rodrigo would object to my going to church sometimes?" she asked. "I say my prayers every day, of course, but I miss attending mass and sometimes I feel the need to confess myself."

"I'm sure you do," Señora Guzmán replied.

"I would have gone if it'd been possible," Nicole said defensively, wearying of the other woman's constant sneers. "For the past year I've been either in prison or in places where no churches were available."

"Here in New Spain we God-fearing, decent women not only have our private chapels at home, but attend church several times a week," declared Señora Guzmán. "Doña Inés, for example, not only never misses mass on Sundays and holy days, but goes to the cathedral to pray every afternoon. That's where she was coming from just now. They say she prays for the soul of her late husband. *Pobrecita!* You could benefit from her example. I confess I can't understand for the life of me how you French with your frivolous, godless ways can profess to belong to the same church as we do!"

But Nicole only half heard her chaperone's tirade of criticism that followed. She was growing more and more accustomed to the elderly woman's recriminations. Besides, she was too engrossed in her own thoughts. The memory of Doña Inés's eyes lingered. It was disquieting to learn that she had yet another enemy in this alien land where she was as much, or more, of an outcast than she had been in her own.

Chapter 46

Only once did Nicole feel she might have made a friend
in New Spain. It was in one of those rare moments when
Escobar left her alone — or rather, was forced to leave
her for several minutes — although she was surrounded
by close to a hundred people and still discreetly guarded
by one of the grandee's men.

They were attending a lavish reception at the *palacio*
in Puebla, and Escobar had insisted that she wear the
gold brocade he had ordered for her — a simple, tight-
bodied gown, its skirt falling in a shimmering cascade
over the farthingale, a fashion still popular with the Spanish aristocracy. The grandee had been reluctant to leave
her even in a room full of people, but on the insistence
of the viceroy, who wanted to see him alone for a moment,
Escobar caught her impatiently by the arm and led her
to an as yet unoccupied table in a corner of the large
hall, where a white-wigged, uniformed lackey stood at
attention.

"Wait here," he said curtly. "If I don't find you sitting

in this exact spot when I return, you'll pay dearly, I promise you."

As he left, he paused to say a few hurried words to the lackey.

"I can see why you hate to tear yourself away from that new mistress of yours," Nicole heard the official tease Escobar as the latter hung back, still hesitant to go into the adjoining room, his eyes fixed on her. "Frankly, I rather expected you to come with Doña Inés tonnight, but I admit your *francesita* is a delicious piece. What do you intend to do with her once you have formalized your *compromiso* with Señora Alvarez?"

"I'm thinking about it," was all Escobar muttered in reply.

"*Bueno*, I suppose you deserve to savor the fruits of your victory now that you have finally beaten that rascal Dawson," chuckled the portly viceroy as he nudged his guest along to his study, "and I dare say your pretty little mistress is the tastiest fruit of them all, *verdad?*

The lackey brought her a glass of liqueur. The chocolate taste was pleasant, but she only took a couple of sips and then sat uneasily in the straight-backed gilded chair, trying to take in her surroundings. She found herself calculating how far she might get if she just got up and walked out of the *palacio* at that moment.

"*Con su permiso, señora.* Allow me to introduce myself — José Luís Ruíz, your humble servant. Would you mind if I sat here for a moment?"

A tall, lean Spaniard with a Vandyke beard and a glass of sherry in his hand was smiling at her from across the damask-covered table.

"I'm waiting for my escort," she replied in her imperfect Spanish.

"Ah, you mean Don Rodrigo?" The impeccably dressed young man flipped up the tails of his rose-colored velvet frock coat and sat down opposite her. "I've been observing you for over a week now. Fortunately, Don Rodrigo has been very kind in offering us numerous glimpses of you since he brought you back to Puebla with him."

Nicole stirred uncomfortably in her chair. "Well, if you know Señor Escobar, you probably also know he won't like it if he finds you sitting here with me on his return," she replied coolly.

The newcomer shrugged his aristocratic shoulders. "This is a public gathering," he said easily. "Why should he object if I sit at a table that has been furnished for the convenience of the guests?"

"Do as you wish, *monsieur*," sighed Nicole, wishing this intruder would go away and let her resume her musings. "I certainly am in no position to stop you. Since you say you've been observing Don Rodrigo and me for a while now, you probably know I'm a prisoner-of-war, and as such, I have no say in the company I keep, beginning with Don Rodrigo."

The young man smiled and nodded his head knowingly. "Yes, I know all about you," he admitted, "and forgive me if I presume to say that it grieves me to see a woman of your obvious breeding and beauty in what must be a very awkward position. Or am I misinterpreting your feelings about your situation? Perhaps you enjoy the type of attention Don Rodrigo showers upon you?"

"I assure you, *monsieur*, I don't welcome the attentions of a man who helped bring about the death of my husband and has made me his unlawful prisoner."

"If I could be of any service —" She felt his hand cautiously brush her arm, and she forced herself to remain perfectly still. She was alone now, so she could not afford to close the door on any possible means of escape without at least considering it.

"I fear there would be too much danger involved to ask you or anyone to take such a risk," she replied carefully.

"I'm not without connections," he murmured through the delicate mustache and pointed beard that framed his sensuous lips. "You have only to command me, *señora.*"

Nicole dared not look directly at him, but as she covered her face discreetly with her fan, she cast him a curious glance. His dark, lean face was not unpleasant. Although the expression she saw there was unmistakable, his appraisal was not as offensive as most. She reminded herself that this was not the moment to discourage anyone who might want to help her.

"I'm hardly in any position to command...." she parried, keeping her head bent demurely behind her fan. If only Escobar would stay away from the table long enough for her to see what this man had to offer her — and the price he would expect for it!

"That's not true," her admirer said quickly as the pressure of his hand increased on her arm. "Try me. Ask what you will."

"As long as I'm a prisoner, I dare not ask for anything," she insisted cautiously.

"Aha! What you're saying is you'd like to escape, is that it?" he said, his brown eyes studying her intently.

Her heart was pounding now, as she tried to keep a tight rein on her wits. How far could she trust this stranger? He probably wanted her for himself, but almost any man would be a better jailer than a sadist like Escobar. Nevertheless, she must proceed carefully. She was glad she was sitting down. It was an effort just to control her voice, much less the trembling of her arms and legs.

"Is it so surprising that I should like to be free?" she asked softly.

"Not at all. If that's what you want, perhaps it can be arranged. Where would you like to go?"

"Are you amusing yourself at my expense?"

"Of course not. Tell me."

"Away from here, out of Mexico. If possible, on a boat bound for ... for some neutral port."

"I see. But what would you do once you got to another strange country, alone and without funds? Would you really be any better off?"

"At least I'd be free," she retorted defensively. "Besides, my husband often instructed me as to what I should do if I ever found myself in such circumstances." The fleeting image of the ruby still hidden, along with her emerald-and-jade wedding ring, in the hem of her ruffled petticoat flitted across her mind, but she had no intention of confiding that secret to anyone.

"And for the sake of supposition, let's say I go to the trouble of helping you reach your destination. Would you have any objection to my accompanying you on your journey?"

For the first time Nicole couldn't hide her bewilderment over the boldness of his questions.

"Accompany me?" she sputtered.

"Precisely." He smiled. "How else could I be sure you arrived safely at your destination?"

"That wouldn't be necessary. It would be too much to ask," she faltered, unable to believe that this conversation was actually taking place here in the midst of the viceroy's gala reception.

"Oh, let me be the judge of that."

"But I have no way of repaying you. At least, not until I'm free," she ventured cautiously. "Of course, if you really helped me, I'd certainly reimburse you for your trouble and expense as soon as I could."

There was that enigmatic smile again. "*No se preocupe tanto.* You're worrying too far in advance," he chided, his hand completely around her arm now. "A beautiful woman is never completely without recourse. The truth is, I hope I'll have won your favor as well as your gratitude by the time we've come to the end of our voyage."

"I'm afraid you're making light of my tragic situation," she hedged. "Thank you for your sympathetic interest, but —"

He flashed his ready smile. "You do me an injustice, *señora*," he laughingly protested. "I really am planning to go abroad within the next month or two, and frankly there's nothing like the company of a lovely woman to turn a tedious voyage into a pleasant holiday."

At that instant Don Rodrigo and his host emerged from the adjoining room, so she cut him short. She could feel the grandee's searching gaze immediately dart across the room to where she sat. Her admirer quickly withdrew his hand from her arm, but she wondered whether he had acted in time to escape Escobar's sharp eyes. As it was, she could see anger twitching in the set of the latter's jaw as he strode toward her.

"I'll be in touch with you," Ruiz whispered as he took up his wineglass from the table and rose.

"But how ...?"

"I'll find a way," he muttered with a sly wink, and was gone.

But as the days went by and she heard nothing from him, she decided he had simply been in his cups and gave up any hope of his helping her.

Chapter 47

So she was enceinte! God help her and her poor child!
Yet in the midst of her panic there was joy. According
to what Madame Baudier had explained to her, Nicole
calculated it must have happened that last passionate night
in July she and Paul had spent together before he left
Pensacola. Just to know that she was carrying his child
lifted her out of the stupor she had been in since the
news of his death had come to her. She felt a glow radiating
within her now. Paul was not completely lost to her after
all! How ironic it was that the love she had shared with
him — that love which everyone in New Spain mocked
and cursed — would be blessed with a child! Her joy
was bittersweet, but it gave her a reason to live, to fight
all the harder.

Now more than ever she had to escape, not only for
herself but for that precious life she carried in her womb.
Paul's child could not be born among his enemies. It
must face its future in the land where its father was honored
and respected as a hero, where it could claim its birthright.
Paul would have wanted no less, and most certainly she

would not rest until she and her child were safely out of enemy hands.

She was doubly glad now that she had hidden the ruby Paul had given her. It would pay for her passage to New England, but first she had to get back to Veracruz and on a ship to some neutral port where she could then find passage to Virginia and get to Paul's lawyer.

And she had to act immediately — before she started to show and while she could still travel. She trembled at the thought of what Escobar might do if he suspected she was carrying Paul's child. The man was capable of such malice that he might try to harm it. Most certainly he would fear — and rightly so — that if the child proved to be a boy, the day would come when he would seek vengeance on the man who had been responsible for the death of his father and his grandparents. Merciful Virgin, protect the seed she carried within her and let it be born free of the stigmas and rancors of the past!

But where could she turn? Who was there to help her find a way out of her present dilemma? Señora Guzman was completely on Escobar's side. No amount of money or pleading for compassion would ever convince her chaperone to help her, of that she was certain. Just the thought of that woman's owlish eyes watching her every movement already filled her with dread, but now it terrified her, for if anyone could detect she was pregnant, it would be that dour Spanish watchdog. No, she must never underestimate her overzealous *dama de compañía* — not even for a moment!

As for José Luís Ruíz, he had never contacted her, so he had either reconsidered his offer and decided it would be too risky, or he had never meant to help her in the first place. Besides, she doubted he would want to take a pregnant woman along with him on his holiday!

Of course, Doña Inés would probably be glad to see the woman she believed her rival removed from the scene, no matter how it might be brought about. The glimmer of an idea flickered across the darkness of Nicole's despair. Perhaps she could turn Doña Inés's jealousy to her advantage. Trying to assuage that jealousy would do little good, yet of all the people around her at that moment, Nicole suspected that Escobar's *prometida* was probably the only person who might be receptive to the idea of getting her out of Mexico with as little fuss as possible.

At least it should be worth a try. She knew there was always the risk that Doña Inés might betray her confidence, but Nicole was counting on the *gran dama's* pride — on the fact that she would think it beneath her dignity even to admit to the existence of Don Rodrigo's supposed paramour, much less discuss such a subject with him.

Of course, there had been moments when she had been tempted to make a mad dash for freedom, to break away from Escobar as he escorted her around town, or perhaps try to give Señora Guzmán the slip the first opportunity that presented itself. That day in the *mercado*, she had certainly thought of running off. But she knew how futile such a mad dash would be if it wasn't well planned. She had to have some kind of a plan. It was important that she get more than a few feet away without being detected or her escape would be doomed to failure from the start. Neither Escobar nor Señora Guzmán traveled alone. Whenever they went outside, the guard assigned to her was always lurking in the background. He would be after her in a moment. What's more, the way Don Rodrigo had flaunted her around town, she would be easily recognized as "that redhaired French harlot" who was Escobar's "prize-of-war."

No, unless she had help from someone who could get her out of Puebla, she didn't have a chance. When she did make her break, she had to have at least the possibility of success. If she failed and Don Rodrigo was alerted to her intent, her chances of getting away again would be even less. And there was the baby. She had to have this child — Paul's child — especially now that he was gone. The baby was an extension of his life, of their love. Dear God, let it look like him!

She had to find a way to speak to Doña Inés alone. Señora Guzmán had said that the "sainted lady" went to church every afternoon. Perhaps she could convince Escobar to let her go to the cathedral around the time she had seen his fiancée that day in the *mercado*. That in itself would be quite a feat, but the most difficult hurdle would be still to come — to convince the enemy who hated her most of all to become her ally.

Chapter 43

Once Nicole had Señora Guzmán's approval to back up her request to go to church, it wasn't too difficult to obtain Don Rodrigo's consent. Of course, she had to bite her tongue and let them each expound on how a sinner such as she most certainly was in dire need of repentance, and though they made her absolution seem well-nigh impossible, they at least commended her for beginning to see the error of her ways.

She did hope to find some solace in prayer, and most of all to pray for Paul and that precious fruit of their love just beginning to bud within her. How she had loved him ... how she *still* loved him! Their time together had been so brief — only a few months — yet she knew it would illumine the rest of her life. Perhaps deep down, she and Paul had always known their happiness would be short. In Paul's profession, death was always a possibility. Perhaps that was why they had loved each other with such passionate intensity.

The cathedral of Puebla was the most ornate church in New Spain, rivaling even the one in Mexico City. Begun shortly after the conquest in the sixteenth century, it had taken almost a hundred years to build, so that the imposing Renaissance fortress style had baroque embellishments from later periods of architecture.

Señora Guzmán had often boasted about how beautiful the church was, but when Nicole entered the cool hush of its interior, she was still not prepared for the dazzling splendor that lay before her. Built on a majestic scale, the cathedral was a breathtaking kaleidoscope of multicolored marble, ceramic, and onyx and great stone pillars arching gracefully into a multivaulted ceiling. Its altars were covered in mantles of gold and its highly polished floors bathed in the jewel-toned light penetrating the stained-glass windows.

There was no service at that hour, so the church was not crowded. Perhaps that was why those who were there seemed to be women of the upper class who probably did not care to rub elbows with the natives. They were accompanied by their chaperones as befit ladies of their station, and all were elegantly dressed, with small lace mantillas on their heads and jeweled rosaries hanging from their tightly laced waists.

Nicole was wearing one of her own prim black brocaded silks that Don Rodrigo had ordered Señora Guzmán to buy for her. With her bright curls caught up under a black lace mantilla, she felt she blended in acceptably with the rest of the women around her.

Eagerly she scanned the cathedral for the haughty figure of Doña Inés, but the latter was nowhere to be seen. Trying to hide her disappointment, Nicole watched as Señora Guzmán instructed Escobar's henchman to wait in the back of the church. Then Señora Guzmán took Nicole by the arm and propelled her down one of the processional aisles.

The confessionals spaced along each side of the church all seemed to be occupied, so the two women genuflected and, making the sign of the cross, made their way to the lavishly sculptured Altar of the Kings and knelt at the rail.

They had no sooner begun to pray, however, when an elderly woman hobbled painfully out of one of the confessional booths and Señora Guzmán nudged Nicole. "Go ahead and confess yourself," she hissed. "God knows you need it!"

"No, I'd like to pray a little first and prepare myself," Nicole whispered back.

The Spanish woman gave an approving nod with her heavily veiled head and for once agreed with her. "Yes, I suppose you really should," she conceded. "I'll go first, then."

Nicole watched the tall, bony woman disappear behind the black velvet curtain and then rose quickly to make her way to the ornate little *capilla* dedicated to the Virgin. Shimmering behind a blaze of votive candles and elaborately dressed in pale blue satin, a golden sunburst around her head, the Virgin seemed to look down on her with a soft smile of compassion. Bedecked with pearls and precious jewels from her wealthy devotees and surrounded by the colorful, childlike *retablos* painted crudely but eloquently by her more humble but equally grateful followers, the Virgin was by far the most resplendent of all the figures in the cathedral. For Nicole, it was like seeing an old friend in the midst of her enemies.

She gave a sigh of relief and knelt again. It was good to be alone with her thoughts at last ... to see the familiar face of the Virgin and be able to bare her soul. The peace and quiet of the cathedral, disturbed only by the faint rustle of silken skirts and the murmur of repeated orations, had a strange, hypnotic effect as the sounds reverberated among the arches all around her.

The only gift she had for the Virgin was the votive candle that Señora Guzmán had bought for her in the entrance to the cathedral. Its single flame sputtered from her tears as she placed it in the rack.

After a special oration for Paul, she prayed fervently for deliverance — if not for her sake, then for her child's. It must not be born among its enemies, at the mercy of the man who had caused the death of its father and grandparents. *Sainte Vierge!* Please let this poor child have a better life than she and Paul had been able to have!

For a moment her eyes were so clouded with tears that she didn't notice that the woman emerging from the nearby confessional was Doña Inés. But now, as she distinguished the unmistakable figure gliding toward her in stiff black taffeta skirts lined with steel-ribbed petticoats, she kept her head bowed and waited with pounding heart until the Spanish woman was about to pass her by. So much depended on the next few minutes. What if Inés just pushed her aside and refused to listen to anything she had to say? Worse yet, what if she made a scene and Señora Guzmán heard? Suddenly Nicole felt very foolish. Her plan was too audacious. How could she think even for a minute that the woman who most hated her in the world would even consider helping her?

Nicole shot a nervous glance at the confessional Señora Guzmán had entered and was glad there were no signs of the elderly woman. Nor was Doña Inés's companion anywhere to be seen. The latter was probably also confessing herself or praying in one of the small chapels set in niches along the side walls of the church.

Rising from the priedieu, Nicole stepped into the aisle and blocked Doña Inés's path. Her throat was so parched now that she doubted any words would come out. Besides, her mind had gone blank. All the things she was planning to say and had practiced over and over again in her mind had evaporated. Her legs felt heavy as they took the few fatal steps forward. But it was too late to turn back. This one fleeting moment could mean life or death for her and her unborn child; she *had* to take this risk.

Doña Inés stared at her, her eyes narrowing until they seemed two dark slivers of obsidian glittering in the dim light of the church. Nicole could feel those stilettos boring through her, as though Doña Inés refused even to acknowledge her presence. The Spanish woman drew herself up to her fullest height and was about to continue on her way, evidently hoping to force the younger girl to give way before her. But Nicole was determined now to use to the fullest these precious moments that destiny had granted her. She extended her hand to detain the Spanish woman.

"Let me pass!" Doña Inés hissed in clipped Castilian, pulling back her arm as though the spot had been singed.

"Please ... *por favor, señora* ... hear me a moment, no more," Nicole implored. "I assure you, I mean you no offense."

"Your very presence offends me!"

"Believe me, I have no designs on Don Rodrigo," Nicole plunged on, determined to say what must be said before anyone might interrupt her. "I'd like nothing more than to find some way to get out of Mexico."

Doña Inés's delicate nostrils quivered indignantly. "And why should I concern myself about what a woman like you wants?" she replied, flipping open her black lace fan and holding it over the lower half of her face so that only the dark, smoldering slits of her eyes looked over its ruffled edge.

"You should, because whether we like it or not, our fates are linked," insisted Nicole. "We basically want the same thing. Help me escape, and both our purposes will be served."

"Don't flatter yourself," scoffed Escobar's *prometida*. Instead of using the respectful *usted* for "you," she was addressing Nicole with the familiar *tú* — a form of speech reserved in Spanish only for intimate relationships or for persons of much lower station. It was a subtle way of insulting her. "I assure you that if and when I want to get rid of a rival, I can easily do so without the necessity of collaborating with her."

Nicole swallowed hard but went on. "I don't doubt

it, but even you must admit that it would be simpler and more effective if you'd just help your unwanted rival steal out of town secretly and be rid of her once and for all, rather than risk incurring your future husband's wrath by taking direct action against his prize-of-war, which seems to be a point of honor with him."

Though Doña Inés was listening in frozen silence, Nicole could tell by the rise and fall of the Spanish woman's ample bosom that her arguments were beginning to reach her. After all, Inés might be burning with rage over her fiancé's negligent treatment of her, but she was no fool. If any harm were to come to Don Rodrigo's mistress here in Puebla, his *prometida* would be one of the first persons suspected; yet if his prisoner-of-war were to escape, it probably would never occur to anyone to think that Inés had been instrumental in effecting it.

"Come to the point, wench," Inés suddenly snapped impatiently. "What exactly are you presuming to ask of me?"

Nicole's heart was hammering again, but she tried to remain calm. "Actually very little," she answered quickly. "I need to get to Veracruz without being recognized and board some ship there headed for a neutral port."

Doña Inés's face remained as expressionless as ever as she fingered the jeweled sheath of her stiletto that hung on a gold chain down the front of her stiffened skirts. Nicole waited breathlessly, the silence weighing more heavily with each passing second. If only she could fathom what was going on in the mind of this enigmatic woman. Would Inés Alvarez cry out and denounce her? Or would she just walk away without so much as dignifying her plea with a reply? Or perhaps she might unsheath her dagger and try to put an end then and there to her hated rival!

"This Tuesday Don Rodrigo will have a *fiesta* for his saint's day," the Spanish woman finally said, her lips hardly moving. "See to it that you're there and ready to act on my signal."

Nicole took an eager step forward, her eyes aglow. "Then you will help me?"

The Spanish woman drew back, as though even the young girl's proximity might infect her. "*Vamos a ver.* I make no promises, but hold yourself in readiness. We'll see." Without a parting word, the dark beauty crossed herself and went on her way, her black lace fan swaying languidly and her countenance as impassive as ever.

Chapter 49

The weekend before his saint's day, Escobar paid her one of his unannounced visits. Nicole could tell at once by his swagger that he was in a mood to taunt her.

Señora Guzmán had no sooner withdrawn than he strutted around a few times and then paused directly before her to announce that his engagement to Doña Inés was now official.

"They announced the banns at mass this morning," he stated pompously.

Nicole didn't know whether this news boded good or ill for her. Personally, she felt that Don Rodrigo and his arrogant *prometida* deserved each other. But she hoped it wouldn't make Doña Inés any less inclined to help her. The latter might feel secure enough now with the formalization of her betrothal to think it was no longer necessary to help her rival get out of the country.

"That means someone else will have to escort you in public from now on," he continued flatly. "And I assured my *prometida* that I'd have you out of this villa by the end of the week. But nothing will really change, of course.

You'll still belong to me, and I'll continue to do with you as I please."

She was wearing a sacque gown of green-and-white striped silk that Paul had given her, with its tightly laced bodice but freely flowing back cascading in loose pleats from her shoulders to the floor.

"And where will I live?" she asked, trying to hide her anxiety.

"Someplace nearby. But don't think you'll be any less my prisoner than you are now. My cousin Concepcion will continue to stay with you, and you'll still be well guarded."

"And my escort?"

"His eyes narrowed to two glittering pinpoints, as though trying to read her innermost thoughts. He seemed to have been waiting for her to ask him that question. "If you're hoping it will be that *criollo* José Luis Ruíz, you can discard the idea," he sneered. "I regret to inform you that I killed your admirer in a duel last week — right after he made so bold with you at the viceroy's reception."

Nicole couldn't believe her ears. It was all she could do to keep herself upright. "You *killed* him?" she echoed incredulously. "My God! But why?"

"That should be obvious. He offended my honor. But then, what does a *mujerzuela* like you know about honor?"

"But there's nothing between us to warrant talk of honor. On the contrary, only hatred binds us to each other."

"True, but he didn't know that, nor did anyone else who saw him sitting with you that night."

"But to *kill* him? By all that's holy, he didn't deserve that!"

"Do you take me for a fool, *señora*? I was well aware of that little flirtation you two had behind my back that night. The lackey who attended you was under orders from me to keep an eye on you until I returned. Do you think I'd go off and leave a slut like you to go about whoring with the guests? Besides, I saw Ruíz drawing his arm away from you as I came back into the room. You seem to lead your admirers to their deaths, *señora*, but then, a man who runs after a *puta* is a fool to begin with and deserves what he gets!"

"But all we did was talk. *Mon Dieu!* That poor man! Was it necessary to murder him?"

"I didn't murder him," Escobar corrected her dryly. "I killed him in a fair duel defending my honor. Do you think I could overlook such an affront to my manhood and let it go unchallenged? And don't give yourself too much importance in the matter. I'd do the same to any man who'd try to steal something that is mine. If a thief breaks into my stable and tries to steal one of my prize mares, or even presumes to ride her without my permission, he should be held accountable for his actions."

Nicole drew herself up. "You'd compare me to your mare? I'm a human being, not an animal!"

"You, *señora*, are a whore," he hissed, catching her by the arm in a sudden burst of rage, "and my comparison is apt. You were made for mounting, and like my mare, whether I choose to ride you or not, you're mine, so no one has the right to use you or even come near you without my permission. Is that understood? Another incident like that one with Ruíz and I'll not only kill the man but horsewhip you as well! I'll not be disgraced by the likes of you!"

Nicole swayed. The force of his hatred was like a living thing bearing down relentlessly on her.

"The same goes for Moreno," Don Rodrigo added, his tone still menacing. "I've asked him to be your escort at my *santo* this coming Tuesday evening, but don't go trying your wiles on him or you'll seal his death warrant. I'm the best blade in Puebla, and he knows it, but he's *loco* enough for you to be tempted to forget it. That's why I'm warning you as well as him not to forget. I'll have my eyes on both of you all night."

"I'm sure Don Heriberto expects a more generous

arrangement than just being allowed to escort me around town," she said, but her voice was so weak she couldn't recognize it as her own.

"I'm sure he does, but I have no plans to share you with anyone at the moment. Of course, if he continues to escort you like a gentleman, without offending my honor, I'll probably have to let him take some payment eventually, but not until I say so. Just bear in mind that if I ever decide to really give you up, you'll face a lot worse than Don Heriberto. Displease me, and I'll turn you over to the Inquisition or send you back to the commander in Pensacola where you can have the distinction of being the only whore in the port. Between the garrison and the ships anchored there, you should be kept quite busy."

Nicole stared at him in disbelief. "I'd never have thought anyone could hate so much," she said accusingly, her indignation renewing her faltering spirit. "You speak of honor, but there's no honor in a man who abuses helpless women the way you do!"

His laugh was ugly. "You're a harlot. Why should you consider my putting you to work at your trade an abuse? Or do you accuse me of abusing you precisely because I have not yet asked you to attend me?"

She paled but held her ground. "If you believe that, then you're a bigger fool than any of the unfortunate men you've been maligning, now that they're no longer here to defend themselves!"

For a moment he stared at her, no longer making any effort to hide the lust that was consuming him. "If I thought . . . if there was a possibility that you could . . ." His voice was strained and raspy. "Perhaps you could make the difference. . . ."

He took a step toward her, but she drew away from him, frightened by what she saw in his eyes.

"But how could you think of getting pleasure from me when you yourself have said time and again that you would never consider touching me?" she quickly reminded him. "I assure you I haven't changed in the least toward you."

"I don't give a damn about how you feel about me," he snarled. "It's what I find myself feeling for you! *Condenada mujer!* You know all the tricks to rouse a man, don't you? You have a whole bag of them, *verdad*? Well, come on, show me how you do it, you little minx — rouse me enough to make me want you in spite of everything. Show me how you made a man like Dawson so *loco* for you that he died on the gallows for trying to get back to you!"

He was on top of her like a wild man now, tearing at her gown with desperate urgency. All control was gone. "I want to see you — all of you! You damn bitch! You have me half out of my mind. I can't sleep at night thinking of how it would be to possess you!"

He dragged her kicking and scratching toward the bed and threw her back on it. With the agility that years of experience had given him, he pinned her beneath him and yanked the lacings of her bodice apart until he had bared the quivering cones of her breasts.

For a moment he held her there, unable to tear his eyes away. "*Caramba, mujer! Qué hermosa estás!* No wonder you drove Dawson to his death! Let me see the rest of you."

He began to tug impatiently at her skirts now, holding off her flying fists with one hand while he forced her gown and petticoats past her hips. "*Qué barbaridad!* he muttered appreciatively, exclaiming as he stripped her ruthlessly, methodically, determined to bare her completely to his bold scrutiny.

Beads of sweat glistened on his broad forehead and his breathing was increasingly labored now. His thick black hair with its streaks of gray had pulled free of the ribbon at the nape of his neck, and he brushed impatiently at the strands that fell into his eyes as he bent quickly over her and ran his hands greedily up and down the inviting smoothness of her bare skin.

She continued to fight, but she knew she was lost. Even if she screamed for help, no one would come. Who would dare to interfere between the master and his captive concubine? Señora Guzmán would probably even smile with grim satisfaction and mumble to herself that her charge was only getting what she deserved.

And then there was the baby! She couldn't let him hurt the baby. If she continued to fight him, he would only become more abusive. Before anything else, she had to survive this moment. The only thing that mattered now was that no harm come to the child. Clenching her teeth, she suddenly forced herself to lie perfectly still.

Taken aback, Escobar paused and looked down at her. "Ah, so you'll cooperate now?" he asked gruffly.

"I won't fight you," she said icily, "but don't expect me to respond."

"Respond?" he scoffed. "The hell with your response! What interests me is that you get a response out of me!" His breath fanned her face as he pressed urgently against her and began to squeeze and claw at her breasts with desperate intensity. "I know how to get a reaction from you, all right," he said angrily as she moaned and twisted in protest. "It's you who should worry about rousing me!"

He ran his hand feverishly up and down her body, all the while bearing down on her with mounting force. He was fumbling with his breeches, and she shuddered as she awaited the moment she had been dreading for so long. Anger and violence were in his touch. He wanted to make her suffer this ultimate act of humiliation. Yet she sensed he wanted more than just revenge — that he desired her in spite of everything, though he hated himself for wanting her that way.

Panic shot through her veins like wildfire. The pain of his hand brutally handling her breasts tore her thoughts into jagged fragments, yet somehow, in the midst of her terror and confusion, she realized something was wrong. The lust was unmistakably there. It was in his eyes, in his accelerated breathing, in the pressure of his body pushing demandingly against hers. Yet something was missing. The hard thrust of his shaft was absent. Though far from being as experienced as Escobar thought she was, she certainly knew enough about men now to know that, much as this one wanted to rape her, he was lacking the wherewithal to do so.

"Al demonio contigo!" the grandee suddenly exclaimed, kneeling back on his haunches and looking down angrily at her. "The devil spawned you to drive men to their doom!" he roared, cuffing her in frustrated rage. "I'd like to ram you from here to hell and back!" He let out a string of oaths, but it was too late. She knew the truth. Don Rodrigo was cursing himself more than her — cursing his own impotence. All his stinging insults had been, in fact, a cloak to hide the real reason why he had been holding himself aloof from her.

"My God! You ... you ..." She caught herself, afraid to put the truth into words, not wanting to invite an even more violent reaction from him.

"And if I am, it's thanks to that damn husband of yours, Paul Dawson. May he rot in hell!"

Nicole sat up, clutching her torn bodice over her smarting breasts, staring at him in open amazement. "But how can you blame Paul for something like that?" she challenged him.

"Because it's true. Up until two years ago, I was perfectly fine — could handle the wenches two at a time! Then Dawson fired that broadside and wounded me. I told everyone I'd been hurt in the thigh, but it was really in the groin. No one must know.... A man of my reputation ..." His voice broke off. "I haven't been able to spear a woman since then.... His voice was the merest whisper.

Suddenly he turned back to her, rage kindling anew in his eyes. "But perhaps there's still one chance left. Perhaps with a woman as beautiful as you ... with some of those whorish tricks of yours ..." He bent toward her once more, but she quickly slipped out from under his knees and jumped off the bed.

"I know nothing about such things," she faltered.

He gave a short, sardonic laugh. "Just the sight of you like this ought to be enough to raise the sap in any man!" he groaned in despair.

"But what about about Doña Inés ... your marriage to her?" Nicole asked, hoping to distract him from coming at her again. "How do you expect to keep your secret from her?"

The grandee gave a scornful shrug of his broad shoulders. "Once she's my wife, she'll have to learn to bear the situation, even as I have had to do," he said harshly, "and she's too proud to say anything to anyone. At least she has a son I can make my heir. I can never have one of my own now. The British sank the ship my wife and only son were on in the last war, and Dawson robbed me of my manhood in this one!"

He walked around the bed to where she stood and towered over her. "As for you, you slut, one word to anyone about this, and it'll be your last! I swear by the Holy Trinity, I'll strangle you with my bare hands if you so much as hint at it."

He glared at her a moment longer, as though he would strike her again. Finally he swung around and stormed toward the door, his shirt flying loose over the top of his breeches.

He paused at the door and looked back at her, devouring the naked perfection of her with anguished eyes, as she reached for her torn garments with trembling hands. "I won't give you up!" he said hoarsely. "No matter what, you belong to me, and I'll find some way to get satisfaction out of you. At least I'll make you pay again and again for what Dawson did to me!"

The door slammed behind him. So Paul had had his vengeance after all! And for a man like Escobar, it was a punishment worse than death! She knew it was more urgent than ever that she get away as quickly as possible. Now that she had discovered Rodrigo Escobar's dark secret, she and her child were in greater danger than ever.

Chapter 50

Heriberto Moreno was in a very good mood. He'd been waiting for this moment ever since he had first laid eyes on Don Rodrigo's *francesita*. Now his goal was in sight. The fact that Escobar had asked him to squire the girl to the festivities that night made it almost certain she would soon be his.

Of course, everyone at Don Rodrigo's traditional saint's day celebration had immediately jumped to the conclusion that the grandee had already turned his mistress over to his friend, especially since the latter was escorting his *prometida* that evening.

Moreno knew, however, that he dare not try to breach the wench yet. Much as he was bursting with desire for her, he didn't want to end up like José Luís Ruís had, mortally wounded on the field of honor simply because Don Rodrigo had considered an advance on his *querida* a personal affront. No, no whore, even one as delectable as this, was worth so high a price.

Nevertheless, Don Heriberto looked approvingly at the flame-haired beauty on his arm and reveled at the prospect of really being her owner. When the day came that she was his to do with as he pleased, this wench would know damn well who her new *dueño* was! He peered down at her cleavage, intriguingly visible through the golden cobweb that formed the lace yoke of her brocade gown. Escobar dressed her brilliantly — gold cloth to encase the perfection of her charms! Every man in the place had his eyes on her. Next to her, all the other women paled. Even Doña Inés, with her regal beauty in black velvet lavishly adorned with silver lace, looked drab next to the warm radiance of this exciting woman at his side. French whores were reputed to be the best.... Well, he'd soon put this one to the test. It couldn't be long now.

"You're magnificent tonight, my dear," he beamed as he possessively covered her hand resting on his arm with his. "I'm the envy of every man in this room."

Nicole kept her ivory-and-lace fan close to her face, trying to shield herself from Moreno's lecherous gaze. If only she could shield her ears from that monotonous nasal drone of his as well! She could feel Don Rodrigo's dark, brooding eyes fixed on her and his friend from where he stood across the large *sala* with Doña Inés standing triumphantly by his side. Now that she knew the truth about Rodrigo Escobar, she shuddered every time she felt his tormented gaze on her. In his strange, twisted way he was burning with a cold, ruthless passion for her, but his desire was consuming him from within. He had been using her as a facade to hide his impotence as well as avenge himself on Paul, yet he had fallen into his own trap. For now that very impotency stood between him and the unfulfilled desire he had come to feel for her. For a man of his lustful nature, that must have been the most unbearable part of all.

Nicole tried to fathom the enigmatic features of Doña Inés's exquisitely chiseled face. The Spanish woman was striking, her alabaster skin contrasting sharply with the thick black coils of her hair as the raging fire in her huge black eyes belied her icy exterior.

At the moment Inés seemed to be holding herself aloof from the scene, pretending not to notice the way her betrothed had never once taken his gaze off of his supposed ex-mistress, yet Nicole was certain that the Spanish woman was keenly alert to everything that was going on around her, even as a sleek panther stalks its prey out of seemingly drowsy, half-closed lids.

Nicole wondered what this haughty Spanish woman would do if she knew the truth about the man she was so eager to marry. She was not the type of person to be patient or understanding, nor was Escobar. Their marriage was certain to be a clash of wills, of one pride pitted against the other. Yes, they were well matched, Nicole thought; the irony made her smile.

She tried to detect some sign of recognition from Doña Inés. Had the Spanish woman decided to help her escape or not? There was nothing to suggest that Escobar's betrothed intended to address so much as a single word to her, much less lift a finger to help her. How would she even be able to talk to Inés again with this lecher Moreno holding fast to her arm and Don Rodrigo watching every move his friend or any other person made toward her?

Vaguely she heard Don Heriberto rattling on at her side. "When you're mine, as I'm certain you will be soon," he was saying enthusiastically, "I'll dress you in silks and satins and show you off to all of New Spain, but when we're at home, I'll keep you clad only in dressing gowns of sheerest muslin and net so I'll be able to feast my eyes on all of you. Oh, we'll have some fine sport together, I promise you. I'll keep you so busy you won't have time to think of any of your past lovers. You'll see, *querida*."

She tried to pull her hand out from under his, but he kept it pinned to his arm.

"And those breasts of yours! *Qué senos tan lindos tienes!* I'll have them raw from *chupándolos!*" He squeezed her hand. "Just the thought of them makes my mouth water!"

Nicole fought to keep her face from showing her disgust. She cast a curious glance around the room, trying to distract herself enough to blot out her repugnant escort's vivid descriptions of his future plans for her — plans which, after her traumatic scene with Escobar only a couple of nights ago, she doubted would ever come to pass.

The grandees assembled there that evening came from some of the oldest families in Spain, and the atmosphere was heavy with the scent of musk and rice powder. The high-beamed ceiling of the hall echoed with the music of full-throated guitars and the polite murmur of the guests paying homage to Don Rodrigo's *santo*. The candlelight reflected in the crystal and brightly polished silver and gold, rendered the room a glittering wonderland. The fabrics chosen by the men and women were sumptuous — dark velvets and silks, an occasional brocade or satin. Precious jewels, powdered wigs, and gossamer mantillas abounded.

Some of the younger people wore their own hair or natural-colored wigs, but the older or more important guests had donned the white perukes or even powdered their coiffures in the formal manner. Of course, Don Rodrigo, as the guest of honor, was appropriately bewigged and bejeweled, though the harsh contrast of his black velvet frock coat with the stark white of his carefully curled periwig was not especially flattering to his olive complexion.

Among the young men standing unobtrusively on the sidelines, Nicole spotted one or two who reminded her of Paul. It was always that way whenever she was in a crowd ... but then she was always thinking of Paul. Even in New Spain there were fair-haired, light-eyed men ... like that slim, haughty-looking gallant with sandy hair and striking blue eyes standing near the punch bowl. But there the resemblance ended. Sometimes it wouldn't even be the coloring but a man's build or simply the way he carried himself or gestured. That was what called her atten-

tion to the tall man in black silk. He was built like Paul
and sometimes even moved like him. She couldn't see
his eyes very well, for he was looking down, but what
did it matter? The sight of his jet black hair and pointed
Castilian beard quickly brought her back to reality. Why
did she torture herself fantasizing this way? She knew
it couldn't be Paul. He no longer lived except in her heart.
A sob choked her as she turned away and lifted her fan
to hide the tears that sprang to her eyes.

Moreno was still in the midst of his soliloquy, oblivious
to her lack of interest in him.

"Not even your mantilla can hide the lights in that
glorious hair of yours," he went on. "When you're mine
and we're alone together, I'll make you wear it loose,
falling over the whiteness of your shoulders and
breasts. . . ."

But now he glimpsed her moist eyes behind her fan
and sensed at last that she was disturbed about something.
"What's wrong, *querida*? You look so pale and wan all
of a sudden."

"I wish you wouldn't hold on to me like you're doing,"
she said, glad to have an excuse to say something at last.
"Don Rodrigo is watching us, and he seems very annoyed.
He can be terribly jealous, as you well know," she added
meaningfully.

Don Heriberto did know, and it was he who paled
now. "You say he seems annoyed?" he asked nervously,
dropping his hand from hers.

"So he seems to me," she replied, taking a few steps
away from him with relief. "I'd hate to see anything unfortunate happen to you just because he thought you were
paying too close attention to me before he's really given
me up."

"Yes, yes, of course, you're right," Moreno agreed, dabbing his embroidered kerchief around the edges of his
white periwig, where beads of perspiration had suddenly
appeared. "Your concern for me pleases me, my dear."

At that moment two Indian servants entered, bearing between them a large clay pot lavishly decorated to resemble a huge five-pointed star with long, colorful ribbons streaming from its fat belly. Immediately the guests relaxed their protocol and began to laugh and joke among themselves, while the guitars left off their nostalgic strumming for a more lively tune.

In the confusion as everyone moved aside to let the servants hang the pot from one of the rafters high above their heads, Nicole took advantage of the occasion to step even farther away from her escort, deliberately mingling with the guests gathering around the *piñata*, as she heard them call it. Instinctively she moved closer to Doña Inés, and as though set in motion by some corresponding mechanism, the Spanish woman slowly began to do the same. Nicole's heart leaped when she saw that Doña Inés seemed to be working her way toward her.

The next moment the rigid figure in black and silver was in there front of her. Nicole opened her mouth to speak, but words caught in her throat as she realized there was no sign of recognition. The Spanish woman continued to glide past her. But in that split second when they crossed paths, Nicole heard a throaty whisper.

"The stables . . . *now!*"

Like a moth that momentarily flits across the face of a lantern, Doña Inés was gone as swiftly as she had come, leaving only the rustle of taffeta petticoats and the scent of heliotrope hanging heavily in the air.

Chapter 51

It had all happened so quickly that Nicole wondered whether she had only imagined those barely audible words hissed in her ear. The instructions, if that was what they were, had been so brief — without any explanation. She stood in a daze, watching Doña Inés lose herself once more in the milling crowd around them.

Suddenly Don Heriberto came up to her. "Ah, my dear, you've probably never seen this custom of ours," he said, drawing her aside. "The guests are going to take turns now to see who can break the *piñata* and bring down a shower of gifts on all of us. We do this for birthdays and the *posadas* at Christmastime. Since it's Don Rodrigo's *santo*, he'll take the first turn with the blindfold and stick, of course."

Nicole realized that this must by why Escobar's fiancée had told her to go the the stables immediately. In the next few minutes Don Rodrigo's ever watchful eyes would be temporarily blindfolded. But how in the world was she going to get rid of this leech, who clung so persistently to her?

She put her hand to her head, and Moreno, noticing purred solicitously, "What's the matter?"

"I feel faint," she replied, quickly seizing the opportunity that his question suggested to her. "Perhaps it's best I go to my room and lie down for a while until it passes." As she spoke, she began to edge her way to where the wide double doors that led to the patio stood partially open to let in the cool night air. Out of the corner of her eye, she saw a laughing group of guests encircling Escobar and urging him to take the first turn, while he protested that such games were better left for children.

"Then I'll accompany you," came Moreno's ready offer.

"No, no," she said quickly. "Don Rodrigo would certainly think the worst of us if he saw you leave the party with me. It's best I go alone. Señora Guzmán is there. She isn't feeling very well herself tonight, but one of the servants can attend me if I need anything."

"But ..."

They were blindfolding Escobar! If only this pest would leave her in peace. She turned to him in desperation. "Please, I only want to refresh myself a little. Perhaps if I can just lie down for a while, I can return."

Moreno's swarthy face suddenly broke into a understanding smile. The wench probably just wanted to relieve herself or was at her time of the month and too shy to tell him the real reason. "*Está bien*," he acquiesced at last, "but at least let me stand in the doorway here and watch you cross the patio to your room."

Doña Inés and several other women guests were turning Escobar around and warning him to watch where he swung the stick when he tried to break the beribboned clay pot. Nicole knew she had to hurry before those precious moments had passed or it would be too late for her to get out of the room unnoticed.

"Perhaps if you'd be good enough to get me some brandy, a few sips might revive me and I'd be able to last the evening out," she suggested. She knew that if he watched her, she'd have to enter her room and, once there, she would not be able to get past Señora Guzmán. It was now or never.

"Ah, yes! That would be even better," he agreed. "You sit right here by the door where you can take in some of the fresh air, and I'll be back as quickly as I can." He grinned encouragingly at her and hurried off, his mahogany-colored frock coat flapping.

The moment he had disappeared into the crowd, weaving his way toward the table of refreshments on the other side of the hall, Nicole gave a sigh of relief and rose quickly from the chair. When he returned, he would probably assume she had taken a turn for the worse and decided to retire to her room after all. She was counting on his fear of Escobar's jealously, however, to keep him from trying to follow her. He would probably wait impatiently but would not risk rousing his friend's wrath by leaving the *fiesta* to go after her. What she most needed was to gain time — enough to be off the villa's grounds before her disappearance was discovered. God grant she could keep a clear head and that everything would go as scheduled. If only her bold captain were here to see her through!

A burst of laughter and more teasing came from the guests clustered around Escobar as they urged him on to swing at the *piñata*. Taking advantage of the distraction, Nicole slipped out the doorway into the cool night.

The large patio was dimly lit by several flickering flambeaux in bronze brackets as a cool breeze gently ruffled the clear mountain air. The closer she came to the stables, the more her doubts plagued her. On just three words muttered fleetingly in the midst of a crowd by a woman she knew hated her, she was staking her entire future and that of her child! She was probably a fool, yet what choice did she have? She had to make the attempt. After Heriberto Moreno's comments that evening, she knew she would have less hope than ever of escaping if Escobar gave her to that abominable rake. So there was no hope there, even if the day might come when Escobar's friend could prevail on him to forgo his thirst for vengeance and give her in reward for services rendered. And what of her poor defenseless baby? The way Escobar loathed anything and anybody connected with Paul, he might even try to prevent a child fathered by Dawson from ever being born!

The stables to the rear of the patio were dark, but she could hear the animals stirring within. Nicole made her way stealthily past several of the private coaches parked in the patio, but no one challenged her. From the sound of clicking dice and gruff male voices coming from the interior of one of the carriages, it was evident that the coachmen and stable boys had gathered to have a *fiesta* of their own with a jug of *pulque* and a lively game of chance.

Once at the stable entrance, Nicole could see a lantern inside. Though the light was particularly dim, she entered apprehensively, not knowing who or what she would find waiting for her. Immediately the pungent odor of manure and sweating horseflesh blended with that of fresh hay. As her eyes grew more accustomed to the gloom, she could distinguish the outline of a small wooden cart with a donkey already hitched to it.

Two men rose to greet her from where they had been sitting beside the vehicle, apparently waiting for her. Nicole was jubilant. Doña Inés had decided to help her after all!

The light was too weak for her to make out the faces of the men. Their bleached white breeches and blouses were only a distorted white blur in the gloom of the stable, but at least their garments helped her see where they were. They spoke to her in low voices, their Spanish broken and untutored.

"You go to Veracruz?" asked the taller of the two.

"Yes, yes," she replied quickly. "Will you help me get

there and book passage on a ship that can take me to a neutral port?"

"Sí, *señora*, we take you."

Desperate as she was at that moment, their reply was enough for her to accept whatever help they could offer her, so when they motioned to her to climb into the cart, she readily obeyed. It was covered with a large piece of canvas, so they lowered the tailgate and helped her crawl in the interior, which was half filled with straw.

Hurriedly she wrapped the woolen shawl she found there around her while they added a few more pitchforks of hay and then bolted the tailgate into place.

As the wheels rattled over the flagstones of the courtyard, Nicole sat back with pounding heart amid the sweet-smelling straw, welcoming its padding. She poked a peephole between the slats on one side of the cart, but she could see very little.

Gradually the sounds of merrymaking faded away, and she knew they must have left the grounds of the villa. With a sigh of relief, she loosened her stays and tried to relax as best she could.

There was no way to tell how long they rolled along, but the road was less rough once they left the cobblestoned streets of the town. She found a canteen of *atole* in the cart, and as she sipped the vanilla-flavored corn milk, a pleasant warmth spread through her. The gentle swaying of the cart as she nestled in the hay gradually relaxed her, and before long she drifted off into a disturbed sleep.

When she awoke, daylight was seeping through the side slats of the cart. They must have been traveling all night. Though their progress was slow, they must have left the town well behind them by now. She was getting hungry and longed to get out and stretch, but she didn't want to delay their journey any more than necessary. The *atole* was cold and lumpy now, but she drank the rest of it. Sooner or later they would have to stop, so she decided to wait and not complain. All she could see through the peephole were rows of adobe houses, so they were probably going through a village.

The rocking of the cart and its dark, close confines reminded her of how it had been in the hold of the ship. But this time, she told herself, it was different. Instead of being on her way to bondage, she was on the road to deliverance. Without Paul it would be a bitter victory, but at least she — and most of all, the baby — would be free. With a sigh she let her heavy lidded eyes close and succumbed to the drowsiness that once more overwhelmed her.

Her sleep was fitful, but when she came to, she realized they had stopped. The hunger pangs were stronger now, and her head felt as heavy as her aching limbs. She peeped out and saw only trees and patches of what looked like late afternoon sky. *Sainte Vierge!* She must have slept through most of the day, too! How could that be?

Suddenly a frightening thought occurred to her. Could the *atole* she had been drinking have been drugged? Her first reaction was one of anger, and she was about to call out in indignation to her escorts and demand an explanation, but then she had second thoughts. Perhaps they had intended her no harm. They might have only wanted to sedate her a little so her tedious and uncomfortable journey would be more tolerable. They were wrong, of course, to have done that without her permission, but what good would it do to argue after the fact? They might abandon her here by the roadside, still days away from Veracruz, and she would be faced with far worse problems. No, she simply would not take any more food or drink from them unless they understood first that she preferred not to be given drugs or herbs of any kind, no matter how beneficial they thought it might be for her.

The cart was rolling over uneven ground now. From the way it progressed, she suspected they had left the main road and entered a little-traveled path in the woods, for there were trees on both sides of them now. Thank God! They were probably going to stop and rest and eat something solid at last.

As she anticipated, they had only gone a short distance off the main road when they came to a stop. This time she heard the soft footsteps of Indians' sandaled feet approaching the back of the cart, and the next minute the tailgate dropped down. Though it was late afternoon now, the daylight momentarily blinded her. All she could see was the silhouette of the man peering in at her through the opening.

"You awake, *muchacha*?" he asked unceremoniously.

"Lift the canvas off and we can get her out of there faster," snapped his companion. "Let's get this over with now!"

Impatiently the second man threw back the top covering.

Nicole stared up into the rugged bronze faces hovering over her. Now that she saw them in broad daylight, she realized they were mestizos, half-breeds of Spanish and Indian blood. There was something about them — something that suddenly disturbed her. The glint in the dark piercing eyes was unmistakably sinister.

"*Mira no mas, hermanito!*" the older one exclaimed.

"Come on, *muchacha*, let's have a better look at you," he said, impatiently pulling her down to the ground before she realized what was happening.

Angrily she pulled herself free of him, trying to regain her balance, but making an effort not to betray how much their attitude was frightening her. "You take too much liberty, *señores*," she sputtered indignantly as she nervously smoothed out her rumpled party dress.

The man who had lifted her out of the cart appraised her coldly. "Well, it seems like we're going to get a real bonus for this job, *verdad*?" he muttered, stroking his chin thoughtfully.

The younger brother stared with equal admiration, his

pockmarked face wreathed in a malicious smile. "Good thing we didn't finish her off until we got a good look at her. *Qué barbaridad!* What we would have missed!"

"She's one of the best hides I've seen, all right," he agreed. "But her kind's always trouble."

A horrible suspicion gnawed at her insides, but she boldly went on. "You were hired to take me to Veracruz, not to drug my drink without my permission, or be so forward as to lay your hands on me as you just did!"

The elder of the two men laughed sarcastically. "We were hired to do much more than that, *muchacha.*" He grinned. "The *gran señora*, she told us you were a *puta* of little value that she wanted out of the way. But she was wrong about one thing. You're at least worth a little special attention before we get on with our business!"

A cold sweat enveloped her. These men were not her saviors — they were hired assassins! Doña Inés had not only wanted to rid herself of a rival, but had wanted final revenge as well!

Chapter 52

The pair was so busy arguing over what they were going to do with her that she caught them off guard. In a desperate burst of energy, she broke away and made a wild dash for freedom, but it was quickly checked. The man with the pockmarked face caught her deftly by the arm.

"Not so fast, *chulita*!" he chided her, ignoring her frantic efforts to free herself from his grip. "I'm not going to slit that pretty throat of yours yet. You be good to me, and I'll stab you with something better than a *cuchillo*!"

He turned to his older brother. "What you say we keep her for a while? Think of it; we can have her all to ourselves — our own private *puta*!"

"*Estás loco*," growled the other, who had already drawn his knife and was fingering the blade tentatively. "The *señora* paid us well, and we'd be fools to cross an important lady like her."

"Bah! How will she know what we do with the wench? After all, what's the difference if we dispatch her now or keep her awhile for our personal use? Either way, the *señora* will be rid of her."

"It's too risky to leave the wench alone in our hut, even tied up. *Mujeres* always bring trouble; you know that."

"*Andale*, Pepe. You know damn well we'll never get another *cuero* as fine as this one again, not even for the pearls of the Virgin!"

The older man studied Nicole for a moment, then grunted. "Well, maybe for a day or two...." he said slowly. "I don't suppose the *señora* would object if we have a little sport with the wench before we complete the job. But after that ..." He fingered the blade of his knife again.

They dragged her between them toward the thatch-roofed hut in the rear of the clearing.

"See what a fighter she is," complained one. "If we try to keep her, she'll be more trouble than she's worth!"

Nicole kicked at him and then sank her teeth into the hand he had around her wrist.

The man spat out an angry oath. "*Condenada mujer!* That does it!" He waved his knife threateningly at her. "I'm going to cut your throat *ahora mismo* — right here and now!" He shoved her to the ground, but his brother pulled her greedily to him, breaking her fall.

"*Qué barbaridad, hermano!* Don't be an *aguafiestas*!" he protested with a flood of his own oaths. "At least let me get a few rides on her before you go throwing a wet blanket on the party!"

The older man shrugged. "All right — *échate*! But take your pokes right here and now, because as soon as we've finshed with this *ramera*, I'm going to dispatch her to hell!"

The younger man lowered Nicole eagerly to the ground and straddled her. "*Bueno*, hold her for me so I can spread her good. Then you can go down on her and I'll return the favor."

He grabbed at her legs, trying to lift her skirts and work his dirty cotton breeches open at the same time.

His brother stood scowling at the marks on his hand, then finally knelt beside him and pinned her arms.

Powerless to move now, Nicole tried to beat down the waves of panic beginning to overwhelm her. She knew she was fighting to save herself and her unborn child not only from abuse but death. These men were assassins. When they finished with her, they were going to kill her.

She tossed her head from side to side, her long, flaming hair lashing the face of the man bending over her, trying to force her thighs farther and farther apart with his knees while he bared his teeth in search of her breasts. Impatiently he caught the hair that was blinding him and pushed it aside.

"Lie still, you *hija de. . .*!"

But the scream that finally came tearing out of her parched throat drowned him out.

"Keep the damn slut quiet!" panted the voice nearest her ear, and a hand clamped over her mouth. She closed her eyes, trying to blot out the horror of that moment, but she knew he was positioning himself for the thrust. She murmured a silent prayer and braced herself. Her baby! God protect her baby!

But at that moment there was a noise behind them — a deep gutteral growl like that of an enraged animal going for the kill. A shadowy form sprang out of the forest and lunged toward them. Something hard and glittering flashed near her, singing in her ears as it cut through the air.

The man on top of her reared up with a startled gasp and hung there suspended for a moment like a pig on a spit, then went limp. Only as he toppled over beside her did she see the sword emerging from his back.

For one breathless instant her rescuer stood high above her, silhouetted against the setting sun like an avenging angel. Then he pulled his bloodstained blade free and turned his attention to the other assassin.

As that ominous shadow of doom fell across him, the

second man paled and began to edge backward, not daring to rise from his knees, yet all the while keeping his dark eyes glued on the bloody sword poised to strike again.

It was then that Nicole recognized the tall, dark-haired stranger. He was the Spaniard with the pointed beard whom she had momentarily noticed at Escobar's *fiesta*. But what was he doing so far outside Puebla? Had he been drawn to the scene by her scream, or was he perhaps another villain with his own motives for intruding upon them?

The terrified mestizo had broken into a run. He crashed headlong into the woods, increasing his speed as he went. But the dark intruder was not willing to relinquish his prey. He plunged in after him.

There was a flurry of startled birds on the wing ... an anguished cry ... then silence.

The Spaniard emerged from the forest, his bloodstained sword in hand. He was making his way toward her, his long legs covering the clearing rapidly.

Instinctively Nicole buried her face in her hands, too drained of energy now to rise from where she knelt on the ground to confront this new menace. True, this man had saved her from Doña Inés's hired assassins, but how could she know what motivated him? She dared not trust anyone in this hostile land. She had risked appealing to Doña Inés and been betrayed. She had trusted the two men with the cart, believing they had meant to help her escape, and here they had been about to rape and kill her!

No, she must remember this lesson and never trust anyone again. Just because there was something about this stranger that reminded her of Paul certainly didn't mean she could trust him any more than the others!

Though she didn't dare look up, she knew he was standing there looking down at her as he sheathed his sword.

At last he broke the silence. "My poor little bobcat,

I can't let you out of my sight for a moment without your getting into trouble!"

Her lids flew open, and she found herself staring into a pair of blue eyes that were very familiar. They were incongruous with the dark hair and beard that framed them, but there was no mistaking them. Had everything that had happened been nothing more than some nightmare then? Was this just another one of those horrible dreams in which everyone ended up suddenly turning into someone else. . .?

"Paul . . . oh, Paul!" she cried and fell unconscious into the arms reaching out to her.

Chapter 53

She was vaguely aware of being lifted and carried into the hut. As the starched ruff of a jabot brushed against her face, the faint scent of sandalwood brought her back.

Her rescuer was about to lay her back on one of the pallets, but she motioned for him to set her down on the chair instead. He continued to keep an arm around her waist to steady her and dropped to one knee beside her. Gently he stroked her tangled hair back from her pale face and kissed the soft curve of her cheek, still damp with her tears.

"Don't be afraid, my sweet. It's all over now. This is Paul. I may have changed the color of my hair and grown a beard, but *c'est moi* ... it's me. I've come to get you out of here."

She reached out to touch his suntanned cheek, then traced the carefully shaped mustache and followed the strip of close-shaven beard that led to a neat point at his chin.

"Paul? Paul, can it really be you?" Her voice was weak and incredulous. In her shock she was still unable to sort out the real from the unreal. But her heart told her who it was before her logic did. In a burst of joy she caught the beloved face between her hands and began to shower it with kisses, repeating his name again and again.

Paul smiled and drew her closer to him, returning her barrage of kisses with ones of his own. "My sweet little Nicole, I'll never let you out of my sight again."

His mouth was hard and firm as he placed it hungrily over hers, bringing her flutter of excited kisses to a long, passionate conclusion. Dozens of questions trembled on her lips, but they were all forgotten in her burning desire to touch and caress him, to reassure herself it really was him, to become one at last with the dream and turn it into reality.

With a cry of unbridled joy, she threw her arms around him and slipped from the chair to his knee. The next moment they were lying on the warm earthen floor of the hut entwined in each other's arms, their lips locked and the hard, vibrant length of him seeking its home deep within her at last.

It was brief but powerful, their bodies racked with their urgent need to reach across the anguish of those past two months and fuse their love once more into one glorious whole.

"Oh, Paul, I never thought I'd be with you like this again," she whispered as she lay in his arms, still clinging to him as though afraid he might suddenly fade away and return to the realms of her fantasy.

He kissed her and rose quickly, pulling her to her feet with him. "My God! I didn't mean to take you like that!" he exclaimed, offering her the chair again while he looked for a lantern to light.

"You didn't mean to take me how?" she asked with mock innocence, but a knowing smile played around the corners of her mouth, still rosy from the passion of his kisses.

"You know ... on the floor like that ... without even

disrobing," he replied sheepishly. "God knows I wanted you to the point of distraction, but after all, you're my wife, not a tavern wench. I should have been more considerate."

She laughed. "And because I'm your wife, we should want each other less? I was as eager as you were, *mon amour*. If you hadn't taken me then and there, I blush to confess I'd have been all over you myself! I'm so happy I ache from the sheer joy of it!"

He gave her a pleased grin and kissed her again, the tip of his tongue lingering on her lips. His passion far from satiated, he reached for her breast, but suddenly he laughed and checked himself. "We'll get on with this shortly," he assured her. "But it will be getting dark soon, and I have to get the horses and bed them down for the night. I've brought two of them — one for each of us — so we can make better time. While I'm gone, why not check around here and see what you can find to eat. You must be starving. I know I am. Don't worry, I won't be long. Now that I've found you, I hate to let you out of my sight for a moment!"

It was dark by the time Paul returned. He had buried the bodies of the would-be assassins and left the horses and donkey in the crudely built stable behind the hut. Meanwhile Nicole lit the only lantern she could find in the one-room dwelling and, using some of the spring water she found in a covered pitcher, put what food she could scrape together — a couple of handfuls of dried beans and a few cobs of corn — to cook in the big clay pots hanging in the blackened fireplace.

The pallets looked so dirty and unappealing, however, that Paul threw them out and brought in fresh hay and covered it with with the blanket he had brought along in his pack. He'd found a jug half full of *pulque*, an almost complete cheese, and two dozen tortillas wrapped in a gauze cloth, which the men had probably bought in the marketplace on their way out of Puebla.

This momentary return to the practical details of everyday living had provided time for the countless questions, so while Nicole melted slices of cheese on the tortillas to ward off their hunger until the pots bubbling in the fireplace were ready, they began to talk.

Paul seemed reluctant, however, to ask her some of the questions most on his mind, so he let her take the lead.

"It's strange to see you sitting there with that dark hair and devilish beard!" she smiled. "You know, I saw you at Escobar's and thought of you, but it never occurred to me it could have been possible.... If I could have seen your eyes, perhaps I'd have suspected, but then I was always imagining I saw you everywhere! Of course, last night I had my hands full...."

Paul scowled. "Aye, I saw it all. Who the devil was that blasted fop hanging on to you all evening? The way he was ogling you, I had all I could do to keep from going up to him and smashing my fist in his face right then and there!"

"Moreno? Oh, he's a friend of Escobar's. But he was only for show. Escobar had him escort me because of his betrothed, Doña Inés. Don Heriberto wanted Escobar to give me to him, but I doubt that would have come to pass." She saw the scowl on Paul's brow deepening and paused, not knowing exactly how to approach the subject of Escobar with him.

"I saw that bastard, too," Paul growled. "He was following every move you and that fellow Moreno made all night. I was at a loss to figure out what was going on there, and trembling so much inside with rage just to see the way the two of them were leering at you, I had all I could do not to throw caution to the winds and carry you out of there by force! Believe me, I had to keep reminding myself to check my temper and bide my time. But then I saw you go out to the patio, and I followed you. As soon as you went into the stables and met the men with the cart, I realized you had already set a plan of escape in motion, so I decided just to follow at a discreet distance and play out whatever followed by ear. I didn't dare stay too close, of course, so when they stopped here in the woods, I had to tether my mounts a little distance away and steal up on foot to see whether you were all right or not. Naturally when I heard you scream, I ran the rest of the way. The bloody bastards!"

Nicole shook her head. "Oh, I didn't hire them," she said quickly. "Doña Inés did. In desperation I turned to her to help me escape, and she was supposed to have arranged for them to get me to Veracruz and put me on a boat going to some neutral port. It was the only thing I could think of to do at the time, since I didn't know you were still alive."

"And the ruby I gave you? And your wedding ring? Do you still have them, or did that bastard Escobar take them from you?"

"He searched my belongings and took everything of value he could find, even the bolts of lawn and linen you gave me, but he didn't find the jewels. I've had them sewn in the hem of my petticoat ever since the Spanish retook Pensacola."

"Good. You were wise, my sweet, to take such precautions. So it was Escobar's fiancée who betrayed you and hired those assassins?"

"She simply paid them to kill me as soon as they got me far enough out of town that no one would know," Nicole said bitterly. "They were going to bury me here in the woods, so I'd have disappeared forever!"

Paul was grim as he sat staring into the fire, his brows drawn together in angry contemplation. "That lady is quite a viper, isn't she? Escobar and that bitch should make a stunning pair!" He reached out as Nicole moved to give him another *quesadilla* and catching her hand, drew her closer to him. "My blood runs cold when I think of the danger you were in. But you should have known

I'd find a way to come and rescue you, my sweet. You know damn well I wouldn't let anyone carry you off like that, much less Escobar! I'd never abandon you. Don't you know that yet?"

"But I thought you were dead. Escobar told me you'd been captured and hanged in Havana. Oh, Paul, you can't imagine how sick with grief I've been!"

She pulled out the little pouch and showed him the lock of blond hair she had been carrying with her all those weeks. "Escobar gave me this as proof. I refused to believe him at first, but when he showed me this, well, I could have sworn it belonged to you."

"It does. They cut that piece and several others off when they captured me. It took half a dozen men to hold me down, but they were determined to get their mementos of *El Diablo Dorado* to send to the authorities in Spain and in their colonies so they could boast of my capture. I was mad as hell at first and made them pay dearly for every piece they took, but after one or two days, I decided to take advantage of their desire for souvenirs. One morning one of the guards came down into the hold to bring us mess. I pretended to be resigned and offered no objections when he asked me if he could take a piece of my hair for his girlfriend. As soon as he bent over with his knife to help himself to a souvenir, however, I wrapped the chain between my wrists around his neck and disarmed him. After that, it was easy. Once I got the keys off him, I freed myself and my men, and we took our Spanish hosts, as well as their ship, completely by surprise. That's the vessel I have now — a three-masted square-rigger called the *Santa Monica*. Maybe we'll re-christen it after you if it gets us safely out of here." He grinned. "Would you like that, sweet?"

But Nicole's eyes misted. "It's true then. You lost the *Avenger*?"

His face saddened for a moment. "Yes, my dear, we lost her — first the storm crippled her, and the Spaniards did the rest."

"My poor darling, I know how much you loved your ship!"

"I did that," he said, heaving a deep sigh. "Although the *Santa Monica* is really a better vessel, I confess I miss my trim little brigantine. But you're more important to me than all the ships on the seven seas, my sweet. What's more, it's probably to our advantage that we have this one now. When we sailed into Veracruz a few days ago, the *Avenger* might have been recognized as mine, whereas the *Santa Monica* was immediately accepted as Spanish. Of course, it's to my advantage that everyone in New Spain thinks I've been hanged, and I'm counting on our getting out of here before the news of my escape arrives here."

Nicole paled. "*Mon Dieu!* You've put yourself in great danger to come into the interior alone like this to rescue me!"

He shrugged his shoulders and smiled. "I stand a better chance of success going it alone. Besides, my men are already taking risk enough just sitting in the bay under the fort guns waiting for me to return, but they're loyal fellows, God love them. I insisted they put this venture to a vote, since there's no profit in it for them, but they agreed to a man to help me rescue you. I guess they figured I wouldn't be much good for anything until I did anyway!"

"But won't your ship attract attention riding at anchor for so long? And so many of your crew members could never convince anyone they're Spaniards. *Mon Dieu!* Are they all wearing disguises like you or . . .?"

Paul laughed. "There's no need for such extremes," he assured her. "I slipped ashore the first night we arrived and left Fernandez in command. He's Spanish and can deal convincingly with the port authorities. But I doubt he'll be bothered too much, since he's telling anyone who wants to come on board that the plague has broken out on the ship; hence all shore leaves have been canceled. In that way everyone in port will give the ship a wide berth and no one will suspect anything if they don't see the crew." He resumed eating, but after a bite or two of the cheese-filled tortilla, he looked across the table at her. "What I can't understand is how Escobar learned about you. Of course, I realize there were few women among the French prisoners at Pensacola, and you, my dear, would attract attention even in a mob, but why didn't the Spanish just assume you were the Baudiers' daughter? I hate to think one of the French officials betrayed my wife to the Spanish after all the help I gave them."

"Oh, no, it wasn't any of them. It was Hanson who told the Spanish commander about me — to save his own neck." She told him how it had happened.

"Damn that Hanson!" Paul's temper flared. "I should have hanged him and been done with it!"

"They wanted to use me as bait to distract you from helping the French defend Mobile Bay, and of course, they hoped they might even be lucky enough to capture you."

"They did try to take Dauphin Island," he told her, "right after Pensacola surrendered. The Spaniards thought they were going to get the whole French colony in one clean sweep, but Sérigny put up a valiant fight and fended them off. The Indians helped, too. Bienville knows how to deal with the redskins and keeps most of them on his side, I'll give him that!"

He poured some of the *pulque* into his mug and offered her a sip, but she took one sniff and wrinkled her nose at it. "Of course, as soon as I got wind of the trouble at Pensacola, I crowded the canvas to get back to you," he went on. "When I learned the port had been retaken by the Spaniards, I immediately went after the ship that was on its way to Havana with the French who had been taken prisoner, thinking you were on it. You can imagine my rage and frustration when the Baudiers told me you'd been taken away at the last minute on orders from the

Spanish commander. Then, when I questioned the Spanish captain of the ship I'd captured about you, he told me Escobar had claimed you as his prisoner and was taking you with him to Veracruz. Well, I needn't tell you I was like a madman. I've only cried twice in my life — the night I lost my mother and father and the day I learned you were in Escobar's hands! I vowed I'd rescue you if I had to go to hell and back to get you."

He leaned across the table and caught her hand, his eyes glittering like sapphires in the glow from the fire. "When I think of how I wanted to protect you by giving you my name and formalizing our relationship — all I did was make you a target for my enemies. Can you ever forgive me? You've suffered so much because of me, and all I've ever wanted to do was keep you from harm!" His voice shook with emotion as he lifted her hand to his lips.

"There's nothing to forgive, my love," she said tenderly. "You had no way of knowing Hanson would tell Escobar about us. Believe me, I wouldn't have wanted to deny our love no matter what happened. I'm proud to say I'm your wife."

"I should have never left you in Pensacola! God as my witness, I'll never forgive myself for that! When I think of all you went through because I wasn't there when you needed me . . ." His voice broke and the table trembled from the force with which he slammed his mug down.

Nicole dished out a plate of beans with a steaming corncob and set it before him. But he caught her to him again. "I couldn't sleep nights thinking of you at the mercy of that son of a bitch Escobar. I thought it wasn't possible for me to hate him any more than I already did, but when I knew he'd taken you prisoner, I couldn't erase from my mind the picture of that sadist touching you, violating you. . . ." His voice was hard and brittle, and the knuckles of his hand were white as he clutched the mug. "But he'll pay, I promise you. It's just one more score I have to settle with him! Once I get you to safety, I'm going to come back here and hunt him down and make him pay for every moment of pain and humiliation he caused you!"

She had never seen him in such torment, not even when he had told her about his mother and father.

With a little cry, she rose and ran to him. "Oh, my darling, there's still so much more I have to tell you," she began, but he held up his hand.

"No, no, let's not talk of this anymore," he begged. "Let's try to forget Escobar at least for tonight."

"But there are things — important things you should know," she insisted. She caught his face between her hands and kissed the hard lines around his mouth. "All I want is for us to get out of this place," she pleaded. "Don't speak of ever coming back here. I thought you were dead and lost to me, and now God has given you back to me. I don't want to risk losing you again! Please, my darling, I need you more than ever now ... *we* need you ... the baby and I ..."

"The — the baby?" He paled. "My God! You're *pregnant*?" He stared at her in disbelief.

She nodded and touched his shoulder eagerly, but to her surprise she felt a violent shudder rack his powerful frame and a low oath rumble in his throat. The murderous look in his eyes startled her, and she dropped her hand from his shoulder.

When he saw the expression on her face, he quickly caught himself and made an effort to control the rush of emotions that was tearing him apart. "My God! You're pregnant!" he echoed as though still trying to digest the news. Then he looked at her and his eyes softened. "It's all right, my sweet, don't worry," he said quickly, circling her waist with his arm and drawing her protectively to him. "I'll take care of you and the child, and I'll even learn to love it because it's yours."

Suddenly she realized what he must be thinking. What

a silly goose she had been to blurt out her news like that without preparing him for it. The poor darling! He thought it was Escobar's!

"I hope you'll also love the child because he's yours as well as mine." She smiled.

He looked stunned. "You mean . . ."

She nodded, smiling gently up at him. "Oh, my dear, it's not Escobar's. It's ours — yours and mine."

"Are you sure?" His face was tight, but he took her hand quickly in his. "Please don't try to spare me," he said huskily. "We've always told each other the truth, and you can tell me this, too. Don't worry, my sweet. I'd never turn my back on you or a child of yours. . . ." The trembling of his arm around her betrayed how much the moment was costing him.

She smiled tenderly and put her finger against his lips. "Oh, how I love you, Paul Dawson," she said, her eyes misting. "Thank you for those words, but fortunately such a sacrifice isn't necessary. The child is yours, my darling . . . the fruit of our love."

Her heart leaped with joy as she saw the expression on his face change to pure delight.

"And I have one other piece of news that should give you at least some satisfaction," she said, taking his bearded face in her hands and lifting it to hers as she stood in the warm circle of his arms. "You've been avenged far more than you know, *mon amour*," she said in a quiet, meaningful voice. "That time you nearly had Escobar two years ago . . . you did more to him than you realized. Your broadside cost him his manhood. He's a miserable, tormented man, consuming himself in his own fire."

Chapter 54

There was a brief shower during the night, but in that tiny hut in a wooded area off the road to Veracruz, Nicole found her world again. While the rain beat on the thatched roof, they lay on their pallet of sweet-smelling hay and renewed their vows by the light of the fire's dying embers.

"We still have a good piece of road to go yet," Paul told her, "and tomorrow we might have more hardships and perils to face, but let's hope the goddess Athena will hold back the dawn for us the same as she did for Ulysses when he was finally reunited with Penelope" — he brushed her face with his lips — "'until he had had his fill of love and sleep in his wife's arms.'" He ended the quote on her lips and gently cupped the fullness of her breast as he molded his loins to hers.

This time he possessed her slowly, tenderly, with a languid sensuousness that reawakened every fiber of her body. There was no need now for him to keep reminding her who it was, as he had done the first time, to erase the phantoms of the past. She recognized every touch of his hand, every brush of his lips, every flick of his tongue.

Her fingers lovingly traced the familiar cords of his muscles as they flexed and vibrated to his passion, and when finally his rhythm accelerated, she gave a shiver of delight and met each thrust with joyous abandon until they were moving as one. The thrill of rediscovery, of reaffirming their love, raised them to even greater heights. No matter what the future held, Paul was there by her side now, and she was grateful for these precious hours with him — hours that she had thought would never come again.

"How I dreamed of this moment when I could hold you close to me again," Paul told her as he lay contentedly on their pallet of hay and cradled her in his arms. "God! How I missed you! From the first day I sailed out of Pensacola, I hated to go down to my cabin. It seemed like a tomb without you. And how I missed your sweet warmth by my side whenever I tried to sleep in my bunk! I love you too much, my little bobcat. I'm obsessed with you!" He kissed the top of the red-gold head pillowed on his shoulder and drew her closer. It was then that he realized she was asleep. With a smile he folded her in his arms and reminded himself how exhausted she must be after all she had been through. And she was expecting now, as well. She was hardly more than a child herself, and here she was about to have a child of her own — *his* child! The very thought of it brought a glow to his world. How this adorable little stray "cub", whom he had taken into his life on an impulse, had changed everything for him! He bent down and kissed her forehead, and she stirred drowsily but didn't wake. How peacefully she slept — like a trusting child, certain that all would be well now because he was there to look after her. If only he would be able to live up to that unconditional love and faith she had placed in him. He was worried about her being pregnant, but it only made her all the more precious to him — if that were possible. He had to get her to New England where she could be safe. He wasn't an especially religious man, but that night he prayed for the strength to be able to protect the treasure — the two treasures — he held in his arms.

The next morning Nicole awakened surprisingly refreshed. With Paul lying beside her, she had rested secure in the knowledge that all was right with her world once more. He had let her sleep while he had prepared the horses for their journey and gone hunting for their breakfast. By the time he had awakened her, he had skinned and cleaned a rabbit and was roasting it in the fireplace. The joy of beginning a new day with each other was enough to make them linger awhile longer on their pallet before folding the blanket and packing it away. While they waited for the rabbit to cook, they made love once again, knowing that this might be the last time they would be able to enjoy such a pleasant interlude together until they were out of New Spain.

They ate part of the rabbit and then wrapped the rest of it in the gauze left over from the tortillas so they could take it with them.

The day was sunny but cool, with the first hint of autumn in the air. The effects of the light showers during the night had just about disappeared, so they made good time for the first few hours. Paul set the pace and tried to keep it steady in order not to tire or jar her. Fortunately she was a good rider, though Paul worried about her riding so long. She assured him that he was being overly concerned and laughingly showed him how flat she still was, since she was not even two months pregnant yet. Nevertheless, he preferred to err on the cautious side rather than take unnecessary risks with her or the baby.

Finally he decided it would be better if she rode seated in front of him so he could hold her braced against him and thus absorb the worst of the bouncing. Now that they were on one horse, however, he insisted that she discard her panniers and all her petticoats except one.

This new arrangement also made it necessary that they

alternate the roans frequently so as not to overtax either one.

Paul was more worried than ever now about delaying too much on the road, for he knew his ship could not stay at anchor in the bay of Veracruz indefinitely without arousing suspicion.

They stopped for a while along a deserted stretch of the road around noon and finished off what remained of the rabbit. A stagecoach passed them, heading toward Puebla and probably from there on to the capital. The driver had waved a friendly greeting, and Paul had returned it, although he would have preferred that he and Nicole had gone unnoticed. Of course, she had discreetly covered herself in the multistriped shawl, which should have made it difficult for anyone to get a good look at her, and he had retouched his hair and beard before they had set out that morning, so they had probably looked like just another Spanish gentleman and his wife or mistress en route to Veracruz.

During the afternoon, while taking another short rest, they had seen someone on horseback headed toward Veracruz, but they hid themselves this time.

They went through a small village of adobe huts, but it seemed almost deserted, for it was the hour when most of the inhabitants were taking their midday meal and siesta. Paul did stop long enough to buy a few tacos from a small street stand that obviously catered to travelers, and Nicole devoured them with relish, joking that her appetite was increasing now that she was eating for two.

But as the day began to wane and they entered another village, a little larger than the previous one, Paul decided to stop for the night.

"It's too dangerous to be on this road after dark, and we and the horses need a good rest. Besides, sweet, you need your nourishment. There's a *diligencia* in this town, so we had better take advantage of the accommodations it offers. There won't be any stagecoach stops after this one for quite awhile."

"Do you really think Escobar might still be trying to follow me?" she asked incredulously. "I doubt he even knows yet that you're still alive, much less with me, so I'm the only one he would be after at the moment."

"From what I know of him, I wouldn't be surprised if he comes after you," Paul replied grimly. "He's just arrogant enough not to want it said that you gave him the slip."

"Don't you think Doña Inés would try to detain him?"

"Yes, I expect she would, but I doubt Escobar would let her or anyone else influence him if he feared his authority or his masculinity might be put to question."

Nicole paled and pulled the rebozo closer around her.

"That's why we don't dare take a coach," he went on as he headed toward the sprawling tile-roofed inn farther down the road. "Not only would we not make good time, we wouldn't have any freedom in our movements. Besides, if Escobar thinks you're alone — and there's no reason yet for him to suspect I'm with you — the first place he'll be looking for you will be carts and public or private carriages."

"Oh, Paul, I'm afraid. Most of all, I tremble to think what Escobar would do to you if he caught you!"

Paul leaned forward to kiss a red-gold curl that had escaped the rebozo. "Don't worry, my sweet, I have two good reasons to fight now. Frankly, if you and the baby weren't my first concern, I'd welcome a confrontation with that bastard once and for all."

"Oh, no, Paul! Promise me we'll go straight to your ship and sail away from this horrid place as quickly as possible."

He laughed. "Don't worry, my pet. I'm just as anxious to get out of this lion's den as you are. I'd prefer meeting Escobar with better odds — on my terrain, not his."

As he neared the entrance to the inn, he whispered,

"Remember now, we're Señor and Señora Chávez. Don't speak; just nod or smile if you have to answer."

She drew her shawl about her head and shoulders, much in the way she had seen native women do with their rebozos, so now her hair and face were completely in shadow.

As the stable boys ran up to attend them, Paul dismounted and helped her down. He said a few words in Spanish and handed the reins over to them along with some coins. The *propina* must have been generous, Nicole thought, judging from the manner in which their huge brown eyes lit up and they dashed about, outdoing themselves to please him. But Paul waved them away in the style of a proud grandee and led her into the inn.

The taproom of the *León de Castilla* was noisy and bustling, half filled with patrons sitting around at tables, drinking hot chocolate or *pulque*, while the clanging of pots and pans and the odor of roast pork announced that preparations were already under way for the evening meal.

Paul's perfect Castilian brought immediate respect from the proprietor, who quickly came forward to meet him. He glanced curiously at Nicole, but Paul's frown was enough to discourage him from continuing his appraisal. Spanish men could be quite touchy about anyone ogling their women, so the innkeeper kept his eyes discreetly averted and hastily led the couple to one of his best rooms.

Paul ordered extra water for bathing and two full-course meals of whatever was being prepared. Then, alone at last with Nicole, he heaved a sigh of relief and hung his sword under his frock coat and vest on the back of a chair near the bed. Finally he carefully checked his pistol and placed it under a pillow on the far side of the large four-poster.

Stretching contentedly, he went over to where Nicole stood looking about the room. "Are you tired, my dear?"

"A little," she smiled, "but I feel surprisingly well."

"Be careful to keep yourself covered whenever anyone is around, even the servants," he warned her. "A good supper and bed tonight and another hearty meal before we set out in the morning, and we should be able to cover a nice stretch of road tomorrow."

"If we were anywhere except in Spanish territory, I could be so happy with you like this," she said, laying her head on his chest.

"The same thought has occurred to me," he said with a twinkle in his eyes, "though I confess riding with you pressed so close against me hour after hour becomes a sweet torment when I can't stop and make love to you along the way. I can hardly wait until we're back on the ship!"

She smiled and shot him a coy look. "Nor I, my love."

He kissed her happily. "By all the saints! My frightened little cub has turned into a lusty wench! You're a bundle of surprises, and I love every one of them!"

She reached up instinctively to run her fingers through his dark hair, but then drew back with a frown. "My hands are all stained from that horrid black dye!" she exclaimed. "How I miss your beautiful golden hair!"

"I'm afraid that, too, must wait until we're back at the ship," he said.

She sighed, but there was still a coquettish gleam in her eye. "With a feather mattress over there, I certainly hope we don't have to wait until we get back to the ship for everything!"

He roared and kissed her long and hard. Then sweeping her quickly into his arms, he carried her to the bed.

Chapter 55

Nicole awakened with a start. In spite of the variety of noises coming from the inner patio and the tavern below, the good hot meal, comfortable bed, and Paul's reassuring presence had eased her into a sound, relaxing sleep.

She was lying half dressed in her petticoat and camisole, as Paul had taught her to sleep when danger was a possibility. They hadn't even drawn the bed curtains, since he always preferred to see at a glance what was around him, especially when he was in a strange place.

The night candle was almost spent, and for a moment she was disoriented by the sight of the dimly lit, unfamiliar room. But even before her eyes could adjust to the semidarkness ... even before she remembered where she was ... she knew something was amiss. Though Paul still lay beside her under the covers, she could feel the tension in every muscle of his body.

Something glittered in the dim light, and suddenly she realized it was a naked sword — its point only a few inches away from Paul's throat!

"This is an unexpected pleasure," came a familiar voice from one of the shadowy forms standing near the bed. "I came to snare a bird and caught myself a lion instead!"

There was no mistaking Escobar's voice, nor the whine of Heriberto Moreno that echoed him.

"Yes, that vendor was right, Rodrigo. Here's our pretty *francesita* doing what best suits her — lying with a man!"

"Get her out of there," Escobar snapped at his friend, still holding his sword on Paul.

The shorter man moved cautiously toward the bed, all the while eyeing Paul warily. However, his eagerness to get his hands on her made him bolder than usual.

Nicole lay paralyzed with terror, watching as the corpulent figure emerged from the shadows and came toward her brandishing an unsheathed rapier. She could feel Paul stir slightly, but what could he really do with Escobar's blade poised and ready to plunge into his throat?

"Is the girl mine now, as you promised?" Moreno whined again. He reached out eagerly for Nicole as he saw no signs of resistance from the buccaneer.

But suddenly Paul threw the covers over the point of Escobar's sword and jumped out of the bed, pistol in hand.

Don Heriberto froze, his arm extended in midair toward Nicole. *"Dios mio!"* he exclaimed, paling under his olive complexion, realizing only too well that he could never lunge with his sword before the pistol went off. "No gentleman would shoot another in cold blood!" he protested.

But Paul's eyes glittered hard as blue quartz.

"From the moment you made your pact with the devil, you sealed your doom," he said levelly.

There was a flash and the pistol sounded. In that split second the Spaniard bolted backward from the force of the ball, and with a look of disbelief on his startled countenance, let his sword fall clattering to the floor. Then he doubled over with a moan.

Paul knew there could be no compromise. He couldn't let Nicole fall into enemy hands. If that happened, they would immediately use her to force him to surrender, and she would be lost.

He turned quickly to Escobar. Already the grandee, with an agility of his own, had slashed his way through the sheet. Before there was time for Paul to prepare the pistol to fire again, Escobar swung his blade and knocked the gun out of his hand, sending it flying across the room.

The sight of her beloved standing defenseless before his adversary brought Nicole out of her paralysis. With a cry she leaped out of the bed and caught up Heriberto's sword from where it lay on the floor. She didn't know exactly what she should do with it, but her movement alone was enough to distract the Spaniard. Clumsy as her thrust was, it served to put him momentarily on the defensive. Even as he dodged her attack with an angry oath, Paul lunged and grabbed his own rapier from where it lay hidden under his frock coat and vest.

"Thank you, my love," he said with a dry chuckle as he rapidly put himself between her and Escobar. From the emerald sparks flashing in her eyes, however, he realized she had every intention of staying there and fighting beside him. "Please, sweet, get out of the way. I've waited a long time for this moment," he said sternly, kicking the chair out of his way and edging her determinedly toward the sidelines, though he never once took his gaze away from Escobar.

The grandee had also resumed his guard and stepped back now to a more favorable position for the deadly contest he knew was about to begin. "I'm only too happy to accommodate you, *capitán*," he said with mock courtesy. "My one regret when they told me they had hanged you was that I'd been robbed of the pleasure of killing you myself. Now it seems I'll have it after all!"

With no further warning, Escobar made a bold thrust, hoping to catch the buccaneer unawares and thus force him to respond so quickly that he might leave himself partially exposed.

But Paul held fast to his guard. He simply kept his

arm still and deflected the threatening blade with a circular movement of his sword — a movement that collected his opponent's blade and obliged the latter to return to his original position.

The two men proceeded more cautiously now, each testing the other's pace and style, feinting to ascertain his adversary's most likely reactions, looking for an opening, for some way of forcing the other to parry in a manner that would leave him vulnerable for the fatal thrust.

But both men were master swordsmen. They knew all the subtle aspects of this complex game of bluff and counterbluff ... of perfect discipline between mind and muscle. It was a deadly form of chess, played at lightning speed. The smallest error in judgment, the slightest miscalculation, could be fatal.

Paul noted early in the match that Escobar, like him, tended to favor the circular parry — keeping his guard position, which made the possibility of finding an opening even more difficult. A doublé, of course, was possible, but then there was always the danger that an opponent as clever as Escobar might only pretend to favor one way in order to lead him into making a wrong assumption — an assumption which could prove costly if he depended on it. There was no way to be sure that Escobar wasn't deliberately deceiving him in order to lay a trap for him, biding his time until the moment when his response would not be the expected one! But one thing was certain; the outcome was going to depend on the speed with which each one reacted.

The room was stifling with its shutters closed to the cool night air, and beads of sweat began to appear on their brows as their breathing grew more labored, their concentration more intense. Nicole watched, still holding Heriberto's sword in her hand, and fighting the temptation to intervene.

The singing and shouting downstairs in the taproom, together with the arrival of an unusually late carriage in the courtyard, had probably masked the shot Paul had fired. She tried to see where the pistol had fallen, but the room was not lit brightly enough to spot it, and she was loathe to tear her gaze away from the dueling men even for a moment. Besides, she had no idea how to reload and fire the gun, even if she did find it.

The clash of the swords grew more feverish, and Paul deftly dodged Escobar's blade as it sliced the air and barely missed singeing the sleeve of his shirt. He had to be careful, too, not to parry always in the same manner, or the Spaniard would be able to predict his methods of defense too easily!

In build, the two men were well matched, and both were fleet of foot. Dawson's stockinged feet moved with a nimbleness that reflected years of scampering up and down rigging and through hatchways and maintaining balance on the swaying deck of a ship. Escobar, too, had spent considerable time at sea, but those years the buccaneer had spent rowing in the galleys probably gave him an edge in thrusting power as well as endurance. The hatred in their eyes charged the bedchamber like shafts of lightning in a summer storm. Each one knew this was a duel to the death. Too much had passed between them for it to be otherwise. The loss of one man's family ... the loss of the other's manhood ... these things could not be easily forgotten or forgiven.

Suddenly footsteps sounded outside the door, and Nicole tightened her grip on the sword.

But when the door opened, it was Doña Inés who stood there, pale and breathless, her black velvet skirts dusty and rumpled and her eyes, dark with rage, shining like a pair of glowing coals.

She glared at the two men, but they were so intent now on their bitter contest that they dared not let anyone or anything distract them.

Suddenly she caught sight of Nicole. Visibly taken aback, she fingered the stiletto hanging in its jeweled scabbard from the chain around her tightly corseted waist. How could this troublesome wench still be alive? She turned her dark, vindictive gaze back to Escobar. And how could her *prometido* continue to make a fool of himself over this French whore? No sooner had Rodrigo discovered the girl's disappearance than he had dashed off with Moreno like a maniac, leaving the guests gaping after them. And throughout it all, there she had stood — the richest, most beautiful woman in New Spain, abandoned and humiliated in front of the cream of Puebla's aristocracy while her betrothed had run after an insignificant harlot! Why, he had already killed José Luís Ruíz because of her, and now Heriberto Moreno lay dead on the floor — another victim of the havoc this slut had wrought!

But the farce was not over yet, for here was Rodrigo dueling with yet another man, and the reason was perfectly obvious! She took a step toward the men.

"Rodrigo!" she called out in a sharp, commanding voice. "Stop making a fool of yourself! She's only a *mujerzuela* — a slut!"

But Escobar didn't cast her so much as a glance. It was doubtful he had even heard her. He was too busy turning away his opponent's latest thrust, which had been too close for comfort.

She stepped closer and called him again. This time the grandee growled his annoyance and shoved her roughly aside. *"En nombre de Dios! Vete, mujer!"* he exclaimed between labored breaths. "For God's sake, woman! Get out of the way!"

Inés colored to the roots of her smoothly parted hair. "By all the saints!" she gasped, her voice hoarse now from the rage strangling her. "You've humiliated me over this strumpet for the last time!"

The slim, finely pointed blade of her dagger flashed in the dim light as she plunged it into Escobar's back.

With a cry of amazement, the grandee turned toward

her at last, bewilderment clouding his dark eyes. But his rhythm had been broken. He saw Paul's sword coming and parried, but not soon enough to block the lightning stroke that followed in the fraction of a second that his guard faltered.

The buccaneer's blade found its mark.

"Damn you to hell, woman! You've undone me!" Escobar groaned as he fell to one knee, clutching the spot where Paul's rapier had penetrated his chest. The blood oozed through his fingers, and he stared down at it in horror, then crumpled.

"Dios mío!" shrieked Inés while Paul stepped back, still breathing heavily, the damp lawn of his shirt clinging to him as he kept his bloodstained sword on guard and waited to see whether Escobar would rise.

The Spanish woman knelt beside her betrothed, trying to stop the blood with a lace-trimmed handkerchief. She looked up frantically at Paul, her eyes wild and accusing. "My God! You've killed him!"

"It seems I have, madam," he said flatly, lowering his weapon at last, "though I assure you I could have done it without any assistance from you!" He wiped the blade of his sword clean with his handkerchief and threw the bloodstained patch of linen on the floor beside his enemy. The taste of revenge wasn't nearly as sweet as he had expected it to be. He had waited over twelve years for this moment — dreaming, planning, even changing the course of his life — and now that it had come, it didn't seem to matter as much as he had thought it would.

Still unable to accept her part in her fiancé's death, Inés suddenly looked up at Nicole. *"Ramera!* This is all your fault!" she hissed, leaping to her feet, her stiletto poised again to strike.

Nicole lifted the sword she still held in her hand defensively, but Paul had already stepped behind the crazed woman and caught her by the wrist, pinning her arm behind her.

"Calm yourself, madam, and drop that deadly little toy of yours," he ordered. "I've never harmed a woman before, but you're sorely tempting me!"

The Spanish woman struggled like one possessed, the black hatred in her eyes fixed on Nicole. "You harlot! Why didn't those men I hired kill you? *You* should be dead, *not* my Rodrigo!"

Nicole met her rage with the green fury of her own eyes. "You're mistaken, *señora.* You've been mistaken all along. I never was Don Rodrigo's mistress, nor could any woman have been . . . not even you. He was impotent. He had been for two years!"

Doña Inés blanched. "You lie!" she exclaimed, the beauty of her face distorted with anger and hatred. "My betrothed has always been known for his prowess with women. Why, he could handle half a dozen whores like you at a time!"

"Perhaps once, but not recently," insisted Nicole. "He may have used me to keep his secret from the public, but he lost his manhood from a wound he received while fighting the *Avenger* a couple of years ago. You would have learned that for yourself, *señora,* on your wedding night."

"I — I don't believe you," the Spanish woman faltered, staring incredulously at Escobar's lifeless figure at her feet.

"You can have him examined if you wish and confirm what I say for yourself," Nicole suggested icily. "But it will probably only make you feel all the more guilty for your own sins. Because of your misplaced jealousy, *señora,* you nearly had me murdered and helped bring about your fiancé's death as well."

"You needn't feel too guilty about Escobar's demise," Paul suddenly interjected. "From the day he caused my parents' deaths, he was destined to die by my sword, and when he dared take my wife prisoner, he only hastened that end."

He took the stiletto from her hand and released his hold on her wrist.

"*Dios mío!* What this wench says can't be true!" she moaned, falling to her knees once more beside Escobar's body.

"I assure you that if it wasn't, and he had violated my wife, I'd have run my sword through his groin instead of his heart," Paul assured her, returning his rapier with a thud to its scabbard.

But Inés no longer heard him. "Rodrigo, Rodrigo," she murmured, suddenly all affection. "She's lying, isn't she? She's just slandering you because you cast her aside when you formalized our *compromiso*. You only came here to help your friend recapture her for himself ... that's what people should know...."

She tried to dab at his wound again with the blood-soaked handkerchief, as though unable to accept that the life had gone out of him. "*Mi pobre amor* — my poor love," she cooed. "People will know how you risked your life to help your friend overtake his mistress and her renegade lover."

Paul motioned to Nicole, hurriedly slipping into his boots and gathering his belongings, even as he whispered, "We've got to get out of here right now before someone calls the watch ... if they haven't already!"

He took Heriberto's sword from her. "We'll keep these," he said, scooping up the pistol from the floor. "They may come in handy before our journey is over."

He put on his frock coat and vest and grabbed his traveling pack, while Nicole started to lace her stays, but Paul motioned to her to hurry and get dressed. She had hardly slipped on the skirt and bodice of her gown than he was pulling her to the door with him.

Suddenly he paused. "I think I'll leave Doña Inés's fancy little weapon here," he said with a sardonic smile. "Then she can explain to the police why one of her fiancé's wounds matches it so perfectly!"

Nicole wrapped herself in the folds of her rebozo once more and followed him obediently out of the room, still in a daze, with her laces dangling, her shoes clutched on one hand, and her disheveled clothing held together with the other. As Paul closed the door behind them, she caught a fleeting glimpse of Doña Inés prostrate over the lifeless body of Rodrigo Escobar.

Chapter 56

By the time they had made their way quietly down the rear staircase and out to the stables, the first light of day was streaking the gray early morning skies. A generous tip from Paul yielded prompt attention from the groomsmen and gave him immediate access to the two freshest mounts on the premises.

For a while Paul rode at a fast clip, holding Nicole tightly against him and keeping hold on the lead rein of the other bay, as he tried to put as much distance as possible between them and the inn. But finally the need to give the horses some relief forced them to seek a secluded spot within the forest that lined the road.

They seemed to have come upon the ruins of an ancient temple, though the site was completely shrouded now in a verdant carpet of rampant vegetation. The gravelike mounds of some long-dead civilization that had flourished here centuries before only added to the unreality of the moment.

"*Mon Dieu!*" sighed Nicole as Paul lifted her down and carried her over to what seemed to be a fallen column crumbling into oblivion. "Did it really happen, or did I only dream that Escobar and Heriberto Moreno are lying dead in our room at the inn? I'm as confused as Doña Inés was when we left her this morning."

Paul paused, the saddle in his hand, as he was about to transfer it to the fresh bay. "She's probably gotten her second wind by now," he said. "That woman has solid rock at her core."

"Do you think she's given the alarm by now?"

"I'm sure she has. I should have killed her, too, for she's bound to send the watch after us, but I couldn't bring myself to kill a woman. God knows I was tempted to ... but I couldn't do it."

"Oh, Paul, so much killing! It sickens me!"

His eyes softened. "My sweet innocent! Do you think I kill for the pleasure of it? We're in a hostile land where one word of information about us could cost us our lives. I may still come to regret my moment of weakness in sparing Doña Inés's life before all this is over!"

"I wonder if she'll ever really accept the truth about Don Rodrigo and the part she played in his death? She's such a proud, arrogant woman."

"Don't waste your time speculating about that one," he said scornfully as he swung the saddle on the alternate horse and began to adjust the straps. "Rest assured, by the time the watch arrives at the inn, she'll have concocted a pretty story to tell them, in which we'll be the villains and she and her grandee friends the victims. I dare say once she's back in Puebla, she'll believe most of her own accounts as to what happened at the inn!"

Nicole was silent for a moment, looking at the leaf-strewn ground.

"At least you've had your vengeance," she said at last. "You caught up with Escobar and finally made him pay for his crimes against you and your family."

He threw a blanket over the other horse and patted it for a few minutes. Then he came over to her side and stood looking down at her. "Yes," he said at last, resting one booted foot on the mound where she was sitting. He gazed admiringly at her, delighting in the way the shaft of sunlight slanting across the clearing turned her bright hair into a tumult of burnished gold about her shoulders. "It's strange how unimportant even that moment of revenge seems now," he went on softly. "Even the fact that Doña Inés's stupidity had a part in it doesn't matter to me anymore. As I stand here looking at you, my sweet, the only thing I care about now is you — you and our child. All I want is to get you safely out of this place so we can start planning our future. It's time to lay the past behind us."

Nicole's eyes were misty pools of placid green. "Oh, yes, Paul. We have every reason to look ahead now."

"We're going to have to be more careful than ever from here on out," he reminded her. "Before we weren't certain whether you were being followed or not, but now we know we are. It will be getting hotter as we get into the lowlands, but you'll have to keep that rebozo wrapped about you, especially over that glorious hair of yours. To see you once, my pet, is to remember you forever. I'm afraid Escobar found us all the more quickly because the street vendor we bought those tacos from was too impressed by you!"

"Perhaps I should dye my hair like you, or at least wear a wig."

"It's an idea worth considering," he admitted, "though it'd take a lot of dye, and I don't have much left ... which reminds me, I didn't have time to retouch my hair and beard this morning, so you should check me before we go back on the road. And we didn't have a chance to eat anything either, so I suppose I'll have to go hunting again."

She reached out and caught his large suntanned hand — the beloved hand that had so often defended and caressed her — and laid her cheek against it, drawing comfort from knowing he was alive and beside her again. He smiled down at her, a little puzzled by her sudden burst of affection, but pleased by it, and bending forward, he kissed her.

Their lips lingered, enjoying the brief moment of intimacy after the harrowing experiences earlier that morning. It was a moment of muted passion ... of simple joy in each other.

But the crack of a twig, the rustle of dried leaves underfoot brought them back suddenly to reality. Paul bolted upright, his sword already halfway out of its sheath. The shaft of sunlight was obliterated now, as a circle of silent shadows closed in around them.

Chapter 57

"Damn it! I was afraid of this!" muttered Paul. He saw the question in her eyes and added quickly, "They're *cimarones* — runaway slaves turned bandits. Be careful. They're desperate outlaws ... cutthroats."

Realizing how outnumbered he was, Paul rapidly calculated that he probably stood a better chance using his wits instead of his weapons. He let his sword drop back into its scabbard but kept his hand resting on the hilt as he turned to face the menacing band of half-naked blacks encircling him and Nicole.

Clad only in dirty white breeches, their brawny, sweaty bodies gleaming like polished ebony, the highwaymen were armed with sabers and machetes. They were enough to strike terror in the hearts of any wayfarer, but Paul held his ground, maintaining a calm she was certain he could not possibly feel in the face of such overwhelming odds.

The Negroes eyed him warily, fixing their eyes on the pistol in his belt and his hand resting on the hilt of his sword. They knew they had him at their mercy, yet he was an adversary not to be taken lightly. He could easily cost them some lives before they subdued him.

Paul's greeting, however, was friendly, though he did not yield an inch of his ground. At first he addressed them in Spanish. Then he began interjecting strange words that she didn't recognize — words she had never heard him use before.

For a moment the Negroes stared at him, their mouths agape and their eyes more wary than ever. It was evident they didn't fully understand him, yet they seemed amazed that they could understand anything at all of what he said — that he was talking to them in a language similar to theirs.

The leader of the brigands, the tallest and most powerfully built of the group, reminded Nicole in many ways of Legarde's overseer, although he was older than Virgo had been. He listened to what Paul had to say, seeming to grasp at least fragments of it.

Suddenly Paul removed his frock coat and vest and handed them to Nicole to hold so he could take off his shirt and stand before them stripped to the waist. Deliberately he turned his back to them and let them examine the scars on his shoulder blades. They moved in closer to him, mumbling one to another, and some even touched him and made grunting sounds.

Meanwhile Nicole stepped closer to him, finding it harder by the minute to hide her fear. But even as he continued to permit the bandits to finger his scars, Paul murmured to her in French, "Please, sweet, whatever I do, say nothing. Just do as I tell you and trust me."

He faced the blacks again, but seeing the disbelief in their dark, cautious eyes, he said a few more disjointed phrases and drew Nicole into the protective circle of his arm. "Forgive me, my dear, but I must do this if we're to come out of this alive," he whispered, and to her amazement, he lowered the neckline of her gown just enough to reveal the brand on her shoulder.

The blacks stared curiously at the fleur-de-lis and once

more made strange sounds among themselves, while Nicole colored self-consciously. She could feel how taut Paul's muscles were, and she realized how tense he really was.

After a few more seconds, he covered her shoulder, but kept his arm around her as he spoke to the guerrillas.

The suspicion, however, was gone from their eyes, and between gestures and broken phrases, Paul continued talking to them in a more relaxed manner. After a few more minutes, they finally motioned to Paul for him and Nicole to follow them.

"I think I've convinced them to help us," Paul told her as he lifted her up on the back of their saddled horse. "They're going to take us the rest of the way to Veracruz by a route through the jungle known only to them."

"*Mon Dieu!* Can we trust these outlaws?" Nicole asked, eyeing the half-naked savages.

"At this point all we can do is hope we can," Paul murmured as he took the reins of her horse and walked beside her. "We really have little choice in the matter. As a gesture of friendship, I gave the leader one of our horses. It was better to give it to them and gain their goodwill than to have them take both and go on feeling hostile toward us. At least they can sympathize with us now because I told them we had been slaves, too, and like them, had suffered the pain and humiliation of the brand and the whip."

"But how could you make them understand you?" she asked bewilderedly. "Wherever did you learn their language?"

He smiled. "I can't say I really know it," he corrected her. "I was just lucky enough to remember a few words that the Negro who was chained next to me on the galley used. Actually, the dialect these blacks speak is quite different from the one my companion spoke, but at least there was enough resemblance in some of the words that I finally could make myself understood."

"Thank God for that!" she whispered.

"Aye, we can well thank Him," he agreed. "And while you're at it, you'd better say a little prayer to that Virgin of yours, my sweet, that all goes well between here and the port," he added as they suddenly plunged into the cool shade of the ominously silent jungle.

In some ways Nicole felt as though she were back in the swamplands of the Louisiana Colony. This jungle was just as thick and green and twisted, but everything seemed more exotic. How long ago that trip down the Mississippi with Paul seemed now!

On the way to the bandits' hideout, their leader, Cumba, explained to Paul that there were at least three such villages of runaway slaves hidden in the jungles between Puebla and Veracruz. Paul got out his bear oil and had her cover every exposed spot of her body with it while he put his shirt back on and anointed himself with the insect repellent as well. She knew him well enough to sense that he was still somewhat leery of their host's hospitality — that he wasn't certain yet whether they were guests or prisoners of the highwaymen.

By the time they reached the bandits' hideout, dusk was falling and the village was aglow with campfires. The odor of frying fish hung appetizingly in the air.

Hugging the tranquil lagoon, with dugout canoes lining its banks and fish nets drying in front of its thatched huts, this little patch of Africa buried in the Veracruz jungles was a poignant replica of the land these runaway slaves or their ancestors had once known.

After Cumba had said a few words to his people about Paul and Nicole, the blacks gathered around to stare with open curiosity at their visitors' mementos of the past and show them their own scars as well. At least half of them — men and women alike — had some visible evidence of past abuse — from ridges left by the lash on their backs to brands on their foreheads or cheeks with the emblems of former owners. The arrogance and cruelty of the grandees was well-known among them, and the fact that Paul was fleeing from the watch because he had killed one of the hated Spanish overlords only helped make him more welcome in the village.

The freshly caught fish, followed by platters of some of the lush tropical fruits of that region — pineapples, papayas, mangoes, and bananas — proved to be an unexpected treat to Paul and Nicole, who were ravenous by that time. When they saw that the brigands meant them no harm, they gradually relaxed and enjoyed the brief interlude of rest in the midst of their dash for freedom.

That night they shared a humble pallet in a one-room hut facing the dark, moon-streaked surface of the placid lagoon, and slept contentedly in each other's arms until the first light of dawn glittered on the water's changing mirror and awakened them.

Cumba and his two eldest sons had agreed to guide them to the coast, and the blacks were up and waiting for them to begin their journey as soon as they had had their breakfast. But Paul was reluctant at first to let her undertake so long a trek through the jungle without a litter of some sort to carry her at least part of the way.

Nicole had laughed, however, and tried to reassure him that she would be perfectly all right traveling on foot like everyone else. Nevertheless, he was hesitant until Cumba assured him that there would be times when they would be traveling in a canoe and she could rest.

"All right," he had finally agreed, "but if you feel too tired to go on, don't hesitate to tell me, and we'll either stop and rest or I'll carry you part of the way."

She was pleased to see how this buccaneer husband of hers, who could kill a villain with the flick of a wrist, could also treat her with such gentleness and concern. Yes, she thought contentedly, Paul Dawson was going to make a fine father for their child.

She braided her hair and coiled it up out of the way under a faded red bandanna that Cumba's wife gave her. Then she donned a pair of *huaraches* and a white cotton tunic and straight underskirt with colorful embroidery, which the shy, soft-spoken mulatta gladly exchanged with her for the gold brocade party dress and matching slippers. Before giving up the ruffled petticoat to use with the gown, however, Nicole removed the jewels from its hem and sewed them into the waistband of the skirt under her new tunic. In the privacy of the jungle, Paul packed away his frock coat and vest and didn't bother retouching his hair and beard. Nicole was pleased to see the familiar gold lights beginning to show through as the boot black dye quickly wore off, but she realized now that the hair caught back at the nape of his neck was much shorter than it had been before the souvenir hunters had gotten to him. But his hair would grow again, and if losing it had helped him live and come back to her, she would have been willing for him to have shaved it all off!

It gave her a warm, secure feeling to watch those familiar forearms and shoulders flexing beneath the lawn of his shirt as he helped the Negroes paddle the canoe or cut their way through the overgrowth. When they had to get out on foot, he and Cumba each carried a pack on his back, while the bandit leader's two sons carried the canoe on their shoulders until they got to another stretch of water.

Though the journey was long and tedious, and the weather hot and humid, it wasn't as bad as she had expected. In many ways her journey through the swamplands of Louisiana had prepared her for this one. At least the land here seemed solid beneath her feet, and their guides knew the way well enough that there were often paths already beaten down for them. The trees and abundant vegetation offered some shade, and once when they paused to rest, the young boys ran off and came back a few minutes later with huge melon-shaped nuts they called *cocos*, which she had never seen before, but the milk inside them proved to be a welcome refreshment from the heat.

That night they stayed at another African village. At first the blacks glared at the white intruders, hostility in their eyes, but after Cumba grunted his explanatory phrases to the village chieftain, the people came around to stare at the captain's whip scars and his woman's branded shoulder. Nicole didn't like being the center of so much curiosity, but Paul quickly warned her under his breath not to forget that they were in the midst of outlaws who could just as soon cut their throats as welcome them as friends.

Once the villagers accepted them, however, the tension eased, and they were invited to join the evening repast. Nicole wasn't certain what kind of meat it was in the stew, but it had a wild, tangy taste that she found quite appetizing, though a bit tough.

A hut similar to the one they had slept in the night before was assigned to them, though this time there was no lagoon in front of it. Cumba and his two sons were taken in by the village chief and his family, who had the largest hut in the settlement.

"Just one more day, my sweet," Paul murmured as they lay back on the fresh pallet that had been prepared for them. "With any luck we'll be on board my ship this time tomorrow night."

Chapter 58

They arrived at the port of Veracruz shortly before sunset, and from the sounds of merrymaking that filled the air, there seemed to be a festival in progress. Paul felt this distraction might be used to their advantage, but Cumba advised him to stay under cover of the forest until darkness had fallen. There would surely be fireworks displays as the night wore on, he told Paul, and if the couple mingled in the crowd, they should be able to work their way unnoticed to the docks and then out to Paul's ship anchored in the bay.

Cumba explained, however, that he and his sons could not accompany them beyond the edge of the jungle. A black man in town after sundown would be too conspicuous, for the law through the Spanish colonies forbade all Negroes to be on the streets after dark. Paul and Nicole's new friends, however, stayed with them until it was time for them to leave their hiding place and go into the town.

While they waited, Nicole helped Paul stain his hair

and beard again, so that by the time the last rays of the sun were gone, she had covered over all traces of gold.

"Cumba says the townsfolk are celebrating the dedication of a new church," Paul told her as she cleaned the traces of dye from her fingers. "About an hour before midnight they'll be setting off a big display, and when the *castillo* goes off, there will be so much noise and mischief on the square that we should be able to get to my ship without anyone paying much attention to us."

"I can't help but be afraid we won't make it!" She confessed. "So many things can happen ... even while we're walking through the town to the docks!"

"Don't worry, my sweet. Just follow my lead and let me do all the talking if we're stopped. Whatever you do, don't let them hear that French accent of yours, and keep that bright hair well covered. While you're about it, you might try keeping your eyes downcast, too." he added teasingly, "though timidity doesn't always come easily to you, I know!"

As they went about their preparations for appearing in public again, Paul continued to converse with the Negro chieftain in a mixture of African and Spanish words and sign language. By the time the two leaders came to their farewells, there seemed to be genuine friendship between them. Each in his own way had come to grips with the destiny that the so-called civilized world had imposed upon him. They could say good-bye to each other, therefore, with mutual respect.

The strings of brightly colored lanterns hanging in the main plaza and the streets around it swayed rhythmically in the warm, steady breeze from the bay as they illumined the night and bathed the revelers in their kaleidoscopic glow.

Every corner had a group of its own musicians. The tinkling of restless harps, the full-bodied twang of guitars, and the beat of marimbas all blended into a strange medley of sounds that set oldsters to reminiscing and youngsters to dancing. Everyone was in a festive mood and strangers hailed one another like lifelong friends. Street vendors offered every form of corn imaginable, from roasted cobs to thick, creamy *atole*, to innumerable varieties of tacos and tomales to tempt the palate. And throughout it all, the multiple juices of the miraculous maguey — that curse or gift of the ancient gods to Mexico — flowed freely.

Nicole clung to Paul's arm as they wended their way through the revelers. A man in a coarsely woven woolen sarape brushed unsteadily against them as he passed, and offered them a swig of his mescal. Paul accepted and offered to buy the rest of the flask from him. At first the native hesitated, but when he saw the amount in Paul's hand, his bronze face lit up and he surrendered the bottle.

Now Paul walked with his arm around her waist, swaggering a little, with the flask dangling from his hand in easy view. "Put your head on my shoulder," he whispered in her ear. "Act a little tipsy, too."

She was glad to lean closer to him. It was comforting to feel his strength at that moment, to know she wasn't alone in the midst of the babel all around her.

A religious procession was wending its way toward them, and the crowd momentarily stayed its boisterous merrymaking to give way to the monks bearing a richly adorned statue of San Mateos. Instinctively Nicole stopped and made the sign of the cross, but Paul edged her along gently, taking advantage of the distraction to make even more progress. He wanted to be in a rowboat on his way to his ship by the time the fireworks started.

Suddenly he felt the eyes of a *vigilante* on him. In his haste to reach the docks, he had probably attracted the man's attention. He had to cover up his failure to stop for the procession with some logical reason! As the official approached them, Paul eased Nicole quickly into the shadows of an archway. Holding the flask of mescal in plain sight, he bent and kissed her long and passionately, running his hand exploringly over her buttocks and arching her firmly against him.

Nicole saw the *vigilante* coming toward them out of the corner of her eye and understood. Holding her shawl tightly around her head, she lifted her hand to his face as though to stroke his hair, but actually trying to hide his features as much as possible.

For a moment the *vigilante* stood looking at them as though undecided whether to call them to task over their disrespect to San Mateos, but then he shrugged his shoulders and joined the people following the procession.

"Luck seems to be with us," Paul grinned, "so let's improvise a little more." He continued to hold her to him a few seconds longer in order to be certain the watchman was out of sight. His lips lingered on hers, and she sensed that the pretense was gone.

"Faith, sweet, but I like these native costumes!" he teased as he released her. "No hoops or stays or starched petticoats! It certainly makes for a pleasant embrace!"

Nicole flushed as she checked the rebozo draped over her head and smoothed her cotton tunic. "Really, Paul!" she chided. "Here we are surrounded by danger on all sides and you're thinking about such things!" Yet despite her anxiety, she was secretly pleased that she wasn't the only one who tingled every time they embraced.

"Luck seems to be with us so far, my sweet," he said as they turned the corner and entered the street that ran along the waterfront.

Rapidly he scanned the broad panorama of the moonlit bay. There were several ships at anchor, their tall, stark masts silhouetted sharply against the night sky. But he froze in his tracks. His was not among them — the vessel he had expected to be waiting there for him was nowhere in sight!

Chapter 59

"Which one is yours?" Nicole asked eagerly.

He hesitated, not wanting to upset her. "It's not any of those," he muttered . When he saw the color draining out of her face, he added quickly, "But don't worry, my dear, I'll get you away from here even if I have to swim out of the bay with you on my back!"

They were on the main walk now, and found themselves being swept along by the crowds through a series of arches that ran across the front of one of the most imposing buildings in the port. Nicole suspected that this was the *palacio* where Escobar had stayed as a guest and she as a prisoner. She had really seen so little of the town at the time and she remembered even less of it now. The only thing she recognized with any certainty was the fort. Her heart froze at the sight of those high turreted walls rising ominously from the reef that jutted out across the entrance to the bay. How often she had looked out of her barred window in despair at the fortress and thought she would never see Paul again! Outlined against the starlit sky, San Juan de Ulua seemed to be brooding over the festive town like a sombre guardian frowning at its children's frivolity.

Paul paused and she waited breathlessly for him to say what he was going to do.

Suddenly he took her by the arm and began to resist the flow of the crowd, edging his way toward the sandy beach where several longboats were drawn up to the shore. There were fewer people there — only a young couple making passionate love in one of the boats, oblivious of everything and everyone around them, and in another, a drunken sailor with a half-empty bottle of tequila in his hand and a large straw hat pulled down over his face, dozing under a sarape.

The nearer Paul got to the boats, the more confident he seemed to become. He quickened his step, tightening his hold on her arm so she wouldn't lose her balance in the soft, damp sand. Nicole, however, was growing more apprehensive by the minute, wondering how far Paul could take her in a stolen longboat that certainly would not last very long on the high seas. Only *le bon Dieu* knew what was to become of them now!

"*Oiga, amigo!*" he called to the man sprawled in the boat. "May I have a word with you?"

She was surprised at the certainty with which Paul approached the mariner. What if the latter proved to be quarrelsome? In his inebriated state he might make a fuss that could draw the attention of the watch! But she had learned to trust her husband's judgment, and the moment the sailor stirred and sat upright, removing the sombrero from his face, she realized why Paul had approached him so boldly. This man was no drunk, nor was he a stranger. He was Fernández! How long had the Spanish buccaneer lain in that longboat, pretending to be in his cups, waiting for Paul's return? The loyalty between Paul and the men who had followed him from the very beginning of his privateering career never ceased to impress her. How could she ever hope to compete with such a bond? Paul belonged to the sea and to the men he had led for so many years. That he had loved her enough to let her into his world at all was a miracle in itself. The day they had been reunited in the forest, he had promised not to leave her again, but that had been in the heat of passion, after they thought they had lost each other forever. Then, too, he had said that before he had known she was pregnant. He probably would want her to sail with him even less now that she was enceinte. And afterward there would be the baby. She ached at the thought of having to be separated from him again. He would never abandon her, of course. She trusted his love completely now, for most certainly he had proven he would risk his life to come back to her. But much as he loved her, he could be so unrelenting once he made up his mind. If he thought she should stay on shore, he wouldn't give in no matter how much she pleaded with him.

"Aye, *capitán*, here I am," Fernández was saying. "I've been hanging around here on the beach some two or three days now, watching out for you. I was beginning to worry something might have happened to you and the *señora*."

"We did have some unexpected problems," Paul said in a rush, "so I had to improvise as we went along. But where's the ship? And the rest of the men?"

"In a cove farther up the coast," Fernández replied. "It was getting too risky for us to go on staying here in the bay. The authorities were starting to ask too many questions. They even wanted to send one of their physicians to check our crew, since we kept saying we had the plague on board. Finally Josh and I called a meeting with the men and we decided the best thing to do was get out of the bay altogether, since we were getting too uncomfortable just sitting here under the noses of the authorities and within firing range of the fort."

Paul frowned "You're right, of course. It was too much to ask them to do."

"Oh, no, *capitán*, we would have gone on doing it, had there been no other way," Fernández quickly assured him. "*Qué barbaridad!* We'd have fought the whole Spanish fleet if we thought it would have done some good, but it seemed better all around just to bail out of a ticklish situation and go to a more deserted part of the coast where we could lie in wait without attracting any undue attention. So that's where they are right now with Josh in command. I volunteered to to stay behind and wait for you so I could take you there as soon as you showed up. I hope you approve of what we did, *capitán*, but it seemed like the right decision at the time ... and you weren't here. ..." The Spaniard's voice faltered as he cast an anxious glance at Paul.

"Of course you made the right decision — and a very wise one!" Paul exclaimed, giving his lieutenant a hearty pat on the back. "I knew I could count on you and Josh to handle things on this end."

He scanned the shoreline and the grim fortress sitting on the long finger of land reaching out into the bay.

"We should get away now under cover of darkness while the fiesta is still in full progress. Doña Inés and the innkeeper must have informed the authorities by now that I'm in the vicinity, and soon the whole coastline will be alerted. How far do we have to go to reach the ship?"

"If we leave now, we should be there before noon tomorrow. It's a good, secluded spot, but the problem will be tonight — getting past the fort and out of the bay."

"Then what are we waiting for? Let's get going!" exclaimed Paul. Even as he spoke, fireworks began to go off in front of the arcade where he and Nicole only a short while before had walked.

He lifted her quickly into the longboat, and the two men lost no time in shoving off.

"Keep your rebozo over your head," Paul reminded her, "and lie back as though you're enjoying a nocturnal boat ride with your sweetheart. Let's hope the fireworks last until we get out of range of the fort."

Fernández cleared his throat nervously. "If you'll permit me, *capitan* ... maybe you'd better get out of sight and let me be the *novio*," he ventured. "The watch might be on the alert for a young girl with a man of your height and build, whereas I could never be mistaken for you even in the dark!"

Paul chuckled. "Right you are again," he agreed. "We'll do better if I hide and let you be the 'sweetheart' until we're out of the bay. From all appearances, you'll probably pass as just a sailor on a moonlit excursion with his wench."

Paul crouched on the bottom of the boat and pulled the canvas over him. Then he told Nicole to lean against him.

The bursts of fireworks were coming more frequently now, as Fernández dipped his oars rapidly into the dark waters.

They glided silently, giving the two ships anchored near the docks a wide berth but hugging the shoreline whenever possible in hopes they would blend in with the terrain. Almost everyone's eyes at that moment were fixed on the brightly lit town nestled in the curve of the bay like a multifaceted jewel glittering againt the black velvet backdrop of the tropical night.

Sounds of music and laughter wafted across the water, and some poor mariner, not fortunate enough to have been granted shore leave that night, joined in with an off-key song of his own from his lonely watch on one of the ships.

Fernández had just about cleared the fort when a challenging voice called to him from the ramparts, demanding to know who he was and what he was doing rowing around the bay at that hour of the night. The Spaniard, however, immediately sat upright so his slight build could be easily seen in the moonlight and shot back a reply in a voice presumably thickened by one sip too many of tequila.

"*Qué diablos, hombre!* Can't a man take his *novia* for a little boat ride in the moonlight without being subjected to the Inquisition?"

"Orders are to challenge everyone," the voice shouted back: "We just got word that *El Diablo Dorado* is roaming these parts."

Fernández gave an annoyed grunt. "And what do I have to do with that blackguard? Whoever said they saw him must have seen a ghost. Dawson was hanged in Havana weeks ago!"

"No, they say now he got away and is here."

"Bah! That's so much bilge water! You're frightening my *novia* with all your talk of pirates!"

"*Bueno*, you'd better not venture too far out," came a second voice. "We don't want to have to fish your bodies out of the bay come morning."

"No, *señores*, I'll stay close to the shore," Fernández assured them condescendingly. "But I promised my *muchacha* I'd let her see the *cohetes* from out here so she can get a better view."

A chorus of laughter resounded from the ramparts, and another voice called back, "*Vaya, hombre!* So you're going to show the wench the rockets?"

"*Cuídate, muchacha!* Be careful, girl!" came the first voice again. "I wager your sweetheart's got a *cohete* of his own to show you, too!"

At that moment the town was suddenly crowned with a burst of glory as the fireworks display officially got under way and a dazzling panorama of lights began erupting high in the sky above the docks. The rapid blasts and the explosions drowned out the final taunts of the guards in the fortress.

"Is that the *castillo* Paul was talking about?" Nicole asked Fernández in her halting Spanish, staring in wonder at the seemingly endless eruption as it spattered the heaven with cascades of light.

"No, no, *señora*." The Spaniard smiled. "Those are just the *toritos* — the 'little bulls.' Each one is made out of papier-mâché with a fierce, painted face on a huge frame and covered with all kinds of fireworks that go off one after the other while someone runs around with it and pretends he's a bull charging into the crowd. It's all in fun, of course, and everybody laughs and tries to fight it as a toreador would. But look — *mira!* Now you're going to see the big one ... the *castillo*, a huge castle of fireworks. You see, it's way up on a pole. That one there must be at least thirty feet high. Watch and see what happens."

He went on rowing, anxious to take advantage of the distraction to get as far away from the fort as possible while the soldiers were busy watching the festivities in the town, but she sat facing the shore, so she couldn't help but see it, and indeed, the spectacle was something to behold.

From what she could see, the *castillo* was like a huge coneshaped pine tree mounted on a long pole that extended high above the rooftops of the town. Covered with all kinds of fireworks — skyrockets, catherine wheels, Roman candles, star shells, clusters, and heel chasers — it was also adorned with dozens of wooden or papier-mâché figures — dancing girls, *vigilantes* and masked bandits, horses, tigers, and bulls — each figure joined and movable, with whole bunches of fireworks attached to them so that, when the fuse was lighted, they all sprang to life. The dancers danced, the animals leaped, and the bandits and *vigilantes* shot off skyrockets with their pistols. For a moment the lights hung suspended in the sky, and then they broke into thousands of sparkling stars that rendered the others pale by comparison. While the cheers of the crowd echoed through the bay the music matched the barrage of the exploding fireworks.

"*Mon Dieu!*" she gasped, her eyes reflecting the glow. "I've seen fireworks displays before, but never like this!"

The Spaniard laughed. "You should see the ones in

the capital and in Puebla for the grandees! This is just a little fiesta, *señora*."

The longboat had cleared the fort now, and they were rounding the tip of the reef, where only a lighthouse stood to mark the end of the natural barrier.

Paul's head emerged from under the canvas, a triumphant grin wreathing his handsome face, and Fernández passed him the bottle of tequila.

"A lovely night for a fiesta, isn't it, *mis amigos*?" he chuckled as he lifted himself up on his elbow and kissed her merrily on the cheek. "I'd say there's reason enough to celebrate wouldn't you?"

Throwing back the canvas completely now, he took a quick swallow from the bottle and then grabbed an oar to help speed them on their way to freedom.

Chapter 60

"What course shall I chart, capt'n?"

"Home, Josh. I've given orders to let out the canvas and head for Virginia . . . home to good old Norfolk!"

Paul filled his lungs with the fresh sea air and lifted his eyes to the starlit skies. They had been sailing since dusk and had had a favorable wind all night, so they were fast leaving Veracruz behind.

Nicole looked up at him from the crescent of his arm and smiled knowingly. How elated he was now that he was back on his ship once more. He had been the same way that day she had run out to him on the deck of the *Avenger* in the midst of battle. There was a part of Paul Dawson that responded to danger. It ignited his faculties, sharpened his wits. At moments like this every fiber of his body was alive and ready to spring into action. He had been born to command, and it came easily to him. When the clear blue of his eyes shone bright with such assurance, she could still see behind them the young boy who had dared defy a nation and set it to trembling at the mention of his name. She loved seeing him this way, with his clean-shaven jaw squared off so resolutely and his golden hair ruffled by the persistent wind. Yet she feared the call of the sea would come between them someday, and the thought of being separated from him again was intolerable.

"We'll stop off a few days at Mobile on the way to Virginia," Paul continued, turning now to her with a smile. "As fetching as you are in that cotton skirt and tunic, my sweet, you need more than one dress. As far as clothing is concerned, I'm afraid you're worse off now than you were that first day I brought you on board my ship. This time I can't even offer you any gowns from women I'd raped and killed!" he teased.

She colored self-consciously. "How I must have exasperated you!"

"No more than usual," he assured her with a playful kiss. "I have some good news," he added suddenly. "Fernández tells me that while he was waiting on the beach for us in Veracruz, a ship arrived with the news that the French had taken Pensacola around the seventeenth of this month. From what they said, it was quite a battle — two hours of hard fighting. The French must be in a jubilant mood. After all, they were the underdogs, so they can be justly proud of their victory."

Nicole's face lit up for a moment and then clouded. "What irony! All we've suffered these past couple of months because of the Spaniards, and now everything is back the way it was! What cruel tricks destiny plays on us!"

"That's true, my dear, but at least we, too, are as we were, with ... how do you French say it? ... a little *lagniappe*!" He patted her flat little belly appreciatively and grinned down mischievously at her. "Fernández also heard that the French caught many of the men who had deserted them in that first encounter with the Spaniards and either executed or sentenced them to the French galleys."

Nicole was thoughtful. "Then it seems everyone has

been avenged," she said at last. "Or will you continue to pursue your vendetta with the Spanish, even though Escobar is dead?"

Paul was suddenly somber. "I couldn't do anything to save my mother and father," he said grimly, "but thank God I was able to rescue you from my enemies. Nevertheless, Doña Inés brought home to me the folly of revenge — how self-destructing it can be. Just as her hatred ended up killing the man she loved, the hatred between me and Escobar nearly cost you your life, and that, my dear, is a very sobering thought." He drew her closer to him and tightened his arm around her. "I suddenly realized that I'd been so busy seeking vengeance on my enemy that I'd been risking the loss of the one thing that was really of any value to me. What a fool I was ... throwing away the future because of the past!"

She looked down at the green glitter of her wedding ring against the whiteness of her hand. The reality of Paul had dissolved the phantoms of the past for her. His love had liberated her from the shackles of the spirit as well as the body. She had known much evil, but there had been good along the way, too, and that good had illumined even the darkest moments of her existence.

"If we're going to be in Mobile in a few days, perhaps we can look up the Baudiers," Nicole said suddenly, elated at the thought of seeing old friends again. "You said they decided to settle there, didn't you? I'd at least like to let them know I'm all right now. And then there's Murielle. I really wish I could see her again. Now that I'm your wife, it ought to be safe for me to go ashore, don't you think?"

Paul smiled. "I've already thought of that, my sweet," he admitted. "And it's also occurred to me that you might like to invite Murielle to go to Virginia with us. This ship is a little larger than the *Avenger* was, so I can let her to have a small cabin for the few weeks of the voyage. Now that you're expecting, you're going to need someone you can trust to help take care of you, and later on, the child. Since you and Murielle are already such good friends, she might make an excellent nursemaid or house-keeper, if she's willing, of course. I'd pay her well, and she'd be treated like one of the family. It would be a good, secure life for her, and I know she'd be a great comfort to you, especially since she's someone from your own country who speaks your language. That way it would be less lonely for you to make the transition to the English colonies."

He looked down at her with a pleased smile in antic-ipation of her enthusiastic approval to his suggestion. To his surprise, however, her eyes were smarting and her lower lip trembling.

Nicole could feel a lump closing off her throat. So it was as she had feared. He was planning to leave her in Virginia and sail away again once he had her settled there! But she was not going to accept his decision this time without putting up a fight.

"Paul Dawson!" she exclaimed. "I know what you're up to, but I refuse to be dumped in Virginia or anywhere else while you go galavanting off again around the Caribbean!"

His brows arched in surprise, then a twinkle crept into his eyes. "Now, you know very well, my sweet, that a fighting vessel is no place for a woman," he said sternly.

"Then I'll dress like a man and fight by your side, if need be!" she replied.

He threw back his blond head, his hair already damp with salt spray, and his hearty, carefree laughter rode on the wind across the open sea.

"Ah, so you're ready to fight by my side, are you?" he teased. "At least it's with me now instead of against me!"

But she would not be cajoled. "I mean it," she insisted. "I can learn to fight. Didn't I help you with Escobar? Or, if you insist, I'll stay locked in the cabin the whole voyage, but please, Paul, I don't ever want to be separated from you again. I couldn't bear it."

His smile was broadening as he listened to her. "Nor I, my sweet. I couldn't bear it, either," he finally interjected softly.

"I positively won't stand by waiting on the sidelines. . ." she began, then she paused, realizing at last what he had said. "You — you mean you agree with me?" she stammered. "You'll take me with you?"

"No, your life is too precious to me to risk it when it's not necessary."

The emerald sparks flashed again. "You mean . . .?"

"I mean, my little bobcat, that it's far easier to keep you by my side than to have to keep running after you every time you get into trouble," he said with a patient smile. "But since you cannot — and I won't let you! — have our child, and God willing, many others, on the high seas, I guess I'll have to stay on land with you."

He was smiling broadly now, enjoying the gamut of expressions flitting across her countenance. But even in the midst of her joy, a cloud of doubt remained. Now that she had won her point, she felt a little guilty. "Oh, Paul, do you really mean it? Can you be happy that way? I know how much you love this life . . . how much your ship means to you. . . ." There was more than the spray of the sea misting her eyes now. "Perhaps I'm being too selfish," she said. "I wouldn't want the day to come when you'd resent me because you felt I'd pressured you to give all this up for me."

His eyes softened. "I love the sea, but I love you and our child in that sweet womb of yours even more," he said tenderly. "I'm weary of fighting. I have better reasons for living now than for dying. For one thing, I want to watch our child grow from day to day and help mold him or her into a fine man or woman. I never realized what a lonely life I led until you came into it."

"And your ship . . . your beautiful new ship?"

"I admit I have a soft spot in my heart for it." He swept a proud look around him from his vantage point on the quarterdeck. "I know I could come to love every board and canvas of this one as I did the *Avenger*. That brigantine was like an extension of myself. But it's gone now, along with the grievances and suffering that gave birth to it. All of that is over with now ... behind us, where it should be. Of course, I'll probably keep a share in this new vessel when I turn its command over to Josh and Fernández, but you and I have too much ahead of us, my dear, to dwell any longer in the past. Our future lies on land now, not the sea. It lies with our child and the life we'll be building together on the plantation I'm going to build for us on the banks of the James River right outside of Williamsburg."

Tears welled up in her eyes. "Oh, Paul, do you think our neighbors, your countrymen, will accept me despite the fact that I'm an *incorrigible*, an undesirable...?"

He chuckled, "Incorrigible you may be, my sweet, but certainly no one could ever call you undesirable!" He pulled her to him playfully and kissed the frown disturbing the smoothness of her brow.

"I'm serious, Paul," she insisted. "This brand on my shoulder ... it won't let us forget ..."

He saw how her usually vivid eyes had turned to the gray-green of a troubled sea. Gently he eased the sleeve down from her shoulder and brushed his lips against the fleur-de-lis. "I for one don't want to forget it," he said softly. "To the contrary, I'll kiss it every day of our lives for having brought you to me. Actually, I'd say a more important question is whether you think you can be happy in my land, which will be your home, too, from now on."

She looked up at the bold profile she had come to love so intensely, and her tears of love and joy mingled with the salt spray dampening her cheeks. "Oh, my dear, as long as I'm with you ... on land ... on sea ... it doesn't matter...."

She molded herself to his warm firmness, smiling up at him through the mist blowing against her face.

"Ubi bene, ibi patria," she murmured softly. "Where one is happy, there is one's homeland!"

The blue of his eyes ignited and he nuzzled her hair, thinking how it shone like the sun even in moonlight. Then he led her slowly back to the privacy of their quarters. As the warm breeze of the Gulf filled the sails high above them, Nicole lost herself in the world of Paul's arms ... the only world she wanted ... the only home she would ever need.

AUTHOR'S NOTE

Two little-known fragments of the history of French colonial America serve as a background for this book and inspired much of its action.

In the year 1719 the Mississippi Delta country was mostly a vast, primitive land. Mobile Bay and, intermittently, Biloxi were the Louisiana Colony's only ports, while a few settlements and plantations around Bayou St. John and along the banks of the Mississippi River were just beginning to take root in the wilderness. New Orleans was still only a clearing in the swamplands with a couple of palmetto huts on it.

At first glance the struggle for Pensacola may not seem to have been one of the important wars of the eighteenth century. Nevertheless, it had a far-reaching effect on the history of America. (In the Treaty of 1721 France agreed to give Pensacola and all other captured towns back to Spain, since she realized she might need Spain's assistance if she was going to hold back the British in America.) But as Glen R. Conrad points out in his book *Immigration and War*, based on *Mémoir of Charles Le Gac, Director of the Company of the Indies in Louisiana, 1718-1721,* if the budding French colony, weak as it was in 1719, had not dared to distract the mighty Castilian lion by striking first and proving it was strong enough to be reckoned with, the Spaniards would have surely taken over the poorly defended French settlements. As a result, what started out in Europe as a minor dynastic war could have ended in disaster for France in America.

With all of the Mississippi Valley and everything west and south of it under Castilian rule, it would have been fairly easy for Spain to have taken over the one small patch left that did not belong to it — the New England colonies.

Although North America, like South America, might have still eventually broken off with the Old World, we would have more than likely ended up with the two Americas united by language and customs, which, though an intriguing premise, would have most certainly left us with a very different culture than we have today in the United States!

Another little-known part of French-American history is the fascinating story of Louisiana's "forgotten brides." At least ten years before the arrival of the revered little Casquette Girls in 1728, who have become such a proud part of New Orleans history, there were others, not so revered, who landed in Mobile and Biloxi whom history disdainfully refers to as "the bad girls." Sent in chains from France to pacify the men in that then all-male colony, these consignments of women of usually shady origin — convicts, prostitutes, and correction girls — form a vital part of one of the most dramatic stories found in the settling of America. The hopelessness of their plight fires the imagination and, in retrospect, indignation as well as compassion, since it is recognized today that so many of them were not the degenerates they were said to have been but rather victims of corrupt officials and unjust laws and courts of that epoch. Nevertheless, historian Herbert Asbury observes, tongue-in-cheek, that the genteel Casquette Girls "must have been amazingly fertile and the earlier strumpets all barren," since none of Louisiana's first families ever admit descent from those initial shipments of harlots!

Although Nicole D'Arcenaux's particular consignment was invented for purposes of telling this story, it was faithfully patterned after numerous others that did exist, and though her experiences with the corrupt official and abusive landowner are fictitious, they certainly could have happened when the conditions of the times are considered.

This early method of enforced colonization used by France was one of its greatest fallacies — a shameful chapter in the history of that country. The Regent — Philippe, Duc d'Orléans, a notoriously licentious man himself — and other exploiters like the canny John Law and the bungling Mississippi Company (later merged into the Company of the West) used everything from flagrantly deceitful propaganda to outright kidnapping to populate the Louisiana Colony.

In an effort to imitate Spain, which had dazzled its prospective colonists with the promise of gold and silver and sent them to the New World in the plan of *conquistadores*, France tried to lure its own people to America with prospects of instant wealth in a land of milk and honey. The steaming swamplands of the Mississippi Delta, however, were a far cry from the rich mining terrains of Mexico and Peru, so the Regent decided there was nothing left to do except populate his undesirable colony with undesirables!

Of course, the policy of sending convicts and debtors to the New World as bond slaves was not limited to France. England used it as well throughout the seventeenth and eighteenth centuries, but in most cases the operation, though sometimes equally callous and cruel, was at least better organized, so the rights of master and servant were more carefully protected. According to historians' estimates, over half the white migrants to America during the colonial period were either voluntary or involuntary bond servants. In New England the majority of such colonists served their sentences or periods of indenture and then went on to become respected members of their communities. (Many even sold themselves, as well as their families, into temporary bondage just to pay for their passage to the New World and get a fresh start.)

Perhaps France's greatest fault lay in its nonchalant attitude toward its colonies. Where Spain sometimes erred in the opposite direction by ruling with an iron fist, France usually ruled with a shrug of its shoulders. Such a lax, disinterested policy unfortunately weakened the Louisiana Colony precisely at the moment when it was struggling to get a foothold on an already difficult terrain and further undermined the loyalty of its unwilling inhabitants — a fact which often brought about additional problems at times of crisis, as it did in the Pensacola War.

During the brief period between 1717 and 1721, however, thanks to the steady flow of human shipments obtained by fair means or foul, the population of the Louisiana Colony increased twentyfold, although how many thousands died in the process no one will ever know!

It was a brutal period in which the innocent, the sensitive, and the unprotected suffered the most. Yet it was also a time when one could still look off into what seemed unlimited horizons and dream of a better future, unfettered by the abuses and mistakes of the past — a time when one could still mold a dream into a whole new world.

Lorena Dureau
New Orleans, La.